W9-BVE-049

Near Mayfield, Kentucky, increased seismic activity is causing farm animals to exhibit bizarre behavior and soil to erupt in fountains of mud.

In Memphis, scientists uncover data that reveals an uplift of the earth's crust, an unusually strong lunar pull, and near-record flood stages along the Mississippi and Ohio Rivers.

Now, a group of specialists will descend into one of the Midwest's deepest coal mines in a race against nature—to prevent a disaster America's heartland is completely unprepared to face. . . .

8.4

8.4

PETER HERNON

JOVE BOOKS, NEW YORK

This is a work of fiction. The events described here are imaginary, although the existence of the New Madrid Seismic Zone and its potential for future activity are acknowledged by government and independent researchers alike. The characters are fictitious. They are not intended to represent specific persons or to suggest that the events described actually occurred.

8.4

A Jove Book / published by arrangement with
the author

PRINTING HISTORY
G. P. Putnam's Sons edition / February 1999
Published simultaneously in Canada
Jove edition / November 1999

All rights reserved.
Copyright © 1999 by Peter Hernon.
Sources for illustrations are given at the end of this book.
This book may not be reproduced in whole or part,
by mimeograph or any other means, without permission.
For information address: The Berkley Publishing Group,
a division of Penguin Putnam Inc.,
375 Hudson Street, New York, New York 10014.

The Penguin Putnam Inc. World Wide Web site address is
http://www.penguinputnam.com

ISBN: 0-515-12713-2

A JOVE BOOK ®
Jove Books are published by The Berkley Publishing Group,
a division of Penguin Putnam Inc.,
375 Hudson Street, New York, New York 10014.
JOVE and the "J" design
are trademarks belonging to Penguin Putnam Inc.

PRINTED IN THE UNITED STATES OF AMERICA

10 9 8 7 6 5 4 3 2 1

For Janice

ACKNOWLEDGMENTS

A number of seismologists, disaster planners, structural and mining engineers, nuclear weapons experts, and others provided invaluable help in researching this book. I here thank several who took extra pains. I tried to hew to scientific fact as much as possible, and I take full responsibility for reworking facts for the sake of fiction; the good people I acknowledge bear no responsibility for how I used the material they so graciously provided.

My thanks to Robert B. Herrmann, professor of geophysics at St. Louis University; James E. Beavers of Oak Ridge, Tennessee, a structural engineer and expert on natural and technological hazards; Bob Neel and Jim Gover of Albuquerque, New Mexico, both alumni of the Nevada Test Site, who explained the art of detonating nuclear bombs underground; Reid L. Kress of the Robotics Systems Division at the Oak Ridge National Laboratory; and Arch Johnston, director of research at the University of Memphis Center for Earthquake Research and Informaion.

Thanks also to a great editor, David Highfill of G. P. Putnam's Sons, and to my agent, Richard Pine of Arthur Pine & Associates. Thanks also to Howie Sanders and Richard Green in Los Angeles.

And special thanks to my wife, Janice.

Will a catastrophic earthquake strike someday on the New Madrid Seismic Zone?

Without a doubt.

The only question is when. Experts don't expect another big one for at least a hundred years, but no one knows for sure and that's what makes seismologists and emergency planners nervous when they talk about the NMSZ.

The ground is still shaking. The fault averages about two hundred measurable earthquakes a year, twenty a month. Every year and a half, it produces a shock of magnitude 4 or greater on the Richter scale. Next to California, the New Madrid Fault in America's heartland is the most dangerous earthquake zone in the United States.

The use of a nuclear device to turn off an expected earthquake has been seriously suggested, especially as a way of "destraining" the sites for nuclear power plants or big dams. The literature on earthquakes produced by underground nuclear explosions is extensive.

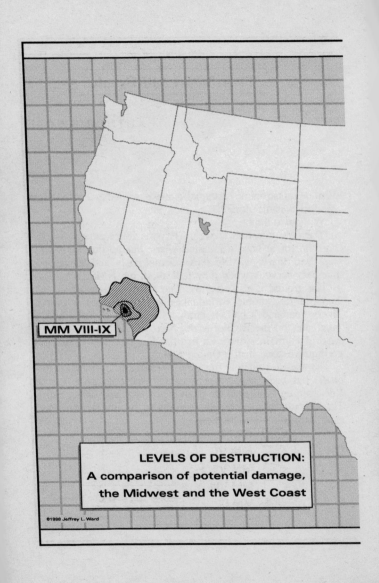

MM VIII-IX

LEVELS OF DESTRUCTION:
A comparison of potential damage,
the Midwest and the West Coast

©1998 Jeffrey L. Ward

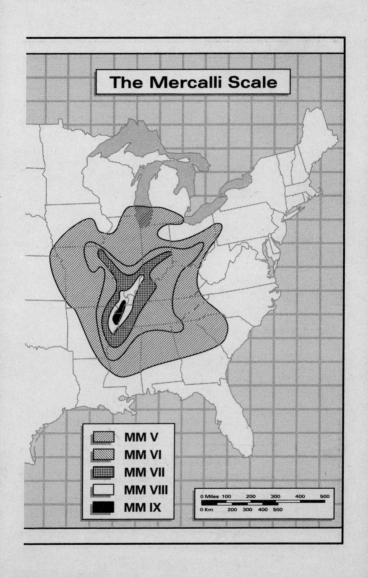

The Mercalli Scale

- MM V
- MM VI
- MM VII
- MM VIII
- MM IX

0 Miles 100   200   300   400   500

0 Km   200 300 400 500

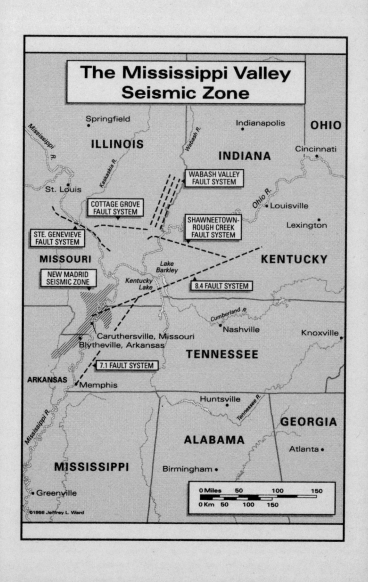

The Mississippi Valley Seismic Zone

Springfield

Indianapolis

OHIO

Mississippi R.

ILLINOIS

Wabash R.

INDIANA

Cincinnati

St. Louis

Kaskaskia R.

WABASH VALLEY
FAULT SYSTEM

Ohio R.

Louisville

COTTAGE GROVE
FAULT SYSTEM

SHAWNEETOWN-
ROUGH CREEK
FAULT SYSTEM

Lexington

STE. GENEVIEVE
FAULT SYSTEM

MISSOURI

Lake
Barkley

KENTUCKY

NEW MADRID
SEISMIC ZONE

Kentucky
Lake

8.4 FAULT SYSTEM

Cumberland R.

Caruthersville, Missouri
Blytheville, Arkansas

Nashville

Knoxville

TENNESSEE

7.1 FAULT SYSTEM

ARKANSAS

Memphis

Huntsville

Tennessee R.

GEORGIA

ALABAMA

Atlanta

MISSISSIPPI

Birmingham

Greenville

©1998 Jeffrey L. Ward

0 Miles   50   100   150

0 Km   50   100   150

A bad earthquake at once destroys the oldest associations; the world, the very emblem of all that is solid, had moved beneath our feet like a crust over a fluid; one second of time has created in the mind a strong idea of insecurity, which hours of reflection would not have produced.

Charles Darwin, reflecting on the devastating February 20, 1835, earthquake in Concepción, Chile

JOHN ATKINS GOT OUT OF HIS MUD-CAKED GMC
Jimmy and felt the wind slice through his parka. He'd pulled
to the side of a country road twelve miles west of Benton, a
small town in the extreme corner of southwestern Kentucky.
Cornfields lined both sides of the single-lane gravel road.
Left standing after the fall harvest, the dry stalks were as
tall as a man.

Atkins was lost. Any other time it might have amused
the seismologist, who'd made his reputation tracking killer
earthquakes around the globe and had never gotten lost. But
not when he was running late and it was his own damn fault.
He knew he should have called ahead and gotten directions.

The night before, he'd flown into Memphis and rented the
Jimmy. He'd driven 150 miles north through Tennessee and
crossed the border into Kentucky earlier that morning. Later
that day, if he could get his bearings, he planned to meet his
old friend Walter Jacobs, head of the Center for Earthquake
Studies at the University of Memphis.

He opened a folding map he'd bought at a gas station and
laid it on the hood of the Jimmy, holding the corners down
against the wind. The gravel road he'd been following for
the last four miles wasn't even on the map, and he regretted
he hadn't taken the time to pick up a good topographical
one before he left Memphis.

Deciding to turn around, Atkins took a final look up the
road, which continued on a straight, rutted line through the

wind-blown fields. There was no sign of a house, turnoff, or barn.

Refolding the map, he heard a sharp, high-pitched sound. Coming from somewhere to his right, it was faint and almost inaudible, but as he listened the noise grew louder. There seemed to be two distinct sounds mixed together: one, soft like wind blowing through dried leaves; the other more shrill.

Atkins strained to hear. It sounded like insects, thousands of them. Maybe locusts. But not in the dead of winter. That was impossible.

Whatever was making the noise was moving fast. In a matter of seconds, the sound had increased in intensity.

Atkins climbed up on the hood of the Jimmy to try to get a better look. He didn't see anything unusual. The cornfields stretched for acres in either direction. The wind stung his eyes. He rubbed them and stared out across the fields, which gently sloped down from low, gray hills. The tops of the cornstalks rippled in the wind.

Difficult to pinpoint, the sounds seemed almost to surround him.

Out of the corner of his eye, he thought he saw movement in the field about forty yards from where he was parked. He stepped up on the roof of the Jimmy. Standing there, he watched in amazement as the tawny stalks of corn fell over. They were making the rustling sound he'd noticed. It was as if a huge blade were slashing through them at ground level.

Something was cutting a ragged swath ten feet wide through the middle of the field. And it was headed in his direction.

Transfixed, Atkins watched as row after row of cornstalks pitched forward.

Atkins thought about insects or birds. Thousands of small birds, chirping loudly. Maybe starlings. He'd heard flocks of starlings before. Their noisy chittering was similar to what he was hearing. And they liked to settle in cornfields and gorge themselves.

But how could birds make the stalks fall over in neat rows like that? It was baffling.

The moving furrow was thirty yards away and looked like it would cross the road directly in front of the Jimmy.

The wind shifted and the noise suddenly became clearer,

more sharply focused. Atkins still couldn't place it, but decided to get back into the Jimmy and start the engine. He didn't want to meet whatever was going through that cornfield without some protection.

Atkins climbed down on the hood and jumped to the ground just as a gray rat ran out of the field and across the road.

It was the biggest field rat he'd ever seen. Two more rats charged across five feet in front of the Jimmy, disappearing in the cornstalks on the other side. Three others followed. All he saw were gray streaks.

Atkins watched, his revulsion mixed with fascination. During a trip to India a few years earlier, a rat had bitten him when he reached under a bed to find his shoes. It was a nasty wound that had become infected. He'd almost come down with tetanus.

More rats fled the cornfield in a panic. Something had to be chasing them.

But what?

The rodents exploded out into the open, four and five at a time. One stopped in the middle of the road and stood on his hind legs. Sniffing the air, its long whiskers twitching, the rat stared at Atkins for a moment before it raced off.

The noise had built to a steady, ear-splitting sound of alarm. As Atkins watched, a row of cornstalks ten feet wide fell forward into the road. A gray, undulating wave of rats swept into view.

Hundreds of them, thousands.

The hairs on his neck standing on end, Atkins ran to the door of the Jimmy. He was stepping on rats, kicking them out of the way, crushing them. One hit him in the chest and hung on, clutching the front of his parka with its claws. He batted it away with a gloved fist. Moving for the door, he tripped and almost fell, just managing to grab the side-view mirror.

The rats kept hurtling out of the cornfield. Atkins opened the door, still kicking at them. They were scurrying under the Jimmy, a dense, squealing mass with long, obscene tails. Atkins jumped inside on the driver's side, killing a rat in the doorjamb when he slammed it shut.

Two rats leaped inside before he got the door closed. Atkins kicked furiously at the floorboards, killing one with his foot. Again and again, he smashed at the other with his fists until he finally broke its neck. Something hit the windshield. First one, then another rat slammed into the glass. Pushed along by the frantic hordes still behind them, they were trying to leap over the obstruction in their path.

Horrified, Atkins sat in the Jimmy as the rats swarmed over it, covering the hood like a moving, gray blanket. In their frenzy, they slammed into the windshield and wiper-blades. Some were trampled by those charging behind them. Nipping and biting each other, many bled from wounds. The vehicle began to sway as waves of rats buffeted the front bumper. Atkins watched some of them scamper across the sunroof.

He tried covering his ears to get rid of the unnerving sound of the rodents clicking their curved yellow teeth. It didn't work. He could still hear the fierce squeaks and the scraping noise their paws made when they ran across the hood and windshield.

Then, suddenly, it was over.

The last of the rats crossed the road and charged into the opposite field. Atkins watched the deep gouge in the corn-stalks move away from him. The rats were frantically racing in a beeline for the wooded hills.

Atkins watched and waited. Nothing was chasing them.

When he reached to turn on the engine, he had to try several times before he could fit the key into the ignition. His hands were shaking too much.

"DID YOU KNOW CHARLIE RICHTER WAS A NUDIST?"

Elizabeth Holleran grinned and kept working with her trowel as she stood next to Jim Dietz at the bottom of a fifteen-foot trench. She'd heard Dietz tell this one before and still enjoyed it.

"That was back in the late fifties when the Seismo Lab was still in that incredible mansion out in Pasadena," Dietz said, scraping the wall of the trench smooth with the edge of his trowel. "I think Douglas Fairbanks owned it back in the twenties. Incredible place. Marble floors, paneled offices, private bathrooms for each professor. They used the billiard room for a library. Laid the seismograms out on the pool tables. It had wonderful gardens. Acres of roses. Charlie and his wife Lillian liked to go out there and walk around in the buff. Not a stitch on. Made a lot of the deans nervous as hell."

"You ever join them, Jim?" Holleran asked.

"He never asked," Dietz said gruffly. "But then Charlie wasn't a very friendly guy. Truth is he was a real SOB. You ever hear how he screwed Beno Gutenberg?"

Holleran had heard that one, too, but she kept digging into the hard dirt without saying a word.

"The two guys were colleagues. One day back in the forties, Beno suggested they use a logarithmic scale to plot earthquakes. That was the breakthrough that helped them come up with the new seismograph. Beno and Charlie worked on it together. Charlie took all the credit, and Beno

never challenged him on it. He was an easygoing guy and
didn't think it was worth the trouble. Fact is that scale should
be called the Gutenberg-Richter scale.''

Dietz took a sip from a jug of water. The floor of the
trench was littered with crumpled taco wrappers from his
lunch. ''Charlie just called it the magnitude scale. But if
you wanted to call it the Richter scale, well, that was fine
with him.''

Dietz had been one of Richter's star grad students back in
the late 1950s. His stories about the great seismologist were
legendary. Holleran and Dietz both taught at Cal Tech's
Seismo Lab. They'd become good friends, working almost
shoulder-to-shoulder in the deep trenches they'd dug with a
John Deere backhoe. Both wore yellow hard hats as they
scraped at the compacted sand and layers of soil. They were
searching for the buried record of past earthquakes.

Their dig was forty-five miles northwest of Santa Barbara
at a place where the Pacific Ocean met the rocky coastline.
A desolate spot known as the Devil's Jaw, the southwest-
ernmost corner of California. Located on one of the many
smaller faults that jut off from the San Andreas, it had produced a magnitude 7.3 earthquake in 1925.

They'd shored the walls of the trench with aluminum
plates that resembled planks of plywood and were held in
place by steel cross-braces. They lowered the shoring into
the trench with a hook and chain then used a hydraulic pump
to press the plates up tight against the earthen walls.

Holleran and Dietz had carefully measured the depth of
each of the soil layers. The technique was like cutting a slice
out of a layer cake. Each slice showed a different geological
period and had recognizable colors and texture: the hard,
yellow-brown color of sand; grayish red clay; boggy peat.
The telltale signs of dry years and floods stood out clearly.
So did the jagged imprints of the big earthquakes—several
of them in the magnitude 7 range.

Both were sweating heavily. It was early January, but the
southern California sun was straight overhead and the temperature was in the mid-seventies. They wore shirts, T-shirts,
and soiled work boots. Dietz, a bearded man in his late sixties, was a full professor at the Seismo Lab, a specialist on

the San Andreas Fault. Holleran was a thirty-two-year-old assistant professor who'd moved to Pasadena after getting her doctorate from the University of California at Santa Barbara.

Nearly six feet tall and slender, she towered over Dietz, who barely nudged five-foot-six. He liked to stand next to her in a classroom and tell the students they were the long and short of it. Holleran kept her thick blond hair tied in back so she wouldn't have any trouble with the hard hat.

With painstaking attention to detail, they scoured the walls of the trench for bits of carbon—fragments of ancient leaves and twigs, bits of wood or coal. When they found one, they gingerly placed it in an aluminum foil pouch. Each fragment, no matter how small, was considered "black gold."

Holleran's specialty was using these small pieces to date when the fault had ruptured in an earthquake. By using radioactive isotope carbon 14 to date the fragments, she could calculate how old the beds of sediment were. Major earthquakes that had ruptured the fault over the millennia had broken these beds, forming offsets—dark tears and creases that stood out in the exposed soil like marbling in a cake. Holleran measured the lengths of the offsets with a steel tape that hung from the top of the trench.

During the last six months, over vacations and breaks, she and Dietz had dug three similar trenches, each one crossing the fault like the rungs of a ladder. They'd identified six great quakes along that short, but potent fracture in the earth, which branched off the San Andreas Fault fifty miles to the east. The oldest dated to A.D. 235. There had been quakes in the time of Muhammad; around 1215, the year of Magna Carta; and about the time Jamestown was founded in 1607. The dates showed, on average, a moderate to heavy quake every sixty years. The last one had struck nearly seventy-five years earlier, which meant the fault was due for a major rumbling.

Later that afternoon when they'd finished for the day, Dietz and Holleran relaxed on a rocky outcropping that faced the ocean. They sat in the sun and drank cold beer with two of their lab assistants, graduate students who worked as go-fers and helped operate the equipment. They shared a cramped trailer that had electrical hookups for a telephone, three computer terminals, and a refrigerator.

Holleran loved this part of California. The desolation of the place, the wild shoreline and plunging cliffs. To the east a sawtooth line of yellow hills retreated into the haze. She liked to walk those hills alone, carrying a couple of sandwiches and a thermos of tea in a day pack. It was hard to believe that Los Angeles was just a two-hour drive straight down Highway 101.

So far that city and the rest of California had been incredibly lucky. The big quakes in 1812, 1838, 1857, 1927, 1940, and 1952, for the most part, had gone off in remote areas such as Devil's Jaw. The 1906 San Francisco earthquake was another matter entirely. The quake, a magnitude 8.2, and the subsequent firestorm touched off by broken natural gaslines, had almost destroyed the city. More than two thousand people died. If the same thing happened today, the death toll would be staggering.

On the wall of her bedroom was an enlarged black-and-white photograph from the San Francisco earthquake. It showed a young woman, hands on her hips, standing on a hilltop, staring out at the burning city as smoke poured into the clear sky. Holleran saw the haunting photo every day. It helped her put a human face on the disasters she'd spent so much of her life studying, helped her keep the cold numbers in the right perspective.

One of the grad students had gone to the trailer for more beers. When he returned, he told Holleran she had a phone call. The man had left a message, a telephone number and his name, Otto Prable.

Dietz said, "Otto Prable! Now there's a name from the past. What do you think that man's worth these days, ten, twenty million?"

Holleran was surprised. She hadn't seen her former professor in more than three years. Prable was a brilliant man. There was simply no other word for it. He'd become a highly paid consultant since he left the university ten years earlier, a geophysicist who was an expert on weather and climate. He'd done extremely well providing long-range global weather forecasts to clients that included some of America's largest agribusinesses and utility companies. He'd made a fortune.

Holleran had taken a couple of postdoctoral courses with him on climatology—how hurricanes, drought, volcanic eruptions, and other natural forces influenced the planet's weather. He was one of the most mesmerizing teachers she'd ever had, a superb lecturer who insisted that his students think for themselves.

He'd been disappointed when he couldn't persuade her to switch from geology to atmospheric physics. She wondered if he had any idea how close he'd come.

Prable lived just a few hours down the coast in Mesa Verde.

Wondering what he wanted, Holleran walked to the trailer and dialed the number. It rang and rang. Just as she was about to hang up, Prable finally answered.

"I've sent you a package," he said without any introduction or greeting. "A videotape and some computer disks. I've also sent you a key to my office. My papers are there. I want you to study the material and do what you think best."

"Doctor, what's the matter?" Holleran said. His voice sounded weak, far off. Something in his tone immediately put her on edge.

"I have pancreatic cancer, Elizabeth. It's terminal. Please watch the video. It will explain everything. It's very important that you do this as soon as possible."

The news stunned her. She hadn't known that Prable was sick.

"Doctor, where's Joanne? Let me talk to Joanne." Holleran knew and liked Joanne Prable. She'd taught English literature at Berkeley. A warm, good-humored woman. She and her husband were inseparable.

Prable didn't answer. Holleran heard his heavy, irregular breathing.

"Please put her on the telephone."

"Read and study all the materials," Prable said. "Promise me that."

"I promise, doctor. Now please put your wife on the line. Let me talk to her." Afraid he was going to hang up, she wanted to keep him talking. She sensed that something was terribly wrong.

"I can't do that, Elizabeth," Prable said after another long pause. "My wife is dead. My dear, beloved Joanne. She wanted me to do it. Begged me to do it. Oh, dear God, and I listened to her."

ATKINS DROVE BACK TO THE BLACKTOP AND FOL-
lowed the road signs toward Kentucky Lake. He'd noticed a
boat marina when he passed near the lake earlier that morning. He wanted to get directions and maybe a cup of coffee.
After what he'd just seen, he figured he could use a good
jolt of caffeine.

He didn't know what to think about the horde of rats.
They were like frightened lemmings charging for the nearest
cliff. He'd heard of rats moving in huge packs but had never
seen anything that remotely compared with what he'd just
witnessed. It was going to be at the top of the list of things
to tell Walt Jacobs.

He and Jacobs went back a long way, since their days
together in graduate school at Stanford. Jacobs had gone to
Memphis after spending a few years in California with the
United States Geological Survey (USGS), the federal agency
responsible for studying earthquakes, volcanic eruptions, and
all manner of seismic hazards. Atkins, who'd just turned
forty-two, was with the USGS's disaster response team. It
was his job to visit the sites of severe quakes and examine
their effects. He'd just returned from a month-long trip to
Peru, where a magnitude 7.3 quake had leveled several villages in the Andes. The *terremoto* had triggered landslides
that wiped the villages off the mountainsides. A couple hundred people had died, most of them in crudely built masonry
homes that fell on them while they slept.

A few days after dropping off his report at USGS head-
quarters in Reston, Virginia, Atkins had flown to Memphis.
Jacobs had invited him to visit what geologists called the
"New Madrid Seismic Zone."

Atkins was looking forward to the meeting. They had a
lot to talk about, especially Jacobs' concern that conditions
were ripe for a potentially serious earthquake in that part of
the country. Shaped like a gigantic hatchet, the fault line
extended roughly 140 miles along the adjoining state lines
of Arkansas, Tennessee, Kentucky, and Missouri. It passed
through parts of five states and crossed the Mississippi in
three places.

Jacobs had faxed him a map that showed the fault with
striking clarity. It was clipped to a notebook that lay open
next to Atkins on the front seat. As he drove, he glanced at
the map again. He still couldn't believe it.

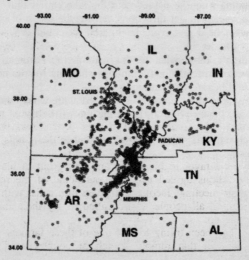

**Earthquakes in the New Madrid Seismic Zone in the Last
Twenty Years**

The map showed seismic activity that had occurred in the
heart of the Mississippi Valley over the last twenty years.

The dots represented the locations of earthquakes over an eight-state area, most of them small, usually less than a magnitude 2 or 3. The hatchet or hammer shape of the fault showed clearly, a darkening where the dots were so thick they overlapped. The handle crossed the boot heel of Missouri and extended into Arkansas. The blade crossed the corners of northwestern Tennessee, southwestern Kentucky, southeastern Missouri, and southern Illinois.

Little known to most Americans, it was one of the most active faults in the world and had produced three of the largest earthquakes on record in North America. The village of New Madrid in the Missouri boot heel was the epicenter for the quakes that struck between December 16, 1811, and February 7, 1812. Thousands of aftershocks had rippled across the Mississippi Valley.

Based on damage reports, all three earthquakes measured a magnitude 8 or greater on the Richter scale.

Atkins found that a little short of staggering.

He was going to meet Jacobs later that day at Reelfoot Lake to discuss the situation. Located forty miles away in northwestern Tennessee, the big lake had been created by the New Madrid earthquakes. Atkins had always wanted to see it.

Along with the scientific data that concerned Jacobs, there'd also been reports of strange animal behavior in the fault zone. Hogs running wild in their pens. Cows butting into each other. Horses slamming around in their stalls. And now rats.

Partly as a favor to his friend and partly out of his own curiosity, Atkins agreed to check out some of the reports before their meeting. Jacobs had given him a list with four or five names, all people who'd called to say their animals were acting up.

Atkins had been trying to find one of these farmers when he got lost on that remote stretch of country road near Benton.

The Chinese had long relied on animals to provide warning signs for earthquakes. In one famous example, in February 1975, a magnitude 7.3 quake hit the city of Haicheng. More than ninety percent of the homes collapsed. Earlier that same day, officials had warned the population that a big quake was imminent. Despite bitter cold, most people moved outdoors. Only a couple hundred people died, and this in a country where it was common for bad quakes to kill thousands. The Chinese partly based their prediction on reports of unusual animal behavior.

Atkins had always been skeptical about using animals as earthquake predictors. And yet the phenomenon interested him and was hard to discount. Maybe animals could sense subtle changes, say, in magnetic fields or feel pressure building up in other unknown ways.

After his encounter with the rats, Atkins was willing to admit he'd been scared, but he still wasn't ready to believe the rodents somehow sensed an earthquake was imminent and were scurrying to get away. He wasn't about to make that kind of intellectual leap. Some other explanation for what he'd seen was possible, but he could talk that over with Jacobs.

He reached Kentucky Lake shortly after 11:00 A.M. He still had plenty of time to drive fifty miles into neighboring Tennessee for their meeting.

THE lake was impressive. Set between steep, forested ridges that had once formed a spectacular valley, it was 135 miles long, the largest reservoir in the world. There were actually two lakes, separated by a slender finger of land about three miles wide that was called, appropriately, the Land Between the Lakes. The other reservoir, Lake Barklay, was only slightly smaller than Kentucky Lake. Both had been created in the 1930s when the Army Corps of Engineers dammed the Tennessee River. Roughly 170 miles from St. Louis to the northwest and 140 miles from Memphis, the lakes were a popular tourist attraction.

Admiring the view, Atkins understood why. He turned off the road at the marina, which was near the northern end of the lake. A small bait and tackle shop and a restaurant were on a floating dock that formed a T in the water.

After parking in a gravel lot, Atkins descended a flight of wooden steps to the dock. He entered the empty restaurant and took a stool at the counter. Moments later a middle-aged woman with striking red hair entered. She wore a gray-and-black-checked flannel shirt and was wiping her hands on her jeans.

Surprised to see a customer, she apologized. "Sorry, I didn't hear you pull up. I was out back checking the bait tank."

Atkins ordered coffee and a piece of cherry pie. The sign behind the counter said it was homemade.

"I guarantee you'll like it," the woman said. "I baked it this morning."

Atkins guessed she was in her early to middle fifties. She had an attractive face and a warm, engaging smile.

He introduced himself, and the woman reached across the counter and shook his hand. "I'm Lauren," she said. "Lauren Mitchell." Serving the coffee and pie, she asked what brought Atkins to Kentucky Lake. "Don't take this as an insult, but you don't exactly look like you came here to fish," she said.

When he explained that he was a geologist with the USGS, Lauren's face brightened.

"Everybody's been talking about all the weird stuff the animals have been doing," she said, freshening his coffee after he took a few sips. "Personally, I don't believe in that. You usually hear the cockamamy animal stories after the quake, not before. This time it's different." She wiped up some spilled coffee with a white towel. "Do you think we're gonna have one?"

Taken aback by her blunt question, Atkins said, "I don't know."

"You live in these parts, you get used to the ground shaking and the animal stories," Lauren said. "We usually get a shaker once, maybe twice a week. Nothing really big although we've had those, too. I remember a magnitude 5 we had six or seven years ago not too far from here. Rocked this boat dock like a bobber."

Atkins mentioned the rats he'd just seen. The memory still made the back of his neck tingle.

Lauren stared at him over the counter, her dark green eyes narrowing. "That's a new one," she said. "That's one for the books. You hear all kinds of stories out here in the country, especially about earthquakes. It's part of the local folklore. Heck, when I was a little girl, my grandpa told me stories about the big one back in 1896. How the ground shook like jelly. How waterspouts opened up in the fields. How the dogs were barking in the middle of the night just before the ground started shaking. You hear all kinds of queer stories. But I've never heard anything like the one you just told me.''

"Have you noticed anything unusual?" Atkins asked. He liked Lauren. She was salt of the earth just like his mother and her people. Farmers mainly from upstate New York. Real people without any pretensions, people who liked to work with their hands and who had roots that went a long way back.

"You mean have I seen any animals doing crazy stunts? No, nothing like that. But I'll tell you one thing—this lake sure has been acting up.''

"What do you mean?" Atkins swiveled in his stool, so he could look out through the curtained windows at the lake. It was three or four miles wide, the far shore shrouded in haze.

"It's been real choppy," Lauren said. "We've been getting waves running two and three feet. I can't ever recall anything like that before. Some days you'd think it was the ocean with a storm blowing.''

"How long has it been like that?" Atkins asked.

"A month or so," Lauren said. "It's quiet right now. But yesterday afternoon, it was kicking up whitecaps like I've never seen. This dock gets bumped around pretty bad in rough water. Come spring, I'm gonna have to retighten all the couplings.''

Moments later, Atkins heard footsteps pounding on the gangplank that connected the dock with the shore. The door slammed open and a young boy ran in, carrying his backpack.

"Grandma, you've got to see this," he said excitedly. "They're all dead." Then he turned around and ran back outside.

"Bobby, what's the matter with you?" Lauren asked, calling after him and stepping from behind the counter. She turned to Atkins. "That's my grandson. His mom and dad were killed in a plane crash just after he was born. My son

was his father. It was a rough time. My husband died about
then. I've raised Bobby myself. He's twelve.''

Atkins watched him out the window. The boy was tall for
his age, almost six feet. A good-looking kid. He wore a blue
jacket, jeans, and red Reeboks.

"You've got to see this," Bobby shouted from outside.
"They're dead."

"What's dead?" Lauren asked. She didn't know what he
was talking about.

Puzzled, she and Atkins went for the door.

"There must be hundreds of them out there," yelled
Bobby. He was so excited and breathless he could barely get
the words out.

"Bobby Mitchell, come here this minute and tell me what
in the world you're talking about."

The boy looks scared, Atkins thought.

"Here, see!" He brought over a plastic bag and emptied
the contents on the decking—half a dozen good-sized frogs
and a three-foot-long bull snake, all frozen stiff.

"What on earth . . . ?"

"They're down by the lake, Grandma. You've got to see."

He was pulling her by the hand. Lauren slipped her coat
on and started to follow him.

"You mind if I tag along?" Atkins asked. He wondered
what the boy had seen.

"No, come on," Lauren said. "This is one time when I
could use some company."

They crossed the gangplank and climbed a short flight of
wooden steps to the parking lot. Hurrying along a tree-lined
path, they followed the boy along the shore of the lake.

"They're over here," he said.

Lauren and Atkins followed him down a narrow trail that
descended steeply to the water.

"This is one of his favorite places," Lauren said over her
shoulder. "In the nice weather he likes to sit on the rocks
and eat his lunch and fish."

They could barely keep up with the boy. The lake was
lapping against the rocks that lined the shore.

"When it gets choppy, you can't even see those rocks,"
Lauren said. "It was like that yesterday. It sounded like the
surf out here."

When they got closer to the water, Atkins stopped in his tracks.

"Grandma, look at them!"

As far as Atkins could see, the curving shore was littered with the frozen bodies of frogs. There were hundreds of them. All of them dead, along with a number of snakes. A big blue racer lay curled up in some brush. Atkins guessed it was at least five feet long. And frozen stiff.

"Here's one," Bobby said. He stood by the edge of the water. "It's still alive."

Atkins went over to look. A frog was struggling out of the mud. It managed to pull itself out and make two or three feeble hops before it stopped moving.

Atkins had no idea what was happening. Frogs and snakes hibernated during the winter. But something had awakened them and driven them up out of the ground.

He saw more frogs emerging from the muck. The shore was covered with dead or dying frogs.

Lauren took her grandson by the hand and started pulling him away.

"Grandma, no. I want to watch. What's happening?"

"I don't know," she said, wishing to God she did.

She looked at Atkins. The playful flicker that he'd noticed in her eyes back at the boat dock had disappeared. Her sharp stare was deadly serious.

"Maybe this man here can tell us," she said.

Atkins swept his eyes along the shore, taking in the numbing sight, trying to make sense of it. He didn't know what to say.

BEFORE SHE LEFT POINT ARGUELLA, ELIZABETH HOL-
leran called the police from the trailer at the dig site. She
described her disturbing conversation with Otto Prable and
her fear that something might have happened to his wife.
Then she told Jim Dietz where she was going in a few hurried sentences, jumped in her car, and headed for Los
Angeles. She went straight down Highway 101, often pushing the speed over eighty.

Elizabeth kept thinking about what Prable had told her and
his strange, almost frightened voice. It was uncharacteristically faint, a whisper.

She made the trip in less than two hours, arriving at Prable's secluded home at dusk. Four police cruisers and an
unmarked blue van were in the driveway. The home was in
Parkside, an upscale neighborhood just north of Beverly
Hills.

Elizabeth noticed that her hands were trembling when she
got out of the car and walked to the front door of the sprawling ranch house. She'd been there a few times before. Prable
frequently hosted parties for his grad students, who gathered
to drink beer and eat cold sandwiches on the rear deck, which
cantilevered off the side of a bluff and offered a sweeping
view of the Santa Monica Mountains.

Elizabeth felt light-headed. She put a hand against the wall
to steady herself.

A detective in plainclothes met her at the door. A sergeant

from homicide. He looked in his mid-fifties, heavyset and balding, with a pockmarked face.

"Miss Holleran, I want to thank you for calling us," he said. "Why don't you come inside and sit down, and we can talk."

Elizabeth followed him into the living room. It was as she remembered it, wide and spacious with a double fireplace. A row of small, hand-painted ceramic dolls stood on the mantel. Native American dolls. Joanne Prable had collected them on their many trips to New Mexico.

Elizabeth heard men's voices in another part of the house.

"Can you please tell me what's happened?" she asked. "I don't think I can take this much longer, not knowing."

The sergeant nodded as if to say he understood. He wore a short-sleeved white shirt that looked too small for his thick arms. His neck bulged at the tight collar. "They're both back in a bedroom," he said. "The woman, Mrs. Prable, was shot once in the head. The man, I assume it's her husband, is lying in bed with a plastic bag over his head. It looks like he swallowed some pills first. There's an empty bottle of Seconal on the floor. One-hundred-milligram tablets. You can go back there in a couple minutes. I'd advise against it, but if you think you can identify them, it'd be a help."

Elizabeth sat there, fighting the urge to scream. It was what she'd feared ever since Prable had called her.

"Could you tell me about the Prables?" the sergeant asked. He had a deep, yet gentle voice. "Do they have any relatives we could call?"

Elizabeth shook her head. "They didn't have any children. Doctor Prable may have had a brother back east somewhere. I'm sure the university would have that in his personnel file."

"What exactly did Prable do?" the sergeant asked. He was writing notes on a small black pad.

"He was a geophysicist. He studied weather systems, climate." Elizabeth could hear her voice, but felt detached from what was happening outside herself.

"Could I ask what you do?"

"I'm a seismologist."

"You study earthquakes?"

"I try to," Elizabeth said.

The sergeant frowned. "Were you here for Northridge?"

"I was out of the country. I was doing some fieldwork in Chile, near Santiago. I missed it." Elizabeth bitterly regretted her bad luck. She'd been in dozens of small shakes before. But she'd never experienced a bad one, and then when it finally happened in the L.A. suburb of Northridge in 1994, almost in her backyard, she wasn't there.

"I was with a traffic detail," the sergeant said. "They sent us out to the I-10 freeway at La Cienega. One of the overpasses had collapsed, broken in two. We took fifteen bodies off it, most of them pretty badly mangled. There were a couple of young kids." He hesitated. "I was born in this state. Earthquakes never bothered me much until Northridge."

Elizabeth had studied the quake in detail. A magnitude 6.7, it had struck around dawn on January 17, jolting much of Southern California, especially the Simi and San Fernando valleys. It killed fifty-seven people, injured more than nine thousand, and left another twenty thousand homeless. It was the most costly earthquake in U.S. history. And yet they'd been exceptionally lucky. The quake's strongest seismic energy was directed away from Los Angeles, out toward the sparsely populated San Fernando Valley. If it had gone the other way, the results could have been catastrophic.

"Was he despondent?" The sergeant's question broke her trance. He was asking about Prable's telephone call, how he'd sounded.

"He said he had cancer and that his wife had begged him to do something. Can I please see them?" She was certain that someone who'd known and admired the doctor and his wife should be with them at a time like this.

The sergeant left the room and returned a few moments later.

"You can go on back," he said. "If you're not used to something like this, it can hit pretty hard. Don't be afraid to sit down if you feel faint."

Elizabeth walked down a long hallway lined with framed photographs of New Mexico. The sergeant led her into the master bedroom.

Joanne Prable wore an expensive blue-and-white dress. Later, Elizabeth remembered how the pleats were crisply folded, how the white pearls and black patent leather pumps looked so carefully selected. She was crumpled on the floor in front of a chair. Her head was turned to the side. Part of her forehead was missing.

"Is that Mrs. Prable?"

Elizabeth nodded, wanting to look away, but unable to.

"She was probably sitting in the chair when he shot her," the sergeant said.

Prable lay on a large bed with a mahogany frame. He was wearing a navy suit and tie. A clear plastic bag was pulled tight over his face.

"Is that him?" the sergeant asked.

Elizabeth nodded. It was the second time in her life that she'd seen a dead man. The first had been her grandfather, who'd lived with her family. He'd collapsed in the bathroom while shaving. An aneurysm had burst deep in his brain, killing him instantly. He'd struck his head on the washstand when he fell, and Elizabeth mainly remembered coming into the bathroom and seeing him sprawled in the narrow space in front of the bathtub with a trickle of blood at the corner of his mouth. She was a senior in high school. He was seventy-six when he died. He'd given her her first rock collection. She still missed him dearly.

The sergeant wanted to know whether Prable had said anything about a note, a will, or any personal papers.

Elizabeth remembered that he'd said he sent her a package with a videotape and some papers and that he didn't want her to tell anyone about it until she'd examined the materials.

She took a final look at her former professor.

"No, he didn't," she said, recalling the desperate sound of his voice over the telephone. "He didn't say anything at all about that."

If Prable was so secretive and desperate to get some kind of information to her, then she felt the need somehow to see it for herself before she mentioned it.

WHEN HE LEFT KENTUCKY LAKE, ATKINS DIDN'T know what to make of it—first the rats, then frogs clawing their way out of the mud. Still skeptical this had anything to do with earthquakes, he had to admit that if they wound up having one, some excellent research material would be available.

More than ever, Atkins was looking forward to his meeting with Walt Jacobs. Following the short-cut directions Lauren Mitchell had given him, he made the drive to Reelfoot Lake in less than an hour. It was in the northwestern corner of Tennessee, 120 miles due north of Memphis. The Mississippi made a sharp S-bend a few miles to the west.

Atkins had arrived at the lake's visitor center before Jacobs. He had a lot to think about as he sat in the Jimmy, which rocked lightly in the parking lot against the buffeting wind.

The day before, he'd arrived at the Center for Earthquake Studies at the University of Memphis. He'd dropped by Jacobs' office on Central Avenue, hoping to catch his friend off guard, but he was teaching a graduate class. The center shared space with the USGS. Atkins found the agency's part of the building and was going to introduce himself when he passed a partly closed office door. He heard two geologists talking to each other.

They were discussing him. They had some of the biographical details right, but not all of them.

Atkins had been to more earthquakes than anyone else on

active service with the USGS, experienced more temblors, seen more of their massive destruction. No other natural force on earth compared with earthquakes. He was haunted by them, obsessed by their power. As a consequence, he was almost constantly on the road, which was how he wanted it. He had no relatives. Both of his parents were dead. His father had been a high school math teacher at a small school in northern Illinois. He'd taken him on extended hikes in the Tetons and Wind River Range, where Atkins had caught the geology bug. He was fascinated by the big mountains and the dynamic forces that had shaped them. He was still in grade school when he knew what he wanted to do with his life.

He'd inherited his father's love of the outdoors as well as his rugged build and thick, dark brown hair. Atkins was six-foot-two and after the trip to Peru, where he'd battled an intestinal bug for weeks, he needed to put on some weight. He'd dropped nearly twenty pounds and it still showed, especially in his face.

"The guy's a legend," Atkins heard one of the geologists say as he stood in the hallway listening. "He's been to every magnitude 6 or better going back fourteen years. Colombia, 1987. Nepal, 1988. Burma that same year. Armenia, 1988. Luzon, 1990. Kobe, Japan, 1995. And those are just some of the highlights. I don't know if the guy's even got an apartment in the States."

"You can have that," the other geologist said. "That's no kind of life."

How true, Atkins remembered thinking. Not much of a life at all, but the only one he knew.

They'd missed one of his trips. The big one. Even now, he could run through the scenes in his head like a movie. He remembered every image, every detail.

On September 19, 1985, at precisely 7:17 in the morning, he'd been in Mexico City.

As he sat in the Jimmy at the Reelfoot Lake parking lot waiting for Jacobs, Atkins closed his eyes and let it play again.

HE felt the tremor hit, a strong one. The ground swayed sharply, right to left. Then it happened again, only more violently. He rolled out of bed and glanced at his watch to check the time. It was like trying to keep his balance on a pitching surfboard. His legs almost buckled. He had to lean against the wall to steady himself.

The bed started sliding across the floor as if pushed by invisible hands.

A lamp toppled over.

A closet door flew open.

The glass shattered in the large window that offered a view of the skyline.

The small hotel trembled. Atkins tried to force himself to think clearly, not to get rattled. The earthquake's tremendous power stunned him. He'd often wondered how he'd react, whether he'd be scared and freeze up. He had his answer. His stomach tightened, and he had to fight back what he knew was fear.

He checked his watch as soon as the heavy shaking ended. The peak intensity had lasted about forty seconds. That was way up at the upper end of the scale. Definitely a major earthquake.

"That's a 7.5 for sure," Sara said, slipping into her jeans. She'd been knocked over when she tried to get out of the moving bed.

Atkins shook his head. "More. Maybe a magnitude 8."

Barely thirty years old, Atkins had earned his doctorate in seismology from Stanford University. He'd led a team of geologists who'd just finished setting up a network of seismographs and accelerometers in a thirty-mile loop that ran into the mountains north of Acapulco in the Mexican state of Guerrero. Prime earthquake country, the Guerrero Gap, as it was called, was due for a major quake.

They'd just returned to Mexico City the day before and had had the good luck to find rooms in a low, two-story hotel outside the damage zone. Atkins and Sara had been living together for the last nine months and were engaged. They were traveling with Brad Garvey, another USGS geologist.

The Mexican capital had taken a pounding. The main damage zone was the bed of old Lake Texcoco, which had been drained. Many of the newer skyscrapers and hotels were located there, built on the lake bed's thick deposit of soft, high-water-content sand and clay. Hundreds of buildings were severely damaged or destroyed. Atkins, Sara, and Garvey went out to survey the damage.

They slowly worked their way through frantic crowds on the Paseo da la Reforma until they came to a new six-story apartment building. The facade, tan brick with large picture windows and recessed balconies, looked untouched, but the entire back end had caved in. It stood there like a Hollywood prop. Rescuers were bringing out the victims on stretchers or carrying them by the arms and legs.

The first aftershock was barely noticeable, a gentle swaying of the ground. Little more than a nudge. The second one, which immediately followed, was much stronger.

"Look!" Sara cried. The apartment building slowly rotated on its foundation, a twisting half turn. One of the side walls bowed out and the upper floor collapsed with a sickening crash. At first there was an eerie silence. The screams followed, coming from deep in the rubble.

Atkins, Sara, and Garvey ran toward the building. They were still able to enter through the front door, which had been pulled from its hinges. They followed two cops into the lobby. Broken timber and drywall blocked the lobby. Plaster dust kept falling. The police quickly retreated. They'd seen enough.

Atkins and the others started picking their way single file up a broken stairway to the second floor. Inching forward, Atkins heard a whimpering voice. A child.

Atkins lost sight of Sara and Garvey as he made his way toward the child, following the sound of her cries. A girl, he thought.

He found her pinned under a table in a smashed apartment. Atkins froze. Something large and heavy crashed down into one of the upper floors. He figured another section of brick wall had toppled. They were on borrowed time.

He smelled smoke. The smell was faint but getting stronger. Atkins inched his way back into the hallway. The odor was more pungent. He could taste the smoke.

The building was on fire.

Atkins shouted for Sara and Garvey. Sara called to him. Her voice sounded far away, muffled.

He nearly tripped with the child, caught himself, and kept going, groping his way back down the hallway, ducking under fallen I-beams. Black smoke started pouring in on him. He began coughing.

"Sara! Brad! Get out of here!"

He heard Sara. Her voice louder, closer.

"We're all right," she said. "We're trying to find a way out."

She was behind a collapsed wall, which must have come down in the last aftershock. Trapped in one of the apartments, they couldn't get back out to the hallway.

Atkins tried to fight his panic.

Sara and Brad were cut off.

"I'll be right back!" he shouted.

"I love you." He heard Sara clearly. "Please hurry."

Atkins managed to get out with the child, stumbling into the bright sunlight. Two men in blood-splattered uniforms, paramedics, ran forward and took the little girl. Atkins looked up at the apartment building. The top floors—what was left of them—were engulfed in flames.

Atkins started back inside.

"*¡Señor, no es posible!*" A cop grabbed him, pulling him by the arm.

Breaking away, Atkins entered the lobby and stopped in his tracks. In the intense heat, his hands instinctively came up to protect his face. He screamed Sara's name and heard wood crackling in the fire. A series of small explosions popped like firecrackers on the upper floors, probably canisters of propane gas going off.

Still shielding his face with his hands, he tried to climb the stairs. The cop, a heavily built man with a strong grip, pulled him back.

The building moved. Two men were holding Atkins, the cop and a soldier. Gripping him by the shoulders and neck, they got him outside and pushed him away from the building.

"Sara!"

He kept screaming her name as the burning building folded in on itself.

John Atkins sank to his knees and wept. He was crying when the next aftershock hit, the strongest yet. Two streets over, a ten-story building fell down in a roar of grinding steel and shattering glass. Atkins didn't notice. He was cursing himself for not having the courage to crawl back into the flames.

A RAP AT THE WINDOW BROKE HIS TRANCE.

Atkins turned and saw Walt Jacobs smiling at him. Jacobs was a round-faced man with an easy manner who liked to smoke a pipe outdoors. He was smoking one now, a bent briar.

Atkins got out and shook his friend's hand.

"So how did it go?" Jacobs asked. "Did any of those reports check out?"

"I never got that far," Atkins said. He described his experiences with the rats and dead frogs.

Jacobs frowned. Unmistakable worry showed on his face. "What do you think about that, John?" he asked.

"I'm not sure yet," Atkins said. "I figured it was something we better talk about."

Jacobs put his pipe in his pocket. His shoulders were hunched in the wind, his collar turned up. "Let me show you something first," he said. With Atkins following, he walked to a tourist overlook that offered a sweeping view of Reelfoot Lake.

"Where's New Madrid from here?" Atkins asked.

Jacobs pointed to the northwest. "About twenty miles as the crow flies."

The small town across the Mississippi in Missouri was near the epicenter for the three monster earthquakes of the last century. The original settlement lay buried under the river.

Atkins found it incredible that the quakes had created the

lake. The gray water spread out before them as far as the eye could see.

"The lake's twenty miles long and a couple miles across," Jacobs said. "Covers almost a hundred square miles."

They stood on a wind-blasted hill. Shivering in the cold, Atkins dug his hands deeper into his pockets. He didn't know why Jacobs had insisted on the walk. They could see the lake just fine from the front seat of the Jimmy, and he was eager to hear Jacobs' thoughts about the chances for an earthquake.

Atkins was aware that the New Madrid Seismic Zone was overdue for a magnitude 6 or greater earthquake and that his soft-spoken, cautious friend was worried about seismic data suggesting the fault was becoming unusually active. The New Madrid System included six, possibly seven intersecting fault segments.

"It's only in the last couple years we've been able to piece together what happened up here," Jacobs said of the 1811–1812 earthquakes. "The last one in the sequence happened on February seventh around three in the morning. It was strong enough to cut across the Mississippi in three places. This ridgeline we're standing on is actually the fault scarp from that last quake. It crosses two major bends in the river over by New Madrid."

He handed Atkins a map showing the locations of the epicenters and their dates and the maximum range of magnitudes.

Using more conservative analysis, the first megaquake at New Madrid was between a magnitude 8.1 and 8.3. Other studies put it as high as 8.6. It was the largest quake in the series. All were a magnitude 8 or greater.

The open-ended Richter scale used a logarithmic progression in which an increase of 1 in magnitude represented a tenfold increase in strength. Magnitude 8 quakes were exceptionally rare. Only nine had been recorded in the twentieth century. The largest, a magnitude 8.6, occurred in 1964 in Alaska.

The short, seven-week time frame for the New Madrid quakes left Atkins in awe. A seismic triple play. In recorded history, nothing compared. He was well aware that, after the

West Coast, the New Madrid Zone in the nation's heartland provided the greatest earthquake risk in the United States.

Atkins tried to imagine the tremendous force of a cataclysm powerful enough to cut across the biggest river in the United States and, in the process, create a lake. The earthquakes had literally ripped the landscape apart. He'd never seen country like this. The topography was almost eerie: flood plains stretching out for miles, steep bluffs looming in the distance, the twisting river.

Jacobs pointed out a dark line of tree stumps in the water, not far from shore.

"Those are cypress trees, what's left of them," he said. "The quake snapped them off like matchsticks." Each tree was broken off cleanly at approximately the same place.

"Reelfoot was the name of a Shawnee chief," Jacobs said. "The Indian name for this country is Wakukeegu, 'land that shakes.'"

"How did the lake form?" Atkins asked.

"The fault throw during the last big quake was twelve to fifteen feet, high enough to dam a creek and cause the land to subside," Jacobs said. "The water just started backing up. We've got maps from the early part of the nineteenth century. This lake isn't even on them."

It was difficult for Atkins even to imagine that kind of uplift, which illustrated the earthquake's tremendous force. He knew that all three quakes had blown geysers of muck and other debris into the sky and turned the ground into a gumbo of mud and water.

Jacobs explained that the New Madrid quakes actually formed six lakes, all of them huge. The Army Corps of Engineers drained four of them back at the turn of the century for farm land.

"How far is St. Louis from here?" Atkins asked.

"About 150 miles."

"And Memphis?"

Jacobs knew what he was driving at, and smiled. "About 120. You've also got Cincinnati, Louisville, Lexington, Indianapolis, Little Rock, Cairo, Illinois. All within a three-or four-hour drive. Then there's Paducah, Kentucky, Cape Girardeau in Missouri, and a couple hundred smaller towns that are a lot closer."

The two headed back toward their cars, rubbing their arms to keep warm in the cold air. The wind had dropped off. Jacobs smiled and said, ''Depending on whether the New Madrid system connects with two or three other faults, you might want to throw Chicago into the mix.''

Atkins tried to let all that register. How many people were affected? Several million at a minimum. The San Andreas Fault simply didn't compare. A large expanse of Southern California west of the San Bernardino Mountains was sparsely populated. If a bad one hit, the quake would affect only one city at a time. Seismic waves triggered by earthquakes along the San Andreas Fault just didn't travel that far. The rock out there was too soft, too fractured.

The great San Francisco quake of 1906 was a good example. It was only a little less powerful than the largest of the New Madrid quakes, but the damage was limited almost exclusively to a 200-mile radius around San Francisco.

It was a different story out here in the Mississippi River Valley, where seismic waves traveled much farther and where cities and towns were more numerous. The shock waves from the famous quakes rang church bells in Richmond, Virginia, and Charleston, South Carolina. Windows had broken in Philadelphia. It was felt as far away as Montreal. The deep rock in this part of the country was older and harder, which meant the shock waves traveled farther. A big one could send perceptible seismic waves radiating for more than a thousand miles.

Jacobs handed him another map. He'd seen this before, but it was still a shocker. It showed how midwestern quakes dramatically differed from those on the West Coast. Earthquakes of similar magnitude were far more damaging in the heartland and their destructive range far greater.

''How many tremors did you say you get on average every week?'' Atkins asked, studying the map.

''Of a magnitude 1 or better, at least three or four. Sometimes they come in clusters of five or six. Lately, the intensities are getting higher. Fact is, I'm getting a little worried.''

Jacobs wasn't sure he was doing the right thing in sharing his concerns with his friend. When it came to trying to predict an earthquake, candor was risky and usually best avoided. But after meeting Atkins, sizing him up, he decided to get it all out in the open.

"I've been here going on twenty years, and I've never seen so many things pile up," Jacobs said. He was carefully watching Atkins, trying to read him.

"You mean precursors?"

Jacobs nodded. "I wouldn't be so concerned if it was just one or two events. But, hell, we've got a swarm. For starters dilatant strain levels are way, way up."

"How much?"

Dilatancy was a measure of increased pressure on rocks as they swelled or dilated with water. Specifically, it was found that water-saturated rocks placed under strain increased in volume during deformation. There was evidence that as the pressure on the rock increased, cracks began to develop and multiply within the rock, the fractures increasing in number as the pressure built toward the breaking point. Laboratory tests were done, squeezing rocks to high pressure using special hydraulic presses. It hadn't been understood until fairly recently that this microcracking occurred in wet, saturated rocks before they'd break under stress. Delicate instruments could measure the expansion or "volumetric strain" of the cracks. There was some evidence that dilatancy increased before a quake.

"Eight, ten percent. We've also got increases in the magnetic fields." Rocks cracking under pressure and then closing again just before a quake sometimes altered magnetic fields.

Atkins asked about radon emissions. The odorless, radioactive gas was trapped within all rocks. When they started to fracture under stress, as just before an earthquake, greater quantities of gas were sometimes released.

"We've got gauges on ten deep wells scattered along the fault line," Jacobs said. "The readings are all up. A few are way up."

"What about P velocities?" Atkins asked.

The idea behind P, or primary, wave velocities was deceptively simple. Earthquake damage is usually caused by three different kinds of elastic waves. Two of them move within the rock itself: the fast-moving primary, or P, wave and the slower-moving secondary, or S, wave. S waves resemble ripples of water moving near the ground surface, ripples that can hit harder the farther out they travel.

The P wave resembles a sound wave and can penetrate both liquid and solids—volcanic magma, mountain granite, or the ocean. When they reach the atmosphere, P waves become sound waves that can be heard by humans and animals, especially dogs. The sound is often likened to a loud, long crack of thunder.

As an earthquake indicator, P waves were important. If rock properties changed before a quake, then the speed or velocity of the seismic waves passing through them also changes. Measurements from previous quakes suggested that P velocities changed by about ten to fifteen percent before a quake.

"The fluctuations are in the twenty percent range," Jacobs said matter-of-factly.

"What kind of uplift are you getting?"

"Over the last three years, four to five centimeters in places. We're running another GPS survey right now." The Global Positioning System was a complex satellite network operated by the Department of Defense. It allowed precise measurements of the earth's topography. By comparing how the ground had changed over time, where it had risen or shifted, geologists could calculate whether stress was building along a fault. An uplift of four or five centimeters was significant.

"Is this what you brought me out here to talk about?" Atkins asked.

"I didn't want to be too direct," Jacobs admitted. "I thought I'd just show you the data, tell you what we've got. Keep the rockets to a minimum."

Atkins understood perfectly. Any talk about earthquake precursors tended to make seismologists nervous in a hurry. It was professionally risky even to bring up the subject. And yet he had to admit that all of these indicators pointed to something going on.

They climbed into the Jimmy, the stiff wind off the lake pushing hard at their backs.

"So what do we do about the animals?" Atkins asked.

Carefully weighing his words, Jacobs said, "I'm just as skeptical about that as you are, John. But there's been so much of it lately. A lot of animals seem to be doing weird things.''

''What about that sheriff you mentioned?'' Atkins said. ''The guy back in Kentucky who had the friend who raised cattle.'' The sheriff had called Jacobs two days earlier and described the man's problems with his herd. They'd been going on for nearly two weeks.

''He just said they were acting crazy as hell,'' Jacobs said. ''It sounds like more of the same. Your rats and frogs. His cows.''

''I wouldn't mind visiting him and trying to hit a couple of the others on that list you gave me,'' Atkins said. He grinned. ''Who knows, there might be a paper we can write about it later.''

''Only if there's an earthquake,'' Jacobs said. ''And I'm not sure about that.''

''Right, you're just worried as hell,'' Atkins said.

His friend nodded slowly and pulled his snap-brimmed cap lower on his head. ''You've got that right, John. I don't like any of this. I'm a scientist. I'm supposed to rely on facts and nothing but the facts. But I don't like the way this feels.''

Before they left the lake, Jacobs said he'd check out some of the names on the list himself. They'd meet back in Memphis late the next day and compare notes.

AT WALTER JACOBS' SUGGESTION, JOHN ATKINS drove up to meet the Graves County sheriff in Mayfield, Kentucky. It was a short trip from Reelfoot Lake, about thirty miles. The sheriff—his name was Lou Hessel—had called the USGS in Memphis a few days earlier to report that he was taking a lot of calls from farmers about strange animal behavior.

Hessel had lived in the New Madrid Fault Zone his entire life and read whatever he could about earthquakes. It was a hobby with him. He'd read about Chinese studies on the subject and thought Jacobs ought to know about all the calls.

Atkins met Hessel late in the afternoon at the ornate, Victorian-era courthouse in Mayfield.

"Why don't we run on up and see Ben Harvey," the sheriff said. "He's been calling me almost every day for a week, telling me his herd of Black Angus are acting crazy. At first it was happening mainly after dark, and Ben thought someone was trying to rustle them. So he spent a couple nights sitting out in the field in his pickup with a shotgun and a cell phone. Then the cows started bellowing in the daytime, too. The old boy's on edge."

"How many calls have you gotten like his?" Atkins asked. After what he'd already seen, he was more than curious.

The sheriff paused as he filled his pipe with a strong-smelling cherry blend. "In my county, maybe twenty-five. You'd think everybody around here was hittin' the bottle.

But this is the Bible Belt. Most of these farmers don't drink anything stronger than Coca-Cola.''

Atkins followed the sheriff's car ten miles into the country. The low, gray skies had given way to sleet and rain. The wiper blades trapped the icy slush at the edge of the windshield. The air was heavy with the smell of wet hay and grass. It was hilly country broken by pastures and cleared fields. The farms were small and well kept. The barns roughsided and black with age. Turning off the blacktop, they drove up a long gravel road that ended at a cluster of barns, blue grain silos, and other outbuildings. The farmhouse, a two-story clapboard home with green trim, was set back in a grove of oak trees. A pretty place.

The sheriff tapped the horn a couple times. Atkins got out to stretch. He walked over to talk to the sheriff, who'd stayed in his car.

"Ben's got close to ten thousand acres," Hessel said. "He's not hurting, not by a mile, but you'd never know it to look at him. He's using a twenty-year-old combine and drives a beat-up station wagon with a couple hundred thousand miles on the odometer. But don't let his appearance fool you. Ben's pretty sharp.''

The sheriff laid on his horn again. The front door opened. A stout, middle-aged woman wearing a blue-and-white University of Kentucky sweatshirt stepped out on the porch.

"He's out behind the pond, Lou," she said. "Bull gored one of his good heifers.''

The woman sounded upset.

"When did it happen, Barbara?" the sheriff asked.

"About an hour ago. The vet's out there with him.''

"Get in with me. We'll go have a look," the sheriff told Atkins. "That's big trouble." Atkins climbed into the front seat. The sheriff accelerated up a rutted road barely wide enough for the car. "That bull's probably worth close to a hundred thousand dollars. Prime breeding stock.''

They crested a hill. A station wagon was pulled over to the side of the road. A gate opened to a fenced pasture. Just inside the gate, two men were standing over a prone animal.

"Al Barden's with him. One of the best vets in the county." The sheriff put on his gray Stetson and snapped shut his raincoat. "I was hoping I wouldn't have to wear this today in the rain. It's brand-new. Hundred fifty bucks."

Atkins got out of the car and followed the sheriff into the pasture.

A man with a broad ruddy face and thick neck raised his hand in greeting. The cow that lay at his feet was a big animal with white and black coloring. Blood was oozing from a fist-sized hole in its chest.

"Lord almighty, Ben, what's goin' on?" the sheriff said.

Ben Harvey stared down at his dead cow. He wiped the rain from his eyes. "One of my bulls just laid into this heifer," he said slowly. "I've got five or six cows down out in the fields. My whole herd's gone crazy. I thought maybe it was anthrax, but Al here tells me no."

For the first time, Atkins noticed the rifle the farmer carried. He held it close to his side against his rain slicker.

The vet, a young-looking man wearing a hooded poncho, shook his head. "It's not just the cattle herds," he said. "I spent the morning with Ralph Bierce. Couple of his big hogs killed each other before Ralph could get out to the pen. I can't find anything physically wrong with any of these animals. I want to get some blood samples, maybe start calling—"

"Gentlemen, we've got company," the sheriff said.

Atkins looked up and saw a massive animal with curved, jutting horns, standing on the hillcrest, a dark silhouette against the sky. The bull pawed at the muddy earth then slammed its head down as if trying to drive one of the horns deep into the ground.

"Ben, I think he's gonna make a run for us," the sheriff said. The vet had already started moving slowly for the gate. Atkins was about to follow him when the bull charged. It came at a gallop, half sliding down the hill, head down, bellowing in rage.

Atkins figured he'd never make it to the car. There wasn't time. The animal was only thirty yards away and coming hard.

The sheriff stepped away from the dead cow and drew his revolver, a long-barreled Smith & Wesson .357 Magnum.

"No, I'll do it!" Ben Harvey said sharply.

In one fluid motion, he brought the rifle to his shoulder,

sighted quickly down the barrel, and fired. The bull pitched backward as if it had slammed into an invisible wall. It fell over on its side and struggled to get up, its thick hind legs pushing into the soggy ground for traction. Another shot rang out, the sound cracking back from the hills. The bull went down hard and didn't move.

Atkins took a couple slow, deep breaths. His legs were wobbly. The sheriff nodded. He felt the same way himself.

"I sent four kids to college for a lot less than what that bull cost me," Ben Harvey said quietly. "I've been around animals all my life, and I've never seen anything like this. I don't get worked up too easily, but I want to tell you I'm a little scared."

IT WAS LATE IN THE EVENING WHEN ELIZABETH HOL-
leran arrived at her condominium in Santa Monica. The private patio and small garden were what had sold her on the
place, that and the fact that the masonry walls were reinforced and tied to steel footings. Not completely earthquake
proof. No building was, but it was as good as you could do.

The big yellow envelope was propped against the front
door. She'd half expected it. She put it on the dining room
table and poured herself a glass of white wine. She sat there,
staring at the package, afraid to open it. Her name and address were care fully printed in black ink in Prable's distinctive handwriting.

Elizabeth checked her voice mail. One of her graduate
students had called twice, a kid from New York who was
sweating through his dissertation. He was working on an
analysis of fault slippage during the 1995 Kobe earthquake.
The port city in Japan had taken a bad hit, a magnitude 7.2.
Along with the Northridge quake, it was a frightening example of what could happen if a moderately big quake struck
near a large city. The damage in Kobe was far worse than
what had happened in Los Angeles.

Elizabeth took another sip of wine and sat down at the
table. She opened the envelope and took out a videocassette,
two high-density computer disks, and a single sheet of white
paper folded in half.

A key was taped to the paper, on which Prable had
written:

Elizabeth, please watch the enclosed video. Joanne operated the camcorder so forgive the occasional lack of focus. All of this, I hope, will be self-explanatory. If you wish to pursue the matter, my papers and the computer system on which I based my analysis are in my office. The key opens the door.

I only recently completed these calculations. If I hadn't been so sick, I would have sounded the alarm myself, done whatever was in my power to bring this information to the right people. It wouldn't have been easy. The USGS, as you know, can be incredibly obtuse. But I would have tried. The cancer has changed everything. I'm too tired.

I'm sorry to draw you into this, Elizabeth. If you find my analysis accurate and choose to do something, it will be incredibly risky. You will be attacked in ways you can't imagine. If I'm correct in my risk assessments, you don't have much time. Good luck and a thousand blessings.

Prable

Elizabeth slipped the video into her cassette player and sat down. When it started, Otto Prable was slumped in a chair. He wore a dark suit and tie, the same suit he'd worn when he took his life. His face was ghastly. Hollow cheeks, deep-set eyes that peered out from the sockets. His skull showed through his skin.

Holding a clipboard on his lap, he smiled at the camera.

"Hello, Elizabeth," he said, clearing his throat. "I don't have much strength and I tire easily, so I want to get right down to business. Joanne is recording all this. Joanne, say hello to Elizabeth."

"Hello there, Elizabeth," his wife said in a light, almost musical voice. "It's bad enough I have to listen to Otto. Now I've got to film him."

It was so strange for Elizabeth to hear Joanne Prable speak her name. She kept picturing her as she lay on the floor of her bedroom. Elizabeth had to force herself to put the image out of her mind.

There were so many other memories of the Prables: party hosts, intrepid tour guides to northern California, and ballroom dancers. They'd taken up dancing fairly late in life, when Joanne thought it would help her husband get his mind off recent prostate surgery. They were both naturals on the dance floor and were soon winning state competitions, even giving lessons. Elizabeth had gone to several dance contests and marveled at how sexy they looked together, Joanne in a tight blue lamé gown with a daring slit skirt and her robust husband in a white tux. That image lingered as did the many times she'd met them casually. Joanne loved literature and art and was continually forcing Prable to read her latest best-selling discovery. A beautiful couple.

Now she saw Prable sitting in what looked like his front room. A large fireplace was off to the side.

"Elizabeth, you know what I do," he said. "I'm a climatologist. I analyze long-range weather patterns and make predictions on how changes in the weather affect agriculture, the amount of grain shipped from the Midwest, or the need for more heating fuel during an unusually cold winter. As a consequence of my work, I've become interested in solar activity. The impact of sunspots and other solar events on our planet and on our weather cycles. More out of curiosity than anything else. At least that's how it started. I began to plot earthquakes according to periods of peak solar activity and found some curious relationships. The eight greatest quakes on record in this century, starting with the San Francisco quake of 1906, all happened at times of extreme solar activity.

"I also plotted," Prable said, checking his clipboard, "these large quakes according to the earth's position relative to the sun. Most happened during perihelion, the period when the sun is closest to earth. The bigger quakes tend to bunch up in the months of December and January and close to perihelion. The northern hemisphere was especially vulnerable, possibly because perihelion falls there during the winter. These were also periods of high tides, and as you probably remember I've spent a lot of time these last few years looking at how the tides affect our weather.

"I find it extremely interesting that the data from the Apollo space missions to the moon show all kinds of lunar earthquakes happening at perigee, the point where the moon's orbit is closest to the earth. That's also a time of maximum tidal pull, and if I'm correct in my analysis, the period of maximum earthquake stress. Clusters of quakes, some of them huge, happen during periods of strong solar activity and tidal pulls.''

Prable looked up and stared directly into the camera. Elizabeth gave a nervous start. He seemed to be staring straight into her eyes.

He managed a weak smile. ''I know what's probably running through your mind about now, Elizabeth. You're thinking, 'Oh, God. Not another tidal stress theory to explain earthquakes.' I understand your skepticism. I felt the same way until I started looking at where these solar and tidal forces were most likely to have some impact. I concluded that a band of latitude running from roughly eighty-two to ninety-three degrees north will be subject to extremely strong tidal forces on or about January twentieth. Then I began to plot areas where stresses were building on known earthquake faults. Weak, unstable places that might be susceptible to tidal triggering. I ran my own computer analysis. Information from the Global Positioning System was especially valuable. The GPS readings showed me how the topography of an area had changed over time—land movement, uplift, and compression. I was able to compare horizontal and vertical displacements with land surveys from the fifties, your basic topo maps. That helped me identify faults where the crust had shifted the most, where stress was building.''

Elizabeth had recently begun using GPS readings in her own work. Geologists had only recently begun to use the satellite system to map topography. The measurement system was based on triangulation. The precision was breathtaking. Locations down to a couple of millimeters could be pinpointed from space. It was possible to track how the earth's crust was moving and changing from one year to the next.

''My conclusion from all this, Elizabeth, the reason I made this tape for you, is that I believe there's a good chance for a serious quake, possibly a magnitude 7, somewhere in the New Madrid Seismic Zone. The topography data shows an unusually heavy buildup of stress there. My projections indicate the greatest likelihood for such a quake will be during a period two or three days on either side of January twentieth. What makes the New Madrid fault particularly interesting to me is its history.

"As you know, it's produced some of the strongest earthquakes ever to happen in the northern hemisphere. These tremors happened after almost two years of virtually no sunspot activity whatsoever. We've just gone through a similar period. It's only been in the last three months that the solar flares and sunspots have picked up again. Heavy solar activity is predicted for January sixteenth. That's four days before the date of maximum tidal pull."

The theory here, never proven but much debated, was that solar flares and sunspots unleashed powerful solar winds, thereby increasing the number of charged particles streaming from the sun. The solar winds could cause turbulence in the earth's atmosphere, turbulence that could affect the planet's rotation. These slight variations in rotation, so the theory went, could trigger earthquakes.

Prable was visibly weakening. He'd slumped lower in his chair and was having difficulty breathing. He looked into the camera and smiled again. It was taking more effort. The pain showed in the tightness at the corners of his mouth.

"I had my last chemo yesterday," he said. "I stopped it. Total waste of time. It knocks the hell out of me."

Prable took a sip of water. "Elizabeth. Please understand that I haven't limited my analysis solely to solar activity and geological stresses. I've also factored in some other data, which I'm more familiar with—weather assessments and river stages. The New Madrid Seismic Zone cuts straight across the Mississippi River, which drains the entire upper Midwest. That region has sustained almost nine straight months of near-record rainfall. The Mississippi and Ohio rivers have hovered at or near flood stage for five months out of the last eleven. It's likely that more water, in the form of melted snow, will come downstream in the next month or so. All that water will increase the stress on the fault, making it more vulnerable to fracture.

"I'll make the rest of this brief. I can't talk much longer. I want you to check my data. Perhaps I've made a mistake, miscalculated somewhere. I don't believe so, and I'm not afraid to tell you that even though I'm dying, it frightens the living shit out of me. If a large quake hit on the New Madrid

Seismic Zone with anywhere near the magnitude of those in the early nineteenth century, it would be a disaster, a national calamity. In my opinion worse, by far, than the Civil War.''

Prable waved his hand at the camera, a feeble gesture. ''You'll have to do what you think best with all of this, Elizabeth. I wish I were there to help. If there's anything to what my wife the Roman Catholic has been telling me these last few months, maybe I will be able to help you. In spirit as they say.''

Prable smiled, a warm, open smile that radiated from his gaunt face.

''I've changed my will. You are now one of my favored beneficiaries. My net worth may come as a surprise. You'll soon be a wealthy woman, Elizabeth. Consider it partial payment for what I've done to you.''

The tape went blank. Elizabeth sat there unable to move, transfixed by what she'd just seen. She closed her eyes and could still see his face.

ATKINS SAT IN THE FRONT SEAT OF BEN HARVEY'S
pickup, watching the cattle. They'd driven to one of his far
pastures. Sheriff Hessel had left to get back to his office
in Mayfield. He was worried about the weather icing up
the roads.

The behavior of some of the animals was bizarre. Cows
normally moved slowly as they grazed. Atkins watched as
the animals—individually or sometimes three and four at a
time—suddenly lifted their heads up from the feed trough
and trotted stiffly in wide circles.

Harvey couldn't explain it. Or hide his concern.

"They've been doing that on and off for a week," he
said. "I haven't got an explanation. Neither does the vet."

"Have you felt any tremors lately?"

Harvey smiled. "We get three or four little shakes a year
around here. You get used to that pretty quick you live in
this country. Five, six years ago there was a good jolt. Maybe
a 5 on that Richter scale. It didn't do any damage to speak
of except maybe snap a few sewer lines and some gas pipes.
And, friend, it never made my cattle go nuts."

Harvey invited Atkins for dinner and drove back to the
farmhouse. Atkins was eager to leave but Harvey and his
wife, Barbara, insisted that he stay. The pot roast was already
in the oven. The delicious aroma of meat, onions, and sim-
mering gravy filled the kitchen.

Barbara drew a glass of water from the tap.

"Smell that," Harvey said, handing the glass to Atkins.

The odor of sulfur was unmistakable. The water was slightly clouded.

"Three days ago that water was clear and sweet," Harvey said.

"Oh, dear," Mrs. Harvey said, looking out the window. "It's finally starting."

The wind came in gusts, and Atkins heard the sleet hitting the glass like handfuls of pebbles.

"You better spend the night, Mister Atkins," Ben Harvey said. "This keeps up, the road's gonna be solid ice. It's really coming down."

Atkins didn't want to put them out. Even more to the point, he wanted to get back to Memphis as soon as possible and start going over Walt Jacobs' data on the New Madrid Seismic Zone.

"Now that the boys are grown and living on their own farms, we've got four empty bedrooms upstairs," Harvey said. "You're welcome to one of them. I wouldn't go out in that."

Although he was eager to leave, Atkins accepted the offer with gratitude. He enjoyed a huge meal, and afterward Ben Harvey got out a bottle of Old Granddad and poured each of them a jigger. They sat by the fire in the farmhouse's spacious living room. When they turned in, it was still sleeting.

A little after midnight a telephone awakened Atkins. Moments later, Ben Harvey knocked on the bedroom door.

"What is it?" Atkins asked, struggling to clear his head. He'd been in a deep sleep.

"Poachers," Harvey said.

The caller was a hired hand who worked for him. He and his wife lived in a trailer on the far side of the farm. He was getting ready to turn in for the night and had looked outside to check if it was still sleeting. He'd seen some lights in the hills.

"I told him to call the sheriff," Harvey said. "I'll head on out there and take a look myself. There's a lot of deer that winter in those hills. The poachers come after them at night with four-by-fours. The bastards use spotlights. You catch a deer in the light, it won't move, and you can pick it off easy. We had a hell of a problem with poachers a few years back. We finally ran them off. At least I thought we had. It looks like they're back in business.''

Harvey put on his raincoat and boots and got a rifle out of a gun case in the family room. He asked Atkins if he wanted to go with him.

''I wouldn't mind the company if you're up to it. You gotta sit out there in the dark and hope they come your way. It can get kinda boring.''

Left unsaid was what they'd do if someone did come their way.

They walked out to the truck and headed down one of the dirt roads that crisscrossed the farm. The sleet had stopped. They had to drive a few miles, the wheels crunching through thick sheets of ice.

Looming ahead, Atkins saw the low hills, snake-backed and dark.

They were still a mile away when a flash of bluish-white light lit up one of the hillsides.

Harvey stopped and said, ''That's no lantern.''

The light alternated from a pale, luminescent blue to reddish-orange. It flashed, then flashed again, lingering for a few seconds with a strong afterglow. The band of light appeared to hover directly over the ridgeline.

''Are there any power lines or buried cables running across those hills?'' Atkins asked.

''Not that I know of,'' Harvey said. He let out a deep breath, trying to steady himself. ''I've never seen anything like that in my life.''

The hillside had gone dark then the lights burst out again, brighter than ever. They seemed to rise from the ground and settle over the tops of the trees, a color spectrum of white, various shades of blue and orange that radiated in waves.

''What do you think's causing that?'' the farmer asked.

''I don't know,'' Atkins said. And he meant it. He'd read about ''earthquake lights,'' but had never seen them before. Most seismologists—himself included—were skeptical about such lights, even in the face of some fairly dramatic reports. The light show—and according to the descriptions, it could be even more spectacular than this—usually happened before or during an earthquake. The entire sky had reportedly lit up like the northern lights just before a powerful quake struck in Italy in May 1976. More recently, twenty-three spottings of earthquake lights were reported in and around the Japanese city of Kobe before the 7.2 magnitude quake on January 17, 1995. Most appeared as streaks of lightning, arcs of light, or quivering fan-shaped bands of color that appeared to rise above the ground.

They differed substantially from the northern or southern "auroral" lights, which were caused by solar storms that sent energy pulsing into the upper atmosphere along magnetic field lines. The auroral lights were usually seen in northern latitudes, more rarely in southern. They tended to be green or yellow. Earthquake lights were usually blue, white, or orange.

Sightings of earthquake lights were plentiful but good photographs of the phenomenon were rare. They'd often been reported along the coasts of northern California or Mexico, frequently just offshore. Their origin remained a mystery. One theory suggested that the main cause might be the discharge of polarized electricity from rocks during heavy ground shaking.

Atkins stepped out of the pickup. Harvey got out on the other side. The lights that continued to hover over the hills were more vivid now. It looked like sheet lightning.

Atkins wished he had a tape recorder to dictate his description. Or a camera.

"Ben," he said to the farmer. "I'll need to get back to Memphis first thing in the morning. I'll take my chances with the ice."

OTTO PRABLE'S OFFICES WERE JUST OFF WILSHIRE
Boulevard in Santa Monica, a low-rise, nondescript building
that he owned. Elizabeth Holleran drove straight there after
watching the video again. She used the key he'd sent her to
open the front door.

Her heart was pounding when she stepped inside. The
walls to the spacious office were covered with graphs and
color-coded maps that showed the earth's topography in
sharp detail. There was also an array of weather charts—
rainfall, river stages, and flood projections from the Army
Corps of Engineers. The most recent reports were only four
days old. And from the way they were filed, it appeared to
Holleran that Prable had worked almost up to the time he
took his life.

On a table that ran the entire length of the room, eight
computer terminals were arrayed. Holleran almost gasped
when she saw them. They were all Sun Spare 10s, exceptionally powerful computers with a prodigious megabyte capacity. They cost around $40,000 apiece. Holleran's department
had only two of the machines, and on-line time was at a
premium. She'd never seen so many of them in one place.

Prable was linked through his computer network to the
National Weather Service forecasting bureau in Kansas City,
the National Oceanic and Atmospheric Administration in
Boulder, the National Geomagnetic Information Center, and
the National Earthquake Information Center.

Most of the data was in real time. His computers—all

were in the "sleep" mode—captured the information the moment it was produced by the host computers.

Prable even had his own analogue seismograph, which was mounted in a glass case next to what must have been his principal work desk, a kidney-shaped expanse of polished cherry.

Holleran also noticed the direct computer linkup with the Global Positioning System.

She sat down at Prable's desk and logged on to his personal computer, using a password he'd provided: GINNY, his wife's middle name. The first file to appear on screen was a series of color images taken by the Solar Maximum Mission Spacecraft. She remembered Prable's controversial ideas about the triggering effects of solar activity on earthquakes. The eight photographs arrayed on the computer's color monitor were a time-lapse chronograph of a recent coronal mass ejection, or CME, from the sun.

It resembled a hazy gas bubble forming on the surface, rapidly expanding frame by frame until it blew up in long tendrils of brilliant white light, the violent birth of a solar windstorm. The CME images were provided by the High Altitude Observatory of the National Center for Atmospheric Research in Boulder.

Holleran clicked onto another icon. Prable had plotted the approach of this solar windstorm toward earth.

Peak solar activity was predicted for January 16, one week away. Prable's computer graphics showed how the winds were expected to affect the earth's magnetosphere on or about that date. When this solar shock wave hit the earth, Prable had calculated that it would set off a geomagnetic storm strong enough to alter the tides as well as satellite transmissions. And possibly set into motion a chain of events that might result in an earthquake somewhere in the New Madrid Seismic Zone.

Holleran scanned the data with increasing skepticism. It had started eating at her even as she watched Prable's video. The relationship between earthquakes and such phenomena as solar storms, the tides, and gravitational pull was simply too remote and unproven for her to take seriously. She'd never been able to buy into such theories, which were far outside the scientific mainstream. She found herself sitting there wondering how a man of Prable's brilliance could have gone so far astray from his original discipline of geophysics. The waste of it all saddened her.

One of the files contained his analysis of stress buildup along the fault. Holleran found that data far more interesting.

Using two-dimensional computer graphics, Prable demonstrated how ground in the seismic zone had experienced a gradual uplift that started approximately a hundred miles north of Memphis. In one three-hundred-square-mile sector, the ground had risen as much as seven centimeters over four years. That was a huge, rapid change. The computer's graphic presentation of this deformation was outstanding. It showed a dome-shaped uplift, which strongly suggested large, horizontal movements deep underground and a buildup of tectonic strain energy.

Holleran switched to a file named: Earthquake Projection Data.

For the rest of the long night, she pored over Prable's computer analysis of an earthquake risk along the New Madrid Seismic Zone. She was impressed by his marshaling of facts. It was an amazing compilation of data, seemingly disparate, but all focused on a single seismic event.

He'd even provided a statistical analysis of the probability of a major quake on the New Madrid Fault. It was crucial information, for without a probability assessment—an indication of the odds of a quake happening—a prediction was meaningless. Holleran doubted such an assessment was remotely possible based on the data he used, most of which she found seriously flawed. With the exception of uplift along the New Madrid Seismic Zone, it seemed to her the assembled facts had little if anything to do with seismology. She found herself repeatedly questioning his conclusions and much of his data.

Holleran sat in front of the computer monitor, fighting the onset of a headache and wondering if his terminal illness had made Prable irrational, even slightly crazy. His earthquake data, in her opinion, had little or no validity. It was almost pseudo-science.

The one exception, the fact that troubled her, was the degree of deformation he'd found north of Memphis. She hadn't been aware of that. It was quite large. She was sure seismologists at the University of Memphis—they had several good ones—were tracking it. She'd met one of them, the head of the university's earthquake center. He was considered the country's leading authority on the New Madrid Fault. She couldn't remember where they'd met. Probably some conference. She'd try to run down his name and call him in the morning or send an E-mail.

It was hopeless trying to find it now. She'd been up too long without eating anything and was starting to have trouble focusing.

Holleran was beginning to understand Prable's last comments on the video—his apology for what he'd done to her. He'd left her with a real mess on her hands—and a disturbing memory. She could still see the look of fear on Prable's face when he described what might happen on the New Madrid Fault. His fear was genuine.

Holleran downloaded his data onto a disk. She'd been up for twenty hours. Her entire body craved sleep. When she could think more clearly, maybe she could sort some of this out.

THE ALARM NEXT TO ATKINS' BED JARRED HIM
awake. He could smell the aroma of strong coffee. Within
five minutes, he met Ben Harvey in the kitchen. They drove
to the hills where they'd seen the strange lights the night
before. They got out there just as the sun was coming up. A
thin sheet of ice covered the ground and trees.

Atkins wanted to make absolutely sure no power lines or
underground cables were buried nearby. They slogged up
and down the steep, frozen hillside, their boots crunching
through the crusty ice. Atkins was looking for any sign of
fissures or grabens, places where the earth had given way to
form sinkholes. He didn't spot anything unusual in the
topography.

Harvey urged him to have breakfast and wait for the sun
to melt the ice. He'd heard on the radio that driving conditions were treacherous. But by 6:00, after thanking Harvey
and his wife for their hospitality, Atkins was heading back
to Memphis in his rented Jimmy. He kept the speed under
twenty miles an hour on the ice-covered blacktop.

Atkins had a hard time focusing on the road and his driving. He kept thinking about the lights and a possible explanation. If it wasn't a shorted-out electric line, what about
swamp gas? That was probably a stretch, but escaping gas
sometimes emitted a shimmery glow that could be detected
at night. The problem was he hadn't smelled anything out
in the field. He wondered if some kind of strange electromagnetic discharge might be another possibility.

He didn't have any good answers. Not about the lights. Not about the rats that had swarmed over his four-wheel-drive in a field or about all those dead frogs and snakes at Kentucky Lake.

Before he left for Memphis, he'd left a message for Walt Jacobs, telling him about the lights and asking him to pull together all of his seismic data on the New Madrid Fault. As soon as he got back to the USGS's offices at the University of Memphis, he'd make arrangements to send someone to Harvey's farm with a camera. He might even go himself and take another look around. If he did, he'd make sure he brought along a good set of topo maps to check the ground elevations.

After half an hour of white-knuckled driving, Atkins passed a sign for the turnoff to Reelfoot Lake. He was passing right through the center of the New Madrid Seismic Zone.

It was a constant struggle to keep the Jimmy on the road. Even the lightest tap on the brakes sent the back end sliding sideways. He crept up to a rural intersection and pulled to a stop. A Tennessee Highway Patrol car, blue lights flashing, was blocking the highway.

The trooper rolled down the window and waved to Atkins.

"Road's closed ahead," he said. "Got a bridge that's solid ice. Had a bad accident up there couple hours ago. A man's dead."

Atkins explained that he was with the U.S. Geological Survey and was in a hurry to get to Memphis.

"This is important," he said. "I'm willing to take my chances."

"Sorry, no can do," the trooper said. He was polite but firm.

There was a truck stop and diner across the road, a white prefab building with a red awning over the door and three sets of gas pumps. A few cars and pickups were parked on the gravel lot.

"Why don't you get something to eat," the trooper said. "Irma does a damn good breakfast. We ought to have the road open in an hour or so."

Atkins nodded and pulled onto the lot. A few years back, he probably would have argued with the cop. His temper had been an issue with Marci, his last steady girlfriend. They'd had an on-off relationship for nearly two years. A long time for him, the longest since he'd lost Sara. He'd come close to falling in love with Marci. Maybe he even had and hadn't realized it until it was too late. She was a lawyer. Petite, long brown hair, a lovely woman. They'd met on the racquetball courts at the YMCA in Reston. She'd finally walked out on him, and he didn't blame her. She was tired of his temper tantrums and sulking moodiness, but mainly tired of him not being there. He'd gone to Ankorah after an earthquake. When he got back to their apartment three weeks later, she was gone. She'd taken only her clothes.

"I recommend her apple pie," the trooper called out.

Atkins smiled tightly and waved. As he got out of his car, he looked across the road. An old church with faded white paint and a tall, graceful steeple was set back from the intersection. A small home, also made of white clapboard, stood next to it. The parsonage. A cemetery wrapped around the church, a fenced yard with hundreds of gray, weather-beaten headstones that tilted at odd angles.

Atkins heard a dog barking. The animal, a black Lab, was standing on the front porch of the parsonage, head back and howling. As Atkins watched, the big dog began pulling at its chain. Straining to break free, it jerked and tugged so hard that it fell over. The dog got up and lunged again, the chain holding it back. The animal's piercing bark was like nothing Atkins had ever heard. It looked frantic to free itself.

The front door opened. An elderly man wearing a blue sweater and holding a newspaper stepped onto the porch to see what was wrong. The dog instantly turned and hurled itself at him, knocking him down. The man fell hard as the dog kept trying to break its chain.

Atkins ran to help. So did the trooper. A woman opened the door and had to slam it shut when the dog charged her. The old man managed to get up on his knees, grab the chain, and pull the Lab over on its side. He unfastened the lead from the collar and the dog was off the porch like a shot. It was acting crazy. There was no other way to describe it.

Dumbfounded, Atkins watched the animal race across the open field behind the church when the ground began to shake. A mild jolt, quickly followed by a stronger one. Instinctively, Atkins began counting: one, two, three. Four seconds before the shear waves arrived. The earthquake's epicenter had to be close. It was a good shake, one of the strongest he'd felt in years.

The ground rocked for over ten seconds. At least a magnitude 7, maybe more, he figured.

Atkins looked out at the field behind the church and couldn't believe his eyes. The undulating ground was moving from left to right in an S wave. It was headed in his direction. Transfixed, he watched it roll toward him—ground, trees, church, the parsonage riding up and down on its crest as it swept by. The wave knocked him off his feet. He'd been on solid earth one moment, in the air the next.

The trooper had fallen to his knees. He pointed across the road to the church.

"There goes the steeple!" he shouted.

Toppling over, the gilt cross going first, the steeple snapped off at the place where it was attached to the roof. Atkins watched it fall. Then the ground began to heave again. There was a deep rumbling, far off, but building louder. Then the earth erupted in geysers of sand and water. Dozens of blowholes spouting muck twenty feet into the air.

Atkins knew immediately what was happening. Liquefaction. The ground had suddenly liquefied or turned to quicksand. He'd never actually seen it happen before, but this was a textbook example, taking place right before his eyes. A stunning display. The force of the earthquake had blasted up a mixture of foul-smelling water, sand, lignite or "brown coal," and other debris from deep in the ground. As he watched, amazed, four or five separate geysers ripped the cemetery open. Clods of muddy earth, bits of wood and peat were blown into the air. Caskets were pushed up to the surface. Entire coffins lay exposed. Some with only the tops or sides or a smashed end visible, poking up through the ground. A few lids had sprung open. Bodies had pitched out. Skeletons. It was horrific.

The trooper shouted, "Do you hear that?"

The ground thirty feet from Atkins opened with a tearing sound and just as quickly slammed shut again. It cracked and groaned like an ice floe breaking up. The grinding noise was loud, unnerving. The fissure was four or five feet across and could have been several hundred yards long.

There was another good shake, less intense than the first. This one shattered the diner's hand-painted plate-glass window. Customers began pouring out of the place.

Atkins ran to help the old man, who was still lying on the front porch of the parsonage. The house had been pushed off its stone foundation and was listing on its side. The crevasse left a jagged crack in the ground that crossed the road at a right angle, splitting the pavement in a wide gash. The offset was a good two feet.

Atkins got the man under one arm, while the trooper took the other. The man's wife had come out to help. Both of them were dazed with fear. The woman said he was a Baptist minister. They both kept staring at the cemetery, eyes clouded, uncomprehending. The ground was littered with fragments of broken caskets, pooled muddy water, and bones.

It took nearly an hour of trying before Atkins finally managed to get through to Walt Jacobs' office at the University of Memphis. He made the call from the diner.

Jacobs, who'd arrived back in Memphis late the night before, gave him the news. The earthquake was a magnitude 7.1, the biggest quake on the New Madrid Fault in 104 years. The epicenter was about thirty miles northeast of Reelfoot Lake, but the seismic energy had radiated due south. Memphis had taken a solid hit.

"We've got some damage here," Jacobs said, struggling to regulate his voice. "The reports are just starting to come in. Sounds a lot like Northridge. We're going to have some casualties."

MOST MORNINGS STARTED EARLY FOR LAUREN
Mitchell, well before six, and this one was no exception.
Even though they'd had an ice storm the night before, the
white bass were running in the main channel and there were
some die-hard fishermen who put on insulated snowmobile
suits and went out after them in bass boats. It didn't matter
how cold or wet it was. Someone was always out on the
water.

Lauren was getting ready to check the fingerlings in the
minnow tank when the first sharp jolt knocked her to the
floor. Her feet came right out from under her and she went
down hard, barely getting her hands up in time to break
the fall.

Another hard shake was followed closely by two more,
each more powerful than the other. The dock lurched up and
down, straining the mooring cables until they creaked and
vibrated. Fishing rods, reels, and other gear crashed down
from their pegs and shelves. Lauren waited until the wild
seesaw motion slowed before she went outside on the deck.

In a matter of seconds, the lake had changed dramatically.
The water churned with whitecaps. Lauren hardly recognized
it. She'd never seen the normally placid water so rough, not
even during the recent spells when big waves were running.
It was boiling out there.

Lauren had to grip the railing hard when the dock began
rocking again. Water washed over the walkways. For a moment she wondered if the marina was going to pull apart or

collapse. That was the first she realized what was happening: they were having an earthquake. And, by the feel of it, a damn good one.

Thank God her grandson, Bobby, had already left for school in Mayfield, she thought. The boy liked to hang out on the dock in all kinds of weather. If he'd been on one of the narrow walkways that separated the boat slips, he might have lost his balance and gone into the water.

It would have been a good time for that geologist to be here. When this was over, maybe she'd give him a call in Memphis. If they were looking for reasons why all those animals were going crazy, they had their answer now. She remembered the frozen frogs and snakes. Somehow they'd known what was coming.

She wished suddenly that her husband Bob were still alive. Maybe he could have made some sense of all this.

God, how she missed the man. She'd never gotten over his death.

Lauren had bought the boat dock nearly twenty years earlier using insurance money she'd received after her husband and fourteen other men were killed in a coal mine accident. They were working in the Golden Orient, the deepest, most deadly mine in Kentucky. A cave-in on level 15 had trapped Bob and the others fifteen hundred feet underground. It took six weeks to get the bodies out. They found all of them in a twenty-foot-long section of tunnel. The air had probably given out in about an hour. Everyone, her husband included, had suffocated, but not before many of them had scribbled notes to their wives and loved ones on scraps of paper and stuffed them in their pockets. She kept Bob's note framed on her dresser. There were only seven words: I LOVE YOU. GOD KEEP YOU SAFE.

A year after Bob's death, Lauren bought the dock and marina. She and her grandson lived on a two-hundred-acre farm about two miles away. They had a stable and three horses. It was a good life. The dock was making a little money. Lauren couldn't complain. Her parents had recently moved to Heath, near Paducah. She was living on their farm. Her dad had decided to move into the city when it got too hard to climb up on a tractor. Her mother hadn't minded at all. She'd jumped at the chance to leave the country.

The dock was still bumping up and down in the rough water. Lauren got a pair of binoculars and focused on the big dam that loomed two miles in the distance. It stretched nearly a mile and a half across the north end of the lake. Kentucky Route 41, a two-lane blacktop, ran right along the top of it.

Lauren couldn't believe what she was seeing. Huge waves were slamming up over the rim of the dam. It looked as though the water was washing right over the highway. She'd never seen anything like that before.

ELIZABETH HOLLERAN HAD GOTTEN UP MUCH LATER than usual. She slipped into a pair of khaki chinos and a denim shirt and went into the kitchen to make a pot of coffee. She normally drank decaf, but not this morning. Groggy with fatigue, she needed a jolt of the real thing. She'd crawled into bed shortly after 3:00 A.M., then had awakened twice, unable to sleep, too agitated by Otto Prable's video and the data she'd seen at his office.

Holleran was trained to be extremely skeptical about any purported earthquake prediction. It was an inbred, almost instinctive defense mechanism. There were too many well-meaning incompetents. Too many psychics. Too many wild-eyed quacks ready to come out of the woodwork and forecast a big quake. She'd come by her skepticism naturally. Her father was a retired biologist who'd taught at Northwestern for nearly thirty years. What she knew about the rigors of the scientific method and self-discipline she owed to him. He'd trained her to rely solely on her own observations and verifiable facts; nothing else mattered. Nothing.

Holleran wanted to go over Prable's data again and examine it carefully with all the critical skepticism she could muster. She wanted to do her best to find the holes that would quickly disprove it. There was bound to be a miscalculation or false assumption on his part, but it might take her days of hard work to ferret it out and she didn't have any time to spare.

She needed to call Jim Dietz. She'd meant to do that yesterday, but had completely forgotten once she started looking at Prable's data. Their plan had been to work the trench at Point Arguello for another two or three days, depending on the weather.

Holleran turned on the radio and got out some breakfast dishes. By then it was past 8:00. Time for the news. She caught something about a strong quake with damage and injuries near Memphis. Holleran dropped her cereal dish in her haste to turn up the volume. Milk and cornflakes splashed onto the tile floor.

The quake had occurred four hours earlier. It measured a magnitude 7.1 on the Richter scale.

That was a pretty big one and right in the New Madrid Seismic Zone.

Right where Otto Prable had predicted a major earthquake was likely to strike.

NEIC: Near-Real-Time Earthquake Bulletin
http://www.neic.cr.usgs.gov/neis/bulletin/bulletin.html

USGS
National Earthquake Infromation Center
Geological Hazards

Products & Services	Current Earthquakes	Earthquake Information
Earthquake Search	Earthquake Links	Station Book

COMMENTS

THE FOLLOWING NEAR-REAL-TIME EARTHQUAKE BULLETIN IS PROVIDED BY THE NATIONAL EARTHQUAKE INFORMATION SERVICE (NEIS) OF THE U.S. GEOLOGICAL SURVEY AS PART OF A COOPERATIVE PROJECT OF THE COUNCIL OF THE NATIONAL SEISMIC SYSTEM. UPDATED AS OF JAN 10 06:35:14 MST. ALL TIMES BELOW ARE LOCAL.

DATE	TIME	LAT	LON	DEP	MAG	Q	COMMENTS
mm/dd	hh:mm:ss	deg.	deg.	km			
01/10	06:22:13	37.46N	88.50W	33.0	7.1Mb	A	New Madrid Seismic Zone
01/09	23:02:15	54.36N	164.05W	22.0	5.9	C	Unimak Island Region
01/09	06:11:50	22.17S	170.51E	16.0	6.2Ms	B	Loyalty Island Region
01/09	10:09:52	37.66N	118.87W	5.0	3.1	A	California-Nevada Border

Stunned, Holleran hurried to her bedroom where she kept her laptop. Within seconds she was hooked into the Internet site for the U.S. Geological Survey's National Earthquake Information Center. Based in Boulder, the center continually updated seismic episodes around the world.

There were already several entries for the New Madrid quake. The epicenter was approximately 120 miles north of Memphis in extreme southwestern Kentucky. The earthquake had hit at 12:22 Universal Time. Some buildings in Memphis had collapsed, and there were early reports of loss of life.

Holleran nervously tapped in the homepage for the USGS Center for Earthquake Research at the University of Memphis. It was the main clearinghouse for the New Madrid Seismic Zone. She watched as a profile of the quake's seismic pattern slowly scrolled down on the screen. It was striking.

The east-west ground motion was exceptionally violent. The P and S waves looked like saw-toothed mountain peaks interspersed with plunging valleys. P stood for the primary wave. It arrived first. The S, or secondary, wave was slower-moving but harder-hitting. Both were body waves, originating in the body of the rock. The amplitude—represented by the height of the wave—was pronounced. The shaking had lasted forty seconds. So the quake was of fairly long duration.

Holleran punched a couple of computer keys and got a model of the P and S waves.

The S waves had continued for nearly fifteen seconds. Their elastic vibrations sheared or twisted rock sideways and moved the earth with an up-and-down, side-to-side motion. The quake's surface waves, the Love and Rayleigh waves, had also been of long duration.

The quake had been felt five hundred miles away in Chicago, where the skyscrapers along Michigan Avenue had swayed slightly. The buildings hadn't suffered any damage, but the oscillations had continued for a full minute. Moderate damages—mainly collapsed chimneys and broken gas lines—were reported in St. Louis about 170 miles away. There were similar reports from Little Rock and Louisville. The quake had been felt in Pittsburgh and Charleston, South Carolina.

Those distances were a little short of incredible to a California-trained seismologist like Holleran.

The radio had an update about injuries in Memphis. Eleven people were dead, crushed in their cars when a section of a highway overpass had fallen. Hospital ERs were jammed and the death toll was expected to rise. An old, river city like Memphis had an abundance of unreinforced brick buildings. Holleran would bet some of them had crumbled like card castles when the first strong waves hit.

Her pulse racing, Holleran took some breaths to try to settle down. Her hands were trembling when she picked up the telephone to call Jim Dietz.

Holleran pressed the auto dialer for the dig site at Point Arguello. Dietz picked up the phone. He'd already been at work for an hour and had gone back to the trailer to fill his water jug.

"Did you hear about the quake in New Madrid?" she asked.

"I just checked out the Internet site at Boulder," he said. "Pretty nice magnitude."

"Jim, I'm not going to make it out there today."

"You finally got that big date, right?" Dietz, as ever, his charming self.

"I'm going to Memphis."

The line went quiet. She began to tell him about Otto Prable.

PILLARS OF THICK BLACK SMOKE FRAMED THE TALL
buildings downtown, the Midwest Bank and Raldo Towers,
as well as the two bridges over the Mississippi. There was
more smoke than Atkins had expected. More fires. He figured
most of them had probably started after the earthquake shattered gas lines. Entering Memphis on Route 61, he'd just
gotten his first good look at the city's skyline.

He picked up Interstate 40 just after it crossed into the
city from West Memphis, six lanes of stalled traffic going in
either direction. The Pyramid, the city's distinctive riverfront
auditorium, was right behind him. A five-story brick warehouse was burning fiercely a couple blocks off the highway.
The dancing flames were giving everyone a hell of a show.

Atkins had a perfect vantage point. He could look right
down Thomas Street from the elevated highway. Fire
trucks—pumpers, snorkels, and other pieces of heavy equipment—encircled the building. It looked solid, thick-walled,
old. Watching from the driver's seat, Atkins worried that the
firefighters were much too close. There was no telling how
much the walls had been weakened or what would happen
in a good aftershock.

Atkins rolled down a window. The wail of sirens seemed
to be coming from a dozen directions at once. The Memphis
fire department was probably stretched pretty thin by now.
Fire was often the big killer in an earthquake. A lot of people
didn't realize that. Even those who should have known better

like building engineers who routinely forgot to turn off gas and electrical power after a quake.

Listening to the sirens—the sound seemed to wrap around the entire city—Atkins wondered how many people had been hit by falling masonry or glass. Rushing into the street during an earthquake was another common, often fatal mistake. A natural reaction, Atkins had done it himself. But it could be deadly around tall buildings.

None of the city's new skyscrapers had collapsed, but the ground waves had made them sway like trees in a strong wind. Some of the windows had exploded, raining glass on the streets.

As he listened to the radio, Atkins knew that the worst damage was centered just south of Beale Street, the famous blues mecca, where many of the homes and low-rise buildings had shifted on their foundations. That's where some of the biggest fires had broken out.

Damage in the city was spotty but widespread. Even Walter Jacobs' office at the University of Memphis had taken a hit. The Center for Earthquake Studies was located in a converted two-story home on the edge of the campus. The chimney and part of the cornice had crashed through the roof into one of the bathrooms. A grad student who showed up early to crunch numbers on a computer in an adjoining room had a close call.

Atkins had gotten a rough description from Jacobs by cell phone. They decided to meet at the scene of a building collapse. Some bricklayers had been salvaging their work on the walls of a discount shopping center. Two twelve-foot-high sections of solid brick had fallen over in one of the aftershocks, crushing the men. Rescuers were frantically trying to dig out any survivors.

All told, a pretty bad quake, but nothing like a big one. You had to experience a magnitude 7.5 quake or greater to appreciate what could happen. Live through one; lose a good friend. Or maybe the woman you wanted to marry. That's how Atkins tended to grade earthquakes. It was his own personal scale of magnitude. Memphis had been rocked, but its 7.1 hadn't been a real killer. It wasn't like Luzon in 1990, or Kobe, or Mexico City.

Still, this one had been something. The image of the ground rolling like an ocean wave stuck in his memory. He'd never seen anything like that firsthand.

It hadn't happened for a while, but as Atkins made his way off the interstate and headed south on Martin Luther King Boulevard, the old memories came back. He remembered the evening before the quake had hit Mexico City. He was powerless to stop the images from coming, or even slow them down. How Sara and he had made love on the small bed in their hotel room.

Atkins had had the feeling then that Sara wanted all of him, and for the first time in his life, he was ready to give it, to surrender to someone entirely. That night he decided he would share his life with her. He would hold nothing back. She understood and responded with her body in a way she never had.

Driving in the slow-moving traffic, Atkins experienced a moment of intense pain. He knew what had happened. It had happened to him before. Seeing the damage, the shattered buildings, and the body bags after a bad quake made the images of Mexico City come sweeping back. The memory of his last night with Sara in that hotel hit even harder. He would never get over it.

He pushed the memory away. There wasn't time for that now.   •

AS Atkins continued south, many of the intersections were blocked by police cars, fire trucks, and clusters of ambulances. He drove by the main entrance to Graceland. The white-columned mansion of Elvis Presley was on a low hill and partly hidden by trees. Two of his private airplanes, a jet and a turbo-prop, were parked on a small plaza across the street. Even after an earthquake, a line of visitors had already formed, waiting for the landmark to open, mainly elderly, silver-haired women who'd descended from a tour bus. They weren't going to let an earthquake keep them from paying homage to the King.

The collapsed shopping center was near the intersection of Presley Boulevard and Raines Avenue. Atkins parked a few blocks away. Police had strung yellow crime-scene tape around the perimeter of the building. Red and blue lights flashed along streets jammed with emergency vehicles.

Rescue workers were digging furiously around the edges of the wall, searching for survivors, probing the ground with sticks and their hands. A couple of heavyset cops were using dogs.

One look was enough to tell Atkins they were probably wasting their time. The entire west wall, about forty yards of brick, had fallen on the workers.

Atkins spotted Jacobs in the crowd. He was hunched over with a cell phone screwed into his right ear. He wore a battered yellow hard hat, a muddy overcoat, and high-topped rubber boots. An ID badge hung from a chain around his neck.

Jacobs waved him over. "Another reporter," he said, putting the cell in his coat pocket. "It's been nonstop since I got up. I've already called Reston and asked them to send us some media people. We're gonna need all the help we can get."

"How many dead?" Atkins asked.

"So far, twenty-six. There could be seven or eight more buried right here. No one seems to know exactly how many were up on the scaffold when the wall fell over."

Atkins wanted to know about aftershocks. These were often more deadly than the initial earthquake, bringing down already weakened buildings with astounding suddenness. He'd seen it happen often enough. The first time was in Mexico City.

Jacobs shook his head. "I've got five people out setting up a PADS network. So far we've had nothing significant."

PADS stood for "portable autonomous digital seismographs." The suitcase-sized devices were used to record aftershocks and track strong ground motion. Some of the instruments were being shipped in from the USGS research center in Boulder. They didn't have enough on hand in Memphis, one of Jacobs' chronic complaints even though he was no longer with the agency. The lion's share of USGS funds and equipment invariably went to California. The New Madrid Seismic Zone had always been a poor sister to the San Andreas Fault. Jacobs didn't dispute that the earthquake risks were greater in California, where they happened far more often. He just wanted to make sure the very real danger in the heartland was also adequately studied. So far, the risk here had not been recognized. The shortages of equipment and staff were glaring.

He handed Atkins a printout from a seismometer.

"The epicenter was right on the Tennessee-Kentucky line. Nearest town is a place called Mayfield. I've been there. It's up by Kentucky Lake. Right smack in the middle of the New Madrid Seismic Zone."

One of the rescuers raised a hand, motioning for the other diggers to stop. They were all firemen. Despite the cold, some of them had taken off their heavy yellow coats and were working in shirtsleeves. They'd just pulled a man from beneath the wall. He was completely covered with mud. Atkins watched as a big, red-faced fireman with a thick beard wiped mud from the man's mouth and nose and, kneeling next to him, began mouth-to-mouth resuscitation. Another man hurried over with a canister of oxygen. They put the mask over the bricklayer's mouth.

The big man got up, picked up a shovel, and went back to work along the wall. He already knew the outcome. After a few more minutes, an EMS technician covered the bricklayer with a green poncho and helped carry the body to an ambulance.

Spectators had gathered, hundreds of them. They were watching the show in hushed silence, pushing in as close as they could. The cops tried to keep them back, but it wasn't easy. There weren't enough of them, nowhere near enough.

That never changed, Atkins thought. Gawkers always turned out in force after an earthquake. So did looters. In Mexico City he'd seen a man break a dead woman's fingers to get her rings off.

"Well, it looks like all your observations were right on target," Atkins said. "Even down to the animals."

Jacobs had actually anticipated the quake. True, it wasn't an exact prediction—he didn't give a time or a precise location or a probability, all key ingredients. And yet Atkins thought his friend still had reason to be proud. So much of their science remained highly intuitive. Jacobs thought conditions were ripe for a quake and had been proven right. That was about as good as the science currently allowed.

"I'd say so," Jacobs said. "We haven't had a temblor that strong since the one I was telling you about back in the 1890s. We were sure overdue."

THE TWA 737 BANKED LOW. THEY WERE APPROACHING
the Memphis airport from the south at twilight, for Elizabeth
Holleran always a beautiful time of the day when the light
was strange and soft. Staring out the window, she saw the
Mississippi curving south in a wide, caramel-colored cres-
cent. Large parts of the city were dark, still without electricity twelve hours after the earthquake. Then the plane banked
again, and she noticed the fires. She counted at least ten
of them.

Holleran had flown from Los Angeles to St. Louis, then
caught a connecting flight to Memphis after a three-hour
layover. She'd traveled light, with a few pairs of slacks,
shirts, and sweaters in her garment bag, and her laptop. Several times during the forty-minute trip, the captain had provided updates about the earthquake. More than thirty people
were dead. Traffic was a mess. Hospital ERs filled to
capacity.

They were lucky, the captain told them in a drawling accent. The quake hadn't knocked out the airport's runway
lights; otherwise they would have had to shut down Memphis International.

Holleran remembered his comment about the snarled traffic an hour later after she got a rental car and slowly merged
onto Airways Boulevard. The woman at the rental counter
had warned that driving anywhere would be difficult—especially at night. They were issuing radio reports every ten
minutes, telling people to stay at home. She advised Holleran

to check into one of the motels near the airport and wait until morning. But Holleran was eager to get to the University of Memphis and try to track down the head of their earthquake center, Walt Jacobs.

She'd finally remembered his name and where she'd met him. It was in San Francisco for a seminar on the Northridge quake of 1994. She doubted he'd remember her. He'd presented a paper on the New Madrid Seismic Zone, and she'd asked a few questions. She'd spent the better part of the day trying without luck to reach him by telephone. She figured this was one night he'd be working late and hoped to find him at the university. She'd brought Otto Prable's data. It was loaded on her laptop.

Ever since she'd heard about the quake, she'd been wondering if he'd made an incredibly lucky guess. Or, more troubling, was there something potentially valid in his data that needed to be examined?

Prable had predicted a major quake a few days either side of January 20. He'd missed it by about a week.

Holleran was inclined to think her old mentor had made a remarkably good guess partly based on a few scientifically solid details, including the rate of ground deformation. That's what she wanted to talk over with Jacobs. If he'd even see her. She wasn't so sure he'd have time to talk about Prable and his admittedly bizarre theories. She still remained highly skeptical, but at the very least, the quake had made her less inclined to write his work off quite as easily as before. She was willing to let someone else examine his data. She owed him that much.

She quickly regretted not taking the advice of the woman at the airport. She hadn't gone six blocks before she hit her first detour. The facade of an old building had collapsed, spilling a deep pile of bricks into the street. Following a single lane of traffic around the obstructions, Holleran had to make a right turn and immediately ran into another detour. Most of the streetlights were out.

Holleran hunched over the steering wheel, straining to see the street signs. She had no idea where she was or in what direction she was going. Fewer cars were on the road. She suddenly realized she was in an inner-city neighborhood, block after block of single-story, low-rise apartment buildings, many with boarded windows. Dozens of people were walking in the street or milling on corners, mostly young men. A few had flashlights or ghetto blasters with the volume cranked up.

The car in front of her lurched to a stop and tried to turn around. Men swarmed around it, rocking the front end up and down.

Stunned, Holleran cut the wheel in a tight circle and floored the gas pedal. Something slammed against the roof. A hard metallic sound. They were throwing rocks at the car.

She turned up another dark, narrow side street. She still had no idea where she was and switched on the high beams. More public housing apartments loomed ahead. More people were out. It was a party atmosphere—blaring rap music, laughter, shouts. She saw someone carrying a torch.

Off to the left, the sky glowed a dull orange. A big fire. She started heading in that direction. There were bound to be firemen and police there. She was angry with herself for being so foolish. She should have listened to the woman at the car rental agency and not tried this at night.

She made sure the doors were locked. She had to slow down again when a car cut in front of her. A slender youth smiled at her from the sidewalk. He wore baggy pants and a baseball cap with the brim bent up. She passed two more men, wearing hooded sweatshirts. One of them gave her the finger.

Don't panic, she told herself. Whatever happens, don't get out of the car.

Something heavy banged against the front bumper of the Taurus and careened off to the side. They'd hurled a trash can at her. Holleran smashed through some more cans and kept going.

They were trying to close the street, lining up side by side and forming a human wall. She punched the accelerator and headed straight for them. A few had to dive out of the way. She heard their obscene shouts.

Gripping the wheel, she sped through an intersection. Missing a turn, she backed up and went down another street. She was trying to get closer to the fire. The flaming sky was brighter, but she was lost in a maze of side streets and cul-de-sacs.

She saw headlights up ahead. Two cars with their doors open were sideways in the street. Six or seven men and women were standing there, arguing. Holleran slowed down.

More rocks hit the car. A man put his grinning face up to the window and shouted, "Stop, bitch!"

Holleran banged up on the sidewalk. As she went around the stalled cars, more rocks rained down on the roof and hood. When she tried to turn back onto the street, the rear tires got hung up. They'd dropped into an open drain. The tires spun, burning rubber. She threw the gears into reverse and began rocking the car back and forth, trying to free the tires.

The man who'd screamed for her to stop had a brick in his hand. He tried to smash the driver's window, hitting the glass again and again. It shattered but didn't break. Holleran buried the gas pedal. The tires spun free, the car swerving as it roared back into the street.

There was more traffic up ahead. The street widened to four lanes. The vapor lights were working. A major intersection. Police cars were clustered on the parking lot of a convenience store. She pulled up next to them and turned off the engine. She sat there breathing deeply. Her hands were shaking.

She smelled smoke from the fire. She was very close to it.

A cop came around to her window.

"You all right?" he asked, stepping back to stare at the car. "Where did that happen?"

"Back there," Holleran said as she got out and explained.

Looking surprised, the cop said, "That's Melrose Gardens. You were lucky you got out of there in one piece tonight. Everybody's out on the streets since the quake. We're getting a lot of calls."

"I didn't see any police," Holleran said.

"You got that right," the cop said. "No way are we gonna go in there without lights and a lot of backup."

Holleran looked at him more closely. He was young, maybe early twenties. He looked scared, and she realized what was frightening him. They'd come close to the collapse of law and order, the prospect of mobs roaming the streets.

"What's on fire?" she asked, putting those troubling

thoughts out of her mind. The wind had changed. The smell of smoke was very strong.

"An old meat-packing plant," he said. "A couple blocks that way." He pointed with a long-handled flashlight. "Gas line broke or something. It's been running at five alarms all afternoon. They're letting it burn itself out."

Holleran looked at the convenience store. The plate-glass windows were shattered. She saw two cops with radios walking around to the back and headed that way without thinking much about it. She needed to walk, get control of her nerves.

She could imagine sitting in front of the fire with her dad and older sister back in Chicago. Her mom in the kitchen, getting dinner ready. "Let me tell you about Memphis. You won't believe what it was like to drive there." She'd describe her arrival in the city. Her father would shake his head and sip his Manhattan. He'd tell her she needed to get a handgun and learn how to use it. It had become gospel with him. He'd even offered to buy guns for Elizabeth and her sister, Mary. And pay for the shooting lessons. Before the day ended, he'd wind up raking over the Democrats and President Nathan Ross, all liberals, and the news media until her mom told him to calm down. Her father was Irish and weepy emotional. He'd cried openly the day she'd scored her first soccer goal. She was in first grade, and it was the last game of the season. Mary was a lawyer, who'd sailed through Duke law and was working for a small but good firm in L.A.

Elizabeth pictured telling them what had just happened and almost smiled at the prospect. It was so unreal.

"I wouldn't go back there, miss," the cop said, hurrying after her. "Couple kids were looting the place after the earthquake. When a cruiser pulled up, they bolted. One of 'em didn't make it out."

Elizabeth went just far enough to look around the side of the building. Five or six cops were back there with flashlights pointed at a window. A heavyset teenager in a white windbreaker was lying spread-eagled across the broken sash. He wasn't moving.

"Where were you trying to get to?" the cop said, still trying to be helpful.

"The University of Memphis," Elizabeth said.

"That's way across town," the cop said. "You really got yourself lost."

Elizabeth nodded, half listening. The sight of the dead looter didn't bother her nearly as much as something else. She'd noticed the cracks in the foundation of the store. Some of them were more than six inches wide. They were huge. Bigger than anything she'd seen in Los Angeles after the Northridge quake.

THAT EVENING LAUREN AND BOBBY MITCHELL HAD
a late supper—cornbread, baked ham, fruit salad. Bobby's
favorite meal. He'd been working so hard lately around the
boat dock, never complaining, that she wanted to reward him.

They lived in a two-bedroom ranch house with cedar sid-
ing set back on a hill a couple miles from Kentucky Lake.
Bobby took care of their two quarter horses, Sam and Rob
Roy. He did most of the work in the stable, cleaning out the
stalls twice a day and laying down fresh hay before he left
for school and, again, after he finished his homework in
the afternoon.

As she set out the dinner plates, Lauren had the radio
tuned to a station in Memphis. It was a call-in show, and
they had a man on from the University of Memphis, a geologist. They were talking about the earthquake.

Memphis still wasn't anywhere near back to normal. Parts
of the city remained without electricity and water. It looked
like the final death count stood at thirty-nine, including seven
bricklayers who died when a wall fell on them. A section of
the I-240 freeway had collapsed at Union Avenue, crushing
a beer truck and its driver. An old warehouse filled with
paint was still burning on Cotton Row on Front Street near
the river.

The geologist mentioned that the quake's epicenter was
near Mayfield, Kentucky.

''Grandma, we've played them in basketball,'' Bobby said.
The small town was only thirty miles to the west.

"Shush. I'm trying to listen, son." The man was talking about aftershocks.

There'd been a couple of them, nothing severe, but definitely noticeable. Strong enough to keep her on edge.

"The biggest we've had so far was a magnitude 3.2," the geologist said in his slow, soothing Southern accent. "The activity appears to be subsiding—at least as far as the bigger aftershocks are concerned. But we could feel minor shakes for weeks, maybe months."

Lauren figured they'd been lucky. Their dock and home had only minor damage. A couple of broken windows. Some cracked plaster and maybe a chimney that would need tuck-pointing. Some neighbors hadn't been so lucky. There were a lot of damaged foundations and broken sewer and water pipes. A farmer over in Campbell, the county seat, had his whole barn collapse. It fell down like a cardboard box.

The damage had been far more severe across the state line in northeastern Tennessee. There'd been reports that people had actually seen the ground moving like the waves of the ocean. She still had trouble believing that.

Lauren went to bed about an hour later. As she did every night, she lay there thinking about her husband. There were moments, especially as she waited in the dark for sleep to come, when she had to fight back her anger at him for getting himself killed. He'd promised he was going to quit the mines, promised it again at breakfast the morning of the cave-in. He'd said he'd had enough. And then he left for work at 5:00 in the morning carrying a thermos of hot coffee and a lunch pail and never came back.

She couldn't help the way she felt, blaming him for leaving her without a husband. She needed him.

Later, when she tried to remember what happened, piece it all together in the right sequence, she couldn't recall exactly what had awakened her. She didn't think it was the aftershock. Not at first anyway. For some reason she woke up and glanced at the clock on her nightstand; it was just after two in the morning. She heard the furnace kick on. It was cold, below freezing.

She'd started to drift off again when the ground began to shake. Her four-poster bed jostled on the hardwood floor, rocking sideways. She sat bolt upright. A framed photograph of her husband fell over on the dresser. Dishes and coffee cups fell from open shelves in the kitchen, shattering onto the floor.

Lauren slipped into a sweatshirt and pulled on a pair of jeans and boots.

She thought the big aftershocks were supposed to be over. This was definitely one of the stronger ones.

Bobby hurried into the hallway with a flashlight. It was the first Lauren realized that their power was out.

"Grandma, my Michael Jordan poster fell down," he said excitedly. The poster over the bed was his most prized possession. He wasn't frightened in the least. This was fun.

The horses were whinnying and snorting out in the stable behind the house. The quake had spooked them. Lauren went to the back door and looked up at a beautiful, starlit sky.

"Listen! What's that sound?" Bobby had put on his school jacket and was standing next to her on the porch.

She heard the deep rumble. The pounding of rushing water. She realized immediately what it was. What it had to be. They'd opened the discharge gates at the dam.

It took a moment for that to register. She'd lived near the lake two years and they'd never come close to fully opening the gates, which regulated the flow of water into the Tennessee River and drove the huge hydroelectric turbines.

The river levels were already at flood stage. The Tennessee was dangerously high, so why were they releasing water? It didn't make any sense. It would only put a lot of extra pressure on the already weakened levees.

Lauren flung on a coat and told Bobby to go back to bed.

"I want to go with you, Grandma."

"No way, José," she said, scooting him back to his bedroom. "You go to sleep, and that's an order. I'll be right back."

LAUREN drove onto the dam—Route 641 crossed right over it—and stopped at the first overlook, one of several places where motorists could pull off the two-lane road and admire the view of Kentucky Lake. There was no traffic at that hour.

Lauren got out of her pickup. There was a strong, cutting wind off the water. She hardly recognized the lake. Whitecaps were running four and five feet high, the action as rough as during the earthquake two days earlier. Spray flew up as the waves hit the broad, curving wall that plunged vertically to the water. The crashing sound was barely audible over the roar of the water pounding through the dam's open gates.

The huge gates—a row of twelve, each the size of a tractor trailer stood on end—were on the opposite side of the dam about midway across the lake. That's where water was released into the Tennessee River, and where the control house and generators were located. At that point, the dam was more than two hundred feet high.

Staring into the blackness of the lake, Lauren saw the lights of the marinas flickering along the far shore. Her own dock and boathouse were up a long cove that ran back about two miles from the dam.

The cold spray stung her face. She got back into the pickup and drove to the powerhouse. To get there, she had to go to the far end of the dam, turn off on a service road, and double back through a series of curves that ended at the parking lot. On the riverside of the dam now, she got her first look at the massive gates. The lake water was ripping through them in long, white plumes, thundering down thirty feet into the wide canal that fed the Tennessee River.

The powerhouse, a three-story building made of gray stone, was built on a shelf close to the riverside of the dam. On the front of the building that faced the highway, the word KENTUCKY was spelled out in big red letters. The facility regulated the flow of water through the locks, which powered the dam's hydroelectric generators.

Lauren parked. She knew one of the engineers there, Tom Davis. He was a hydrologist with the Tennessee Valley Authority. He and his wife lived up the road from her. They'd built a log cabin with a monster deck. They all went to the same church, United Methodist. Lauren recognized his pickup. Another car was next to it.

The lights were on inside the building. Lauren went into the control house, a room with large windows that overlooked the river. No one was there. She heard someone climbing up the ladderlike stairway that descended to the lower levels, where the dam's mechanical works were located. She'd taken several tours of the place. You could actually get inside the inner walls.

Tom Davis came up the metal steps. His face was ashen. Mouth slack.

"Tom, what's going on?" Lauren asked.

He walked past her to a panel of gauges. Spotlights illuminated the open gates and the torrents of rushing water.

"We almost lost her," he said, leaning on both hands against the control panel. "I swear to God. We almost lost the dam."

Lauren stared at him. Her legs felt unsteady.

Tom Davis kept talking in the same low, almost sleepy voice. Lauren wasn't even sure he knew she was standing there.

"I was up here when that last quake hit." He turned toward her, and Lauren saw the bright glitter in his eyes. "I heard one of the walls cracking from the strain. An inner wall down by the waterline."

Lauren leaned against a counter and let it hold her up. She wanted, needed, to sit down. The only chair was the raised stool at the control panel. Tom Davis was gripping it hard.

"I opened the gates to get the level down," he said, his voice soft, almost inaudible. "We've got to get the pressure off the wall. I don't know how much longer the dam can hold."

Two men hurried up the stairway from the lower level, their boots clanking on the metal steps. They wore hard hats. One of them was talking on a cell phone. They stopped in their tracks, surprised to see Lauren.

"Lady, you've got to leave," one of them said. He wore a windbreaker. His close-cropped black hair was streaked gray at the temples. A big guy in a white shirt and tie at 3:00 in the morning. Broad shoulders. He looked to be in his early fifties.

"I don't think so," Lauren said. He reached for her arm, his jaw set. She pulled away from him.

"They're with the Seismic Safety Commission," Tom said in that same strangely detached voice. "They've been out here looking at the dam since the first quake. They came straight over after that aftershock."

The man in the windbreaker shot him an angry glance and told him to keep quiet.

"You have to leave," he repeated to Lauren.

"Don't even try to lay a hand on me," she said.

The other man had put the cell phone in his pocket. He was younger than his partner, a little shorter. "He wants the gates closed," he said. "He wants it done now." He sounded as if he couldn't believe what he'd just said.

"Do it," barked the man in the windbreaker, turning to Tom Davis.

"Who the hell are you?" Lauren said.

"Shut the goddamn gates!" the man shouted at Davis, getting right in his face.

"You want to lose this dam?" Davis said. He was about sixty years old, a small man with glasses and thinning hair. He gripped the back of the stool as if his life depended on it. "You want to take responsibility for that, for what will happen?"

"Shut the fucking gates! That's a direct order."

"No," Tom Davis said in a slow, steady voice. "I want that in writing."

Lauren saw flashing lights outside. Two highway patrol cars had pulled into the parking lot. Men started piling out. Doors slammed.

Three troopers entered the powerhouse. They wore gray jackets with black belts over the shoulders and Smoky the Bear hats.

"Get this woman out of here!" the man in the windbreaker snapped. His voice was high-pitched and hoarse, almost a scream.

The trooper glanced at Lauren. She knew several state police officers, but not him.

"Are you the guy with the earthquake safety commission?" the trooper asked. The man in the windbreaker showed him an ID.

Turning to Lauren, the trooper said, "Ma'am, you've got to leave this building and get off the dam." Even as he spoke, he was opening the door for her.

"They want Tom to close the gates," Lauren said, trying to explain what was happening, what was at stake. She felt light-headed, breathless. Then angry at the strong-arm police tactics. ''The dam has been damaged. He's afraid it will give way unless the water's released to ease the pressure.''

Saying nothing, the trooper led her outside and told one of his men to escort her off the dam. Immediately.

As she walked to her pickup, a trooper was in lockstep right at her elbow. He looked nervous and didn't say a word. More police cars were driving onto the dam, blocking both ends. They were closing it to traffic.

Lauren opened the door to the pickup and slid behind the wheel. She started to say something, to try one last time to make the trooper understand what Tom was telling them. Then she paused and listened. At first she didn't realize what she was hearing.

Silence. The roar of the water going through the gates had stopped.

IT WASN'T MUCH, A GENTLE CREST ON HIGHLAND
Avenue about thirty feet high and three hundred yards long,
but crucial ground in analyzing what happened during the
earthquake. Culp's Nursery was located there—a couple of
glass greenhouses and a small lot for seedlings and other
plants. The earthquake had shaken them so badly that the
walls had disintegrated. The small store that had sold garden-
ing tools and other supplies looked like it had imploded.

Atkins and Walter Jacobs had gone there to take a look.
Sensors at the University of Memphis about two miles away
showed some of the strongest vertical shaking ever recorded
during an earthquake at that small hill. The results were so
unexpected that they'd rechecked the instruments to see if
they were properly calibrated. Slow S-wave velocities and
soft soil conditions were a deadly combination. The ground
had shaken like a bowl of jelly. Fortunately, no one was
there when the quake hit. The only casualty was a dog, a
big Rottweiler the owner kept on the premises for security.
A stone planter had toppled from a shelf and split the animal's skull.

The velocity of the secondary or S waves as measured in
meters per second astounded Atkins. He'd never seen anything like it—even at the scene of far bigger quakes. The
hill had experienced severe vertical shaking for nearly thirty
seconds with an S-wave velocity of 150 meters per second.
More typical readings were anywhere from 250 to 800 meters per second with shaking of a much shorter duration. In

soft ground, the slower velocities triggered more severe shaking.

S waves, as Atkins well knew, were tricky and far more damaging than P or primary waves. Distortional, the S waves moved with a side-to-side shearing motion that could make the ground move either vertically or horizontally. P waves, by contrast, traveled faster, but moved in only one direction. Both were "body waves," meaning they moved upward from the earthquake focus underground, the hypocenter, to the surface.

"Can you imagine what would have happened if a hotel had been up here instead of a nursery?" Jacobs said as they picked their way through the rubble.

The hill was at the southeastern end of Memphis. Atkins and Jacobs had set up three portable seismographs there to record the aftershocks, which were occurring with increasing frequency after a slow start. They'd already had a magnitude 4.1 and two in the 3.6 range. The biggest, a magnitude 5.1, had hit earlier that morning near Kentucky Lake.

The Culp's Hill seismographs were among thirty instruments the Center for Earthquake Studies and USGS were installing around Memphis. Another forty had been shipped in from California and were being added to the network that already existed on the New Madrid Fault. These would be scattered over a huge area that included Little Rock, St. Louis, Chicago, Cincinnati, and Memphis. The instruments were linked to a central computer that funneled the seismic data straight to computers at the University of Memphis.

Several teams of scientists had been dispatched from the agency's offices in Menlo Park and Golden to help with the setup. Several of Atkins' colleagues from the Earthquake Risk Assessment unit at Reston, Virginia, had also been sent to the quake zone.

With heavy support from the University of Memphis, which had the most scientists in the field, and the USGS, the show was being coordinated by the Seismic Safety Commission. The group was composed of scientists and structural engineers from the five states most directly involved—Missouri, Illinois, Tennessee, Arkansas, and Kentucky. Walt Jacobs and several on his staff were members. The person in charge, a geophysicist named Paul Weston, had been appointed by the governor of Kentucky.

Atkins had never met Weston, but he'd heard a lot about him the last few days, primarily from Jacobs, who didn't like the man.

"He's smooth as silk, but he can be an arrogant bastard," Jacobs said. "And that's just for starters. It gets worse the longer you know him."

Weston had solid academic credentials, a doctorate in geophysics from Stanford and postdoctorate work at MIT. He'd taught at the University of Kentucky. Jacobs explained that he was politically well-connected, especially with Tad Parker, the governor of Kentucky. Many considered Parker a top contender for the presidency. He'd already set up a campaign committee and was starting to get some national publicity. Parker had lobbied to get Weston put in charge of the Seismic Safety Commission.

Weston had insisted that the commission—and not the Center for Earthquake Studies or the USGS—was handling the earthquake investigation. The group's first meeting was scheduled to start within the hour at the USGS offices at the University of Memphis.

Atkins and Jacobs had stayed longer than they'd planned on the hill and were running late. Absorbed by his thoughts on the S-wave velocities, Atkins barely spoke during the drive to the university. The extraordinary S-wave velocities could only have been caused by some unusual ground structure, say, a layer of soft sediment that made the waves diffuse and expand. Atkins wanted to run a computer simulation of the seismic data they'd already harvested. He didn't like those S-wave velocities at all. They were way too low, way too destructive.

When they got back to the Center for Earthquake Studies, they had trouble finding a parking place. Television sound trucks were lined up four deep along Cottage Avenue, the main campus thoroughfare. Security police had kept the reporters a block from the center's complex located in a pair of run-down, two-story brick homes that faced Cottage. Once private residences, the homes were in bad need of repair—everything from painting and recaulking the windows to fixing the furnaces. The USGS shared space with the earthquake center in a cluttered warren of rooms and hallways that had been partitioned and converted to offices.

As Atkins and Jacobs cut across the front lawn, a television reporter, who'd managed to slip past police, intercepted them.

"Do you think any more big ones are coming?" the young, heavily made-up woman shouted, jabbing a microphone in Atkins' face.

He tried to ignore her and kept walking, but she pushed the mike closer.

"Are you expecting some more aftershocks?" She must have been wearing a thousand bucks' worth of clothing. A designer suit, short skirt, and red pumps, despite the cold.

"We'll have a news conference soon to try to answer some of those questions," Atkins said, trying not to snap at her. The reporters had a job to do, but they could be totally irresponsible. He despised ambush TV interviews.

"Right," the woman said, a surly edge to her voice. "You aren't going to tell us shit."

Atkins shrugged and pushed past her cameraman.

"Nice lady," Jacobs said as they entered the earthquake center's building through the front door.

"Charming," Atkins said. He saw Guy Thompson approaching. Just the man he wanted to see. Thompson was from the agency's hazards evaluation office in Reston. Thompson was wearing his usual Western shirt, faded jeans, and lizard cowboy boots. A CD player was clipped to a belt with a huge silver buckle shaped like a bucking horse. Thompson spoke with an Oklahoma drawl. He'd received his Ph.D. from the University of Oklahoma and could name every Sooner running back since the days of Bud Wilkinson. He was expert in using computer programs to simulate the ground motions of quakes. There was none better.

"John, you old vagabond. How long you been here?"

Atkins shook Thompson's hand and told him he'd arrived a day earlier.

"You got your imaging program up and running yet?" he asked.

"Even as we speak," Thompson said, running his hands through his thick, black hair that he wore to his shoulders. He was a pure-blooded Cherokee and proud of it. He and

Atkins had stepped into an alcove to get out of the flow of traffic. The narrow hallways were jammed with filing cabinets, bookshelves, and storage boxes. The offices were crowded, the atmosphere electric as old friends greeted each other and caught up on news and gossip.

It always struck Atkins at such moments how small the world of professional seismology was. Everyone knew everyone else. What they were working on, the hot research, the rising stars. It was a small, closed society with no more than 125 real players, names that counted.

Thompson led Atkins to a large office, a former family room that had been converted into mission control for the Memphis earthquake. A half-dozen high-powered computers had been set up there. Thompson was in charge of all database programs, graphic presentations, and fault analysis.

"We're just starting to plug in the S- and P-wave data," he said. "We'll have some pretty pictures real soon. Another twenty, thirty minutes."

The "pictures" were computer images or simulations of what had happened along portions of the New Madrid Fault during the quake. Using techniques similar to medical CT scans, Thompson and his team of scientists were able to analyze sound and other waves generated by the earthquake and harvested by the seismometers. Seismic waves passing through a fault commonly slowed down. Their motion patterns could be used to map out the zones surrounding the fault. Thompson's computer programs were able to draw three-dimensional pictures of what was happening deep underground. He mapped the fault's outline by piecing together the faint echoes of seismic waves as they were reflected from buried rock layers. This provided a picture of the structures that produced the echoes. In some cases, you could actually see the fault itself.

Atkins told Thompson he wanted him to feed in the seismic data from Culp's Hill. He thought they'd have enough for him to work with by early morning.

"Sure, no problem," Thompson said. "It's gonna get interesting around here real soon."

ELIZABETH HOLLERAN PEERED INTO THE BATHROOM
mirror. Her light gray eyes looked red and puffy and she
dabbed them with cold water. She'd had less than four hours'
sleep and looked as bad as she felt. It was nearly 3:00 before
she'd found a motel, a Best Western five miles south of
Memphis. Motel space was at a premium.

She turned on the television and caught the end of the
news. With all the closed highways and detours, the morning
commute was a disaster. Gridlock gripped the city and by
7:00 A.M. the mayor had gone on the radio asking people to
stay home. A helicopter beamed back live video of the fires
that were still burning.

The bathroom had a small hotplate for making coffee.
After drinking a cup, Elizabeth called Walter Jacobs' office.
He wasn't in so she left a voice mail message. By late morning, after getting good directions from the motel manager,
she set out for the university. Instead of trying to drive
through the city this time, she looped around the outskirts
on I-240 and came up Perkins Road, which got her to within
a couple blocks of the campus.

Police were keeping the news media away from the earthquake center. Elizabeth tried to explain who she was to one
of the campus cops. She showed him her faculty ID from
Cal Tech, but got nowhere.

Without proper identification, no one was allowed in the
building. Period.

A wave of anxiety hit her. It had happened several times

already, ever since she'd arrived in Memphis and seen the damage up close. The thought kept hammering at her that they were still approaching Prable's date of maximum seismic stress. She knew that it was highly unlikely anything else would happen, that there'd be another earthquake. Prable's methodology remained highly suspect and questionable in her opinion. But the fact remained he'd come eerily close with his prediction for a major quake on or about January 20. At the very least, she wanted to show Prable's data to Jacobs.

If he'd let her.

She had her doubts about that. With a crisis on his hands, he wasn't likely to be too open to hearing what she had to say.

Deep in thought, she barely felt the tap on her shoulder.

"Are you Elizabeth Holleran?" It was a slender young woman with freckles and braided hair. She had a backpack slung over her shoulder. She held out her hand sheepishly.

"I'm Amy Price. I heard you give your name to that cop. I'm a grad student here in the geology department. I just finished reading your paper in my earth seismology class. The one about the trenching you're doing on the San Andreas Fault. It really sounds cool."

Her words came out in an excited, self-conscious rush. Elizabeth was genuinely flattered that Amy was so obviously happy to meet her. The kid was even blushing. Then Elizabeth had a thought. She told her that she needed to get into the earthquake center's building to see Walter Jacobs. That it was very important. She wanted to know if there was another entrance.

"No problem," Amy said, happy to be of service. "Follow me."

She led Elizabeth behind the two homes that served as offices for the earthquake center and the university's geology department. The center occupied one house, which it shared with the USGS. The geology department the other. A driveway and narrow expanse of lawn separated them.

The geology building wasn't guarded. Amy took Elizabeth through the back door and led her into the basement.

"I think half the department is already down here," she said.

"Doing what?" Elizabeth asked, puzzled by the trip through the basement.

Amy smiled and said, "Trying to listen."

The two homes, she explained, had once been the university's student health center and were connected by a tunnel. As many as ten grad students were sitting on the narrow flight of steps that led up to a door that opened directly inside the earthquake center's building. The door was closed, but not locked.

"They're having a big meeting up there about the earthquake," Amy said, lowering her voice to a whisper. "We're trying to hear what they're saying."

"It just got started," one of the students said, a heavyset kid with shoulder-length hair tied back. "They're all in Walt Jacobs' office."

THE SEISMOLOGISTS SAT IN WHAT HAD ONCE BEEN
a front room. Plywood boards covered the windows that had
broken during the earthquake. The atmosphere was tense,
expectant. The eleven people in attendance included some of
the biggest names in earthquake research. Four, including
Atkins and Guy Thompson, were with the USGS. Walt Jacobs represented the Center for Earthquake Studies.

As chairman of the five-state Seismic Safety Commission,
Paul Weston led the group. His first order of business was
to swear all the participants to secrecy.

"I don't have to tell any of you how important that is,"
said Weston.

He turned the meeting over to Guy Thompson. Atkins
noticed he'd tied his long, black hair in a ponytail. He'd also
changed shirts. He was wearing another Western number that
was a bright blue satin. He still had his CD player clipped
to his leather belt and a pair of headphones looped around
his neck.

Thompson apologized to the group in advance. He was
making the final adjustments on his projector. "This might
be a little rough," he said. "We haven't had time to smooth
any of these images out, to enhance them. I'm seeing this
for the first time myself."

The seismic P- and S-wave patterns recorded during the
quake and fed into his battery of computers produced an
image none of the participants had anticipated. As it was

projected on a large screen on the wall, there were audible gasps.

The two-dimensional image—a dark line overlaid on a topographical map—showed that the New Madrid Fault, or at least a major branch of it, extended much farther south than anyone had imagined. It looked like the southwest arm of the fault extended nearly twenty miles south of Memphis. Originally, that segment was thought to have ended roughly forty miles to the north of the city. Nearly sixty miles long, this weak spot deep in the earth had been there all along, hidden and unnoticed, waiting to come to life.

Atkins and the others were shocked. The New Madrid Fault had nearly doubled in size.

One of Thompson's computer-enhanced graphics showed a cross section of the earth's crust.

"You can see how the velocity and direction of the waves changed as they neared the surface," he said, studying the computer images on the screen. The lights were dimmed. The seismic waves had changed direction and picked up speed and power when they hit different rock layers. There appeared to be an unusually thick layer of soft sediments deep below Culp's Hill.

"That's the kind of focusing effect that can double, sometimes triple the velocity of the surface waves," Thompson went on. "That's why the shaking was so severe in that part of the city."

"Can you delineate the fault any better?" asked one of the geologists from the University of Memphis.

Shaking his head, Thompson said it was too far down in the crust, nearly thirty kilometers. His imaging techniques were a lot like CT scans and sonograms. The images were created by piecing together faint echoes as the seismic waves were reflected from buried rock layers and faults. The images were rarely sharply defined; at best the fault could be seen only indirectly.

"About all we can say for sure is that the major pulse of seismic energy traveled in a southerly direction along a previously unknown fault. The epicenter near Mayfield, Kentucky, was the likely trigger." He projected a map of Tennessee, Kentucky, and Missouri on the screen.

"The seismic waves really picked up velocity when they

hit faulting deep below the Memphis area. It was like ringing a bell.''

The surprising thing to Atkins was that the damage hadn't been far worse. The miles of sediment that covered the fault must have deflected or diffused the seismic energy. The exceptions were at places like Culp's Hill, where it had literally burst through the crust.

Thompson used the analogy of spokes on a wheel. What he called the Memphis Fault was a new spoke of the New Madrid Seismic Zone.

Walter Jacobs said, ''This is going to scare the hell out of a lot of people. How do we tell the public that Memphis is sitting right on top of a newly discovered fault? Anybody got some ideas on that?''

Atkins noticed the slight catch in his friend's voice. His face was gray. The fear in the room was almost palpable. Atkins felt it, too.

''None of this goes public. That's out of the question,'' said Paul Weston. ''There'd be an unnecessary panic.'' It was the first time he'd spoken, the voice deep, strong, authoritative. Atkins was struck by his dark eyes, how they focused and rarely blinked. The man was impeccably dressed in a dark gray suit, vest, and wingtip oxfords. Most of the other earth scientists in the room were considerably more casual in their clothing. Jeans, loose-fitting sweaters, and Vibram-soled hiking shoes predominated. Weston looked more like a banker than a geologist.

''We need to make sure of our data before we make any public announcements,'' Weston said. ''I can speak for the entire commission in that regard.'' He repeated his earlier admonition that none of this discussion leave the room.

''I disagree here, Paul,'' Jacobs said, swallowing down the thickness in his throat. ''Half the people in this city live in brick homes. There isn't one high-rise downtown that's built up to California's earthquake code. We get a major shake, these people are gonna be buried. We got to let them know.''

''I've never thought it was a good idea to withhold information from the public, even when it's potentially alarming,'' Atkins said. ''I'd rather err on the side of giving them all the data they can use. Even the most minimal things, like how they can reduce earthquake hazards in their homes.''

Weston looked up from his papers and seemed to be taking in Atkins for the first time. His brow furrowed. ''It's not a question of withholding information. It's making sure that it's accurate.''

''I'd say Guy Thompson's computers have already done that,'' Atkins said testily. He could tell that Weston didn't like this line of discussion.

''What about aftershocks?'' another geologist said impatiently. ''That was a pretty big jolt this morning up by Kentucky Lake. A magnitude 5.1. I'd like to set up an array of seismographs to see what's happening.'' The idea was to saturate the area with instruments to get a precise read on the depth, direction, and intensity of the seismic activity.

''I couldn't agree more,'' said Guy Thompson. ''We've had at least forty small tremors up there since five this morning, none of them much more than a magnitude 2, but a real swarm.''

''Let's be sure to check the dam up there,'' Jacobs said, irritated with himself for just remembering that important detail.

''I've already taken care of that,'' Weston said.

Relieved, Jacobs nodded his head. ''Glad to hear it. That's one place we sure don't want trouble.''

''Are we prepared to talk about energy projections?'' one of the geologists asked. He'd been sitting quietly in a corner, writing notes furiously. He was young, late twenties, and wore a garish sweater. Atkins recognized him, but didn't remember the name. He was from the University of Chicago.

Measuring how much energy remained locked in elastically strained rocks was a complicated, time-consuming procedure, but it was vital to calculating whether the potential for another big quake was still stored in the ground, whether it was wound up like a coiled spring.

Someone suggested doing a GPS survey to measure any horizontal or vertical displacements in the crust. The Global Positioning Satellite system allowed for minute measurements of changes in the earth's surface, one of the best ways to check for rock strain. If the crust was rising, or uptilting, it meant energy was still stored in the ground.

"Anyone know when the satellite system's back on-line?" Atkins asked. An unusually large solar flare had shut the system down several days earlier. Fallout from the flare had also played havoc with power grids along the East Coast.

"Four more days," said a voice at the back of the room. "The solar wind is still very strong. None of the satellites are operational."

Atkins turned around to see who'd just spoken. A woman was leaning against the wall in the back of the room. She had straight blond hair and was wearing a denim skirt and tweed jacket. Good-looking, about thirty. A briefcase and laptop were slung from her shoulder. No one had seen her enter.

Everyone in the room was dumbfounded to see Elizabeth Holleran standing there, wondering where she'd come from, how she'd gotten in.

Weston rose halfway out of his chair. "This is a private meeting."

Holleran recognized three or four of the men from conferences they attended together. One of them came to the rescue. She vaguely remembered him.

"Hi, Elizabeth," said one of the USGS geologists who'd flown in from California. "This is Doctor Elizabeth Holleran of Cal Tech and about the best trencher I've ever met. She's doing some great carbon-dating work on the Pacific Coast near Los Angeles. Had a dynamite paper published on the subject a couple months back in *Earth Sciences*."

"I want to know how she got in here," Weston said, his voice laced with anger.

Holleran apologized for the interruption. She explained about the tunnel and the door.

Weston got up, hurried to the door that led to the tunnel, and pulled it open. He saw the assembly of grad students, sitting on the steps. "I want you all out of here immediately," he said, slamming the door and locking it.

"They really couldn't hear anything," Holleran said, sorry to get the students in trouble. It was impossible to hear through the closed door.

Weston repeated his request for Holleran to leave. "I'm sure you can understand why we're meeting here and why we must insist on strict secrecy. You weren't invited."

"I need just five minutes," Holleran said. "This is important." She'd been wondering how she was going to do this ever since she got on the airplane the day before. She figured the best approach would be straight on, just lay it out and try not to fixate on the huge professional risk she was taking.

"I've been given data that predicted a major quake on the New Madrid Fault sometime around January twentieth. What I keep asking myself, what I can't get out of my head, is whether the earthquake you just had down here was a foreshock to an even bigger event."

Atkins could only stare at her. Is she really serious about this? he wondered. Jacobs and the others had the same reaction.

Holleran, strangely, started to relax. Without hurrying, she began with the telephone call she'd gotten from Otto Prable three days earlier; then she quickly and concisely summarized his data on maximum solar activity occurring on or about January twentieth, a window that coincided with a period of extremely strong lunar pull. It was Prable's opinion that these powerful forces could trigger a quake in an area already under maximum stress. And based on earlier GPS readings that indicated an uplift in the crust, the New Madrid Seismic Zone was clearly under stress. Holleran likewise mentioned Prable's observations about strong changes in electromagnetic fields and the extended period the Mississippi and Ohio Rivers had been near flood stage, exerting steady pressure on the fault.

"I know how implausible this must seem," she said in conclusion. "I've only managed a brief look at Dr. Prable's probability analysis. I've brought all his data with me."

She'd spoken for about four minutes without interruption. But everyone in the cramped, overheated room was transfixed.

Breaking the silence, Walt Jacobs asked, "Is Prable the guy who used to teach at Cal Tech?"

Holleran nodded.

"He was a physicist, wasn't he?"

"Geophysics."

She started to say more, but Paul Weston angrily interrupted. "This man Prable isn't even a seismologist, and you're telling us he predicted the earthquake.'' He shook his head derisively. ''You've taken quite enough of our time.''

Holleran knew she needed ice in her veins to pull this off. It was turning ugly, but she'd blow everything if she lost her temper.

''Otto Prable's analysis says a period of maximum stress will occur sometime around January twentieth. That's nine days from now. You've just had a major quake. I'll tell you this, that magnitude 7.1 sure caught my attention back in Los Angeles. A moderately large earthquake exactly where he said one was likely to happen. Professionally, I think his methodology sounds like science fiction. I didn't even take it seriously—until that quake. I still believe it was probably luck. He made a good guess, but let's assume, for discussion, that maybe he was on to something, as totally far-fetched as that sounds. Didn't you have a magnitude 5 just this morning somewhere around here? I keep asking myself, could these be foreshocks?''

She let that thought hang there a moment, staring each man in the room straight in the face. They were all watching, waiting. Paul Weston kept lowering his head and frowning.

''At the very least I'd want to see what Prable had to say,'' Holleran said. ''I'd want to look at his data just to be on the safe side. I'm sure it will be badly flawed. But I think it would be negligent not to examine it. The man was brilliant. I've got his entire computer file on CD-ROM disks. We can download it right here.''

She caught John Atkins' amused half-smile. The look irritated her. It was as if he were telling her, You've got yourself into a fine mess, girl, so what in the hell are you going to do to get out of it?

''What happened to Otto Prable?'' Atkins asked. The name was familiar. He thought he might have met him at a seminar. Weston and some of the others looked pretty bent out of shape. Atkins couldn't help admire how well the woman was handling herself even if what she was saying sounded completely off the charts.

''He's dead,'' Holleran said. ''He was in ill health. He took his life.''

Livid, Weston slammed a fistful of papers down on the desk. He'd had enough.

"I'll be writing a letter to your department chairman about this," he said. "That's a promise. Now will you leave immediately, or do I have to call the police?"

"That's not necessary," Holleran said. She picked up her briefcase and laptop. "My department chairman is George McGintry. I suggest sending him an E-mail. It'll be faster."

AS SOON AS THE EMERGENCY MEETING ENDED AT
the University of Memphis, Seismic Safety Commission
Chairman Paul Weston got into a waiting car. He was driven
to an airplane hangar set back in a remote corner of Memphis
International Airport. Weston was escorted to a rear door,
where a young man with a cell phone and a clipboard ushered him inside.

Tad Parker, the governor of Kentucky, had landed only
minutes earlier. His private Learjet was parked in front of
the hangar.

Two other men were waiting in the empty, unheated building. Stan Marshal, the older and more nervous of the two,
was a seismologist, a big man who wore a snap-brimmed
cap. Mark Wren was both an engineer and a geologist. They
worked for Weston and had just returned from Kentucky
Dam. Their overcoats were buttoned to their necks. It was
cold enough inside to see their breath.

Parker had flown in from Frankfort, the Kentucky capital.
His presence in the city was a secret.

The governor, always immaculately groomed, was wearing
one of his trademark double-breasted suits. A big man, six-
foot-four, he'd retained the athletic good looks of his youth
when he was a starting point guard for the University of
Kentucky basketball team. A conservative Republican, Parker had been elected governor twice by huge majorities and
was starting to raise serious money, much of it from Wall
Street, for a run at the presidency. Insiders figured he had a

good chance. Kentucky's economy was booming, thanks in large part to Parker's decidedly low-tax, pro-business stance. The incumbent, President Nathan Ross, was unpopular. Parker was on a roll.

He'd delayed a fund-raising trip to California to talk to Weston. Only his closest advisers were aware that he was in Memphis.

The governor curtly greeted the geologist. He'd worked hard to get Weston appointed head of the powerful five-state Seismic Safety Commission. Two of his biggest campaign contributors, the CEOs of major engineering companies, had lobbied for Weston so he'd done them a favor, albeit reluctantly. He found the man's coolness off-putting. Parker didn't like Weston, but he had no reason to criticize his performance. He seemed competent and on top of things.

The commission, unique in the country, crossed both state and federal lines and had complete authority to assure that new public buildings and structures met seismic safety standards. They were also in the process of retrofitting some older structures, including several major bridges across the Mississippi. Their jurisdiction also extended to the big TVA dams in the five-state region.

"What's the situation at Kentucky Dam?" Parker asked.

Weston said, "We've got some cracks in the base wall. They opened up after the main shock. We're trying to get them repaired and reinforced as quickly as possible. It's nothing that can't be handled."

He'd spoken with slow deliberation. If anything, he almost sounded upbeat about it.

"You're sure those cracks can be repaired?" Parker asked.

"Yes, governor," Weston said in his crisp, efficient voice. "It's going to take a couple weeks to do it right. We've moved a lot of heavy equipment in already. I should mention that people are starting to talk. They know there's a problem at the dam. One of the marina operators up there, a woman, is making some noise. She's talking to people. Wants a public meeting."

"What's her name?" Parker asked, interested.

"Lauren Mitchell."

"Maybe she's right. Maybe we ought to have a meeting," Parker said, considering the idea, weighing its possibilities.

"Let people know what's happening. Tell them the truth. That there's been some damage, but it's being taken care of and there's no danger. You have any problem with that, doctor?"

"None, sir. I couldn't agree more."

Parker's eyes locked on Weston, drilled into him. "You think we could have another bad quake up there any time soon? A big one strong enough to knock out that dam?"

"I don't believe so."

"Is that a hedge?"

"It wasn't meant to be, sir," Weston said. "The statistical odds are hugely against another strong quake. In terms of seismic energy left in the ground, it's almost an impossibility."

Parker made his decision.

They'd repair the dam as rapidly as possible. He wanted the work completed in two weeks. He didn't care what it cost. He'd get the other governors to go along and approve the funding, a state-federal match. The governors had to vote to approve expenditures to repair earthquake damage. They'd also need the TVA's okay, but that had never been a problem.

Parker raised another subject. "Should we consider an evacuation from the towns below the dam until the repairs are finished?" he asked.

"I don't think that's necessary, governor," Weston said. "The cracks aren't a threat to the dam's structural integrity. I think an evacuation order would cause unnecessary hardship and create panic."

Parker mulled it over and said, "All right. Keep me informed."

The meeting was over. Within moments Parker was back on board his Learjet, getting ready to return to Kentucky. He'd put off that fund-raiser to California for a few days to give him time to tour the quake damage in his state.

Relieved to see the governor depart, Weston knew he hadn't been totally forthright. He'd downplayed the damage at the dam and was lucky Parker hadn't pushed him for more information. The cracks—five of them—were thirty feet long and leaking. They were running pumps to keep the water level low enough inside the dam's inner wall to make the repairs.

He was going to send Marshal and Wren back there immediately to make sure the work was completed as quickly as possible. They were pushing their luck, and they knew it.

THE FAMOUS MEMPHIS "DRY" RIBS WERE THE SPE-
cialty of the house at the Blue Sax Grill, a Beale Street
institution. With a panache that was part of the atmosphere,
the waiters served steaming platters of meat rubbed in spices.
Located on the ground floor of an old drugstore, the place
wasn't cheap. John Atkins had gone to the Blue Sax for an
early dinner to avoid the crowds. A tall waiter with mahogany skin and a white apron took his order and shouted a few
clipped words to the kitchen: "Half order, beer."

It was only late afternoon, but Atkins wanted to turn in
early. He'd declined Walt Jacobs' invitation to join him and
his wife for dinner at their home. He was exhausted for one
thing. For another, they both needed to get up before dawn
to catch a helicopter for Mayfield, Kentucky, just across the
Tennessee line. He and Jacobs and a team of four other
seismologists were going to set up an array of seismometers.
They wanted to place fifteen instruments on a line running
roughly from the extreme southwestern tip of the state due
east to Kentucky Lake.

The area had been extremely active with aftershocks. They
hoped to get more precise readings on exactly what was
happening deep in the ground. The biggest jolt so far was
the magnitude 5.1 earlier that morning.

The waiter had just brought his order, placing the heavy
plate piled high with ribs in front of him, when Elizabeth
Holleran introduced herself.

"May I join you?" she asked.

Atkins hesitated, trying to suppress a groan.

"If you'd rather not," Holleran said.

"No, please. Sit down," he said, gathering up the newspaper he'd been trying to read in the dim light. He cleared a space for her. "It's just been kind of a rough day." He didn't want to get into an analytical debate with this woman over sunspots, tidal forces, and earthquake predictions. He was way too skeptical. Way too tired.

"One of the USGS people told me where I might find you," she said, sitting down.

Atkins pushed back in his seat, waiting for her to begin, wanting to get this over with.

"Would you mind if I ordered something to drink?" Holleran asked. She'd already had quite enough of the attitude in his voice. She felt like telling him to shut up and just listen. But this was too important. She had to be more diplomatic.

"Sure, why not?" Atkins said. He stopped his waiter and asked for another beer. The man quickly returned and banged a frosty mug down on the scarred wooden table without saying a word.

"That's a waiter with personality," Atkins said sarcastically. "They give the place its Southern charm." He was already thinking how to get out of this as quickly and politely as possible.

"Jim Dietz told me to say hello," Holleran said. She'd just spoken to him on the telephone. "We're working together on the Point Arguello project."

Atkins had taken a couple advanced seismology courses from Dietz at Cal Tech. They'd stayed in touch. Atkins liked and respected his intellect.

"Did Jim know what you were going to do down here?" he asked.

Holleran nodded. "He said I was out of my mind." She took a sip of beer, a big one.

Atkins smiled in spite of himself. She reminded him of an eager graduate student. Maybe a little older, but not much. Late twenties or early thirties. Not bad-looking. Better up close than in that conference room, which was good enough. In fact, she was damned fine-looking, sitting there on the edge of the chair in a green jacket and black corduroy slacks. No makeup at all. Didn't need it.

Atkins complimented her on her papers describing the dig at Point Arguello. He'd read both of them. It was solid research by someone who'd spent months in the field and wrote with authority. He noticed Elizabeth's smooth, deep tan. This was a woman who wasn't afraid of hard work or getting out in the sun. But he wasn't about to waste any more time than absolutely necessary listening to her talk about Prable and sunspots.

Elizabeth put down her beer mug. She wanted to get started while she still had the nerve. "I need someone to look at this data," she said. "I was hoping that maybe you could—"

Atkins put up his hands. He'd been expecting it. "Now hold on," he said. "I heard what you said this afternoon. I don't want to get involved in that."

"Otto Prable was a superb scientist. We need to look at his data. I know it's probably a waste of time. But if you'd just—"

"Why me?" Atkins said. "Why not that guy who introduced you this afternoon? Go to him. I can't help you. I don't want to help you. I think Prable just got lucky."

There was a moment when Elizabeth started to unravel, felt the panic slip out. She was putting her reputation on the line with a complete stranger who was acting like an asshole. She forced herself to calm down.

Atkins helped. His brusque question snapped her out of it. "You think Prable predicted the magnitude 7.1 we just had? Or was that only a precursor? I can't keep it straight. And what was that date for maximum exposure? January twentieth?"

Elizabeth didn't like his condescending tone. This was becoming far more difficult than she'd hoped. "Prable said there was a high probability of a severe earthquake," she said, regulating her voice. "We've had one moderately severe quake already and several strong aftershocks. I think we ought to see what the man was talking about."

"But he wasn't even a seismologist," Atkins said.

Elizabeth looked at him, focusing her thoughts. "No," she said, not fighting the anger this time. "He wasn't a seismologist. He wasn't even a geologist. And I say, thank God! I've never met such a group of backbiting hypocrites. Have you ever stopped to think that our vaunted profession has *never* made an accurate earthquake prediction? Not a single one in all these years. Here's someone who isn't a seismologist, and we're quick to knock down his data sight unseen because he didn't have the right pedigree. Dammit!'' She pounded her fist on the table. People glanced at them. Even the glassy-eyed waiters looked momentarily interested.

She started to get up, snatching the straps of her briefcase. To hell with this, she thought. Dietz had been all wrong about Atkins. He was a total jerk. She'd try someone else. Maybe Jacobs.

"No, please," Atkins said, motioning for her to sit down. "Don't go."

Elizabeth Holleran took a breath. She sat back down again. Her eyes were flashing.

"The key issue, it seems to me, is to run a probability analysis of Doctor Prable's data," she said, keeping her voice low. "I doubt it's accurate, but after what's happened down here, I'd sure want to examine it. He's talking about a period of maximum stress in another nine days. All my training and instincts tell me he's way off base, that his work is seriously flawed. But I keep asking myself, what if in some crazy way he's right? It doesn't leave much time."

"And you think he might be right?"

There was that irritating smile again, she thought.

"As a seismologist, I think that's highly unlikely. But you had to know him, his intellect and integrity. I don't see how we can afford not to check his theory out."

She was still angry and a little dismayed with herself for wanting to continue talking to this man. She'd read about Atkins. She guessed he was in his mid-forties. He had a creased, ruddy face and big shoulders and hands. The nose was all wrong, pushed slightly off center and flattened at the bridge.

She took out two computer disks and laid them on the table.

"It's all right there," she said. "I would have asked Jim Dietz to take a look at them, but there wasn't time. After that 7.1, I wanted to get right down here."

Atkins noticed it first, how their beer glasses started shaking. It was almost imperceptible, then the movement became more pronounced. The glasses were rattling, jiggling on the table. The beer splashed out of them. The ground lurched, a sharp sideways motion. Not much, but strong enough to knock a plate-glass mirror down from the wall. It shattered on the floor.

Atkins figured a magnitude 3. Nothing major, but the restaurant erupted in screams. After the last few days, everyone was on edge. Even a minor aftershock was enough to start a stampede. People knocked over tables as they pushed and shoved their way to the front door.

"They're going to run right over us," Atkins said, sliding the table back against the wall. They were near the door, right in the path.

He slipped Elizabeth's computer disks into his jacket pocket. There was another moderate shake, stronger than the first. A row of liquor bottles fell off the shelves behind the bar. Broken window glass rained down onto the street from the building's upper stories.

"Don't . . . go . . . out . . . there!" Atkins shouted. He heard the glass exploding on the pavement outside. "Stay off the street! You're safer in here."

It didn't do any good. A heavyset man, who'd left his wife behind in his rush to get out, elbowed his way toward the door. An elderly woman fell, and Atkins had to push back two people who started to step on her. Elizabeth grabbed the woman by the shoulders and pulled her out of the way.

There was a pileup at the front door. Blows were being thrown as a couple dozen people frantically tried to push and shove their way outside. Atkins had seen it all before in Mexico City. The dead stacked up five and six feet deep around the doors of the high-rises. Trampled. The faces battered beyond recognition.

A solid-looking man in his mid-fifties, white hair and black blazer, collided with Elizabeth. In his haste to flee, he'd looped his arm through the strap in her briefcase. He was pulling her down.

Atkins slammed the man against the wall, freeing Elizabeth's arm. Eyes bulging with fear, the man swung savagely at Atkins' face. Ducking under the blow, Atkins hit him in the jaw and stomach, hard punches thrown from the shoulder. The man sat down, his back sliding against the wall.

Many of the patrons cowered under tables. The light fixtures over the tables were swaying. Atkins saw it, felt it in the restaurant. The quake had been nothing at all. But it was making people snap.

SEEN FROM THE BELLY OF THE HELICOPTER, THE plowed muddy fields looked dotted with sandpiles. It was shortly after dawn, and they were clipping along the cotton fields of the Missouri boot heel at two thousand feet. In the shadowy light, it was easy for Atkins' eyes to play tricks on him.

The strange starburst markings on the ground were a yellowish, powdery-white color. When the light was better, he noticed that the impressions looked smooth and feathered at the edges. Some were huge. They peppered the floodplain that spread out for miles on either side of the Mississippi.

His face glued to a porthole window, Atkins kept clapping his hands, trying to warm them in the biting cold. The team of six geologists on their way to southwestern Kentucky sat on bench seats in the helicopter's unheated cargo bay. The big olive-green chopper belonged to the Kentucky National Guard.

Atkins knew he was looking at sand blows, but he'd never seen any that compared with these. Each one of those white splotches was a scar, the remains of a miniature volcano that had blown up during the great quakes of 1811 and 1812. The ground beneath them had turned to quicksand.

"Looks like the whole damn boot heel blew up," Atkins said, shaking his head in disbelief as he tried to imagine what it must have been like.

The sand blows, the result of massive liquefaction, were among the most dramatic evidence that remained of the

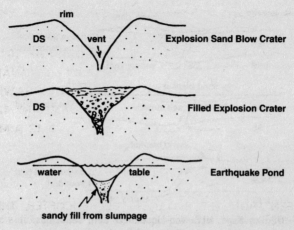

Sectional Views of Extrusive Sand Features

earthquakes that had also formed fissures and deep craters. There'd also been widespread landslides. The area of severe liquefaction covered 48,000 square kilometers, making it one of the largest earthquake liquefaction zones in the world. The only rival was in the Ganges river plain of India, the result of Himalayan earthquakes.

Liquefaction occurred when an earthquake shook wet soil that was loosely packed and fine-grained, usually a mix of clay and sand. It turned into a dense liquid that resembled quicksand. If the pressure was heavy enough, sand and water were pushed to the surface with such explosive force that they formed sand volcanoes or sand blows. Many were eight to twenty feet across. Some were well over a hundred feet. The hardened conical sides of the sand blows eventually disappeared, leaving all those white marks on the table-flat countryside.

The process had always fascinated Atkins. Jacobs opened his laptop and punched a few keys. The screen displayed various examples of the bizarre sand features, which he showed to Atkins and one of the National Guardsmen who sat beside him.

Jacobs gave directions to the pilot over a headset micro-

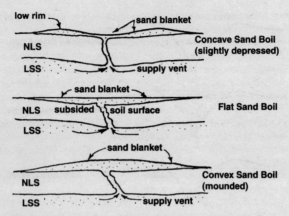

low rim — sand blanket

NLS

LSS — supply vent

Concave Sand Boil (slightly depressed)

sand blanket

NLS subsided soil surface

LSS

Flat Sand Boil

sand blanket

NLS

LSS — supply vent

Convex Sand Boil (mounded)

DS=Dry Sand; NLS=Non-Liquefiable Soil; LSS=Liquefiable Saturated Sand

phone. Atkins tried to wake up. He'd barely arrived at the airport on time.

On the way, he'd stopped off at the earthquake center. He got there at 4:30 A.M. and left a detailed E-mail message for Guy Thompson. Against his better judgment, he asked his friend to try to do a probability analysis of Prable's earthquake projections. He also asked him to check the data against Jacobs' observations. He'd left the two computer disks Elizabeth Holleran had given him. Convinced it was a waste of time, he'd told Thompson to try it only if he had the time. That wouldn't be easy. Thompson was already working eighteen-hour days.

Atkins suddenly regretted what he'd done. Guy would have plenty of reasons to blow up, and he couldn't blame him.

He remembered again how he'd stood in the street with Elizabeth Holleran after they left the Blue Sax. She thanked him for pulling that man off her. But she was still completely focused. She asked him again if he could have someone do a computer analysis of Prable's earthquake data. A tough, good-looking young lady. But he still wished he hadn't given those disks to Thompson. As soon as he got a chance, he'd try to call him and tell him to forget it.

Jacobs said, "We're going to fly over the world's largest sand blow then swing north about twenty miles to New Madrid."

Atkins saw the lightly shaded patch on the ground before anyone else. Shaped like a funnel, the tapered end curved toward the river.

"Is that it?" he asked, stunned. The sand blow was immense.

Jacobs nodded. "There's so much sand down there they call it 'the beach.' "

A rural road stopped abruptly at the edge of the area and veered around it at a sharp right angle.

"It's a mile and a half long," Jacobs said. "And about a half mile wide. The ground's littered with debris from the quake—fragments of coal, lignite, charcoal. When that one blew, it must have sounded like someone had opened a pipe straight to hell."

Atkins didn't doubt it and tried to imagine what it must have looked like when the ground started to erupt and boil. Something out of *Inferno*. Towering geysers of muck thrown up thirty, forty, and fifty feet from deep in the earth. The noise must have been deafening.

"Hang on. We're going to climb," Jacobs announced to the geologists, whose eyes were riveted on the ground. The helicopter shot up like an elevator, leveling off again at about four thousand feet.

Atkins saw it first, but he'd been looking for it. Jacobs had tipped him off earlier. The famous Boot Heel Lineament. The largest visible surface feature left by the three quakes of the early 1800s. A faint line that ran like a reddish-brown ribbon about eighty miles across the Missouri boot heel. The name came from the shape of the small wedge of extreme southeast Missouri that dipped into Arkansas.

"No one knew about it until 1988, when a grad student was studying some satellite photographs. Jumped right out at him. We still don't know much about how it was formed. The best explanation is that it somehow reflects the actual fault deep below it."

"What's the tower off to the left?" Atkins said, almost

shouting to make himself heard over the droning chop of the rotors.

"Power plant, one of the biggest in Missouri," Jacobs said. The smokestack was belching puffs of white smoke across the pink horizon.

Atkins started to say something. Jacobs grinned. "I know. The lineament runs right beneath it. I'd call that poor planning."

"Any nuclear plants around here?" Atkins asked.

"Nothing in the immediate fault zone," Jacobs said. "But if you move a couple hundred miles east, the TVA's got two nuclear plants on-line. Sequoyah and Watts Bar. Both are over near Chattanooga."

Atkins didn't even want to consider the problems a nuclear reactor would present in a powerful earthquake. So far, that had never happened anywhere in the world. But it was only a matter of time. Back in the 1970s, a magnitude 5.3 quake hit about twenty miles from a nuclear plant in Humboldt, California. The plant wasn't damaged, but the Nuclear Regulatory Commission decided to close it anyway. The issue of what would happen to a nuclear power plant—especially the hot core—in a strong quake was one of many unanswered questions. They were nowhere close to solving it.

The helicopter banked right and crossed the Mississippi a few miles south of the power plant. The shadowy line in the ground disappeared at the edge of the river, which twisted in a long S curve.

"That's one of the most powerful rivers in the world," Jacobs said. "The last of the New Madrid quakes cut right through it. Pushed it around like a kid playing with wet sand. Every time I think about a natural force that strong, it kinda takes my breath away."

THE UH-60 BLACK HAWK PUT DOWN AT A SMALL
National Guard airfield north of Mayfield, where Seismic
Commission officials had arranged to have three Ford Ex-
plorers waiting out by the runway. The geologists formed
two-member teams and fanned out across the southwestern
quadrant of Kentucky, the area that had continued to show
intense seismic activity.

Within thirty minutes of landing, Atkins and Walt Jacobs
were on their way in a rented blue Explorer loaded with three
portable seismographs. They had a long day ahead of them.

The teams wanted to set up an array of twelve instruments
on a 120-mile line running roughly from the Mississippi
River east to Kentucky Lake. The plan was to have the network up and running within fourteen hours, which meant a
grueling day. Each team had three or four stops to make,
many of them in remote, rugged country.

There was an unspoken sense of urgency. The recent
tremor that had struck near Kentucky Lake was the strongest
since the magnitude 7.1 event two days earlier. Sixty-eight
small quakes had been logged in that area during the last ten
hours, most of them a magnitude 2 or less, so weak they
couldn't be felt.

The geologists wanted to harvest as many seismic waves
as possible, then use them as earth probes to create computer-
enhanced images of what was happening in the ground. It
was an unprecedented opportunity to study the crustal rock.

Everyone knew this chance would last only for a short time. They had to gather the data now, before the quakes ceased.

After the discovery of the previously undetected fault that ran south beyond Memphis, Atkins wondered if the strong ground activity in western Kentucky indicated the same thing. Was it possible they'd find another branch or segment of the New Madrid Seismic Zone?

He'd spent much of the day thinking about that and was still mulling over the possibilities as he and Jacobs sped due east on the Sam Purchase toll road. The hazy sky of the early morning had given way to beautiful afternoon sunshine. It was just over forty degrees. Fine weather. Jacobs was driving, pushing well over the sixty-mile-an-hour speed limit. He had a bluegrass CD blaring in the stereo. The sound went perfectly with the rugged countryside.

They were on their way to their last stop—an abandoned coal mine. They wanted to set up one of the portable seismometers underground. This would eliminate the possibility that the instrument would pick up any "background" noise such as automobile traffic. Jacobs had already arranged the trip with the company that owned the mine. The Golden Orient plunged two thousand feet into the ground, one of the deepest mines in the state.

Atkins kept returning to the foreshock-aftershock issue. Were all of these recent miniquakes the gradual winding down of the magnitude 7.1 event? Or were they building to an even bigger earthquake?

He'd been arguing it with himself ever since his meeting the night before with Elizabeth Holleran. He had major doubts about the foreshock theory. He'd already talked it over with Jacobs that morning. It didn't fit with the historical record, which seemed to mitigate against another big quake any time soon on the New Madrid Fault. The recent pattern there was clear. One moderately big quake seemed to occur every ninety years or so.

But Atkins couldn't quite forget the glaring exception: the three quakes of 1811–1812, each of them a monster.

Jacobs had calculated that up to fifty percent of the elastic strain energy remained stored in the rocks after the first quake in the famous New Madrid sequence—enough to trigger two more huge quakes. It was a sobering statistic, one that Atkins couldn't overlook.

As he sat in the Explorer's passenger seat working over all this, Atkins also realized he wanted to see Elizabeth Holleran again.

It was a surprisingly strong feeling, and it explained why he hadn't gotten much sleep that night, less than four hours, the first time in a long time anything like that had happened.

Ever since he'd lost Sara, he'd found it hard to relax with another woman, to spend time and make the emotional commitment to get to know someone better. He knew what the problem was; a doctor he'd seen had explained it to him: He was still grieving over Sara's death. The powerful feeling had lasted for years. This desire to see Elizabeth Holleran was totally unexpected.

Jacobs turned off the toll road and drove north about ten miles. They were near the small town of Kaler about fifteen miles northeast of Mayfield. The mine had been closed for more than twenty years, Jacobs explained. There'd been a fire. Some miners had been killed.

"I don't know the details," Jacobs said. "But it must have been pretty bad. They reopened it a couple years later, but then air pollution regs closed them down again. Too much sulfur in the coal. Most of the mines in this part of the country had to shut down for the same reason."

"How far down do you want to set up the seismometer?" Atkins asked. He wasn't looking forward to this.

"A couple hundred feet," Jacobs said. "That ought to filter out all the surface noise. You don't gain anything by going much deeper."

A gate blocked the private road to the mine. The facility covered five miles of forested hill country. One of the arms of Kentucky Lake was twenty miles due east.

Jacobs called the mine's security office with his cell phone. Ten minutes later an elderly guard arrived in an aging pickup. He wore a holstered pistol and red suspenders. His cheeks and chin were covered with white stubble.

"I been expectin' you all morning," he said curtly, getting out of the truck to unlock the gate. "Follow me."

"Friendly guy," Atkins said softly.

"They warned me about him," Jacobs said. "He's been

here forty years. Lost his job when the mine shut down. Stayed on as a guard.''

They drove up a gravel road that dead-ended at a parking lot. The mine entrance was inside a corrugated metal building with massive doors. A ten-story derrick that operated the elevator cables towered over it.

With each of them gripping the seismograph's metal carrying case, Jacobs and Atkins followed the guard through a side door. The old man flipped a breaker switch. Overhead lights flashed on. Atkins heard heavy machinery groan to life somewhere above them, high up on the derrick tower.

The elevator was a metal cage large enough to accommodate fifty men.

The guard handed each of them a scuffed miner's helmet.

"The levels are marked on the wall in red numbers," he said. "Just push the buttons to go up or down."

"Are you going with us?" Atkins asked.

"No, sir," the guard said. He hesitated. His tone softened. "I don't think you boys ought to be going down there."

"Why not?" Atkins asked. The man was staring at them, wide-eyed, not blinking.

"Something ain't right." He looked like he wanted to say more but changed his mind. "You get in any trouble, hit the big yellow button on the elevator control panel. It'll sound an alarm."

"What happens then?" Jacobs asked.

"I'll call for help," the guard said. "You'll have to wait 'til it gets here. That could take a while."

He slammed shut the elevator's metal grill. Jacobs pressed the red button for Level 2. The cage started down with a rust-grinding lurch. There were twenty levels, descending two thousand feet. A single light bulb burned over their heads.

"I wonder what he wanted to tell us," Atkins said.

"I'm kinda glad I didn't find out," Jacobs said. "Mines spook me enough as it is. I never could have worked in one."

As they slowly descended, it occurred to Atkins that this was the deepest he'd ever gone into the earth. A geologist for more than twenty years, he'd spent his entire life on the surface. The profession hadn't taken advantage of these man-made deep spots in the earth.

Reaching Level 2, they carried the seismograph about twenty feet into the coal tunnel. They could see only as far as the lights on their helmets penetrated the darkness. It was cool, almost cold, the only sound being the steady dripping of water from the rocks.

They got the battery-driven seismograph up and running in about ten minutes. Jacobs plugged a small laptop computer into the unit. It was an analogue machine. The seismic activity appeared digitally on the computer screen.

"Jesus Christ, John! Look at this," Jacobs said, playing a flashlight on the screen. "This ground's alive."

The readouts startled Atkins. He'd never seen such intense seismic activity. All of it was way under magnitude 2. The waves were too weak to be felt, but they were coming in ten- to twenty-second intervals.

"I can't wait to get a directional reading on this," Jacobs said. They'd need to let the seismometer run awhile to harvest enough data to get a precise fix on the source of the waves and their direction.

Atkins felt something brush his cheek. He looked up and saw coal dust falling from the ceiling of the shaft.

"Do you smell that?" Jacobs asked.

Atkins straightened up. He smelled the faint, unmistakable odor of rotten eggs. Hydrogen sulfide. The foul gas that made the air around Hawaii's Kilauea volcano so tough to breathe. Atkins had been to the volcano several times. He'd recognize that distinctive odor anywhere.

Hydrogen sulfide was usually associated with volcanoes. Pockets of the gas formed deep underground and were released like champagne bubbles during eruptions. There'd been reports of strange odors seeping from the ground. He remembered how the farmer, Ben Harvey, had complained that his well water smelled bad.

"We must be getting some venting," Jacobs said, referring to a natural vent or crack that allowed the odors to escape from the ground. But that didn't explain what was causing the smell.

"Hold on, listen!" Atkins said.

A faint rumbling came from the depths of the mine. It

was hard to pinpoint the exact source, like trying to locate a sound underwater. It seemed to be coming from all directions at once, the sound rising up from the deep earth—distant, strange, unreal.

Atkins had never heard anything like it. He had an overpowering urge to get out of there fast. He felt trapped.

A loud groan reverberated in the tunnels, the sound echoing back off the walls, building like thunder. Then, as abruptly as it had begun, the rumbling stopped. It was as if someone had thrown a switch. The silence was total.

Atkins felt his heart pounding in his chest. He was pouring sweat. It stung his eyes. He'd kept waiting for a tremor, tensing for it.

"Maybe we ought to go a little deeper," Jacobs said.

Atkins looked at his friend for a moment. Neither spoke.

"All right," Atkins said. "Let's do it."

They picked up the seismometer and computer and got back into the elevator cage. Jacobs pushed the button for Level 10, halfway to the bottom of the shaft. The big car started to descend. They were going down another eight hundred feet.

The farther they descended, the stronger the smell became. By the time they reached Level 8, both of them had pressed handkerchiefs over their noses and mouths. The odor was almost overpowering.

Jacobs waved his hands to indicate they'd gone far enough. He was coughing.

The elevator cage was open on the sides. Atkins touched the rock wall. The rough stone was almost hot. Then he noticed that his feet were getting warm. The cage's steel floor was heating up. Warm air was blasting up from the bottom of the mine shaft.

LAUREN MITCHELL WAS THE FIRST TO SPEAK AT THE public meeting, which was held that evening in the over-heated gymnasium at Mayfield Senior High School. With a population of ten thousand or so, Mayfield was one of the larger towns in extreme southwestern Kentucky. Memphis was about 120 miles to the southwest. Approximately three hundred people were jammed into the high school's small auditorium—men, women, children, all of them sitting nervously on bleacher seats or folding chairs, or leaning against the walls.

Lauren had organized the meeting virtually single-handedly. She'd talked to everyone she could think of about what she'd seen at Kentucky Dam. It hadn't taken long to spread the word, and she'd gotten some help from the local radio station.

Lauren wasn't the only one who'd heard the water blasting through the dam's big gates. A lot of people who lived along the Tennessee River—some as far as five miles from the dam—had been awakened by the pounding roar. Many of them were in the gym. So were about a dozen sheriff's deputies and state troopers, who stood in the back.

Paul Weston and two other members of the Seismic Safety Commission sat at a table at the head of the basketball key. Weston, as usual, was formally dressed—suit, crisp blue shirt, paisley bow tie. Governor Tad Parker had ordered Weston to hold the meeting that evening. Parker, who was in the state capital at Frankfort, expected a full report.

Television crews from Memphis, tipped off about the session, had their cameras and lights on as Lauren walked to the stand-up microphone in front of the table. She wore jeans and a brown leather jacket and was holding a legal pad.

"I want to know, we all do, what's going on," she said. She described what she'd seen and how Tom Davis, the hydrologist in charge, had told her they'd almost lost the dam.

"We've spoken to Mister Davis," Weston said. "He tells us he doesn't recall making such a comment."

"That's not true," Lauren said, struggling to keep her voice calm. "I know what I heard. What I don't know is why someone would want to make Tom change his story. And where is Tom? I asked him to come tonight, and he told me he would. Have you already gotten to him?"

"That dam's never been safer," Weston said in a warm, friendly voice. "We've had four engineers go over it from top to bottom. We made another inspection just this morning. There are several minor cracks on an interior wall that need some patching. Those repairs are now being made. Everything else looks in fine shape."

"If they were just minor cracks, why did Tom open those gates?" Lauren persisted.

Weston nodded understandingly and said, "I know some of you must have wondered what was going on up there during the draw off. Well, the fact is that Mister Davis was perfectly justified in opening the locks. He thought he had a . . . problem after that last quake. We may have some disagreement over what exactly he said to Ms. Mitchell here, but the bottom line is he did the right thing. Maybe he overreacted a little. In hindsight, we could have handled all this better. Let people know what we were doing and why. That's why the governor was so eager to arrange this meeting tonight. He wants everyone here to know he understands how inconvenient it is for you folks to have 641 closed. We'll get it open as soon as those repairs are made. Shouldn't take more than a few more days, but we want to do it right."

"What if there's another earthquake?" Lauren said. "We've been getting shakes out here every day. Is that dam going to hold if we get another good one?" She got a round of loud applause. Many of those in attendance were farmers or people who owned small businesses along the Tennessee River. Marina operators like her, grocery store and gas station owners, who depended on tourists. Men and women alike, they favored flannel shirts, work boots, and quilted parkas.

"I can speak to that question," Weston said. "I know you're all concerned with the series of aftershocks we've been experiencing. That's normal after a strong earthquake. The seismic activity could keep up for weeks or even months. But there's no evidence we'll get another big quake in the magnitude 7 or greater range any time soon. I'd stop worrying about that. It's not going to happen."

JOHN Atkins and Walter Jacobs had arrived at the gym just after Lauren Mitchell walked to the microphone. They'd driven to Mayfield straight from the mine after Jacobs got a cell phone call from Weston's office, asking them to attend the meeting.

Atkins remembered Lauren from his visit a few days earlier to her boat dock and hadn't forgotten the unnerving sight of all those frogs and snakes crawling out of the frozen ground near the lake. Surprised to see her, he was interested in what she was saying, but his mind was preoccupied.

Jacobs and he hadn't had a chance yet to discuss with anyone what had happened in the Golden Orient. They wanted to return first thing in the morning with additional instruments to measure the heat and magnetic fields that were being generated in the mine. There were examples of such phenomena in the literature, but they were extremely rare. The ground was highly unstable.

At the very least, Atkins wanted to install a strain meter to see if he could get any readings that might help them analyze how much energy remained stored in the crust.

Standing there in the back of the gym, he remembered the heat, the strange, overpowering smell, and the sound welling up from the deep rock. Mainly he remembered how scared he was in that open elevator cage during the agonizingly slow ride up to the surface. They'd gotten the call to head back to Mayfield just about the time they'd climbed into the Explorer.

Distracted by his thoughts, he watched Lauren standing at

the mike. She obviously wasn't buying what Weston was telling her. Neither was anyone else in the gym. They all looked skeptical, worried. The children had picked up on the current of fear in the room. Some of the littlest ones were crying.

Atkins noticed a woman in an olive-green trench coat get up from a seat in the back of the gym and approach the microphone. She had dark blond hair.

Elizabeth Holleran.

She walked up to Lauren Mitchell, who was still standing at the mike. Paul Weston's sudden anger was clear to see. It could be felt, measured.

Holleran smiled at Lauren and introduced herself. She nodded to the men seated at the table. Some of the same faces she'd addressed yesterday.

"You're doing very well," Holleran told Lauren, smiling at her. "Would you mind if I ask a few questions?"

"Not at all," said Lauren, who looked pleased to get the help. "Be my guest."

"This is starting to get interesting," Jacobs whispered to Atkins. He was struck by Holleran's poise as she approached Weston and the others. She was cool, steady under pressure.

"Doctor Weston, there's a simple way of determining how serious the damage was to the dam. Then we can assess what's been done to repair that damage. Could you tell us if there was any sideways movement or settling?"

"You have no standing before this panel," Weston exploded. His earlier warmth completely gone, he looked like he wanted to come up out of his chair. "I promise you that I'm going to lodge a formal complaint with the head of your department at Cal Tech."

"It's an easy question, really," Holleran said, ignoring the threat.

"Why don't you answer the lady's question instead of barkin' her down," someone shouted from the back of the auditorium.

"Damn right! Answer her question!" shouted another.

Atkins enjoyed watching Holleran in action and found himself wanting to cheer. It was a simple, albeit crucial question. She deserved an answer.

Holleran said, "For the benefit of anyone here who might

not know this, the shock waves from a big earthquake like the one three days ago can cause large structures such as dams to sway or settle. A sideways movement greater than, say, seven or eight centimeters could cause serious damage. You'd need to do major repairs, provided repairs could even be made. It's the same thing with settling. If the dam settled only a few centimeters, there's no real harm. But if it was greater than seven, eight, or nine centimeters, you could have major, possibly fatal damage.''

Weston's reddening cheeks looked windburned. He was leaning forward in his chair, arms folded, trying to appear patient, under control.

"This woman isn't qualified to make . . .''

He was shouted down.

"Answer her question! Did that dam move sideways or settle?''

Several other loud voices were yelling for answers.

"We don't have any information on that,'' Weston said, changing his tone, trying to become more conciliatory. "The engineers who did the inspection are still working on their report.''

You better be right about that, Atkins thought. The one duty a seismologist owed the public at a time like this was absolute honesty, even, in his opinion, at the risk of starting a panic. He doubted Weston was telling these people everything he knew.

A few in the crowd starting whistling. "You're lyin',' mister,'' someone yelled. "You got to know what's happened to that dam. Hell, you just told us the engineers just finished inspecting it.''

"The information will be made available at the appropriate time,'' Weston said, sitting back in his chair. He'd regained his composure. Hands palm down on the table, he looked at Holleran, his gaze unflinching.

"Do you remember what happened in the San Fernando Valley in 1971?'' she asked.

"Oh, come on,'' Weston said. "The two situations aren't the same at all.''

"Let's hope so,'' Holleran said. She explained for the audience's benefit that in 1971 an earthquake in the San Fernando Valley almost breached the Lower San Fernando

Dam near Los Angeles. It came perilously close to failure and forced the evacuation of eighty thousand people. A thin wall of dirt was all that separated the valley from 15 million tons of water.

"The governor wants you all to know he's making absolutely sure the dam is safe," Weston said, forcing a smile. He figured he better end this as quickly as possible. "We'll be back to you with more information, everything you want, as soon as we get it." He gathered his papers and started to stand up.

A heavyset bearded man in a down vest grabbed Weston's arm. Two state troopers immediately ran toward him.

"Here it comes," Atkins told Jacobs.

The man pushed one of the troopers away. Two others grabbed him from behind. Then everyone was up. There were shouts, screams, the slam of folding chairs being overturned. Someone threw a punch. The deputies and troopers moved in to restore order.

ATKINS approached Elizabeth Holleran, who was talking to Lauren. They turned and walked quickly out of the gymnasium. Atkins followed. He wanted to see if Holleran was all right. One of the troopers had given her a pretty good shove, trying to get at the bearded farmer.

He caught up with Holleran and Lauren at the far end of the parking lot, which was jammed with cars and pickup trucks. He saw them stop next to a late-model station wagon with its headlights on and engine running. They were talking to the driver.

The woman sitting behind the wheel saw Atkins approaching. She stopped talking, backed up quickly, and drove off the lot, gravel flying from the rear wheels. She almost sideswiped another car that was also trying to leave.

Atkins said to Holleran, "Are you okay? I saw what happened—"

"That was the wife of the hydrologist who works out at the dam," she said, interrupting him. "The man who told Lauren the dam was in trouble." She started to introduce Atkins to Lauren Mitchell.

"We've already met," he said, shaking Lauren's hand. "I was out at her boat dock the day before the quake."

"He wants someone to go to the dam right now," Lauren said. "He says the damage is a lot worse than anyone's letting on. He thinks it's all a cover-up, that the cracks can't be repaired."

She explained that the hydrologist had left a door open so that someone could slip inside the dam for a firsthand look at what was going on. The catch was that they'd need a boat to get to it. The door allowed access to an equipment platform and was on the side of the dam facing the lake.

"How can you get out there?" Atkins said.

Lauren said, "I've got a boat. It's a little rough out on the water, but I can take you."

"When?" Holleran asked.

"How about right now."

Taking Lauren's car, they drove to her marina. She gave each of them a snowmobile suit and slipped into one herself. It would be bitter cold on the lake.

"How long has it been this choppy?" Atkins asked as they walked along the boat dock. They were heading to the roofed enclosure where Lauren's twenty-foot outboard was tied up.

"Ever since the first earthquake," she said. "It'll calm down for a while then kick right up again."

The lake was about three miles wide at that point. Far off in the darkness, Atkins thought he could make out tiny pin-pricks of lights on the opposite shore. The water slapped hard at the dock, splashing over the wooden walkway. Floating on oil drums, the dock was rocking, pitching up and down like a buoy. Atkins had to grip the handrails tightly to keep his balance.

He didn't doubt that the repeated aftershocks were causing the water turbulence.

He looked out at the lake. He wasn't looking forward to going out there in an open boat.

"We'll need to be real careful when we get up near the dam," Lauren said, handing each of them a life vest and showing them how to tie it on. "The water's pretty rough on that end. We don't want to get caught in the current up there."

Lauren climbed down into the V-bottom and started the big 150-horsepower Mariner outboard, which roared to life in a plume of blue smoke. She sat at a steering wheel in the middle of the cockpit. Holleran sat on a bench seat in the stern.

Atkins untied the bowlines and hopped aboard. The current spun the boat around like a wood chip. Lauren gunned the engine and pulled away from the marina. They had to go about two miles down the lake. Atkins sat next to Holleran and tried to keep his face out of the spray that kicked up over the gunwales every time they plowed through a wave.

Lauren was as good as her word. It was a bone-jarring ride made all the more uncomfortable because she hugged the rocky shoreline, where the wave action was rougher. She wanted to keep out of open water as much as possible so they wouldn't be seen as easily. About halfway to the dam, the main channel forked. Lauren steered down the smaller arm, where it would be even harder for anyone to spot them from the dam.

The trip reminded Atkins of some rafting he'd done on the Colorado River back in his grad school days. They ran Class IV white water all the way down the canyon.

Holleran was holding on to her seat for dear life. Every time they pancaked down on a wave, they were almost pitched off their seats. She had to shout to make herself understood over the engine.

"You . . . can . . . hear . . . it!"

In the distance, Atkins heard the waves hitting the dam, the noise carrying over the roar of the outboard.

They finally came out of the long cove. The dam loomed up in front of them three hundred yards away. A massive, chalk-colored wall of rough stone and sloping, poured concrete. Streetlights illuminated the top where the two-lane highway ran.

Lauren cut her speed and let the waves and current wash them into an eddy about forty yards from the western end of the dam. A narrow, curving spit of land jutted out at a right angle from the base of the dam and served as a breakwater, creating a pool where boats could anchor. It was relatively sheltered from the lake's open water.

Skillfully handling the wheel and throttle, Lauren eased up close enough to the shore for Atkins to jump out and tie the bow lines to a mooring post. A thick stand of pine trees shielded them from view from the dam.

They'd have to climb up a wall of broken stone to get to the door that Tom Davis had left open. The door opened from the inside and gave access to heating and air-conditioning units located on a steel platform that jutted from the dam's outer wall. It was about forty feet up from the water.

Lauren stayed with the boat. Holleran and Atkins started climbing the pile of broken rock, carefully working their way across the face of the dam to the platform. They were soon out over the water, the waves crashing below them against the wall of stone.

Holleran, a strong climber, easily made it to the platform and pulled herself over a low railing. Atkins was right behind her. She opened the metal door. Slipping inside, they found themselves in a darkened service tunnel.

Atkins was relieved to get in out of the biting wind and cold. Water poured off his snowmobile suit. He wiped it from his face and eyes.

Turning on flashlights, they walked about thirty yards down the tunnel. There they heard heavy machinery, the pounding of pneumatic drills and truck engines. It sounded like a construction site. The tunnel—it was more of a cat-walk—ended at a ladder. They climbed down to a lower level about twenty feet below them.

They were inside the huge double wall of the dam. The space was about fifty yards wide at the base with concrete walls that soared up on each side, tapering in the darkness high above them.

From the catwalk, which was in shadows, they were able to peer around a pillar of reinforced concrete. The scene below almost made them gasp. Five cement trucks were lined up bumper to bumper. At least thirty men, maybe more, were working under the bright illumination of portable lights. Drills and jackhammers were pounding. Blue and orange sparks showered down from tall scaffolding where six men were welding steel reinforcement plates against the wall.

Atkins pointed to the wall that faced the lake. Four large cracks fanned out across the concrete like the tributaries of a river, each of them more than fifty feet long. Water was seeping from two of them. They were pumping it out. It was impossible to tell how deep the fissures were. One of them extended into the wall. One of them looked at least six inches wide.

"I wouldn't call those minor surface cracks," Holleran said, shouting out the words. She remembered how Weston had described them a few hours earlier.

Realizing at once what those gaping cracks signified, Atkins felt a cold fear well up in him. The dam was in serious danger of failure. If another moderate to strong quake hit before they finished making the repairs, it was going to collapse. He wasn't a structural engineer, but he didn't see how it could survive. He couldn't begin to comprehend what it would mean if those walls gave way and the lake water poured out into the Tennessee River.

"Weston must have known this," he said.

He couldn't believe, seeing this, that the man had lied so blatantly.

"Let's see if we can get a little closer," Holleran said.

"That's not a good idea," Atkins said. "They might see us."

"You can stay here, but I'm going," Holleran said firmly. "I want a better look at those cracks."

"Are you always like this?" Atkins said angrily. He felt like grabbing her so she couldn't move.

"You're damn right I am," Holleran snapped. She'd had enough of Atkins' arrogance. She'd put up with it at the restaurant in Memphis, but not here.

She'd just started to reach for the ladder to descend to another catwalk when the ground shook. The tremor lasted four or five seconds. Maybe a magnitude 3, Atkins thought.

They scrambled back up the ladder to the service tunnel. They hit the door on the run and got out on the equipment platform. They were scrambling over the railings when someone shouted at them from the top of the dam.

"Don't move down there!"

"Keep going!" Atkins yelled to Holleran, who was in front of him.

There were more shouts from the dam. Someone had a bullhorn. A booming, amplified voice ordered them to halt.

Lauren already had the engine revving when they reached the boat. Atkins untied the lines and jumped in. Lauren gunned the outboard and turned in a tight circle. She shot out of the protected eddy and headed back into open water.

"We've got company," she shouted over her shoulder.

Two boats were angling toward them across the lake. They were coming from the opposite end of the dam. Even in the darkness, Atkins saw the white rooster tails the engines threw up behind them.

Lauren had the throttle wide open. She was still hugging the shore, fighting the strong current. This wasn't even going to be close. The boats were going to overtake them long before they got back up into the cove.

Suddenly they were pitched sharply to the left. It was as if something had given the boat a hard sideways shove.

Holleran and Atkins both understood what had happened. Another quake had struck, stronger than the one they'd had a few minutes earlier.

The effect on the lake was instantaneous. Waves rose up in front of them. The suddenness of it all was breathtaking.

Lauren turned in toward shore. It wasn't far. Maybe thirty yards. Atkins and Holleran were bailing with their hands. The boat had taken on a lot of water when it was pitched to the side. They'd almost swamped.

"Get your life jackets strapped on!" Lauren screamed at them. "Do it now! Make sure they're tight!"

Atkins looked across the lake. He could see only one of the boats. It had flipped over on its side and was heaving up and down in the waves, stern up. He couldn't see anyone in the water. There was no way anyone could survive out there, even in a life jacket. It wasn't much better closer to shore.

A wave crashed over their boat, flooding the engine. They began to roll over.

"Get out and try to hold on to the side," Lauren yelled as they all went into the water. "Stay with the boat! Whatever happens . . . stay . . . with . . . the . . . boat!"

Atkins and Holleran worked their way to the same side of the hull as Lauren. They began kicking, trying to keep the shore in view as they rose and fell with the waves. They were being pulled farther out into the lake.

"We've got to try to swim for it!" Atkins shouted.

"I don't think I can," Lauren said. "Can't move . . . I can't move my arms."

Her teeth were chattering. It was hard for her to talk. Hard to think in the cold. Wet and chilled to the bone, she'd been freezing ever since they'd left the dam. She was losing the feeling in her legs and arms. Her body chemistry was starting to shut down.

Atkins looped his arm through the straps of her life jacket.

"Go for it, Elizabeth!" he shouted.

The boat was lifted up on a swell. Atkins got a good look at the shore. He fixed on a tree. It was barely ten yards away. So close he could see the individual branches hanging out over the water. He tucked up his legs and pushed off as hard as he could against the side of the overturned boat. He saw Elizabeth do the same and then she was lost from view.

"Kick!" he screamed to Lauren. "Kick as hard as you can. Keep kicking!"

The water was very cold. Atkins tried to keep his eyes locked on the tree. Every time a wave lifted them up, he tried to get his bearings, focusing on a point midway up the trunk. He told himself to keep staring at it. His arms were starting to get heavy. He didn't know how much longer he'd be able to keep this up. He could feel Lauren next to him. She was kicking, flailing with her arms. They weren't making any headway. The waves were driving them into the shore, then pulling them back out.

Gripping the straps of Lauren's life jacket, Atkins started thrashing with his right arm. He kept kicking. He thought he was going to drown, that his clothes and boots were going to pull him down. He kicked with his legs and beat at the water with an arm that felt like a lead weight. They were closer to the rocks. He bit down hard on the life jacket strap and clawed his way toward them with both arms, trying to keep his head up.

His right leg grazed something in the water. Rocks. He touched bottom with both feet and pushed off and managed to grab hold of a tree root that was sticking out of the bank. He held on to it until he caught his breath, then pulled and fought his way up onto the muddy ground, dragging Lauren with him.

Collapsing there, he rolled over on his back and felt his legs start to cramp. Sick to the stomach, he coughed up some water and vomit. His legs cramped, the pain stabbing into his calves like nails. He realized he would have drowned if that had happened a few seconds earlier. He kept looking up at the black sky, his left arm clasping Lauren's life jacket. He spat up more water. It was good to breathe.

"Are you all right?" Lauren was on her knees, looking at him, her hands cradling his head. She was shivering in the cold air.

He nodded and clenched his teeth against the pain in his legs. The cramps started to ease off.

He saw Holleran. She was hunched over behind them, kneeling on the ground. Water was pouring off her clothing. Her long hair hung limp over her shoulders. She was the first to get up.

"I don't see them," she said. "They just disappeared."

Atkins, still sucking air into his lungs, didn't understand. Then he realized she was talking about the two boats that had been chasing them. Pulling himself up to a sitting position, he looked out at the lake. The waves were as tall as any he'd ever seen in the ocean. He could hear them beating against the dam, the sound carrying back to them over the water.

The moon suddenly appeared from behind the clouds, a full yellow disk.

THEY walked from the lake to the highway and then in their sodden clothing followed it about a mile to Lauren Mitchell's marina, where they dried off and huddled in front of a propane space heater. They put on new snowmobile suits.

Atkins knew he needed to do something about the dam, start warning people that the damage was far worse than anyone was letting on. First he called Guy Thompson in Memphis. Thompson was excited. He'd been working with Prable's earthquake data nearly nonstop for a full day.

"I've run his probability assessment over and over, and I've got to tell you, John, I can't punch a hole in it," he said. "His correlations look right on."

Thompson had found only one shortcoming with Prable's projections. He'd made an error in calculating solar activity, one of the indices critical to his prediction of a major earthquake along the New Madrid Fault. He wasn't to blame for the mistake. The National Oceanic and Atmospheric Administration had only recently issued a correction in an earlier projection of sunspot activity.

Prable had based his calculations on a date for a peak flare occurring on or about January 20. That date had now been revised.

Thompson told Atkins the rest of it.

"Peak solar activity and flares will occur later today, John. The projection is for a larger number of sunspots than anticipated. The solar wind's gonna be howling. Plasma density levels are going to spike. We're gonna get a real heavy gravitational pull."

Atkins did some mental calculations. That would be about 4:00 in the morning. He quietly mentioned this to Elizabeth, who just stared at him and nodded. Wrapped in a woolen blanket, she was just starting to warm up.

"So what do you make of this?" Thompson asked.

"I don't know," Atkins said. "I wish to God I did." He was still reluctant to put much credence in Prable's data. The effects of solar activity and gravitational pull on earthquakes simply weren't known. It was all new territory.

"Something's happening in the ground," Thompson said. "The seismographs are really picking up over in your area."

Atkins stood by the telephone, aware of Thompson's silence on the other end of the line. As his mind raced, he felt that someone was sitting inside his body, that someone else was holding the phone. He had a pestering fear about how he'd feel when he was back inside himself again.

THEY'D just taken off from Mayfield and swung out to the east a few miles before the UH-60 pilot pointed the nose of the National Guard helicopter due south and leveled off. It was 12:25 A.M. The sky had cleared. The moon and stars blazed in the darkness. Walter Jacobs and two other seismologists were flying back to Memphis to get more seismic equipment. Jacobs wanted to run some measurements in the coal mine.

Unable to find Atkins after the meeting at the gymnasium, he'd decided to leave without him. This was too important to wait. He wanted to be back at that mine first thing in the morning.

Jacobs and the other two men, both USGS geologists, were

seated on benches in the rear of the big helicopter. A crewman, a young soldier bundled in a hooded parka, was up by the closed cargo door, staring out the portholes.

He was the first to notice it—a rippling wave of bright, bluish-red light that seemed to rise out of the ground and hover over the dark hills.

Then the pilot saw it.

"Sweet Jesus," he announced over the intercom. "Check out the light show off the starboard side."

The pilot, a retired Air Force major with extensive flying time, barely got the words out. He'd never seen anything like it. Unearthly, strangely beautiful lights pulsing in broad shimmering bands that grew in strength and intensity. Shades of blue, white, and reddish-orange swirling and streaming ever higher in the eastern sky.

"Is that the northern lights?" the crewman asked, speaking into his radio headset.

"No way," the pilot said, his voice sounding brittle over the speaker. "This is much brighter, stronger. And it's coming from the east, not the north."

Walt Jacobs had unfastened his safety harness and crawled up to the porthole. The crewman moved away so the geologist could take a look. The lights were streaking like neon.

"What is it?" the crewman yelled, shouting to make himself heard over the droning rotors. Jacobs kept staring out the porthole.

"What are you seeing out there?"

Jacobs couldn't take his eyes away from the spectacle. He heard himself say, "Earthquake lights."

JOHN ATKINS ALSO SAW THE LIGHTS. THEY TOOK his mind off his disturbing conversation with Guy Thompson. The pulsing colors lit up the windows of Lauren's bait-and-tackle shop, where he and Elizabeth sat near a propane space heater, trying to get the aching chill out of their bones.

The dancing lights arched across the horizon, or moved in zigzag bands of blue, pale white, and orange.

Atkins explained the phenomenon to Lauren. Rarely seen and largely a mystery, the lights were associated with earthquakes. They were possibly caused by polarized electricity in near-surface rocks or by electrical charges in the air. No one was sure. Atkins couldn't believe the dazzling intensity of the colors. What he'd seen a few nights earlier on that farm near Mayfield didn't compare to this.

The lights shimmered in brilliant, iridescent waves that shot across the sky in long, streaming bands of color.

The lake was boiling, the waves crashing over the dock and pier, which rode up and down on floating steel drums. The cables groaned loudly. Lauren worried the dock was going to pull apart.

"How much time do we have?" she asked.

"I don't know," Atkins said, glancing at Elizabeth. If Prable was correct in his analysis, maybe only a few hours. But he still wasn't convinced that Prable had it right. The effects of solar disturbances and tidal pulls on the earth's

crust had been debated for years—without any clear-cut result. "Maybe we'll have a better idea . . ."

Lauren angrily cut him off. "What good are you people?
You're supposed to be experts on earthquakes, but you can't
tell me whether we're in danger, or how much time we've
got left. I've got two parents living near Paducah. If the dam
goes and all that water hits the Ohio, that city's going to be
wiped out. We need to warn them."

"She's right," Elizabeth said. "We've got to assume a
major quake is imminent."

Atkins agreed. By training, geologists were reluctant to
make predictions about earthquakes. It was so easy to be
wrong, and mistakes could have deadly consequences. But
this wasn't any time to be overly cautious. He'd seen the
cracks in that dam.

"Assuming Prable's right, and Guy's crunched the right
numbers, we've got maybe four or five hours," he said.

"Can you call the sheriff?" Elizabeth asked Lauren. "Get
him out here. Tell him what's going on."

"You bet I can," she said eagerly. "He's an old friend.
He'll come." Once they'd made a decision to do something,
anything, she immediately felt better.

Atkins wanted to hurry back to Mayfield and get the
equipment in the Explorer. They needed to set up seismographs and other instruments. He wanted to be ready. If a
quake hit, that data would be vital.

"How are we going to get back?" Elizabeth asked. She'd
left her car in Mayfield.

"Take my Blazer," Lauren said. "I've got a pickup I
keep down here at the marina. After what you did, pulling
me out of the water, it's the least I can do." She was just
starting to get the warmth back in her legs.

Elizabeth glanced out a window at the lake. She opened
the blinds for a better look. Still not trusting her eyes, she
asked Lauren if she had a pair of binoculars.

Atkins didn't need binoculars. He could see the strange
glow in the water with his naked eyes. The murky green
light appeared to be coming from the depths. It was as if
bonfires were burning far below the surface.

"What . . . is . . . that?" Elizabeth asked.

Atkins shook his head. "It might be a strong electro-magnetic charge emanating from some great depth," he said. "Or maybe escaping gas or heat." He frowned. Earthquake lights were one thing. The bizarre glow in the water was even more baffling. He admitted he didn't have a clue.

THE LIGHT SHOW—THE PULSING HUES WERE AL-
most psychedelic—kept blazing in the sky. If anything, the
colors were more vivid as Atkins held the gas pedal to the
floorboard of Lauren's aging Chevy Blazer. It was hard not
to stare at the dazzling spectacle as he pushed the speed over
seventy miles an hour on the two-lane highway, ignoring the
icy patches as he covered the last ten miles into Mayfield.

They were in extreme southwestern Kentucky, about thirty
miles from the Tennessee line and another 120 miles due
north of Memphis. The Mississippi River was just to the
west. Atkins was glad he'd put Kentucky Lake far behind
them.

"What about those lights in the water?" Elizabeth asked.
She hadn't been able to get them out of her mind.

Neither had Atkins. "My best and probably wrong guess
is that some hot gases are venting from a deep fracture in
hard rock maybe fifteen or twenty miles down," he said. "It
could be some kind of hot phosphorous that's reacting with
the cold water."

"Or maybe radon," Elizabeth said. The inert gas was radioactive. It's sudden release was a recognized precursor of
big quakes, but she was unaware of anything in the literature
that described such a large venting.

"Who knows?" Atkins said. "It's got me stumped." His
heated-gas theory didn't satisfy him. The subject was one of
the first things he wanted to discuss with Walt Jacobs or
Guy Thompson as soon as he could raise them on his cell

phone. He'd tried repeatedly during the last hour. So had Elizabeth. The reception kept breaking off.

Elizabeth had leaned back in her seat with her arms folded, trying to keep warm. The Blazer's decrepit heater, even on full blast, put out only a trickle of warm air. She touched Atkins' hand.

"I'm sorry I snapped at you back at the dam," she said. She'd been wanting to tell him that.

"Forget it," Atkins said. "You were right back there. Sometimes I can get a little obstinate. The next time, just tell me to count to ten and keep my mouth closed."

Elizabeth smiled, and Atkins realized how good it felt to be with her. Just sitting next to her gave him pleasure. That feeling—the joy of simply being in a woman's presence— had been missing from his life for a long time. He was looking forward to getting to know her better.

They pulled off at the Mayfield exit. Atkins rolled up to a railroad crossing just as the red lights started flashing and the metal gates clanked down. A whistle blew far down the tracks. As the train rounded a curve, they saw the bright headlight of the diesel.

"He's really highballing," Atkins said as the freight train roared past them, the wheels banging on the rails.

The crossing blocked the main road into Mayfield. The town looked deserted. The rotunda of the courthouse and a church spire loomed in the darkness.

Later, Atkins remembered having had the presence of mind to check his wristwatch when it started. They both heard a deep, low-pitched rumble, the sound blotting out every other noise, even the rolling clatter of the freight train. The noise seized control of their brains, nerves, senses. Invaded them and drove out everything else. Stronger than thunder, the roar seemed to rise straight from the ground.

It was 2:16 A.M. Atkins scribbled the time on the palm of his hand with a ballpoint.

Elizabeth looked at him. They both knew what that sound meant.

"This is it," she said.

The rumble kept building in intensity. Atkins had heard about the loud ground thunder once before, in Armenia in 1988. A magnitude 7.8 that leveled four cities. Survivors recalled that when the rumbling stopped, a moment of calm followed. It was like the eye of a hurricane before the shaking started.

Atkins tried to break it down into science. The sudden compression in the ground also compressed the air, causing the noise. The stronger, more violent the compression, the louder the sound.

It occurred to him at that same moment that they were much too close to the railroad tracks. He slammed the gear into reverse and floored the Blazer, the tires squealing on the pavement as he backed away.

The train kept passing in front of them, a blur of boxcars, gondolas, tankers. Then with an explosive burst that startled him, Atkins was driven upward in his seat so hard his head slammed into the roof.

"It's coming," he shouted to Elizabeth, who was trying to hang on to her seatbelt shoulder strap.

The Blazer was pitched up and down in rapid, bone-jarring movements. The left door sprung open, and Elizabeth almost fell out. Atkins pulled her back inside.

"Oh, yessssssss!" she said. "This one's real."

They were shaken from side to side, the heaving ground slamming them together hard, shoulder to shoulder. The Blazer rocked back and forth, then up and down. The entire chassis was swaying.

"This is a magnitude 8 for sure," Atkins shouted.

Elizabeth said, "More."

Atkins had backed up about twenty yards from the railroad crossing before the earthquake hit. He realized it wasn't far enough.

"Get out!" Atkins yelled. They were still dangerously close to the train. Many of the derailed freight cars and tankers had been thrown on their sides. Still coupled together, they were writhing like a dying snake, metal grinding on metal.

Atkins and Elizabeth both staggered out of the Blazer and were instantly knocked down by the wavelike ground motion. Atkins recognized the P waves. Shooting up from the deep earth, the first seismic waves to hit after an earthquake struck, they were capable of traversing both the mantle and crust.

Atkins had experienced strong shaking before and knew it was only starting. They hadn't seen the worst of it.

He laid out the sequence in his mind. They were feeling the P waves, which had the strongest velocity and speed of all seismic waves and were the first waves a seismograph recorded. They resembled sound waves and could boom like thunder when they hit the surface. They spread out as they moved up through the ground, pushing and pulling at the rock.

The slower, harder-hitting S waves would arrive next, a series of violent sideways movements that sheared the rock at right angles and could knock hell out of the ground and anything standing on it.

The P and S waves were called body waves because they originated in the body of the rock deep underground. They moved up from the hypocenter of the earthquake to the surface.

A second group of waves, surface waves, followed the body waves. These were the real killers. Slower moving than the P or S waves, they were the last to be picked up by a seismograph. They were named after the two men who discovered them: Love, a mathematician, and Rayleigh, a physicist. Their motion, which resembled waves rippling across a lake, was confined to the ground surface.

The Love wave moved the ground from side to side in a powerful whipsawing action that destroyed the foundations of buildings. They arrived before the Rayleigh waves, which resembled waves rolling across the ocean. The Rayleigh wave made the ground billow, rocking it up and down in a series of rapid undulations.

The two groups of waves, body and surface, created an incredibly powerful one-two knockout punch.

Atkins' only thought was to get farther away from the wrecked train. Some of those cars were probably loaded with oil, natural gas, or some other inflammable chemical.

Supporting Elizabeth by the arm, Atkins managed to stumble forward a few steps before the next strong shake knocked them down again.

"Try to crawl," he said.

The ground was still moving in sharply defined waves. These were probably S waves, Atkins thought. The freight cars were swinging out in an arc, fanning back and forth in rhythm to the ground's wildly oscillating surface motions. Atkins glanced back just as a boxcar whipsawed across the road and flattened the Blazer.

The ground shaking had intensified. The rapid back-and-forth undulations were remarkably powerful.

Atkins smelled something. Three oil tanker cars were burning. Black smoke climbed high over the trees.

Another tanker blew in a bright flash of fire.

"We've got to get away from here before the whole thing goes up," Atkins said.

Supporting each other, sometimes crawling, they moved away from the wrecked train. The ground was still heaving, the jolts so severe and frequent it was impossible to stand.

"Listen," Atkins said.

A new sound.

The earth had started to rip apart in a fissure that cut across the railroad tracks and swept up into Mayfield. Atkins had seen the ground do the same thing three days earlier during the magnitude 7 quake, but it didn't compare with this. As rocks moved and sheared apart deep in the ground, a huge trench was forming, opening up right before their eyes. As the earth split open, the noise was deafening.

Atkins tried to get his bearings. He looked toward the town and saw the church spire rocking back and forth, silhouetted against the black sky. Worried the earth was going to rip open right under them, he got back on his feet and helped Elizabeth stand up. Just as they were getting used to the left-right ground movement, the seismic waves changed direction. The shaking, stronger than ever, shifted to right-left. Atkins guessed they were starting to feel the surface waves. It was hard to distinguish among the different waves when you were caught up in an actual quake.

"John, look!" Elizabeth said. She'd dropped to one knee to keep her balance.

He turned as the ground broke open under the upended train and swallowed a string of boxcars.

Four or five cars just disappeared.

The foul odor that poured from the opening smelled like sulphuric acid.

Then, as abruptly as it had begun, the earthquake was over.

The fissure slammed closed, the sound reminding Atkins of an avalanche only more abrupt, the rumble of snow crashing down a mountainside. It left a jagged scar with a two-foot shelf, or offset. It was as if a carving knife had ripped long slashes in the ground.

Atkins' wristwatch showed the shaking had lasted four minutes and five seconds. Elizabeth agreed with that time. If it was anywhere near accurate, it had to be a record.

The main thrust, Atkins guessed, had driven one side of the fault sharply upward. He figured this "hanging wall" was considerably higher than the other side of the fault.

"I think there was some strike-slip displacement," Elizabeth said. This was horizontal, or back-and-forth, movement along the fault. The direction of the slip had followed a left-lateral motion, meaning each side of the fault had moved left relative to the other.

Freight cars and tankers littered the tracks. Some were piled on top of each other, crushed and flattened. Another tanker blew up, an orange-white ball of fire shooting high into the sky.

Keeping their distance, Atkins and Elizabeth cautiously moved around the end of the train. They needed to get to the Explorer, which Atkins had left parked at the Mayfield High School about five hours earlier. It was only a few blocks away.

LAUREN MITCHELL AND BOBBY MET SHERIFF LOU
Hessel at an all-night convenience store just outside Gilbertsville. The resort town was three miles down the Tennessee
River from Kentucky Dam. Just below the dam, the Tennessee was more of a canal than a river. It broadened considerably at Gilbertsville, where it made a long, graceful curve
before heading downstream toward its juncture with the
Ohio River.

Hessel had known Lauren and her parents for years. In
his early fifties, he had thinning black hair, high cheekbones,
and gaunt cheeks. He didn't like wearing a uniform and was
dressed in a ski sweater, jeans, and boots. He and Lauren
had attended high school together. They'd even dated a few
times back then, nothing very serious, an occasional movie
in Paducah or a boat trip on Kentucky Lake. Hessel's wife,
Judy, was a good friend of Lauren's.

The sheriff listened quietly and sipped coffee from his
thermos as Lauren described what Atkins and Elizabeth had
seen inside the dam and her own close call out on the lake.
He'd driven over from Mayfield as soon as she'd called.
He'd never seen her like this, almost frantic.

"We've got to let people know the dam's in danger of
failing!" Lauren was practically shouting in his face. "They
won't have a chance . . ."

The sheriff glanced at his watch. It was about 2:15 A.M.

"You two get in the car," he said. "We'll start right here
in Gilbertsville. Then we're going to do some hard driving.

We'll head down to Reidland, then cut across the Highway 101 bridge into Paducah. We've got some ground to cover. I know every deputy, volunteer fire chief, and ambulance dispatcher in two hundred square miles. They'll help us get the word out. We gonna raise some hell.''

Bobby got in the back of the patrol car and Lauren had just opened the passenger-side door when she noticed the lights on the parking lot. The poles had started to sway.

"Look at that," Hessel said.

Then the ground exploded. Knocked off her feet, Lauren fell across the hood of the car. Another violent shake sent her staggering backward. She landed hard on her side.

The sheriff tried to get out to help, but the car was rocking up and down with such force he was pinned to his seat. The plate-glass window of the convenience store shattered. A young woman working there stumbled out the doorway, screaming and holding her hands to her ears, trying to blot out the thunder coming from deep in the earth. The parking lights were swaying so hard the poles snapped off at the base.

"There's . . . your . . . earthquake!" Hessel shouted, holding on to the steering wheel with both hands.

He was trying to sit upright in the bucking car, which started rocking side to side—hard, rapid movements that made him clench his teeth. He looked in the back seat. Bobby's eyes were wide open as he gripped the front seat and tried to hang on.

The shaking finally quieted. And the noise. Hessel wasn't sure how long it had lasted, but he felt like he'd taken a physical beating. His left shoulder was going to be black-and-blue from being slammed repeatedly into the car door.

"Listen!" Lauren said, picking herself up off the ground.

The sheriff heard it—a loud, rending crack, followed by a roar that was different from the earthquake.

Hessel realized what he was hearing.

It was rushing water, a flood.

"The dam's gone," he said. He started the car's engine. "Get in, girl! We're going to make a run through Gilberts-ville. Try to give those folks a warning."

Two miles upstream, the mile-long dam had given way. First the exterior walls had broken and split outward, the water rushing through the cracks, rapidly widening them. The steel flood gates were pushed aside as the water boomed through the jagged breach. The hydrologist on duty in the dam's powerhouse had sounded a warning siren moments before he fled for his life. The wail of the siren was drowned out by the rushing water.

Gunning his engine, Hessel raced into Gilbertsville. He didn't know how long it would take the water to reach the resort town, which was spread out on low hills near the western shore of the Tennessee River.

Not long, he figured. Maybe a couple minutes.

The river ran through a narrow, twisting valley until it emptied into the Ohio at Paducah, fifteen miles downstream. The highway was on high ground. The sheriff thought they might make it to Paducah ahead of the flood, but he'd have to drive like hell on a treacherous, two-lane road.

Siren blasting, they tore into Gilbertsville. Lauren operated the portable bullhorn. Hessel headed down a steep road into the heart of town, which had been shaken to pieces.

Lauren tried to keep her nerve up by concentrating on her job. She didn't want to think about her own home and the boat dock.

"The dam's out!" she said, her amplified words booming into the darkness. "Everybody get out! There's a flood!"

The horror of what she was seeing almost choked off her words. Many of the buildings had collapsed. Some still stood with entire walls sheared off. Roofs had caved in. Walls had buckled. The shaking had set off car alarms.

A few people staggered through the wreckage. Thrown from their beds, they looked dazed, in shock.

The sheriff swerved around downed power lines that hissed and threw white sparks, splintered trees, smashed houses. He headed back up the hill that led out of town, racing toward the highway. They'd done all they could.

Lauren looked back up the valley toward the lake. She saw the glint of something silver-white in the darkness. It was massive and moving fast.

"Here it comes!" she said, watching the flood wall roll into view.

The leading edge, a crest thirty feet high, was pushing smashed barges, pleasure boats, and a pile of twisted logs.

"I see it," the sheriff said, glancing in his rearview mirror. He realized this was a race they weren't going to win.

THE JARRING STRENGTH OF THE AFTERSHOCK stunned Atkins and Elizabeth. Incredibly powerful, it knocked them down in the road.

"That was at least a mag 7," Atkins said, pulling himself up off the ground. His clothing, caked with mud, had frozen solid in the cold air. The temperature had dipped below freezing.

"Aftershocks in that range are unbelievable," Elizabeth said.

"It's not like California, is it?" Atkins asked.

"It's not like anything since maybe Alaska," she said. The monster Good Friday earthquake that had struck Anchorage in March 1964 registered a magnitude 8.6. The epicenter was under Prince William Sound, a hundred kilometers away. Parts of the shoreline had risen as much as ten meters. But even there the aftershocks didn't compare with these.

The earthquake had knocked over Mayfield's two main power transformers and toppled a string of electrical towers. Even in the dust and murky darkness, Atkins and Elizabeth could make out the dimensions of the disaster. On the Modified Mercalli Intensity Scale it would have scored the maximum value, a XII.

Developed in 1902 by the Italian seismologist G. Mercalli, the scale assigned intensity values based on observations of physical damage on a scale that ranged from I to XII.

Atkins knew the definition for Level XII by heart:

Damage total.
Waves seen on ground surface.
Lines of sight and level distorted.
Objects thrown into the air.

The grim description fit Mayfield perfectly. As in Gilbertsville, twenty miles east, people were already out in the
streets, wandering with flashlights amid the rubble, broken
glass, and smashed foundations that had once been their
homes. Many of the frame and brick houses looked like
they'd been blown up. The damage was extensive, the debris pulverized.

They'll have plenty of dead here, Atkins thought as Elizabeth and he made their way through the ruins of what had
once been an attractive town of 10,000 residents. They were
heading for the high school where he'd left the Explorer.
Located in the center of town, it was only a few blocks from
the railroad tracks, but it would take nearly an hour for them
to cover the distance.

Atkins shuddered when he considered the potential car-
nage in Memphis. Barely 120 miles due south, the southern
city was known for its fine old brick architecture. So was
St. Louis, 150 miles to the north. All those unreinforced
brick buildings were certain death traps.

The United States wasn't ready for anything like that, but
from what he'd seen in Mayfield, the time of innocence was
over. This quake was a killer.

Two-story homes had been knocked off their foundations.
Trees were down everywhere, snapped off at the base of
their trunks. Water gushed from ruptured fire hydrants, filling
the gutters and sewers to overflowing. Atkins knew that
wouldn't last long, only until the water left in the shattered
mains ran out. After that, the town would be without fresh
water for drinking—or fighting fires. And fire was almost a
certainty after a big earthquake, a fact often overlooked even
by survivors.

The worst damage was centered around the courthouse and
senior high school. The school buildings were destroyed. At
first glance, the courthouse looked as if it had miraculously
escaped damage. The huge gold-painted rotunda appeared to
be in one piece.

Then Elizabeth saw what had happened.

"It collapsed in on itself," she said.

The post–Civil War five-story building was now only three stories tall. The other two, crushed together, weren't even visible. Elizabeth had seen the same thing in Northridge, California, where an entire four-story apartment complex, more than five hundred units, had folded up. That one area was where most of the deaths had occurred.

The ground lurched again, a strong vertical movement. Atkins looked up at the darkened courthouse just in time to see it pancake to the ground in a cloud of dust and flying bricks. For a few moments, the onion-shaped rotunda balanced precariously on the rubble, then tilted to the side and shattered.

"We've got to get some instruments set up," Atkins said. "These aftershocks are really something."

Getting into the field was his immediate, overriding priority. Any seismic data they gathered about the location and strength of the aftershocks would be crucial in plotting what had happened underground. And more important, in figuring out what could still happen. Atkins had one seismograph left in the Ford Explorer he and Walt Jacobs had used. He wanted to get it hooked up and running.

Nearly one hour after the quake had struck, they found the Explorer parked in the lot behind the smashed high school. A large tree, it looked like an oak, had toppled next to it, covering the hood with its branches, but not causing any serious damage. Elizabeth's rental car wasn't as fortunate. A forty-foot television aerial had collapsed, slicing it in two.

WITHIN FORTY MINUTES OF THE QUAKE, THE NAtional Guard helicopter dropped Walt Jacobs and the other seismologists at the University of Memphis. The big UH-60 Black Hawk barely touched down before it peeled off after getting an urgent medical evacuation request from a nearby hospital that had sustained severe damage.

Staggered by the widespread destruction he'd seen—it was all around him—Jacobs wasn't himself when he finally made radio contact with Atkins and Elizabeth. He'd been criticized for equipping each team that had gone to southern Kentucky with a shortwave radio.

He'd insisted on it and taken the heat for the modest extra expense. Now he was vindicated. The quake had destroyed the telephone and cell phone systems, knocking over relay towers and snapping land lines. Communications had broken down throughout the Mississippi Valley.

Without the shortwave, Jacobs wouldn't have been able to talk to the two geologists closest to the quake's epicenter.

But this was no time for self-congratulation. It took him nearly an hour before he was finally able to raise Atkins on the radio. Noticing the red light blinking on its console, Elizabeth had switched it on as Atkins changed into dry clothing in the back of the Explorer.

Jacobs got right to the point.

"It was a magnitude 8.4," he said, his voice strained. "It hit at exactly 2:16 in the morning. The epicenter was five miles west of Blytheville, Arkansas. That puts it at the northwestern axis of the new fault that runs south beyond Memphis.''

Atkins slid into the front seat. He'd heard what Jacobs had said about the magnitude. He wasn't surprised.

"Do you think you two can get over to the epicenter?" Jacobs asked.

"If we can find a way across the river," Atkins said. "Any chance of getting a helicopter?"

"None," Jacobs said. Civilian and military helicopters—anything that could fly—were making emergency medical rescues. They were already overwhelmed.

It was absolutely essential they get instruments set up near the epicenter as soon as possible. Strong motion seismographs would help pinpoint the locations of the aftershocks and determine the depth of the focal point. By recording the distribution and pattern of the aftershocks, they could estimate the potential for more damage.

"In case you can't, we've got some more options," Jacobs said. "They've got some strong motion seismographs at Arkansas State University over at Jonesboro. I'm sure they'll be setting them up as soon as they can get into the field. I know two of the seismologists over there. They're only forty miles from the epicenter, and they're good people, so don't try anything stupid trying to get there, John. We'll be all right.''

The transmission started to break up with static. The radio went silent for a few moments. When Jacobs came back on the air, Elizabeth said, "What's happening in Memphis?''

There was another burst of ground static. When it cleared, Jacobs said, "Memphis as we knew it no longer exists." He made no attempt to conceal his emotion. "You have no idea what it's—''

The voice was suddenly lost in static. Elizabeth glanced at Atkins.

"As I look out my office window on Cottage Avenue, I can see fires to the east," Jacobs said. "I can hear sirens all over the city. Most of the university buildings have been heavily damaged." The library, dormitories, and student center had been shaken to pieces.

"Our own building is missing part of its northern wall," Jacobs said. He started to mention Kim So and lost it.

Slumping back in his chair, it took him a few moments before he could trust his voice over the air.

One of their best graduate students, Kim had been in the computer office early that morning, crunching data about the New Madrid Seismic Zone. A piece of the brick chimney had fallen through the roof, crushing her skull. They'd found her lying near her computer.

"Walt, how's your family?" Atkins asked. He remembered that Jacobs had told him his wife and daughter lived in the city.

"I don't know," Jacobs answered. His throat was so dry he could hardly speak. "I haven't been able to get through to them. It's a brick house, John. A goddamned brick house, and I'm a seismologist. I'm supposed to know better!"

Then, for a few minutes, they lost contact with Memphis.

"Where did he say the epicenter was?" Atkins asked. He had a topo map spread across his lap and a dome light on.

"Just west of Blytheville." Elizabeth had already checked the map. The epicenter was about fifty miles south of New Madrid, the focal point of the first of the massive quakes in 1811–1812.

Atkins looked for the closest bridge across the Mississippi. There was one at a small town in extreme southern Missouri. Caruthersville. Crossing to the Tennessee side of the river near Dyersburg, it was about forty miles southwest of Mayfield and ninety miles north of Memphis.

Atkins wondered if the bridge was still standing.

BOBBY MITCHELL STARED OUT THE PATROL CAR'S
rear window. They'd just rounded a curve, hugging the west
shoreline of the Tennessee River, which flowed through a
deep valley cut. Bobby was watching for the first sight of
the flood wall.

"What do you see, boy?" the sheriff shouted, his eyes
locked on the blacktop. He was driving dangerously fast.
From the highway, it was a one-hundred-foot drop through
trees straight to the river. They were racing toward Raitland,
Kentucky, the next town in the path of the flood surge. Paducah was only fifteen miles away.

"I can't see anything," Bobby shouted.

"You sure can hear it," the sheriff said. He had his window down. The approaching flood was a steady roar in the
distance.

Lauren was trying not to think about what had happened
at Gilbertsville. She wanted to block it forever out of her
mind. There was no way the town, or anyone in it, could
have survived that massive wall of water.

At Hessel's urging, she tried to raise the police dispatcher
in Raitland. The radio scanner mounted on the dashboard of
the car hissed static. Lauren pressed the search button. A
woman's voice came on the air.

"That'll be Georgetta Williams," Hessel said. "Tell her
to put her husband Bob on. Let me talk to him."

Lauren did so. There was a long burst of static. "Bob's

dead,'' the woman said in a dull monotone. "He's lying out in the street. A power line fell on him."

"There's a flood coming your way, Georgetta," Hessel said, grabbing the microphone. "The dam broke at Kentucky Lake. You've got to get out of there."

The woman's shrill laughter stunned Lauren. Coming over the static of the police radio, it sounded disembodied, ripped from her soul.

"Sure," she said, still laughing hysterically. "I'll go get my husband, and we'll get the car and leave."

The radio clicked off.

Hessel punched the gas pedal. The patrol car's high beams were boring into the darkness. He was racing straight down the yellow lane divider. He could tell the softer aftershocks by the way the car vibrated. He felt the shaking in the steering wheel.

They hit Raitland a few minutes later, turning off the highway and heading down a long, steep street, their siren going full blast. Most of the town was laid out on a crescent-shaped plateau just above the river.

Lauren leaned out the window with the bullhorn.

"Evacuate now! The dam's gone at Kentucky Lake!"

She kept repeating the warning as the sheriff maneuvered through the wreckage. The damage was extensive. Just like Gilbertsville, Raitland was a wasteland of broken glass, shattered brick walls, and collapsed buildings.

Lauren realized it was useless. Those who even heard her warning were too disoriented or stunned to respond. And there wasn't time. The flood would hit them within minutes. The town was going to be swept away.

An elderly woman ran into the street right in front of them, waving her arms. Hessel braked hard, barely missing her.

"Lou!" the woman screamed. "It's Dave. You've got to help me."

The sheriff climbed out of the car. "Is that you, Mary Beth?" It was the wife of his cousin, Dave.

Seeing her more closely, Elizabeth realized the woman wasn't elderly at all. Early thirties. She looked older because her face and hair were powdered white from plaster dust. A red gash crossed her left cheek.

"You're bleeding pretty bad, Mary Beth."

The woman touched her cheek and stared almost absent-mindedly at the blood on her fingers.

"Where's Dave?" the sheriff asked.

"The ceiling fell on him. Please, Lou. He's hurt bad."

The house was across the street. The front porch and part of the roof had collapsed.

Hessel said softly, "All right, Mary Beth. I'm coming." He turned to Lauren. "I'm going to stay here," he said. "See what I can do to help. You get on up to Paducah and tell them what's heading their way. Then you and the boy get the hell away from there."

Hessel hurried over to his cousin's smashed home. The woman had already disappeared through the front door. Wanting to help, Lauren followed the sheriff. She told Bobby to stay in the car.

The two-story frame house had shifted on its foundation. Hessel went inside. His cousin lay in the living room, pinned on his stomach with a joist beam across his spine. He was bleeding from both ears.

"I think my back's broken," he said between gritted teeth.

Seeing Lauren behind him, Hessel grabbed her by the shoulders, hard. "Dammit, Lauren. I'm staying with my people. You get out of here. Now!"

Lauren kissed Hessel on the cheek then ran back to the patrol car. Sliding behind the steering wheel, she made a tight U-turn and raced back toward the highway. The ground started shaking again as the car nosed up onto the two-lane.

"Grandma, there it is!" Bobby shouted from the back seat.

Lauren didn't look behind. She didn't have to. She knew the flood water was crashing toward them down the valley. She could hear it.

DICK MARSDEN POURED A CUP OF HOT COFFEE from his thermos and settled back comfortably in his captain's chair. Only two cars were loaded onto the ferry that every other hour crossed from the Tennessee shore to the Missouri side of the Mississippi, then back again. It was the last run of the night. The gangplank had been pulled in and the metal gate secured across the ferry's open bow.

They'd shove off in two or three minutes. Running ahead of schedule, Marsden had time for a quick cup of coffee.

The view from the pilothouse was impressive, even in the dark. The Mississippi was nearly two miles wide, nothing at all like it was at St. Louis. Marsden had worked on fleeting barges there for nearly twenty years. The river at St. Louis—narrow and fast flowing—was like a muddy canal.

Down here near the Missouri boot heel, it was a different story. Three miles upstream, a new four-lane suspension bridge crossed the river. Marsden could just make out the red aircraft warning lights on the top of the span's superstructure. The bridge handled all the interstate traffic crossing from Dyersburg, Tennessee, to Caruthersville, Missouri, where motorists could pick up Interstate 55. To the south, it was 90 miles to Memphis. To the north, St. Louis was 160 miles away.

The ferry mainly served locals who worked in Tennessee and used it to shave commuting time from their homes in Missouri.

Marsden had just set his coffee mug on the instrument

console when the first shock wave hit, throwing him out of his chair so hard his forehead struck the steering wheel. The blow stunned him. The ferry had risen sharply in the water, pulling at its moorings as if a giant hand were trying to pick it up. Then it fell, the hull slamming down again.

Trying to stand on unsteady feet, Marsden gripped his seat so he wouldn't be knocked over again. He watched in disbelief as waves appeared suddenly on the river, six-foot swells rolling from shore to shore. Grabbing a pair of binoculars, he looked upstream toward the bridge. He saw the glint of headlights midway across the deck. Probably a long-distance trucker.

Then, unbelievably, the bridge's long center span snapped in two. Marsden saw the truck, its long trailer outlined in yellow lights, plunge into the river. The deck and part of the superstructure fell right on top of it, throwing up a wall of spray.

The shaking hadn't let up. Every time Marsden tried to stagger out of the pilothouse, he was knocked against the bulkhead.

The cars parked down on the deck were bouncing around like toys, sliding back and forth as the ferry pitched and rolled.

Only minutes earlier, a big three-decker towboat lit up like a Christmas tree and pushing a long string of coal barges had glided by, heading downstream toward Memphis. Marsden watched as the same towboat went by him again, this time heading upriver. It took a moment for his dazed mind to comprehend what he was seeing.

The current was pushing the barges and tow backward.

Across the river, on the Missouri side, large sections of the bank were falling into the water. So much of the shoreline was caving in over there that it looked like a landslide.

His deckhand staggered through the doorway. His face was pale. "The river's full of whirlpools," he said.

Marsden barely heard him. He had his binoculars on the towboat and barges rapidly heading upstream toward the sunken bridge. Then, as he watched, the tow disappeared.

There was no other way to describe what happened. The tow went first, dropping out of sight. Then the string of barges, the last one lifting up, red running lights still ablaze as it nosed up and vanished from view.

When the shaking finally stopped, Marsden went out on the narrow bridge next to the pilothouse. The river was still wild. The deckhand was right about the whirlpools. A big one had opened up, swirling like a huge inverted funnel just downstream from the ferry. Marsden focused his binoculars on where the barges and towboat had disappeared. It was over two miles upstream out toward the middle of the river.

Marsden saw a line of boiling white water and realized what he was looking at. It was the foaming edge of a sharp drop-off.

There was a waterfall out there.

WEARING A WHITE LABORATORY SUIT AND CLOTH boots designed to prevent potentially lethal sparks, Fred Booker mentally ran through the final checklist before climbing into the firing bunker. He was in the Shock Wave Laboratory in one of the cavernous brick buildings at the Oak Ridge National Laboratory's top-secret Y-12 plant. Booker was getting ready to fire the cannon, which was technically called a two-stage, light-gas gun.

Protected by twenty-foot-high fences topped with razor wire and guard towers manned by marksmen with automatic weapons, the Y-12 plant was one of the most secure research centers in the United States. Formerly built to produce uranium for the Manhattan Project in the early 1940s, it had evolved into a cutting-edge engineering laboratory equally capable of redesigning on an emergency basis the propellers for a nuclear attack submarine, building a better beer bottle, or making major breakthroughs in robotics. The facility spanned two and a half miles and contained some 250 buildings.

Booker, a young-looking sixty-seven-year-old physicist, had worked for the laboratory since the late 1970s. Oak Ridge was in the foothills of the Smoky Mountains in eastern Tennessee, twenty miles south of Knoxville. He'd fallen in love with the country. It was where he'd started a new career. Where his wife, Mary, had divorced him. He didn't blame her. She'd never been able to count on him. He was always in the laboratory working, while she had to raise their two ruggedly independent daughters. Mary lived in Knoxville, and they'd remained friends.

A tall, slightly stooped man with close-cropped gray hair and intense gray eyes, Booker kept fit by taking rambling hikes in the mountains. He also liked to paddle his battered Old Town canoe on the nearby Clinch River.

His colleagues considered him a workaholic, irascible, but brilliant.

Soon after getting his Ph.D. from the University of Chicago, Booker had joined the Lawrence Livermore Laboratory in southern California. He'd spent nearly a dozen years helping Livermore design nuclear bombs and had become a recognized master of the arcane art of ''boosting'' weapons—making them more powerful by layering thermonuclear fuels in the bomb's ''physics package,'' greatly enhancing the weapon's destructive impact.

When Booker ended his career at Livermore, he was in charge of the laboratory's underground nuclear tests in the famous ''Area 51'' at the Nevada Test Site. He'd spent entire months on bomb ''shots,'' living in dusty trailers, traveling into Vegas on the weekends. None of it had helped his marriage, which had begun to unravel during his stint at the NTS.

Needing a change, he joined the nuclear engineering staff at ORNL.

Semiretired, he stayed on at Oak Ridge as a consultant and was helping with test shots in the Shock Wave Lab. The firing was done in a remote corner of one of the mammoth buildings once used to separate uranium-235 from natural uranium. Since the end of the war, these Alpha and Beta buildings had served other purposes. The Shock Wave Lab was in the old Alpha building. Painted a dull red like so many of the other buildings at Y-12, it was made of concrete reinforced with steel rods. Its dimensions were prodigious, 543 feet by 312 feet. The labyrinth of piping and equipment the uranium-enrichment process required accounted for these oversize buildings, many of which still lined First Street at the ORNL complex.

Booker had helped design a refitted naval cannon that had been lengthened and retooled to fire a pellet-sized piece of iron at twenty thousand miles an hour into a target—a vacuum impact tank. The 140-foot-long gun resembled a rifle barrel outfitted with a huge silencer. The barrel rested on a series of metal supports. The lab actually used two cannons, depending on the purpose of the shot. One fired at a slightly higher speed. They were lowered into place by an overhead crane. In nanoseconds the guns generated colossal temperatures that matched those at the center of the earth, thereby offering a glimpse of what pressures were like at the iron core of the planet, where the temperature was over twelve thousand degrees Fahrenheit.

A key ingredient in these firings was the explosive propellant. Booker had shaped the special compound himself, a mixture of nitroglycerine and nitrocellulose, which was also used to detonate nuclear weapons. The explosive charge drove a sixty-pound piston that squeezed hydrogen gas down the barrel.

The shots were done in the early morning when the building was deserted. The sound of the projectile moving at thousands of miles an hour and hitting the impact tank wasn't much—the metallic clink of a coin pitched into a coffee can. But the shock wave that followed was a hummer. On previous firings, windows had been blown out of adjoining buildings. Doors had flown open, and floors had shaken.

The firing was done from a bunker of reinforced concrete located near the impact chamber. The bunker was a gray blockhouse about six feet high and eight feet long. Outfitted with an array of equipment, it had steel doors and a window slit covered with shatterproof glass.

"How's the VISAR checking out?" Booker asked one of the two geophysicists he was working with, a young Ph.D. named Ed Graves. VISAR was the acronym for Velocity Interferometer System for Any Reflector. It was used to measure shock waves.

"All go."

"What about the pyrometer?" The device measured high temperatures.

"Up and running," said the other geophysicist, Len Miller. With the ORNL for twenty-five years, he was their leading "deep earth" specialist.

"What about the camera?" They used a rotating mirror

streak camera with a xenon light source to measure shock velocity.

"Ready," said Miller.

"Let's do a shoot," Booker said. He sat at the computer terminal that monitored the firing systems and various recording devices. He rapidly went down the checklist one more time. Miller sat next to him and would do the actual firing. He removed the cover from a red toggle switch.

"Here we go," Booker said. He started the countdown from ten.

He'd reached six when a powerful ground tremor almost threw him out of his chair.

"Dammit, Len. It wasn't time."

He thought that Miller had accidentally fired the cannon. Then the floor shook again, even harder. Booker pressed a button that disarmed the gun.

"Boys, we've got ourselves an earthquake," he said.

The first two shocks had been very strong, but the next one was even more violent, knocking all three men out of their seats.

"We've never had a quake in this part of the state," said Graves.

"We're sure . . . as hell . . . having one now," said Miller, gritting his teeth as he spoke. "I'd put this . . . way up on the Richter."

Booker was used to earthquakes. A few mild shakes out in the Nevada desert, just enough to rattle the windows. Nothing like this.

"I don't know how much longer the building can take all this shaking," said Miller. He was astounded by the length and intensity of the tremors.

"These walls are two feet thick and reinforced with steel," Booker said. The Alpha building was a virtual fortress, designed under top secrecy to house an electromagnetic process for enriching uranium for the A-bomb. It had been built in segments, like a honeycomb with each segment consisting of four walls and a separate roof. The segments or "rooms" fit together like the interlocking pieces of a puzzle to form the building. The Shock Wave Lab was in one of these 100-by-200-foot rooms.

A chunk of concrete as big as a piano hit the bunker and shattered. It was part of the roof.

The ground was still shaking—a strong lateral motion.

More concrete rained down on them. Then, after several long minutes, the ground quieted. Booker carefully opened the bunker door just wide enough to glance up at the roof. He could see black sky through the gaping holes.

"Let's get out, now," said Miller.

"We can't," Booker said. Large pieces of the roof blocked the only doorway out of the building. They were trapped. And the ground was starting to shake again. One jarring tremor, followed quickly by another.

"The first aftershocks," Miller said. "This is one mother of an earthquake."

Scrambling out of the bunker, Booker put his back to the bulky steel impact tank located within a foot of the cannon barrel. He strained to move it.

"Give me a hand," he said, gasping.

"What are you doing, Fred?" asked Graves. He started pushing the heavy tank, putting his back to it until they'd moved it off to the side, away from the barrel. The cannon now pointed directly at the wall.

"We're going to try to shoot our way out of this damn place before the building collapses," Booker said.

The three men hurried back into the firing bunker and strapped themselves into their seats.

"You ever done anything like this before?" asked Graves. His face was ashen.

"Can't say I have," Booker said. He scanned the instrumentation panel, making a few minor adjustments. The compressed gas levels were fine. They could fire the propellant.

"You ready, Len?"

"You want to run the countdown?"

"Just do it!" Booker shouted.

Miller threw the toggle switch. The cannon fired with that strangely muffled sound, but the concussive impact of the projectile blasting into the wall was crushing. The entire building shook. The shock wave lifted Booker a few inches out of his seat.

He opened the bunker's steel door and cautiously peered

out. The cannon had blasted a four-foot hole through the concrete wall.

"Let's go for it!" Booker shouted. He followed the other two men through the hole, bending at the waist to squeeze through. It was pitch-dark outside. The lights that made the Y-12 compound glow like a city were off. The tremors continued in rapid succession. It was hard to walk.

They hurried away from the damaged building. It was cold and they didn't have overcoats. Sirens wailed all around them. Three fire engines hurtled down the street.

Booker knew where they were headed. The containment park.

The mercury once used for lithium enrichment was stored there. Lithium, the lightest metal, had two naturally occurring isotopes, lithium-6 and lithium-7. Lithium-6 was used to make tritium, the gas that did such a nice job boosting the explosive power of nuclear weapons.

The Y-12 plant had required huge amounts of mercury—in the peak years between 1951 and 1963, over a third of the available world supply. Most of what remained was kept in jug-shaped steel flasks stored in concrete vaults in the containment park. Other volatile chemicals were also kept there in large quantity, methylene chloride and fluorine among them.

If any of that storage caught fire . . .

Booker couldn't even try to comprehend what that would mean.

ATKINS HELD THE SPEED AT SEVENTY. IF HE WENT any faster, the Explorer had a tendency to slip out on the curves. The toll road that ran south from Mayfield to the Tennessee border was empty of traffic and in good shape.

Elizabeth had the map open on her lap. They'd head south another thirty miles into Tennessee and pick up Route 412, which would take them to the bridge at Caruthersville.

Atkins had the radio on. There was heavy static. Most of the local stations had been knocked off the air. Occasionally, they were able to pick up big stations in Philadelphia and Chicago, which were broadcasting one appalling bulletin after another. Heavy damage on an unprecedented scale was reported throughout the Mississippi Valley.

Riverfront Stadium had partly collapsed in Cincinnati. The city's Delhi Hills section had been hit hard. The Columbia Parkway was in shambles.

The Muddy Fork district in Louisville was on fire. The Interstate 64 and Interstate 65 bridges over the Ohio River were down.

In Lexington, Kentucky, the Civic Center and many of the buildings along Broadway Avenue were badly damaged. Fires were spreading across the downtown business district.

The worst news was from St. Louis. The city had taken a huge hit. A major hospital in the West End, Bernard-Parks, had collapsed. There was live radio coverage from a young woman who broke down on the air as she struggled to describe the devastation.

"Eight floors have collapsed, the entire west wing," the woman said. "The emergency room was crushed. It's just gone. At least forty people were in there, mainly mothers with sick children." The reporter was losing it. "I can hear people trapped in the rubble screaming. There's absolutely no one to help. No ambulances. No police. It's almost impossible to get anywhere in the city. So many buildings are down."

One horrifying bulletin followed another.

Little Rock's Cammack Village and the Allsopp Park District were burning. Buildings were down on both sides of the Arkansas River.

In Chicago, glass from shattered high-rise windows had rained down on Michigan Avenue. Some buildings had collapsed in the Loop. The Shedd Aquarium on Lake Shore Drive was damaged.

Atkins turned off the radio. He was supposed to be a professional. He knew what to expect—or thought he did. This was far worse than anything he'd ever dreamed possible.

"With damage as far north as Chicago, we've got more than one fault in play here," he said. "This thing has spread a lot farther than the New Madrid Seismic Zone. It's triggering other faults."

"There's plenty of precedent," Elizabeth said. "Remember Landers–Big Bear?"

The 1992 quake in Landers, California—and its unusual consequences—had come as a complete surprise to seismologists. At magnitude 7.5, it was the biggest quake in the state in four decades. A series of faults in the remote Mojave Desert suddenly came to life, causing strong shaking over much of southern California. The main event in Landers was followed three hours later by a second big quake, a magnitude 6.5 near the town of Big Bear thirty miles away and located on another fault.

"I was with a team that examined the sequence," Elizabeth said. "There was no question that the Landers quake touched off Big Bear. There was a whole string of surface ruptures. The slippage just kept moving from fault segment to fault segment. If that had been central Los Angeles instead of the sparsely populated Mojave, it would have been catastrophic.''

But nothing like this, Atkins thought. Los Angeles and southern California had never seen anything like this. And likely never would.

''If this one is triggering other faults, we've got a big problem,'' he said. It was his personal nightmare, one shared by most seismologists. That a big quake could set off others like a seismic blasting cap.

Hundreds of buried faults were scattered throughout the Mississippi Valley and the Midwest. Only a few were still considered active, including the New Madrid Seismic Zone, which wasn't even the largest. Any of them could suddenly ''switch on.'' And no one knew how many faults remained undiscovered.

That was seismology's dirty little secret. A big one could strike virtually anywhere, anytime in the heartland, near any large city. Any fault could suddenly come to life.

If that happened, there was no telling where it might stop. Potential disaster lurked everywhere. A series of faults ran all the way from the Mississippi Valley up the Eastern seaboard. Few people realized that, or understood how vulnerable large sections of the country were to earthquakes.

''We're going to need some good GPS data,'' Elizabeth said. The Global Positioning System was the fastest way to see how much the earth had moved up or down—how much the crust had deformed. Measurements obtained by GPS satellites could show how far the seismic energy had spread or, more important, if it was still spreading.

The degree of deformation would also indicate how much seismic energy remained in the ground, a major clue in determining whether another big quake was likely.

Atkins also wanted to get some SAR data off the satellites. Synthetic Aperture Radar interferometry was a satellite technique that produced highly detailed, high-resolution radar maps of the earth's surface. Not as precise as GPS data, SAR had the advantage of mapping a much larger geographic area, producing images that covered a sixty-mile-wide sector on each pass. It was the quickest way of determining how much the earth had deformed over broad areas.

Getting good seismic data in the next few days would be

crucial. That's why Atkins wanted to do everything possible to get his portable seismograph set up near Blytheville. Their best bet remained those geologists at Arkansas State University. Jacobs had mentioned them during their brief radio transmission. They were closer to the epicenter than anyone. Atkins hoped they'd gotten some instruments set up. It would be a big load off his mind to know they were up and running. They needed to be operational over there as soon as possible.

He was driving on Tennessee Route 51. They'd skirted Dyersburg, passing within six miles of the largest town in extreme northwestern Tennessee. The sky in that direction had a strange orange glow.

Atkins knew what it meant. So did Elizabeth.

Dyersburg was on fire.

They picked up Route 412. They were about ten miles from the Mississippi and the bridge. The rolling, wooded countryside was slowly flattening out, becoming delta bottomland the closer they got to the river.

Elizabeth lowered her window to get a blast of cold air to help her stay awake.

"Do you hear that?" she asked.

Numb with fatigue, Atkins was concentrating on keeping the Explorer on the twisting, two-lane road. He hadn't heard a thing.

He rolled down his window. The air had a strong sulfurous smell. He suddenly had to grip the wheel hard as the vehicle pulled sharply to the right. They almost swerved into a ditch.

Another aftershock.

"Listen!" Elizabeth said.

Slowing down, Atkins heard it. Loud cracks that sounded like cannon shots.

He realized what it was. Trees were snapping.

The ground shook harder. The odor of sulfur was stronger. There was a strange whistling sound, loud and piercing, almost like a steam kettle.

"The ground's liquefying!" Atkins shouted. "We've got to get out of here." As far as they could see in the darkness, the fields on both sides of the highway looked like they were boiling. Jets of black water shot up from holes that had opened in the ground, some with a distinctive cone shape.

Monster sand blows, the larger ones were fifty yards across

and were spouting off like geysers, blowing clouds of muck and hot vapor into the sky.

A gaping sand blow opened directly ahead of them, swallowing a section of the highway. Braking hard, Atkins tried to get around it. The Explorer's rear tires sunk into oozing mud and spun.

Atkins slipped into four-wheel drive and punched the gas pedal. The tires pulled free.

He floored it.

They risked getting stuck repeatedly in the heaving earth. The ground kept erupting. Heavy, carbonized fragments of long-buried trees blasted into the air. Some shot out like missiles. Chunks of hardened peat flew up, peppering the roof of the Explorer. A piece of wood the size of a suitcase cracked the windshield.

They had to keep going. Atkins barreled down the road. The Explorer bounced hard, slamming into a dip. The ground was shaking and bursting open. Muddy water kept shooting up from the sand blows. Trees continued to splinter.

Atkins didn't think they were going to make it. Then, suddenly, they were out of the worst of it. The road was firmer. Despite the open window and cold air, Atkins was sweating heavily.

A few miles later they came to a sign for Interstate 155 and the bridge. The approach was just up ahead. A sign showed the turnoff for a ferry. Two cars with flashing blue lights blocked the road. Tennessee state police.

"The bridge is out," one of the troopers said. His voice was subdued, strained. He stepped up to the mud-splattered Explorer and Atkins got a better look at his face. A young man, maybe mid-twenties. He looked scared. "The center span fell into the river."

Atkins saw where the main span had collapsed. It looked like a half-mile section was missing. Most of the superstructure had fallen into the river. Incredible. Severed suspension cables dangled from one of the support towers that remained standing.

The wind changed and Elizabeth heard something, a strange new sound.

"What's that?" she asked.

"That's a waterfall, lady," one of the troopers said.

LAUREN CLENCHED THE STEERING WHEEL WITH
both hands, the siren of Lou Hessel's patrol car blasting as
they approached the outskirts of Paducah. They had to cross
the Route 60 bridge over the Tennessee River. Lauren
dreaded the passage. The old, narrow two-lane bridge with
a dogleg halfway across was nearly a mile long. She'd never
liked driving on it, especially at night.

Bobby sat in the rear seat, trying to catch a glimpse of
the flood heading toward them. So far, they'd managed to
stay in front of it. Paducah was the end of the line.

Lauren thought the crest was a couple miles behind them
and coming fast. She was focused on a single thought. She
didn't want to be out on the bridge when the water hit it.

"Bobby, can you see anything?" she asked.

"Not yet," he said, rubbing his eyes. He blinked and
stared into the darkness, looking upstream for what he knew
was coming.

The bridge was just up ahead, the black superstructure
outlined against a smoky haze. As they roared up the elevated approach ramp, Lauren got her first good look at Paducah, a city of twenty thousand residents, the largest in
western Kentucky.

Fires had broken out in the central business district. But
the real inferno was raging on the Illinois shore, just below
where the Tennessee flowed into the Ohio. It was a solid
sheet of fire. An oil storage depot had gone up in flames.
The tanks were burning fiercely.

Lauren's mind raced. Her plan was to skirt the downtown district, cut over to Interstate 24, and take the Hinkeville Road exit, going west. Her parents lived ten miles out in Heath. All she wanted to do was find them and get away.

They were almost up on the bridge. The span was separated into three sections supported by concrete pilings driven deep into the riverbed. The car's high beams bored down the middle of the two-lane deck.

"I see it!" Bobby cried out.

Lauren glanced to the right, looking upriver.

It's huge, she thought.

The leading edge of the flood had swept around a bend in the Tennessee. It was going to hit the bridge broadside. The surging water had covered the last ten miles downstream a lot faster than she'd expected.

Lauren was doing fifty miles an hour when she reached the sharp bend where the deck made a jog to the right. She was going too fast and clipped a guardrail, smashing out a headlight before she got the car back under control.

She took another glancing look at the flood and froze. The wall of water was nearly as high as the deck of the bridge and no more than fifty yards away. It looked like it was going to wash right over them.

Lauren punched the gas pedal. They'd passed the half-way point.

There's no way we'll make it, she thought.

The roar of the water resonated in her ears.

The bridge shook sideways as the flood smashed into the concrete supports. Amazingly, it withstood the initial shock. Water poured across the roadway, causing the car's tires to lose traction. The rear fender banged against a railing.

Another heavy blow rocked the bridge's superstructure. This time the supports buckled.

"Roll the windows down!" Lauren screamed to her grandson. "If we go into the river, try to get out of the car."

Give me another twenty seconds, Lauren prayed. Please. Just twenty seconds.

There was another sharp vibration. Something heavy had slammed into one of the supports like a battering ram.

The roadway sagged and started to pull apart. A gap opened in front of them. Lauren hit the brakes, the tires spinning on the wet steel surface. She steered the car into the guardrail, hoping to slow it down. The heavy patrol car bounced off. She turned into the railing again, shearing away a fender. The car spun around a full 180 degrees and stopped.

"Get out!" Lauren yelled to her grandson, who scrambled out of the back seat. She opened the glove compartment and snatched the pistol Sheriff Hessel had told her about, slipping it into a coat pocket.

The car had stopped within yards of the gap that had opened in the roadway. The bridge had pulled apart at one of the places where the steel sections that comprised the roadway were bolted together. The opening was about five yards wide.

Lauren saw that they were no more than thirty yards from the end of the bridge. The only way to get there was a narrow catwalk that ran along the side of the superstructure. Used for maintenance, it extended over the river. They'd have to climb over the outer railing and step down to it.

"I can't do this!" Bobby cried.

"Sure you can," Lauren said. She climbed over the railing and, with her back to the water, lowered herself a few feet onto the slippery catwalk. She helped her grandson down. The catwalk was open to the water. A single handrail was bolted to the side of the superstructure.

Lauren looked up at the patrol car. The lights were still on. Then the bridge lurched and the car started sliding toward the gap in the roadway.

Gripping the railing with one hand and her grandson with the other, Lauren watched as the car fell through the opening and disappeared in the churning water below them.

"Keep going!" she told Bobby. "Don't look down!"

With their backs to the river and holding on to the wet handrail, they slowly sidestepped their way down the catwalk.

Something large hit one of the supports, which shuddered at the impact. Lauren saw what had caused it—part of an electric tower swept downstream by the flood. At least fifty feet long, it was dragging its tangled wires behind it.

The jolt of the collision almost knocked them into the river. One of Bobby's feet slipped off the catwalk, and he fell down on his knees. Lauren grabbed him by his belt and pulled him back up.

After they inched their way past the gap in the roadway, they climbed back up on the bridge and started running toward the end. Lauren felt the pilings move under them.

"Hurry, boy!" she shouted to her grandson.

They had another ten yards to go.

Another five.

They'd almost reached the end when the roadway started to pull away from the approach ramp.

"Jump!" Lauren screamed. Her lungs ready to burst, she put an arm around her grandson, who'd started to lag behind. She shoved him hard just as the deck gave way beneath them. Their momentum carried them forward. She landed on top of Bobby on the approach ramp, skinning her knee.

She lay next to him, gasping for breath, staring at the sky. She reached over and squeezed her grandson's hand. She'd come so close to losing him. A matter of inches. They'd been so lucky. She closed her eyes and started to cry, the tears stinging her cheeks in the cold air. She loved and needed Bobby so much. She'd lost her husband and survived. If she lost her grandson, she wouldn't want to go on living. She realized she and the boy were in the fight of their lives. As she lay there, still holding his hand, afraid to let go, she swore to herself that no matter what happened he was going to come out of this alive.

Bobby sat up.

"It's going!"

Lauren pulled herself to her feet just as the bridge broke into three sections and started to lean toward the water. The surging flood knocked it over. A single concrete support at the middle was all that remained standing. Part of the super-structure lay on its side, still visible. A mobile home washed downstream was impaled on one of the steel girders. So was the smashed wall of a frame home.

"Look over there!" Bobby said, pointing toward down-town Paducah and the Ohio River. Just below Owen's Island, where the river narrowed slightly before it swung by the city, the fire had spread from shore to shore.

More fires had broken out in the Lowertown district.

Lauren had little time to worry about Paducah. They

needed to get off the elevated approach ramp, which was supported by steel trusses. She wanted to be clear of it before the next aftershock hit.

She started down the sloping incline with her grandson when a car pulled onto the ramp and started in their direction.

"Stop!" Lauren screamed, waving her hands over her head. "The bridge is out! Go back."

The car kept coming. It had its high beams on and was headed straight toward them.

ATKINS PARKED THE EXPLORER ON A GRAVEL LAND-
ing that overlooked the Mississippi. It had been a little over
two and a half hours since the earthquake. The aftershocks
had been frequent, some of the jolts very strong. Most were
in the magnitude 6 range, Atkins figured. He and Elizabeth
got out of the vehicle and took their first look at the river.
It was a good two miles wide. And, incredibly, running
backward.

The spectacle was beyond anything in his experience. He
was reminded again of the immense power of a natural force
strong enough to breach one of the biggest rivers in the
world. Cut right across it!

Atkins guessed that the fault line had broken through the
surface somewhere downstream, creating a barrier or hanging
wall that was causing the river to back up. That very thing
had happened during the sequence in 1811–1812. The tremendous uplift of one of the monster quakes had blocked
the flow with several barriers that sent the river roaring
backward.

And somewhere out there, it may have also created a
waterfall.

They couldn't see it. Atkins remembered what Walt Jacobs
had told him about the history of the big quakes in
1811–1812: the fault's uplift had formed a roaring waterfall,
possibly two of them in mid-channel.

As he stared into the darkness upstream, Atkins' eyes
began to play tricks on him. The only thing he could make

out clearly were the steel girders of the fallen bridge. The twisted superstructure jutted out of the river.

Atkins didn't see a waterfall and began to wonder if the troopers were wrong.

"Can you hear it?" he asked Elizabeth.

She shook her head. The rushing water and wind merged into a shrill background noise.

While they were trying to figure out what to do next, another radio transmission arrived from Memphis. It was Jacobs. The hiss of static made it difficult to understand him. There was a lot of ground interference. Then the noise cleared up.

"Arkansas State isn't sending anyone to the epicenter," Jacobs said. "A lot of buildings are down there. They can't get to the equipment." There was another long burst of short-wave static.

Atkins sat in the Explorer, staring out at the river. He didn't know what to say. His mouth was suddenly dry.

"John, I don't know what to tell you to do." It was Jacobs again. The transmission was starting to break up. "Use your . . . judgment."

The radio kept crackling with static. Atkins reached behind him and turned down the volume.

"I've got to try to cross the river," Atkins said, looking at Elizabeth. "We've got to get a seismograph up and running." He pounded his fist against the dashboard. "Look at that water out there!"

"Maybe we can get the ferry to take us across," Elizabeth said.

"Forget the 'we,' " Atkins said. "You're not going."

Elizabeth shook her head. "It's not up for discussion," she said sharply. "We're both going."

"Dammit, no way," Atkins said, pounding the dashboard again.

Elizabeth hit the dash just as hard. "Dammit, yourself!" she shouted. "Don't play mas macho with me, Doctor Atkins." Her eyes were flashing.

Atkins remembered the mistake he'd made with Sara. He'd blamed himself for years for letting her go with him into that heavily damaged building in Mexico City. He should have insisted she stay outside, forced her if necessary.

They'd taken a huge risk together, and lost. He didn't want it to happen again, but he understood he was powerless to stop Elizabeth from coming with him.

Atkins sat there a few moments, trying to collect himself. "All right," he said softly. "I wish to God I could make you change your mind, but all right."

He backed away from the overlook and headed up the narrow road toward the ferry landing. He drove the two miles in silence, glancing out at the river, trying to see it in the darkness. Even with the windows up, he could hear the rushing water.

When they got to the ferry, it was riding up and down on her mooring cables. A two-decker. Not a big boat and square-sterned, it looked like a floating white box. There was room on the bottom deck for about ten cars.

"What do you think?" Elizabeth asked.

"I'm thinking I don't want to do this," Atkins said. He didn't want to cross that river, but had no choice. Getting that seismograph up and running was about the most important thing anyone could do right now. They needed to know what was going on along the fault, how much energy it was releasing, what the aftershocks were doing. He had to try to get over there.

Getting out of the Explorer, he followed Elizabeth aboard the ferry. Hanging onto the chain-link railing for dear life, they climbed a narrow flight of metal steps to the pilothouse. He noticed a dark, massive shape looming out in the water maybe fifty yards downstream. As his eyes focused better in the dim light, he realized it was an island. A big one hugging the Tennessee shoreline. The ferry landing sat near the upstream end of the island.

They were startled by the distant sound of something crashing into the water.

"What was that?" Elizabeth asked.

A voice in the darkness said, "Nothing much. Just part of the Missouri shore falling into the river. It's been like that for the last couple hours."

It was Dick Marsden. He was standing in shadows next to the wheel, holding a pair of binoculars.

Atkins explained who they were and why they wanted to cross the river. He told the captain they needed to set up their strong-motion seismograph as close as possible to the earthquake's epicenter. The device was designed to operate near the source of an earthquake without being knocked off scale by the shock waves. Atkins tried to explain as carefully as he could why they needed to get across the Mississippi. What was at stake.

Marsden laughed. His eyes were bloodshot. His skin mottled. Rotund and badly overweight, he wore a dirty blue jacket and watch cap. Atkins guessed he was about sixty years old.

"I've been living on this river nearly my whole life, and I don't recognize it," Marsden said. "It's calmed down some in the last few minutes. The waves have dropped off. But you go out there now, it's even money it'll drown you."

"We've heard about a waterfall," Elizabeth said.

"As best I can tell, it's a couple miles upstream, about mid-channel," Marsden said. "When the wind's right, you can hear it real good. Sounds like Niagara Falls out there."

He handed her the binoculars.

Adjusting the eyepiece, Elizabeth focused on a faint, curling line of white water far out in the channel. Even with the binoculars, it was too far away to make out clearly. It reminded her of rapids and was apparently the edge of the waterfall.

"How deep is the drop-off?" she asked.

"I can't tell," Marsden said. "You can't get a good look at it from this side."

"Captain, will you take us across?" Atkins asked again. "We need to find out what's going on in the ground. You're the only one who can help us."

"What if I lose this boat?"

Atkins didn't even try to answer. He was asking a stranger to risk everything.

"Is that an island just downstream?" Elizabeth asked.

"That's Chandler's Point," Marsden said. "It's mainly a wide sandbar with a lot of timber."

"How long is it?"

"Maybe a mile and a half, two miles," Marsden said.

"What's the river like down at the far end of the island?" Elizabeth asked.

"It narrows a little. The current really booms along down

through there. No telling what it's doing now. Lady, what are you getting at?''

"Could we head up between the island and the shoreline, then cut across the river when we get to the end?'' Elizabeth asked. "That would put us nearly four miles upstream from the falls and we'd be trying to cross at a place where it's narrower.''

Marsden rubbed his hand across his stubbled chin, thinking it over, trying to figure out what to do. He squinted out at the river through the broad windshield of the pilothouse, then clasped his binoculars to his eyes. "It might work,'' he said. "There's enough water running up the chute between the island and the shore, and it doesn't look like the current's too bad. But when we get to the end and make the cut into the main channel, the old man's gonna hit us a ton.'' He kept staring through the binoculars at the black water. "This ferry belongs to the state of Tennessee,'' he went on. "I probably need to talk to some damn lawyer first.''

He took another long look. Finally, he said, "Jimmy, get ready to cast off.'' The first mate was standing in the open hatchway. "We're going to make a crossing. At least we're gonna give it a try.''

Atkins took Marsden's hand and shook it. Then he and Elizabeth hurried back to the Explorer.

"That was very good,'' Atkins said. "I'm glad you listened to me and stayed behind.''

"I'll probably regret it when we're out there.''

It took a few minutes to drive across the pitching gangplank and tie the Explorer down. The mate chocked the tires securely, front and rear, with blocks of wood. The other vehicles had already been driven off. Their owners didn't want any part of trying to cross the Mississippi.

"Let's do it,'' Marsden said, talking into a loudspeaker.

Atkins and Elizabeth made sure everything in the back of the Explorer was securely lashed down, especially the seismograph and shortwave radio. Then they joined Marsden in the pilothouse. He had both diesel engines revving at full rpms and wanted as much power as possible when they slipped out into the current.

"Cast off,'' he said into the loudspeaker.

His deckhand untied the bow and stern lines. Marsden

pulled away at full throttle from the shore and got the ferry headed up in the chute between the sandbar island and the Tennessee shoreline. The current was stronger than he'd expected, and the water was running deeper. The trees were thick on the island. It was impossible to see through them to the main channel on the other side.

"Current's running maybe five knots through here," Marsden said. "I've never seen it that strong. *Agnes* isn't going to like it once we get around that island." He glanced at Elizabeth, who was standing next to him. "I call this rust bucket '*Agnes*.' It's my wife's name. It can get lonely out here at night, and I like to have somebody to talk to. The beauty of it is *Agnes* can't talk back."

Fifteen minutes later they were nearing the downstream end of the island. "We're coming up on it now," he said.

They came out of the chute, and Atkins sucked in a breath when he saw the Mississippi spread out in front of them. A broad expanse of dark, fast-moving water.

Marsden gripped the pilot's wheel with both hands. He was leaning over it, staring out the window at the river. "Oh maaaan!" he said. "This is some current. I don't know if I can hold her. *Agnes*, baby. We're gonna need every bit of power you've got in you."

As they came around the point of the island and entered the main channel, they hit the current that was pushing back upstream. The force was substantial. The ferry was swept nearly half a mile upstream before the propellers seemed to bite the water. Fighting the wheel, Marsden got the boat straightened out and angled into the current.

He had both engines running full open and was barely making headway.

"Damn, take a look downstream," he said. "Here's trouble."

Riding low in the water, three dark shapes emerged from the gloom. Barges. They'd come around a bend in the river and were bearing down on the ferry. One of them was on fire.

"Oil barges," Marsden said. "There's a fleeting area a couple miles downstream on the Missouri side. One of the big fuel tanks probably blew up and set them on fire. I thought I heard an explosion a while back. They must have broken their moorings and floated upriver.''

The barges were spread out far enough to make it difficult to maneuver around them. It would be like running an obstacle course.

''I'm gonna try to steer through them,'' he said.

''Do you have enough power?'' Atkins asked. He'd noticed how the engines were laboring. They sounded ready to burn up.

Marsden shrugged. ''Let's hope so, son.'' He made a slow, careful turn, trying not to lose control in the strong current.

''Come on, *Agnes*,'' he said softly. ''You can do this for me.''

The ferry was handling better. Working the wheel and throttles, Marsden skillfully maneuvered out of the way of the lead barge, which was burning from two hatches.

''We've got another problem here,'' Marsden said, playing the controls like a keyboard, hands flying. The other two barges were still heading toward them. They'd drifted apart. The closest one was bearing down on them on a collision course.

''That's getting pretty close,'' Atkins said, measuring the distance with his eye. The barge was about one hundred yards away and rapidly closing.

''I'm gonna need a little more power, *Agnes*. You got to put out for me, old girl.'' Marsden was wrestling the wheel. The engines were wide open. He cut a look at Atkins. ''I'm not sure I can get out of the way.''

THE CAR WAS CREEPING AT A SNAIL'S PACE UP THE
middle of the ramp. Lauren saw the driver hunched behind
the wheel. An old woman.

"Stop!" she screamed.

Running down to meet the car, she grabbed the door handle and managed to pull it open. The woman still gripped
the steering wheel. Running next to the car, Lauren pushed
in next to her and got a foot on the brake pedal. The car
finally stopped. Lauren jammed on the emergency brake.

"Didn't you see the bridge was out?" she said, angrily
turning toward the woman. She'd almost gotten both of
them killed.

The old woman sat there, not moving. She wore a winter
coat and had a green stocking cap pulled low over her eyes.

"Are you all right?" Lauren asked.

"I guess so," the woman said. "I don't see too well at
night anymore. Cataracts."

I guess not, Lauren thought. She noticed that the woman's
glasses were as thick as soda bottles.

"What were you trying to do?" Lauren asked, feeling her
anger drain away.

"Girl, don't you know we've had an earthquake?" the
woman said. "I was trying to get out of town and must have
got myself turned around." In the dim light, the woman
looked at least eighty years old. Her eyes were cloudy, and
she had gray skin like etched leather.

"My name's Milly Drew," the woman said. "I'd be

obliged if you'd drive me home. I should never have tried a stunt like this. I guess I just got scared.''

The ramp swayed in one of the repeated aftershocks.

''Bobby, get in Missus Drew's car,'' Lauren said, opening the back door. Her grandson scrambled in.

Lauren moved into the driver's seat. She backed down the approach ramp and got the car turned around. She recognized the model—a 1963 Chevrolet Impala. She'd learned to drive in one. But this looked brand-new. White exterior, red seats.

''The car belonged to my boy,'' the woman said. ''He died some years back, and I never got around to selling it. My husband's dead, too. He was a smoker.''

''Where do you live?'' Lauren asked.

''On Old Benton Road near Interstate 24,'' the woman said.

It was close, a couple miles.

Lauren hit the gas pedal and the car instantly shot forward. The acceleration almost took her breath away. Then she noticed the crossed-flags emblem on the steering wheel. It was a 327.

Mrs. Drew had a muscle car.

Lauren turned onto Route 62, heading away from downtown Paducah. Five minutes later she pulled into the driveway of the woman's home. It was a one-story white frame house that looked beautifully maintained. A front window was broken and the porch sagged, but the place didn't look badly damaged.

''I'll be all right,'' the old woman said. ''I've got plenty of food and a daughter who lives in town. I don't know how I can ever repay you for what you did.''

Lauren hesitated, then said what had been on her mind ever since she'd stopped the car on the bridge.

''There is something you can do, Milly. Let me borrow this car for a couple days.''

''Honey, you can have the damn thing,'' the woman said. Lauren promised to pay her. ''You're sure you'll be all right here alone?'' she asked.

''Don't worry about me,'' the woman said. ''I hope that old car gets you where you want to go.''

Bobby helped the woman climb up her front steps. They left her there, sitting in a swing chair on the porch wrapped in an overcoat and wearing her green cap. She waved to them as Lauren backed out of the driveway.

A few minutes later they were racing down Route 62, headed due west for Heath and her parents' home.

Paducah was burning behind them. Lauren could see the glow of the fires in the rearview mirror. The road was in bad shape, and there was more traffic, people trying to get out any way they could. Many of them were driving like maniacs. Several cars lay overturned on the side of the road.

"Someone's hurt back there," Bobby said as they passed another wrecked car.

Lauren had seen two bodies lying in the grass. She didn't slow down.

She was grateful for the big Chevrolet. It was fast enough to keep them out of trouble. The pavement was badly damaged, and some of the cracks were two and three feet wide. She had to slow down and pull around them.

They were almost to Heath when she ran into the first roadblock. Several cars were pulled to the side. Two cops with red flashlights flagged her down and told her to turn around. The road was closed. Something had gone wrong at the uranium plant, one of them said.

Lauren was vaguely familiar with the plant, which processed enriched uranium for weapons and nuclear reactors. It covered nearly forty acres.

Like most from the area, Lauren didn't know the specifics of what went on there and didn't wait for the cops to explain what was wrong. She gunned the Chevy and roared away, laying a long black streak of rubber on the pavement.

She ran into the next roadblock four miles later. It was on the outskirts of Heath. This time the men were heavily armed and had a barrier across the road. There were five or six of them, and they were dressed in strange-looking coveralls.

"What's that over their faces?" Bobby asked.

They were wearing gas masks.

THE FIRST STRONG TREMOR HAD JOLTED GOVERNOR
Tad Parker and his wife out of their bed in the third-floor
bedroom of the governor's mansion. A heavy mahogany
bookcase crashed to the floor, narrowly missing Parker's
head. He was vaguely aware of his wife's screams.

Parker tried to stand, but the shaking sent him sprawling.
He tried again and was upended so violently it knocked the
wind out of him.

Frankfort, the capital of Kentucky, was about 230 miles
northeast of Memphis and roughly midway between Louisville and Lexington. All three cities had felt the earthquake
that had struck Memphis three days earlier. There had been
a lot of property damage, mainly cracked foundations and
fallen chimneys, but no one had been killed.

But Parker knew this one was deadly.

He crawled to the door, got to his knees, and tried the
light switch. The electricity was out.

Parker cursed himself for drinking too much wine at dinner. He'd met with his campaign advisers and had allowed
himself to be overserved, something he rarely did. He usually
stuck with one small glass of burgundy. This time he'd had
four or five and had only recently gone to bed.

As the ground shook, glass shattered in the pair of French
doors that opened onto the bedroom balcony.

The chandelier in the dining room jingled like a wind
chime as it swung back and forth. Then it fell with a splintering crash of broken glass.

Large gilt-framed pictures were knocked from their mount-ings. A china cabinet pitched over, spilling nineteenth-century Wedgwood and French crystal onto the floor.

Crawling on all fours, Parker cut his hand on a fragment of glass.

"Tad, we've got to get out!" his wife screamed. She tried to hold on to the bed's headboard, but the heaving ground action sent the massive four-poster sliding across the floor, knocking her legs out from under her.

Parker was as frightened as he'd ever been in his life.

When the earth finally stopped moving, he sat with his back against a wall, too stunned to get up. He stayed there with his wife next to him for five minutes before he finally managed to get dressed in the dark, slipping on a pair of trousers and a pullover.

He got a flashlight from the bathroom. The mansion was a shambles. Wide cracks had opened in the walls.

The ground started shaking again.

Parker realized those must be aftershocks. They had to get outside.

With his wife following in her bathrobe, a coat thrown over her shoulders, Parker hurried down the grand staircase to the first floor. He went out the front door just as a car from the Kentucky State Police pulled into the driveway.

A young officer got out. He delivered the terrible news with crisp professionalism.

"The dam at Kentucky Lake is gone, sir."

Parker felt as if he'd been kicked in the teeth. He slumped against the open door.

That can't be true.

As he tried to comprehend the immensity of what he'd just been told, Parker struggled to follow what the trooper was saying. He'd already moved on to another subject—the Department of Energy's Gaseous Diffusion Plant at Paducah.

Parker knew it well. He'd lobbied hard to keep the plant in operation amid rumors that the DOE wanted to phase it out.

He squeezed his hands to his temples and tried to think clearly. It was so difficult, but he had to focus.

"The plant manager called, sir," the trooper continued. "He wants Paducah evacuated."

"What are you talking about?" Parker stammered.

"They have a leak of some kind. He said something about poison gas."

Parker had just toured the uranium-enrichment plant with a delegation of Japanese visitors. He knew how they shot uranium in the form of uranium hexofluoride gas through a series of ceramic and steel separators, which filtered out impurities. The pipes ran for miles it seemed and were forty inches in diameter.

He remembered what one of the plant engineers had told him: The biggest danger was the accidental release of gas. When mixed with oxygen, it was lethal. The separators were sealed under pressure. If they ruptured, they'd go off like Roman candles, spewing clouds of poison gas.

"Will you authorize it?" the trooper asked.

Authorize what? Dammit, man. Just let me think, Parker thought.

The trooper was staring at him, waiting for an answer.

"The evacuation," he said. "They want to do it right now."

The ground shook, just enough to make Parker clutch the mansion's porch railing. He sat down on the front steps. He was suddenly aware of how bright the stars were. The sky was filled with stars.

He'd never seen them so bright. Then he realized why: all the lights were out in Frankfort. The city was in total darkness.

MARSDEN GAVE THE FERRY AS MUCH POWER AS the engines offered. At such driving rpms, he worried about burning them up. The barge was a hundred yards off their port bow. Marsden tugged on the steering wheel. The ferry slowly responded, nosing away from the hulking shape that was riding low in the water and rapidly bearing down on them.

"We might just make this," Marsden said.

Picking up speed slowly, the ferry was making plodding headway against the current.

Atkins turned to take another look at the approaching barge and saw a sudden burst of flames. Almost simultaneously, there was a strong explosion. Slammed to the deck, Atkins struggled to his feet. The ferry, engines open wide, was making a rapid turn as the current shoved it upstream. Large pieces of the barge, hurled far into the water, burned with a white intensity.

Elizabeth was on her knees, bent over Marsden.

"He's unconscious," she said. "He must have hit his head on the radio console." Marsden had a deep gash just above his left eyebrow. Elizabeth pressed a handkerchief on the wound.

Atkins grabbed the steering wheel and tried to get the ferry back on course, headed downstream. It was no use. They'd swung around too far in the current and were facing upstream, toward the waterfall. The engines weren't powerful enough to get them turned around again.

In a matter of minutes they were swept past the island and the ferry landing they'd left thirty minutes earlier. They were being pushed quickly upriver.

In the dim, gray light, Atkins could just start to make out the rough outline and dimensions of the waterfall. What he saw left him speechless.

The rim or edge curved toward the Missouri side of the river and appeared to be five or six hundred yards long. The water below was boiling. He saw clouds of foam rising up over the falls.

Atkins realized in amazement that he was gazing at the scarp of a fault that had pushed up from the depths and breached the Mississippi. That thought riveted his attention as much as the sight of the waterfall. He could also hear it now, a pounding roar. He thought again of a thrust fault and what it did beneath the earth, how the hanging wall moved sharply upward while the footwall dipped. Thrust faults were common in mountain chains, but exceedingly rare in this part of the country.

Elizabeth had managed to stop Marsden's flow of blood. "I don't believe I'm really seeing this," she said, looking out the pilothouse window at the river. She was as moved as Atkins. The force of the cataclysm, seen up close, was beyond anything in her experience.

She pointed out how the height of the waterfall—they were still too far away to see it clearly—appeared to drop off sharply at both ends. On the side closest to the Missouri shore, the drop looked considerably lower. And the water below it was less turbulent.

Their only chance, Atkins thought, was to try to get close enough to the Missouri side so they could go over the falls at its lowest point. There was no way to avoid going over. But if they could maneuver to where the drop-off was minimal, they might be able to slide over without too much risk. At least such was his hastily formed plan.

Atkins told her what he was going to try.

"How far is it?" she asked.

"A mile. Maybe a little more. Here we go." He swung the wheel over and aimed for the shore. If he could keep the speed up and stay ahead of the current, he might be able to steer instead of being shoved along by the river.

Atkins kept heading toward a cluster of tall trees on the Missouri shore that he was using as a marker.

The sky was lighter. It was the hazy twilight before dawn. Atkins noticed how the quake had ripped long, gaping chunks out of the shoreline.

When they were four or five hundred yards from the falls, he got his first good look at it and almost froze up. It was the biggest thrust fault he'd ever seen, or ever read about. Far below the surface of the earth, there'd been a strong vertical displacement of the rock, driving one side of the fault upward, the hanging wall, while the other side, the footwall, dropped. The sharp upward movement had created the waterfall.

He thought it was forty feet high, maybe more.

"We're coming up on it," he shouted.

He kept the ferry angling toward the Missouri shore.

They were almost there. Another two hundred yards and they'd be right on top of it. Realizing they were going too fast, Atkins threw back the throttles and tried to straighten out the bow.

At the last moment, just as they were approaching the edge, he saw that the drop-off was at least ten feet. Better than forty, but still not a safe drop. They were going to take a hit.

"Here we go!" he yelled. "Hang on!"

The ferry nosed over and slammed down in the water in a tremendous burst of spray.

Afterward, he had only fragmented impressions: the stern up in the air, suspended. The jolting impact as the bow crashed down in the churning water. The way the ferry pitched dangerously on its side, almost capsizing. Mainly, Atkins remembered his shock when he looked down the length of that curving wall of water as it poured over the huge upthrust in the middle of the river.

But he had no time to do much more than glance at this spectacle—and at the wreckage of the towboat and barges that had gone over earlier and were capsized in the swirling water. He was fighting to control the steering wheel as the ferry rocked in the powerful eddies below the falls.

They made a complete circle, then another, the ferry pitching wildly, threatening to tip. Water crashed over the lower deck. Atkins worried they'd be sucked into the vortex of boiling water at the base of the waterfall. A great whirlpool had formed there at mid-river, where water pouring over the edge of the scarp collided with the downstream flow from the bridge. He threw the wheel hard to starboard and leaned on it until slowly, a few yards at a time it seemed, they were out of danger.

The Missouri shore was less than a hundred yards away. Atkins steered in that direction. Much of the shoreline around the ferry landing had collapsed. Only a few of the piers were still intact. There was no way to tie up there.

Elizabeth managed to rouse Marsden. "Where are we?" he asked, getting up groggily. "We're hardly moving." Then he saw the waterfall off to the right.

"We went over that?" he said, blinking his eyes.

"Can you get us into shore?" Atkins asked.

Marsden took the wheel and sized up the situation. A few minutes later he'd nosed the ferry into an overhanging section of riverbank that hadn't collapsed. The current, even in that close, was exceptionally strong and he had to keep the engines running at full power to hold the bow into the shore so his deckhand could jump off and tie up to some trees. It took a few minutes before he had the bow and stern secured.

"Thanks for the ride," Marsden said, smiling at Atkins. "Sorry I missed it."

He followed them on unsteady legs down to the deck. The Explorer had come through the pounding with a four-foot dent along the passenger side, but it was essentially in good shape. Atkins was relieved when the engine started. He'd been worried about water getting under the hood and short-circuiting the electrical wiring.

The view of the waterfall from the pier was breathtaking. The roar of the water pouring over the edge made it hard to talk without shouting.

"Can we give you a lift somewhere?" Atkins asked.

Marsden shook his head. "I better stick with *Agnes* here," he said, grinning. "I wouldn't want something to happen to her."

He disappeared for a few moments. When he returned, he carried a pump-action Remington shotgun, which he handed to Atkins. He also gave him several boxes of shells.

"No arguments," he said. "You take this with you. Someone might want to try to take that Explorer. A good four-wheel-drive vehicle is gold at a time like this. I wouldn't let it out of your sight."

Atkins started to refuse, but Marsden almost shoved the shotgun into his chest. "It's loaded. Just flick the safety off, pump it, and fire." He gave Elizabeth a plastic trash bag filled with a few loaves of bread, some canned food, and soda.

Atkins laid the weapon on the back seat. "Good luck, then," he said, smiling at Marsden.

"And to you, friend."

Using an electric winch, Marsden lowered the off-ramp. They'd be able to drive right onto solid ground. The ferry was tied up at the edge of a muddy soybean field about half a mile from the highway.

FRED BOOKER WATCHED HOW THE STRONG WINDS
blowing down from the foothills of the Great Smoky Mountains affected the fires. Sheets of flame shot up whenever the wind stiffened. The earthquake had severed the gas lines, which were burning fiercely all over the Y-12 complex, probably ignited by sparks from fallen wires.

Electric cables and transmission wires were snapping all around him. Streams of white-red sparks were going off like rockets. Broken wires crackled on the ground.

Booker was alone. The two other men he'd been working with at the Shock Wave Lab had left the complex. Staying behind a line of fire trucks, he'd gotten as close as he could to Building D-4 at the western edge of the complex.

Dating from the Manhattan Project, D-4 had been used for end-stage enrichment of U-235 uranium. The biggest structure in the containment park, it was 640 feet long and 412 feet wide. Liquid mercury and the uranium and plutonium cores of mothballed nuclear weapons were stored there in special lead-lined bunkers. There was no danger of an explosion, but if they caught fire, the leaking radiation would be deadly.

It was definitely a hot zone. A firefighter's nightmare.

The quake had knocked the hell out of D-4 and many of the other cavernous buildings that lined Carbon Avenue. A section of the front wall and roof had collapsed.

And to Booker's amazement, the ground was still shaking.

This damn thing isn't over, he realized.

Four fire engines had pulled to within fifty yards of D-4. Mechanical aerial ladders were spraying long, arcing jets of foam on the roof and walls.

"I want everyone evacuated within a one-mile perimeter of this building," a fire captain said.

Booker recognized the man from the frequent safety meetings he'd attended before he retired. He was in charge of Y-12's disaster response team. His name was Tim Duncan. Like the other firefighters who'd gathered around him, Duncan wore a white radiation suit. In his fifties, Duncan was a short, heavy-chested man with a walrus mustache. He looked stunned by the scope of the disaster and was trying his best not to show it.

"I'd feel a hell of a lot better if I could get a good layer of foam down on those mercury storage tanks," Duncan said. He wasn't about to send any men into the building, not with the ground still shaking and the risk of a mercury explosion or a radiation leak.

Booker stepped forward and showed his ID. Duncan recognized him. The physicist was still wearing his thin, antistat suit from the Shock Wave Lab. With all the adrenaline pumping, he wasn't even aware of the biting cold.

"I might be able to help you," Booker said. "Send someone down to the robotics lab. Jeff Burke will probably still be there. Have him bring Neutron down here."

Duncan looked puzzled.

"That's one of the new robots they've been working on. If you need to check out the inside of D-4, it can get the job done. It might even be able to spray some foam."

Twenty minutes later, a dark gray Dodge van pulled up behind the fire trucks. Jeff Burke got out, and Booker helped him lift the robot out of the back.

Neutron had none of R2D2's cuteness. All business, it vaguely resembled a television-sized metal box equipped with a computer screen, viewfinder camera, and a high-intensity spotlight that could be electronically raised or lowered. Depending on the terrain, the robot used either wheels or tractor treads. Made of a titanium alloy, it was equipped with two six-foot mechanical arms that could easily lift two thousand pounds.

Its lightweight frame was attached to a Hawkin Directional

Platform, which permitted it to swivel quickly and easily in a tight circle.

Neutron was still experimental, but Burke had worked out almost all of the bugs.

Duncan explained what he needed. He wanted the robot to spray as much fire-retardant foam as possible on the mercury and plutonium storage areas. Burke knew exactly where they were located in D-4. He'd direct Neutron's movements by remote control and follow them on camera.

He used joysticks to operate Neutron's arms and clawlike hands. Turning on the robot's power supply, Burke had it pick up two of the big sixty-gallon foam canisters, which he and Duncan strapped to its back. The robot would operate the nozzles with its mechanical hands. The way the pincers gripped the equipment was eerily lifelike, Booker thought.

"Let's do it," Burke said.

Neutron rolled slowly to the front of the building, which resembled a ten-story warehouse. The front was made entirely of reinforced concrete painted a muddy red. With Burke working the controls, the robot tapped in a special code on the security lock, opening steel blast doors one-story tall. It then entered D-4, a powerful spotlight attached to the camera illuminating the way.

Burke followed Neutron's progress through the building from a laptop television monitor. D-4 was open virtually all the way from the ground floor to the roof. The acres of floor space were subdivided into hundreds of separate storage areas.

Neutron advanced down a long, dimly lit corridor, turned, and kept going until it came to a fifty-yard row of wooden skids. The steel tanks of mercury were laid on their sides in sturdy wooden frames and looked like oxygen canisters.

"We're in position," Burke said. "Here's where it gets tricky."

Booker kept his eyes glued to the television monitor as the robot methodically began moving up and down the line of skids, covering them with a thick layer of white foam.

"Now where?" Burke asked.

"Send him down the corridor to your left," Booker said. "There's a fire door at the end and another security keypad. The plutonium beds are on the other side."

The ground shook. The building seemed to buckle inwardly.

"Everyone back!" Tim Duncan shouted into a bullhorn. "Get away from there. Now!"

The succession of heavy aftershocks had severely weakened the already damaged building. Afraid one of the walls would collapse on his men, Duncan ordered everyone back at least three hundred yards from D-4.

"Forget the robot," he shouted to Burke and Booker, who hadn't moved from their advanced position near the front wall. They were about fifty yards from the door. "You're too close."

Burke shook his head. "No can do. I'll be out of communication range with the robot. That's one of the glitches we haven't quite worked out. Our range is limited to about two hundred yards."

The ground rocked again. Booker actually felt himself lifted up and down as the earth rolled under his feet.

There was a shudder, then the sound of heavy chunks of concrete slamming to the ground. Part of D-4's flat roof had caved in.

Booker measured the distance to the building with his eye. If the front wall came down, they'd never get clear in time. He resisted an overwhelming urge to run.

THE SUN WAS STARTING TO COME UP, REVEALING
a chilly gray sky and a landscape that had been torn apart.
The sights of cataclysmic liquefaction were everywhere.

Atkins and Elizabeth drove in silence, lost in their thoughts
as they surveyed the devastated countryside. They were on
Route 61, which paralleled Interstate 55 a few miles to the
east. They'd pulled off I-55 when they encountered their first
collapsed overpass. They had to drive out into a muddy field
to get around the wreckage and wouldn't have made it without the Explorer's four-wheel drive. Radio reports said every
overpass had been knocked down in the quake zone. Until
the debris could be cleared, the major north-south interstate
was all but cut off.

No more than ten miles from Blytheville, Arkansas,
they were nearing the quake's reported epicenter. Memphis
was about eighty miles due south. Atkins tried to increase
the speed, but it was impossible. There were too many
obstructions.

Trees were down. Sand blows, volcanic in shape, were
still erupting, blasting geysers of mud, carbonized wood, and
stone into the air, but not with their earlier force. And the
sound they'd noticed most of the long night—the howling
roar of the earth cracking open and venting—had all but
ceased.

Pushing hard to get to the epicenter, Atkins had to stop
frequently to pull around cracks in the highway surface, some
of them two and three feet wide. All the delays were mad-

dening. They'd gone nearly four hours without getting a seismograph up and running at the epicenter. That was
unforgivable. With each passing hour, they were losing precious data.

In some places, the road looked as though a ditchdigger
had cut a deep trench across it.

Despite his increasing sense of urgency, Atkins stopped to
inspect one particularly large sand blow. Measuring several
hundred feet in diameter and perfectly cone shaped, the
crusty sides were about four feet high and had already hardened. Steam was still drifting out of the opening.

Elizabeth slowly approached the side and cautiously
touched the steam vapors. She quickly withdrew her hand.

"It's almost boiling," she said.

"There's got to be a strong thermal element at play here,"
said Atkins. He was still wondering about the strange light
that had made the depths of Kentucky Lake shimmer. It was
possible they were caused by thermal disturbances in the
crust.

"I hope they're setting up some good strain-rate databases
in Memphis," Elizabeth said. They needed to know how
much energy had been released.

She also hoped they'd gotten the GPS and Radar Interferometry Systems operating again. The satellite data would
help them measure with minute precision how much the earth
had shifted or risen. And, more important, whether it was
still rising, a telltale sign that seismic strain energy continued
to build in the ground.

There was so much they needed to know. The greatest
need was for seismic information that would help them
gather precise data about aftershocks. Where they were hitting. And how often.

The strong-motion seismograph they wanted to install near
the epicenter would help them pinpoint the magnitude of the
fault that had ruptured. With any luck, it might also show
whether any previously undiscovered faults had been
activated.

A single seismograph was, at best, of limited usefulness.
They needed to set up a whole array of instruments, but that
would take time. The seismograph in the back of the Explorer was the best they could do.

Elizabeth was eager to do some trenching along the fault line. If there was ever a time for serious paleoseismology this was it. They might be able to find some clues about what had happened deep in the earth in the ancient past. She wanted to know how often big quakes had occurred—and at what intervals. The data could help them calculate whether or not the massive quake they'd just experienced was likely to be followed by another killer.

Elizabeth didn't like to consider that possibility, but the history of the New Madrid Seismic Zone showed that it had happened before.

More traffic was out—mainly cars and pickups and, unbelievably, a few eighteen-wheeler rigs trying to avoid I-55. Atkins figured it wouldn't be long before the authorities closed all highways in the area to everything but emergency vehicles.

Ever since they'd crossed the Mississippi, the change in topography had been striking. The rolling, forested terrain of western Kentucky and Tennessee had given way to country as flat as any desert. They were passing through the Missouri boot heel, a sliver of the state that dipped into Arkansas.

It was part of the Mississippi Embayment, which started roughly where the Ohio River merged with the Mississippi and broadened out in an inverted U to the Gulf of Mexico. The embayment contained the famous Reelfoot Rift, a weak zone in the middle of the North American plate where the earth had tried to pull apart 600 million years earlier. The New Madrid faults were part of the residual scar tissue.

Atkins knew that the northwestern edge of the embayment, the section they were driving through, was the most interesting geologically. The land, an ancient flood plain, was used mainly for agriculture—soybeans and some cotton. The main characteristics were drainage ditches, grain elevators, irrigation pipes, and vast fields crisscrossed with rows of poplar trees.

They crossed the Missouri state line into Arkansas. Blytheville was four miles south, right on Route 61. The epicenter was another five or six miles due south. Atkins took a bypass to get around Blytheville. For the last few miles, they'd noticed dark smoke hanging low on the horizon. The black smudge looked frozen on the gray winter sky.

It was Blytheville burning.

"How many people live there?" Atkins asked.

Elizabeth checked the map. "About thirty thousand," she said.

It was a much larger town than he'd imagined. He doubted a single building had escaped serious damage and thought, again, about casualties. They were going to be horrific.

Five miles later, the smoke was still visible. Atkins turned west on an unmarked country road. He drove another mile, passing a pair of dark-blue grain silos that had been upended by the earthquake. Corn had poured like gold from the gaping cracks. There wasn't a house in sight, just cotton fields that had been picked nearly two months earlier and were still white with cotton the machines had missed. It was bleak country.

"What about here?" Atkins asked, pulling to a stop on the shoulder of the road.

They'd reached the approximate location of the epicenter.

Elizabeth nodded. "Look up ahead," she said.

About a hundred yards down the road, the blacktop had been split wide open. Large pieces of broken pavement were stacked up against each other in overlapping layers. The fissure had gouged the road at a right angle.

Atkins and Elizabeth got out of the Explorer.

"Do you smell that?" Elizabeth asked.

"Ever since we hit the Arkansas line," Atkins said. The strong odor of sulfur was heavy in the cold air. It was the same smell he'd noticed the night before.

The offset was large. Nothing like what they'd seen on the Mississippi, but still striking. The ground on the far side of the highway, the hanging wall, was at least four feet higher than on their side.

The fissure—it was six feet deep—ran as far as the eye could see in either direction, west to east.

"That looks like classic strike-slip horizontal tearing," Elizabeth said, walking to the edge of the fissure. "The right lateral movement must have been incredible."

Shielding his eyes against the wind, Atkins had no doubt that the faulting had generated some monstrous seismic waves.

"I'd suggest we set up around here," he said.

Somewhere below them, at the hypocenter of the quake, probably at a depth of over five or six miles, one of the major faults in the New Madrid Seismic Zone had ruptured with a tremendous explosion of energy.

This was ground zero.

"THE ROAD'S CLOSED. YOU'VE GOT TO TURN around."

The speaker wore a white environmental-hazard suit and a hooded face mask. He was with three other men, similarly dressed.

"I've got to get to Heath," Lauren said. "My parents live there."

"There's been an accident at the uranium plant," the man said. "Some gas leaked out. We're trying to get people evacuated to the west."

"What kind of gas?" Lauren asked. She knew the Department of Energy operated a huge plant near Heath but had only a vague knowledge of what was done there.

Another man approached. He held a radio in his right hand. Lauren noticed that they were all wearing sidearms.

"Just turn around and get the hell out of here," he said angrily.

Lauren looked up the road that led toward town. It was wide open.

She nodded to the man.

"Bobby, get down," she whispered to her grandson. Then she punched the accelerator and swerved around the barricade. The big 327-cubic-inch V-8 roared as she cut back onto the highway. She glanced in the rearview mirror. No one was chasing them. Good.

She drove another half mile and made a turn. She planned to enter Heath from the back in case the main road was blocked. It was a small community. Only a couple hundred people. Her parents' home was on the eastern end, a split-level ranch. Happy to be off the farm near Mayfield, her mother had fallen in love with the place.

Lauren was puzzled by the evacuation. She didn't see any cars on the road. Maybe everyone had already left, she thought.

There was a sudden bright flash in the early morning sky. It was off to the right, a couple miles east. "What was that?" said Bobby, who'd also noticed the burst of light. It looked like a Fourth of July rocket, a long tail of white smoke, then a brilliant red flash.

Later, she would learn there'd been an explosion at the uranium enrichment plant. The massive pipes that carried uranium hexofluoride gas under pressure had cracked open during the earthquake. Pieces of an electrical generator had ignited and gone off like rockets.

"Listen to that," Lauren said. She heard a rapid series of distant explosions.

Bobby pointed toward the east. A helicopter was bearing down low over the treetops headed in their direction. It slowed and hovered directly over their car. It was about twenty feet above them. Painted in white letters across the drab olive fuselage were the words DEPARTMENT OF ENERGY.

A spotlight blinked on beneath the chopper, blinding them.

"You're in extreme danger," an amplified voice boomed out. "Poison gas is drifting in this direction. Turn around at once."

The message was quickly repeated, then the helicopter moved off, climbing rapidly. It was headed due east, toward the uranium processing plant.

"There it is!" Bobby yelled. They were on a slight rise. A chalky cloud, so faint as to be almost indistinguishable in the predawn gray, was drifting toward them. Still several miles away, it seemed to spread out as it rose higher in the sky.

Lauren already had the Chevrolet turned around. At the first fork in the road, she headed south. The two-lane black-top was torn to hell and the car's chassis and springs took a beating, but she kept the speed at fifty miles an hour.

She glanced at the fuel gauge, the first time she'd remembered to do so.

The red needle was nudging toward empty.

She knew there was a small town up ahead. Hammonds. It had a gas station.

When she arrived, ten or twelve cars and trucks were pulled in close to the station's single tank. The owner was operating a cash and carry business. His brick filling station was in shambles, but the lone pump was still working. He carried a rifle in the crook of his arm.

Lauren figured she'd driven about thirty-five miles since the helicopter had warned them. Surely they were out of danger, but she kept nervously watching the sky for a yellow cloud.

When it was her turn at the pump, the owner asked for cash in advance. Twenty dollars a gallon. Dressed in a soiled hunting jacket, he had a full black beard and was chewing a plug of tobacco.

"Dammit, Tom. This ain't right and you know it. You're robbing folks."

The man who was waiting in line behind Lauren had gotten out of a battered red pickup. His voice was laced with anger.

Lauren had fifteen dollars. She handed it to the man with the rifle.

"Please," she said. "Just let me have two gallons." That would be enough to get home.

"You heard the price. That'll buy you three-quarters of a gallon." He pumped it out to the nickel.

"Tom, some people are going to die if they can't drive," the man behind her said. His words were cold, hard. He was bareheaded, maybe sixty years old, and had a leathery face.

"Mind your own business, Harris," the man said. "I'll run my business how I see fit."

More angry words were exchanged. The bareheaded man took a few steps closer to the station owner, pulled a short-barreled pistol from the pocket of his jacket, and held it to the man's head. The owner's eyes bulged. He dropped his rifle.

"Take five gallons, lady," the man said. "Then you and the boy get the hell out of here."

THE CLOUD OF DUST SHOWED CLEARLY ON BURKE'S television monitor as he followed Neutron's progress through the massive building. A piece of the concrete roof had almost fallen on the robot.

"That was close," Booker said.

Burke nodded, studiously working the controls. Neutron had opened the fire door and moved into another part of the D-4 building. The uranium and plutonium storage areas were divided into dozens of separate vaults.

With Burke operating the control panel, Neutron began pouring a thick spray of foam over the storage bunker. There was just enough left in the canisters for one good soaking.

The ground shook again. Another bad one, the movement was horizontal, a sharp back-and-forth motion. Booker saw the front wall of D-4 start to buckle.

"Get out of there!" the fire captain shouted at them over a loudspeaker. "Pull back!"

The huge building was teetering.

"What about it, Jeff?" Booker asked his friend. If that front wall fell, they'd be crushed.

"I'm not leaving the robot," Burke said. "I've got seven years of work tied up in that machine."

They were experiencing a swarm of aftershocks, each stronger in intensity. Another part of the roof fell in. Booker heard it crash loudly to the ground.

The walls were starting to sway.

"Come on, Jeff!"

Burke hadn't moved. Booker doubted he'd even heard him as he hunched over his laptop monitor, manipulating the controls.

Booker was getting ready to grab his friend and pull him to safety when he saw the robot emerge from the rubble. Rolling through a cloud of dust, the machine was using its powerful mechanical arms to clear a path through a pile of concrete and twisted steel that blocked D-4's front door.

"I was worried about the durability of the metal framing," Burke said, still staring at his computer keyboard. "I don't think—"

"Jeff, let's go!"

Burke started after Booker. Moving quickly on its omnidirectional platform, the robot followed them.

ATKINS GLANCED AT HIS WATCH. IT HAD BEEN WELL over four hours since the quake, and they still didn't have a seismograph up and running at the epicenter. He clenched his hands on the wheel of the Explorer. It was incredible, from his perspective the geological equivalent to suffering a heart attack and waiting four hours before checking into the hospital for some tests. He could feel his chest tightening, the pressure building at his temples.

Distant seismographs were recording the aftershocks, but there was no substitute for having an instrument right at the epicenter. They wouldn't miss any of the smaller aftershocks that way, the swarms of magnitude 2 and 3 earthquakes that other seismographs might not pick up. Knowing about those small quakes was important in gauging how much seismic energy remained locked along the fault.

They simply had to get it up and running. It was damned important. Atkins felt like grabbing the seismograph, running out into a field, and setting it up. Just pick a spot. Any spot.

Stop it, he told himself. They needed to find a suitable place or they'd blow everything.

He threw the Explorer into reverse, backed up a couple hundred yards, and turned down a dirt trail he'd noticed a few minutes earlier. He wanted to get off the main highway. He drove slowly, looking for a place. A quarter mile down a muddy path for tractors, he crossed a dry creek bed. A weather-beaten picnic table was off to the side under a stand of poplars. It would make a good platform for the seismograph.

"How about right here?" he said.

"Looks fine," Elizabeth said. Within minutes, she had the instrument hooked up. She was much more skilled than Atkins with the seismograph. About the size of a briefcase, the rugged device was powered by two small solar panels and also had a backup battery pack. The data was digitally recorded on disk.

Atkins ran a quick field test: the starter, pendulum, and timing circuits were all functional as was the backup analogue recording drum and film. Elizabeth plugged a laptop computer into a port on the side of the machine so they could monitor the data visually. The battery supply was good for forty-eight hours.

Atkins wished they'd brought along a gravimeter, a portable machine that could measure changes in gravitational strength triggered by the rise or fall of the land during an earthquake. The instrument could also detect variations in rock densities and was another tool to try to zero in on how much strain energy remained locked in the ground.

That remained one of their chief objectives. There'd been two big earthquakes on the New Madrid Seismic Zone in three days. The first a magnitude 7.1 event. Then the monster that had struck earlier that morning.

Atkins and Elizabeth both knew the history of the fault. The triple of 1811–1812 haunted them. Three magnitude 8 or greater earthquakes in a little over a month. More than anything, they wanted to know if another major quake was possible. That's why they were so intent on gathering as much data as they could on latent seismic energy.

Their plan was simple: stay put long enough to get a complete run of seismographic data.

Atkins thought their food supply would last three or four days. Then, somehow, they'd have to find a way back to Memphis. With the telephone lines knocked down and no way to transmit the data in real time by computer modem, they'd have to take it back physically.

Atkins tried to reach Walt Jacobs by shortwave radio. He wanted to report their location, but couldn't get through to Memphis. There was too much static and background noise, which meant heavy use of the two-band shortwave circuits. With virtually all other means of communication knocked out, the shortwave relay bands were overloaded.

By then it was late in the morning and freezing cold. A ten-mile-an-hour wind was blowing straight out of the north. Atkins and Elizabeth huddled in the back of the Explorer. Worried about running out of gas, they didn't dare operate the heater, but they were tempted. Atkins could barely feel his feet.

To shield themselves as much as possible from the wind, he'd parked against the deepset bank of the creek. A thick stand of poplar trees provided some cover. The seismograph was on the table about twenty yards away. Impervious to the weather, it was in a bright-orange case fashioned from heavy-duty PVC plastic.

Atkins was grateful that the ferry captain had given them some food. He opened a can of corned beef and made sandwiches.

"How about lunch?" he asked, popping open two cans of lemon soda. "And maybe dinner later tonight."

Elizabeth smiled. "Why, Doctor Atkins, are you asking me for a date?"

"You bet."

"I'll be free anytime after seven. Just drop by."

They both laughed. It was the first chance they'd had just to talk. There hadn't been much time for casual conversation. And Atkins wanted to get to know Elizabeth better. If he could get through these next few weeks, which were going to be rough, then he could try.

Elizabeth's hair was tied up, and her nose and cheeks were red from the cold. She looked wonderful.

Atkins had taken the last bite of his sandwich when he heard a noise. It sounded like the whine of a dog.

He stepped outside. The sound was louder. Something moved in the thick bushes near the creek bank.

"What is it?" Elizabeth asked. She'd also gotten out of the Explorer.

"A dog, I think. A small one."

He walked closer to the creek. The seismograph's carrying case was a splash of bright orange on the table. He heard more whining and a few soft barks. The sound was farther up the creek and seemed to be coming from both sides.

Atkins heard the bushes move again as if blown by the wind.

They got back in the Explorer.

"There must be a couple of dogs down there," he said. "They probably smelled the food."

BY midafternoon, the weather—cold, clear, and windy—hadn't improved. Snapping her coat collar around her neck, Elizabeth went to check the seismograph.

Atkins stayed in the van. They were taking turns, visiting the instrument every hour. In less than six hours, they'd captured more than 120 small microshocks, almost all of them in the magnitude 2 range or less. Three had registered a magnitude 4. The ground at the epicenter remained incredibly active.

The time seemed like an eternity to Atkins. He was as anxious as he'd ever been in his life to get a good run of seismic data shipped back to Memphis so it could be analyzed. He also hoped Jacobs had made arrangements with someone, somewhere, to get more instruments shipped out here. They needed an entire array of seismographs, twenty or thirty of them, to get the best possible picture of what was happening below ground.

The seismograph they'd set up on the picnic table was about the size of a small briefcase. Packed in a padded carrying case, it was designed to record only the strongest ground motions. Like most instruments, it relied on a pendulum system. The inertia of the suspended pendulum lagged behind the frame, which moved with the earth. In older seismographs, a pen or stylus attached to the pendulum captured this movement on paper. Atkins and Elizabeth were using a modern machine that converted ground motion into electrical signals that could be amplified and recorded on paper, magnetic tape, or directly into a laptop's memory system. The device was programmed not to go off scale during a severe quake.

Atkins watched Elizabeth walk across the gravel creek bed and bend over to check the laptop. She punched a few keys and jotted some numbers in a notebook.

Waving to him, she motioned for him to roll down the window.

"I'm going to walk up the creek," she shouted, cupping her hands. "Maybe the bank will show the offset."

Atkins nodded. Almost dozing, he realized how incredibly tired he was. Elizabeth's resiliency astounded him. He craved sleep with every muscle of his body. Not Elizabeth. She didn't show any signs of slowing down at all.

Closing his eyes, he must have fallen asleep for a few minutes. Something had awakened him. He wasn't quite sure what. He nudged his elbow into the door frame to get more comfortable in the freezing Explorer.

Then he heard the same low whine he'd heard earlier. A dog barked. In his foggy brain, he thought the sound seemed far away. Then it happened again—loud and close. A bark, followed by a deep growl.

Wide awake, Atkins jumped out of the Explorer and started running up the creek bed. He wanted to find Elizabeth. Then he remembered the shotgun. He went back and got the weapon from the backseat. He checked the magazine. The Remington was fully loaded. Seven double-ought shells. It was a 16-gauge pump. Marsden, the ferry captain, certainly liked his shotguns to have a kick.

Atkins had done a lot of hunting with his father and was a fairly good shot. He released the safety, racked a shell into the breech by pumping the slide, and slipped his finger in the trigger guard.

He wanted to call her name, but something told him to keep quiet. He was aware of movement in the brush in front of him. Crows had been cawing in the upper branches of the poplar trees that lined both sides of the creek. They'd become silent.

Atkins trotted up the creek bed. He heard another growl. The animal was concealed in the trees to his right. He swung the shotgun in that direction but couldn't see anything. He rubbed his eyes, which were watering in the sharp wind.

He walked a few more yards up the twisting creek bed. Barely five yards wide, it was filled with gravel, sand, and dead leaves. The high banks were overgrown with vines and dense brush.

He heard a low, deep growl.

That's one hell of a big animal, he thought.

Another dog barked, then another.

Damn! How many dogs are out here? Atkins wondered. He walked faster, trying to be as quiet as possible. Sweat trickled down the small of his back.

The ground twitched and rolled slightly. It was the strongest aftershock since they'd arrived at the epicenter. Atkins' brain automatically pegged the magnitude at 4.

The tremor unleashed a chorus of frenzied barking. The sounds were just around the next bend in the creek bed.

Hugging the overhanging bank, moving slowly so his boots wouldn't crunch on the gravel, Atkins peered around a clump of vines.

Looking upstream, he sucked in his breath.

Elizabeth was standing in the middle of the creek bed. She slowly bent down and picked up a couple of rocks. There were at least eight dogs in the creek, or up on the bank, animals of all sizes, shapes, and breeds. Elizabeth faced four of them as two others slowly circled around behind her.

The wind changed and Atkins was hit with the overpowering stench of rotting flesh. Farther upstream, he saw the mangled carcasses of at least twenty cows piled into the creek bed. They'd probably panicked during the earthquake, stampeded, and fallen in. The steep drop-off at that point was nearly ten feet. They'd piled on top of each other.

The dogs were feasting on the bloated carcasses.

Atkins still didn't know how many others were hidden in the woods.

He heard that soft distinctive whine again and this time he saw the animal that was making it. The dog, some kind of mixed breed, had the size and bulk of a German shepherd. It was in a crouch, its brown, unblinking eyes locked on Elizabeth, who was coolly facing the other animals, talking to them in a soft, steady voice. The big dog must have scouted them out earlier in the day.

Atkins remembered the rats that had swarmed over the Jimmy and the crazed bull he'd encountered on a farm near Mayfield, Kentucky. The seismic activity certainly had an explosive effect on some animals. No other explanation made sense. Atkins figured most of the dogs were pets. The quake had probably destroyed their homes and maybe killed their owners. Dogs were more likely to survive the initial shaking. And it wouldn't take long before they started hunting for food in packs.

He guessed the dogs had been drawn to the creek by the smell of dead cattle.

Picking up a few slivers of dried grass, Atkins released them in the wind. The grass blew back toward his face. Good. He was downwind.

He wanted to take out the mixed-breed, the apparent pack leader, but Elizabeth stood directly in his line of fire. She took a slow step backward. The dog moved in closer. It was growling, head low to the ground, hackles up.

Three more dogs leaped over the edge of the bank and joined the two circling behind Elizabeth.

Do it now, Atkins told himself.

He'd been too slow with Sara. The memory flashed before him. If he'd reacted more quickly, maybe he could have reached her before the fire swept through that building in Mexico City. The self-doubts had haunted him for years.

He stepped into the open. Aiming quickly, his first blast took out two dogs, who disappeared in red puffs as the buckshot blew them to pieces.

"Lie down!" he shouted to Elizabeth, who threw herself onto the gravel.

Running, stumbling on the uneven ground, Atkins got closer and fired from the waist. Two booming shots. The pack leader rolled over, part of its head missing. Another animal took a load of steel shot in the side and was thrown up the creek bed.

The other animals scattered. Atkins tried to count them as they disappeared into the brush. At least a dozen. And he doubted he'd seen all of them.

Elizabeth got up and ran to him. "I don't know where they came from," she said. "I looked up and they were all around me."

They jogged back down the creek toward the Explorer. Atkins looked behind just as five dogs came out of the brush.

Incredible, he thought. They're following us.

The pack was led by a mastiff with a broad, white head. Flecks of foam flew from its mouth. Barking once, it charged them.

Atkins swung the shotgun around and fired twice. The impact stopped the animal in mid-stride and killed another as it tried to scramble up the bank.

Atkins widened the weapon's choke to give him a broader shot pattern. He had two more shells left and wanted to make them count.

They climbed into the Explorer and locked the doors.

"You okay?" he asked.

Elizabeth sat there, trying to catch her breath. Her face was flushed. "I'm fine," she said. "Now I know why I've always been a cat person."

As they watched from the front seat, several dogs emerged from the woods and began fighting over the carcasses of the dead animals. Small dogs that looked like terriers, the viciousness of their attack was all the more striking.

"From here on, I'll take the seismic readings myself," Atkins said. "I don't want you going down there again. I don't think those dogs have gone."

He wondered if the animals could sense something.

So did Elizabeth. "Do you think maybe they know something we don't?" she asked.

WALT JACOBS HAD INSTINCTIVELY DROPPED UNDER his desk when he felt the first tremor. A strong aftershock sent part of the cornice and front wall crashing into his office. The shattered bricks narrowly missed him, pulverizing a wooden table where he'd stacked books and papers.

The converted house, one of two occupied by the university's Center for Earthquake Studies and the USGS, showed signs of imminent collapse. Cracks, some wide, had appeared in most of the load-bearing walls.

Jacobs had seen enough.

"Everybody out of here!" he shouted. "We're moving into the annex. Now!"

Located behind the other offices, the single-story, wood-frame building was shaped like a military barracks and contained the earthquake center's library, a few classrooms, storage areas, and a workshop. Jacobs and the other seismologists had slept there the night before. The center had a supply of camping gear for field trips—sleeping bags, inflatable mattresses, butane stoves, water purification kits, and other equipment that would prove extremely handy in the days and weeks to come.

The annex, which also housed a set of four seismographs, had been nudged three inches off its foundation, but had held up fairly well. It took several hours to move the computers and the most critical files and databases from the other two buildings.

Jacobs and six other staff members had made it to the

center. So had four of the USGS geologists who'd flown into Memphis after the first quake. Several graduate students had also shown up.

Earlier that morning, Jacobs had privately asked two of the students to try to reach his house in East Memphis to check on his wife and daughter. He hadn't been able to get in touch with them and was starting to worry. He wanted to go himself, but knew his overriding responsibility during the crisis was to keep the earthquake center up and running.

The students, both Ph.D. candidates, a young man and woman, readily agreed. It wasn't going to be easy. Jacobs lived more than ten miles away, in the Germantown area. They'd have to walk.

Jacobs thought of his wife, Susan, and daughter, Lisa. His memory focused on a day before the earthquakes, their last real morning together as a family. They'd had breakfast at the kitchen table, in front of the bay window that Susan loved, the detail that had brought them to buy the house five years earlier. Susan had reminded him to stop at the supermarket on his way home and pick up some milk. He remembered how good she looked, with her long black hair tied back. He should have complimented her, told her how much he loved her. He regretted bitterly that he hadn't done that. He whispered another silent prayer that they were safe.

Later that morning, he made his first extended tour of the campus. The scope of the disaster staggered him.

Most of the university's brick buildings had been severely damaged. Some had been knocked to pieces. Walls and roofs had collapsed. The Feldman Memorial Library, a new five-story building, was a pile of bricks, glass, and books.

The worst damage was along Dormitory Row, where the student high-rises were located. Two of the four dorms had collapsed. One of them, a ten-story building, had snapped in half. The other lay on its side, virtually intact. Some of the survivors had been able to climb out of the windows and jump to the ground.

But many of the two thousand students who lived in those buildings were dead or seriously injured. Some had horrible wounds, and no one to treat them.

Students and a few campus police officers were climbing

through the rubble looking for survivors. Screams seemed to come from a dozen different directions at once.

Jacobs saw a pair of bare legs sticking out from under a section of drywall. He thought he saw one of the legs move and started to pull away a covering of debris.

Stopping immediately, he opened his mouth to cry for help, but no sound came out. He fell to his knees and vomited.

Jacobs took another look at the gaping face. The girl's hair was brown and matted.

He heard someone come up behind him. A young man.

Still on his knees, Jacob waved the youth away and tried to warn him not to come any closer. It was too late. The student already had taken a good look.

"Oh, God!" he cried, and put his hand over his mouth. He dropped next to Jacobs and retched.

Jacobs saw a man he recognized, a middle-aged doctor who lived in the neighborhood. Wearing a gold jogging suit and carrying a small black bag, he was moving around the piles of brick and glass, trying to help the injured.

Jacobs called to the man, but his voice was thick with bile. He was fighting to control his stomach.

He finally got the words out.

The doctor came over, took one look at the body, and angrily said, "Don't waste my time with the dead!"

On the way back to the earthquake center, Jacobs had to stop several times. He felt weak, drained, and couldn't remember when he'd last slept.

When he got to his office, he found Guy Thompson. He was still having trouble with his stomach.

"Any improvements with our communications?" he asked.

Thompson frowned. "Nada, but all is not hopeless."

Overshadowing their many other problems was the need for information on what was happening in the ground. The quake had knocked out telephone lines, which meant they couldn't access data from their PADS network. All but a few of the seismic instruments were linked to the office by telephone lines. So were the handful of GPS monitors they'd only recently installed at sites in western Tennessee and Kentucky.

Two of the six GPS units and four of the seismic instruments operating in the New Madrid Seismic Zone transmitted data by radio wave, but the radio towers had been knocked down or otherwise disabled. The units were still recording data but there was no way to send it back to Memphis.

"We're going to have to get out in the field and collect it ourselves," Jacobs said. "And that's a bitch with all the roads torn to hell and the bridges out."

It angered him that they'd never considered the importance of arranging for a helicopter to retrieve data. They also needed to do flyovers of the earthquake zone to see what the ground looked like. Pretty basic, but hopeless. No helicopters or planes were available.

They'd repeatedly tried the military and national guard, but every available aircraft continued to be used for emergency medical flights.

Jacobs bitterly remembered the many disaster planning sessions he'd attended. The assumption had always been that a quake, even a big one, wouldn't knock out all the land lines. Everyone figured that patchy telephone connections would somehow survive and that they'd be able to receive at least some real-time seismic data.

Their assumptions had proven all wrong, every damn one of them. When they needed precise seismic information the most, it wasn't available.

Thompson reported they'd had better luck keeping in touch with the USGS earthquake evaluation center in Boulder. Thanks to a system called "packet radio," they'd been able to use a special radio modem technically called a Terminal Node Controller, or TNC. The device connected to a two-way fifty-watt shortwave radio receiver and could hook up to a computer terminal.

They could send and receive computer data through "packets" of radio waves. Jacobs remembered how some staffers had thought the system was a waste of time and money. But it was paying for itself in gold. The major shortcoming was that it was agonizingly slow. Using packet radio, a computer could send at only 4800 baud per minute. Even a discount department store computer could transmit at 9600 baud.

Still, it was something. They had two TNC units up and

running. They also had a "fly away" satellite hookup. Jacobs had set up the suitcase-sized device on a courtyard bench just outside the annex. The opened lid of the forty-pound unit served as the antenna. By adjusting the compass and punching in the right code coordinates, they locked in on a satellite so they could transmit. A laptop computer was patched in with a keyboard and eight-inch video screen. Once they uplinked with a satellite, the unit functioned as a telephone. They could also send and receive computer data.

The only problem: it wasn't working.

Intense solar flares had knocked it out along with the Global Positioning System.

Jacobs angrily threw across the room a chunk of plaster that had fallen on his desk.

"We're operating blind here!"

He thought, again, about Atkins. It had been hours since they last talked. Jacobs wondered if his friend had made it to the epicenter and gotten his seismograph set up. There'd been reports that the bridges over the Mississippi from north of Memphis five hundred miles to Hannibal, Missouri, were either knocked down or heavily damaged. Every one of them.

Jacobs hoped Atkins had been able to cross the river. They needed his data. Among other things, it would help them gauge the depth and size of the fault that had triggered the monster quake.

Guy Thompson cried out: "Hey, I just got an E-mail through to Boulder." His laptop was hooked to one of the TNC units. Thompson was wearing a cowboy hat with an eagle feather tucked in the band. He'd also put on another Western shirt, bright red with pearl buttons. "They're trying to send a team here, but the Memphis airport's out of service." He looked at Jacobs. "They say the control tower's been knocked over. Demolished."

"Any more on the exact location of the epicenter?" Jacobs asked. With their seismic network in shambles, they had to rely on USGS in Boulder for precise information.

"No change. It remains approximately ninety miles north, northwest of Memphis. Longitude ninety degrees west. Latitude thirty-six degrees north. Right at Blytheville. It's been felt as far north as Montreal."

The location corresponded with data from their own seismographs, which were running on an emergency power generator. They had a bank of four rolling drum instruments. The first big shock wave had knocked all of them off scale. Since then they'd recorded three major aftershocks in the magnitude 7 range and dozens of minor temblors.

Jacobs knew where and when the quake had occurred, but he still didn't have the complete picture. He wanted to know the depth of the epicenter. That alone would tell them a great deal about seismic wave propagation, the shape of the fault, its size.

The emergency traffic they were picking up off the short-wave channels was catastrophic.

Memphis General Hospital was out of service. Several major buildings in the medical complex had collapsed. Only one of the city's hospitals could still admit patients, and it was overwhelmed with the seriously injured. National Guard units were trying to set up a first-aid station at Forrest Park. There were desperate calls for plasma and blood donors.

"Here's some good news," Guy Thompson blurted out. "I just got through to Boulder again."

"I could sure use some," Jacobs muttered.

"The National Aeronautics and Space Administration just sent out a bulletin," Thompson said. "The GPS system is coming back on-line, and the tracking stations are back in business."

Every seismologist in the annex clapped and whistled. Jacobs closed his eyes. Yes, good news. But tempered by the realization that with telephone lines down, they still needed to get out in the field to collect the data.

The constellation of twenty-four satellites had been out of service for the last five days, the result of severe solar flares. Their precise measurements would show to the millimeter how much the earth's surface had been deformed by the earthquake, how much it had risen or fallen. That would help them set up a strain-field pattern, a way of calculating whether seismic energy was still building.

Unlike the sophisticated array of GPS stations scattered along the San Andreas Fault, only a handful had been installed along the NMSZ, where they were more difficult and costly to set up. It was crucial that each GPS platform remain stationary, a constant problem in the soggy Mississippi Valley. The instruments were anchored with steel rods driven deep into the ground. Each unit was equipped with an SSE receiver and antenna; the receivers were mounted on surveying tripods.

The system was expensive and most USGS funding went to southern California's network, a continuing source of irritation to Jacobs, but a fact of life. Quake-prone California always got the cake; the other parts of the country got crumbs.

Maybe that's going to change, Jacobs thought bitterly.

"Walt, we just got through to Atkins on the shortwave," one of the seismologists shouted. "You're not going to like what he's got to say."

ATKINS SPOKE QUICKLY, FORCING HIMSELF TO BE concise and brief. He didn't know how long they'd have a clear communication channel open with Walt Jacobs in Memphis. The static-plagued shortwave band was proving increasingly unreliable.

He'd just spent the last hour with Elizabeth examining readouts of the seismic wave patterns they'd downloaded straight from the seismograph into their laptop.

Dogs were still prowling around the Explorer. They'd heard barks along the bank of the creek, but none of the animals had shown themselves.

As he spoke with Jacobs, Atkins tried to keep his voice calm, professional. The readings had worried him.

"I've never seen peak accelerations at this level occurring so long after the main seismic event," he said into the radio's microphone.

The seismic tracings indicated a series of sharp peaks and valleys representing the ground's vertical and horizontal shaking. The secondary and surface waves showed vertical accelerations nearly seventy percent that of gravity. Vertical accelerations of fifty percent the rate of gravity were considered large.

The measurement, known as "acceleration due to gravity," was nothing more than an attempt to show how fast and hard the ground was shaking by comparing it with known gravitational forces. The baseline measurement was the speed with which a ball falls, an acceleration assigned a value of

1g. That's the same as racing a car 100 meters from a dead stop in four and a half seconds. Moderate earthquakes produced acceleration rates of .05g to .4g. The rate here was .7g. That was considered huge.

The acceleration rates were troubling enough, but Atkins was also worried about the consistently strong aftershocks—and what they might signify. During the last seven hours, they'd had at least eight quakes that he estimated in the magnitude 5 range, strong enough to rock the Explorer on its axles.

Jacobs confirmed the aftershocks. The seismographs in Memphis had recorded every one of them.

"It looks like the epicenters are bunched roughly forty to fifty miles northeast of us," Elizabeth said.

They could do only the roughest field calculations. By measuring the time difference between the arrival of the quake's primary and secondary waves, they were able to compute how far the epicenters were located from them. The calculations were based on the differing speeds of the waves. Both left the earthquake focus at the same moment, but the faster-moving P waves reached the seismograph first, followed by the S waves. The delay in arrival time was proportional to the distance traveled by the waves.

Atkins knew that Jacobs realized what all this meant: the probable existence of another new fault branching out from the New Madrid Seismic Zone. It was the only logical explanation for such a tight bunching of aftershocks that were apparently outside the main fault system.

The radio clicked back on. "John, we're looking at the same information right now," Jacobs said. "We're going to have to confirm it, but it appears the epicenters are clustered in northwestern Tennessee and western Kentucky anywhere from thirty to forty miles east of Kentucky Lake." The seismographs running nonstop in the library annex had recorded all of them.

Atkins detected the strain in his friend's voice. His own throat tightened as he explained his concerns. Based on this preliminary data, the NMSZ—once again—had become dramatically larger. Three days earlier, after the magnitude 7.1 event, they'd discovered a new fault running south of Memphis.

And now this.

Elizabeth said, "There's no evidence the faulting process is slowing down."

The seismic shock waves were coming far too often for that. The epicenter near Blytheville, the one they were sitting on, continued to generate dozens of microquakes. Then there was the much stronger ground shaking to the northeast. With such instability, the elastic forces in the ground could snap again—at any moment.

"Have you been able to get through to any other seismic stations to nail down the epicenters?" Elizabeth asked.

"We're working on it," Jacobs said.

To fix the exact position, data from seismographs at three or more different sites would have to be plotted. The epicenters were the points where the rippling seismic waves overlapped.

Jacobs expected another data transmission soon from the National Earthquake Center in Boulder. Sophisticated computers were analyzing seismic readings from dozens of instruments scattered around the United States and abroad. That data as well as information recorded by seismographs in Memphis—and now near Blytheville, Arkansas—would fix the exact location of each epicenter.

This, in turn, would help them delineate what appeared to be another new fracture jutting off from the main New Madrid Seismic Zone.

Atkins had a map of the NMSZ spread open on his lap. It overlaid a map of the Mississippi Valley. The fault zone was shaped roughly like a hatchet, with the blade running across the intersection of Missouri, Arkansas, Tennessee, and Kentucky. The massive quake they'd just experienced had exploded about midway down the handle, which dipped seventy miles into eastern Arkansas, paralleling the Mississippi River.

The major aftershocks suggested a new branch extending from the top of the hatchet up through northwestern Tennessee well into Kentucky.

If it held up, the expanded fault zone might run roughly four hundred miles. A long S-shaped series of cracks deep in the earth, extending from just below Memphis, crossing the Mississippi from west to east around Caruthersville, and continuing to within 150 miles or so of Lexington, Kentucky.

"It's the dynamics at work here that worry me," Elizabeth said. "How one major event, the 7.1 quake of three days ago, triggered a series of aftershocks that set up another major event, and now we're getting more aftershocks."

"Liz, what are you saying? That these aftershocks could be leading up to another big one?" Atkins said. Despite his concerns about a possible new fault and the power of the aftershocks, he thought that was going too far. "I know what I just said, but it's way too premature to start a discussion like that. This could all be part of the normal wind-down after a major earthquake. We could be in for some rough aftershocks for weeks. I know what the seismic history here is. Walt's told me all about it. But those big quakes happened nearly two hundred years ago. Right now there's no way we can say all these aftershocks are leading up to another major hit. I'm betting when we start to get some GPS data in, we're going to see the deformation has started to taper off."

"I remember how skeptical we all were about Doctor Prable's data," Elizabeth said. "If we had moved more quickly, started an analysis when we—"

"Then what?" Atkins said. "What would we have done? Warned the public? Made an earthquake prediction? Come on, Elizabeth. Don't go second-guessing yourself. We'll have lots of time later to take a close look at Prable's data and see what we can learn from it. I'm still not convinced it wasn't one of the best scientific guesses in history."

"If we don't pay attention to those aftershocks, we could find ourselves making the same mistake twice," Elizabeth said sharply. She didn't like Atkins' patronizing tone.

Atkins raised his hands apologetically. He didn't want to get into another argument. Not at a time like this, especially after everything they'd been through.

Then he suddenly remembered that he hadn't checked the depth of the focus. It was his oversight. He'd completely forgotten and remembered it only as an afterthought. Any other time an omission like that would have seemed incomprehensible.

Their seismograph readings indicated the "focus," or source from which the big quake had emanated, approached a depth of ninety kilometers. That was incredibly deep. Most killer quakes that struck California originated from foci in the upper ten kilometers. The place where the fault had slipped near Blytheville was buried deep in hard crustal rock, the perfect incubator for enhancing the power and reach of seismic waves.

The radio static hissed. It was Jacobs' voice again. "We've got to get your data back here."

Like Jacobs, Atkins and Elizabeth wanted to feed all the information into one of Guy Thompson's computer modeling programs so they could calculate the true breadth and depth of the faulted area. Combined with GPS data on ground deformation, it would help them gauge the potential for another major earthquake.

"How does it look to you?" Atkins asked Jacobs.

"I'm worried, John. I'd be a liar to say otherwise."

Jacobs was afraid to reveal the real extent of his fear. He still didn't know what had happened to his wife and daughter. It had been hours since he'd sent his two grad students to check on them.

Changing the subject, he asked, "How are you two doing out there?"

Elizabeth said, "Except for some wild dogs, just fine."

PRESIDENT NATHAN ROSS HAD FELT THE TREMOR
as he sat reading in a wing chair on the second floor of the
White House. He was trying to slog through a CIA report
on Cuba, something he'd put off for days. It was hard going,
dense with statistics and pro-and-con recommendations on
resuming diploma tic relations with Castro. Ross was starting
to drift off to sleep. A sudden strong shaking snapped him
awake. The windows in the doors that opened onto the Tru-
man Balcony rattled in their frames. Alarms and warning
bells started going off throughout the White House.

Ross had been in an earthquake once before during a trip
to San Francisco when he'd been governor of Illinois. This
was much stronger. It seemed incredible, the second quake
in three days. That very morning, he'd read a preliminary
Federal Emergency Management Agency report on the earthquake that had damaged Memphis.

He was already moving toward the door when the Secret
Service agent posted outside rapped on it sharply.

"It may be an earthquake, Mister President. We're not
sure yet." The agent had his gun out, a black, short-barreled
Uzi. Two other agents ran down the hallway of the presidential living quarters, weapons drawn. The doors to the building
were being sealed off.

Ross headed for the stairway. He never waited for the
elevator if he could avoid it. The thing took forever.

"We confirm an earthquake. A big one somewhere in the
Midwest. We're just starting to get some reports," another

Secret Service agent called out from the bottom of the long, curving staircase. He had a cell phone in his right hand, a weapon in the left.

"Have the NSA's duty officer meet me in the Oval Office," Ross said as the agent, a young man in a sharply creased gray suit, trotted along behind him.

Ross had never liked the stiff formality of the Oval Office, its *Architectural Digest* sterility and overwhelming sense of history. He hurried through the president's study into the small office, which was dominated by the ornately carved mahogany desk owned by Teddy Roosevelt when he was police commissioner of New York City. It was a god-awful piece of furniture that Ross had never gotten around to getting rid of.

He buzzed the switchboard.

"Get me Steve Draper," he said. Draper was his national science adviser. Ross anticipated he was going to need some technical help. He knew instinctively that if he could feel the shaking in Washington, the country had just been rocked by one hell of a strong earthquake. Much bigger than the one that had hit near Memphis. He needed the best scientific minds he could gather.

There was a knock on the open door.

"Mister President, we've got some information from the National Earthquake Center in Boulder."

Ross motioned in Betty Lou Davis, a newly minted Harvard Ph.D. from DeKalb, Georgia, who was an aide to the national security adviser. She'd drawn the graveyard shift and was out of breath from hurrying over from her office in the West Wing's basement with two assistants, who stood behind her, yellow legal pads at the ready.

"The earthquake registered a magnitude 8.4, Mister President. Its epicenter is somewhere in eastern Arkansas. Roughly the same area that experienced that magnitude 7 quake a few days ago. This one really hammered them. It's been felt over a huge area. Upstate New York, the Canadian provinces of Quebec and Ontario." She hesitated a moment. "Your home state of Illinois has taken a pounding."

"What about casualties?" Ross asked.

"We don't know yet, sir," Davis said. "We're having

trouble getting through to Memphis, Little Rock, and St. Louis. Communications are completely knocked out.''

''We intercepted a cockpit transmission from the pilot of a TWA 747 who was on his approach into St. Louis,'' one of her assistants said. ''He aborted the landing when he lost all contact with the ground. The runway lights went out. All of them.''

Ross sensed that Davis was worried.

''What else, Betty?'' he prodded.

''The pilot stayed in radio contact with the people in the control tower,'' she said. ''We've got it on tape, Mister President. The tower was shaking. You can hear them screaming.''

"IT'S GONE. THE WHOLE THING'S GONE," BOBBY
said in astonished disbelief as he stared at what was left of
the Kentucky Dam.

Lauren thought her grandson was going to burst into tears.
She almost did herself, but didn't want him to see her sobbing. They'd arrived in Benton a few minutes earlier and
had driven straight to the lake. The small town was in shambles, but the damage there was nothing compared with this.

The huge steel gates and the high wall of concrete and
crushed rock that supported the elevated highway had been
washed away. The lock and dam on the far shore were completely inundated. The powerhouse had disappeared. It was
as if the dam had never existed. The water in the lake was
flowing straight into the Tennessee River.

The water level had dropped about forty feet, but the lake
surface was still turbulent. The swells were running two and
three feet with whitecaps.

Lauren drove down the gravel road to their boat dock and
marina. Anticipating the worst, she still wasn't prepared for
what she found.

The dock was gone, vanished.

She got out of the car and walked closer to the lake. She
saw the blue roof of the restaurant about thirty yards out in
the water. Attached by cables to the shore, it had been pulled
into the lake when the water level plunged. The pier and
boat slips had disappeared.

Bobby put his arm around her waist. They held each other,

not speaking, staring dumbly at the sunken restaurant and dock. Everything they'd worked for, the sixteen-hour days, her savings. It was all underwater. Their insurance wouldn't come near paying for the loss.

Staring at the wreckage a few minutes longer, Lauren took the boy by the hand and walked back to the car.

"We're going home," she said. Maybe she could think there, figure out what they'd have to do to survive and how she could find out about her parents, whether they were still alive. She was so tired. All she wanted to do was lie down and let sleep come.

Lauren finally felt the emotional release. Living through all this wasn't easy. She whispered a quick prayer of thanksgiving to God for sparing Bobby. She'd lost her son, daughter-in-law, and husband, and didn't want to lose her grandson. She couldn't begin to think about how she'd survive if something happened to him. So far, they'd been incredibly lucky. If she found their home smashed to pieces, it wouldn't matter.

On the way home, she stopped at Goode's Convenience Store. It was just off Route 641 near the western side of the lake.

The front windows and the glass door were shattered.

Elizabeth knew Vern Goode and his wife, Gloria. Vern also had a gun-and-ammo business and did a brisk trade during the hunting season. The metal, prefab building had two sections—one for the convenience store, the other for the gun shop.

Lauren told Bobby to stay put. She slipped Lou Hessel's .357 magnum into a jacket pocket. She didn't like the feel of the place.

"Vern," she shouted, gripping the heavy pistol in her pocket. "You hear me, Vern?"

No one answered, so she stepped inside the convenience store. The exterior of the one-story building was in fairly good shape. The walls were bowed out slightly, but that was about all. It was different inside. Shelves were knocked down, and part of the ceiling had fallen. The light fixtures dangled from wires. Almost all of the merchandise was missing—canned food, soft drinks, bread, milk, liquor.

She walked next door to the gun shop. The door hung open on broken hinges.

"Vern, it's Lauren Mitchell," she called.

She slowly stepped inside. The gun cases were smashed. Everything in the shop had been removed—the rifles and shotguns that had stood in racks behind the front counter; the boxes of ammo; the pistols that had been displayed in glass cases. The cash register.

She took a couple of steps and stopped. She was standing in something sticky. It was dark in the narrow store. Lauren opened a window blind and in the thin light saw a dark stain that had spread out on the floor from behind one of the counters.

"Vern!" she shouted. "Gloria. Anybody here? Please come on out. It's Lauren."

She moved toward the counter, one cautious step at a time. The black stain looked like a puddle of motor oil.

Lauren peered around the counter. Vern Goode and his wife lay faceup on the floor. Both had been shot in the head.

Lauren leaned against the wall and closed her eyes.

Someone had killed them for the guns and ammunition. Lauren didn't doubt it for a minute. A weapon was worth its weight in gold now.

She wondered how long they'd been dead. She wanted to bury them and look for the daughter, but there wasn't time. It was getting late in the day, and she wanted to be back at her home before the sun went down.

If there was trouble, it would come in the dark.

THE SUN WAS BARELY UP WHEN ATKINS AND ELIZA-
beth got a shortwave transmission from Walt Jacobs in Memphis. He told them that Paul Weston had arrived at the earthquake center with two other members of the Seismic Safety
Commission. They'd come in a National Guard helicopter
provided by the governor of Kentucky. That same chopper
was headed their way to pick them up.

Thirty minutes later, a UH-1 Huey with Kentucky National
Guard markings landed near the creek bed. Carrying only
their portable seismograph and laptop, Atkins and Elizabeth
were happy to get off the ground. Some of the dogs had
gotten bolder during the night and were moving back into
the open.

As soon as they were airborne, the pilot motioned them
forward to the cockpit. The crew chief, a young corporal
with a blond mustache, gave them headsets so they could
talk over the droning roar of the engine.

The pilot explained that Jacobs had a message for Atkins:
he wanted him to enter a building on the Memphis riverfront
and retrieve data from an array of seismic instruments set up
in the basement and on the roof.

Atkins let that thought register. He'd forced himself to
enter dozens of earthquake-damaged buildings since Mexico
City. It had never been easy.

"It's the headquarters for some travel agency," the pilot
said. "The Blake Building. It's at Main and Vance Street,

facing the river. Landing anywhere near it's going to be a bitch. That part of the city is pretty torn up.''

Atkins remembered Jacobs talking about the building's unique construction, how it had been specially designed to withstand earthquakes. Its ''base isolation'' technology relied on shock absorbers made from a rubber and lead composite that were shaped like an accordion and placed in the foundation and at key joints; they allowed the building to remain nearly stationary while the ground moved beneath it. Because of its potential survivability during a big quake, the building's owners had agreed to let the university's earthquake center equip it with an array of seismographs and other instruments. It even had a GPS satellite receiver anchored on the roof.

The helicopter wouldn't be able to wait for them, the pilot explained apologetically. They were under strict orders to return immediately to Kentucky as soon as they put them on the ground. They were assigned to a medevac unit that had been working around the clock ever since the earthquake.

The flight to Memphis took forty minutes. They flew straight down the Mississippi, which had spread out three and four miles in places, swollen by the flood. Atkins knew it was going to get worse; as soon as the massive surge from Kentucky Lake hit the Mississippi at Cairo, it was going to blow out a lot of levee walls.

''Maybe I better prepare you for this,'' the pilot said as they approached Memphis. ''A lot of the city is pretty much gone.''

They saw the distant wall of black smoke long before they had Memphis in view.

''Those are mainly gas and oil fires,'' the pilot said. ''A lot of pipe lines cross the river around Memphis, ten or eleven of them. They all broke and some of them are still pumping out gas and oil. The river's an inferno. It's burning from Mud Island thirty miles downstream. Oil storage tanks blew up. They're still going off like torches. You gotta be real careful flying down there.''

Sitting on a bench seat, Elizabeth looked out a porthole and recognized the familiar S bend in the river, the beginning of the sweeping curve the Mississippi made as it passed

Memphis. She'd first seen it as her plane from Los Angeles made its landing approach. That seemed like months ago.

Moments later, she got an up-close look at the city. The panorama of destruction was unlike anything she'd ever seen in the United States. All three bridges across the river, the Interstate 55, I-40, and the railroad bridge were down; some of the massive concrete pilings were still standing, but there were gaping holes where the decks had buckled and fallen into the water.

The Mississippi was on fire below the smashed I-55 bridge; that's where the oil and gas storage terminals were clustered on the Memphis side of the river. The burning tanks were throwing shafts of black, billowing smoke a thousand feet into the sky.

Hugging the Memphis shoreline, the pilot pointed out a heavily damaged building. "That used to be the Pyramid," he said.

Atkins had never seen the city's distinctive convention center and sports arena complex. Shaped like a pyramid, the tapered sides were covered with thin sheets of metal that shone brilliantly in the sunlight. The top floors had collapsed neatly, telescoping together like the sections of a segmented drinking cup. The broad base, which covered a full city block, remained intact.

They flew over the city's famous Mud Island, which angled out from the riverfront. The monorail that carried passengers to the island's shops, restaurants, and museums had been smashed; three wrecked cars still dangled high in the air.

Drifting, dense smoke obscured the broad view of the city as it stretched far to the east. Then the wind changed and the curtain parted.

"I don't believe this," Elizabeth said, staring down at the cityscape. The larger fires seemed concentrated along the riverfront, where most of the high-rise buildings and renovated cotton warehouses were located. Many of the tall buildings along Main Street looked damaged; a few had collapsed entirely, spilling against other buildings, knocking down entire walls. Some had lost only their upper floors.

There were fire trucks and ambulances down there, their red and blue lights flashing up through the swirling smoke.

"How are emergency vehicles getting around in all that?" Elizabeth asked.

"They're not," the pilot said. "Most of the streets are blocked." He pointed off to the port side. "You see that big yellow building over there to the left? That's a children's hospital. It looks like the walls are standing, but most of the floors have caved in. We flew over it on the way to pick you up."

Elizabeth glanced at Atkins and shuddered. America's luck had finally run out. She realized that the death toll from this earthquake was going to be huge. With the exception of the 1906 quake in San Francisco, the ones that struck in southern California had largely been glancing blows along the edges of major population centers. The real disasters, the ones that leveled entire cities, had struck elsewhere—Chile, or Italy, or Japan, or Armenia, or Mexico.

This time it was different.

"I'm going to put you down fast," the pilot said. They were nearing the landing zone he'd picked. "I'm sorry about that, but some of those buildings are still falling down in the aftershocks. It's gonna be real tight down there."

He explained that the travel building had a keypad locking system. He tore a piece of paper off the clipboard strapped to his leg and handed it to Atkins. It had the numbers.

The pilot slowly began to descend through the patchy smoke. "I'm going to try to set you down on that parking lot." They'd have to drop down between the building and another, taller one that had lost its upper stories. Curtains flapped in the smashed windows.

The crew chief patted Atkins on the shoulder and gave him a thumbs-up. "Get ready!"

As the helicopter descended between two buildings, its rotors were dangerously close to the walls. There was no margin for error. The pilot, a veteran of the Gulf War, was superb. They descended slowly, steadily.

Atkins looped the straps of the seismograph and laptop around his shoulder. The crew chief gave Elizabeth a small backpack. "K-rations, flashlights, and a couple bottles of water. It's the best we can do."

They were about four feet off the ground when Atkins saw the men. Maybe ten of them. They'd come out of nowhere and were running for the helicopter, arms raised, screaming for help.

"Jump, now!" the crew chief shouted.

Crouching at the cargo door, Atkins and Elizabeth leaped for the ground. The men frantically rushed past them. Two of them grabbed on to the bottom edge of the open door and were lifted up as the copter started to climb. Legs kicking, they fell from about fifty feet. Both hit the ground hard and didn't move.

Atkins grabbed Elizabeth's hand. They ran for the travel building.

"What do you have in the backpack?" someone yelled at Elizabeth. "You got any food? Hey, asshole, listen to me." A man moved toward them. He wore dark slacks and a torn overcoat; he was big and heavy, well over six feet tall.

Atkins ignored the man, who was with three others. Their faces were streaked with dirt. They were moving toward Atkins, who fumbled with the security keypad at one of the building's side doors.

"Just give us the backpack," the tall man said.

Atkins tried to remember the keypad numbers the pilot had given him. He fumbled in his pocket for the sheet of paper. Finding it, he punched in a sequence of five digits and pulled on the handle. Nothing.

He handed Elizabeth the paper and faced the men. They kept coming. Atkins picked up a piece of broken pipe lying in the rubble.

Atkins noticed the butcher knife the big man was holding tight to his side. He'd give him another few yards then go for his head with the pipe; he wanted to take him out fast.

Gunfire exploded above them, the bullets kicking up rocks near the feet of the men who were approaching Atkins and Elizabeth. The group broke up and ran for cover.

Atkins looked up and saw the helicopter hovering over the roof of the building. Leaning out the cargo door with a rifle, the crew chief was covering them.

Atkins waved to him.

Elizabeth had the door open. He jumped in behind her and slammed it shut.

THE FIRES HAD BEEN BROUGHT UNDER CONTROL OR extinguished at the ORNL's Y-12 plant. Engineering teams were out inspecting the damage, trying to determine which buildings had to be demolished. It was dangerous work because of the frequent, strong aftershocks. A bad one killed two engineers when a steel I-beam fell as they tried to check out the "Mouse House." The eight-story building contained the biology division and got its name from the 125,000 mice kept there as laboratory animals.

Fred Booker scoped out the damage through a pair of powerful Zeiss binoculars. He stood on the deck of his home in the hills that overlooked the plant. Except for losing electricity and having a couple of large windows broken, his tightly constructed, well-anchored A-frame had come through the quake virtually unscathed. Booker got his water from a well operated by a gas-powered pump; he also had an ample stock of canned foods. And Jack Daniel's. He was in fairly good shape to sit things out.

Booker planned to go back to Y-12 later in the day and offer whatever help he could.

Meanwhile, he had two houseguests—Len Miller and Ed Graves, the young geophysicists he'd been working with in the Shock Wave Laboratory before the quake. They lived in Knoxville, forty miles to the east; Booker had put them up when they were unable to get home.

Both were worried about the flurry of aftershocks.

"There's still a hell of a lot of strain energy in the ground," Miller said.

"It's hard to figure," said Graves. He'd borrowed one of Booker's jackets and was standing on the deck in the bright winter sunlight. "Mid-plate quakes like these are damned near impossible to understand. I keep asking myself if something in the lower crust is putting stress on the faults."

"My guess is it's a hotspot," Miller said. Hotspots were well known to geophysicists. Born deep in the earth's mantle, the layer between the crust and core, they were thermal plumes, gigantic bubbles of molten rock that rose from two thousand miles underground. As much as a thousand miles across and often shaped like the mushroom cloud of a nuclear blast, hotspots played a vital role in keeping the planet from turning into a chunk of space ice.

Graves and Miller likened the earth to a boiling pot of oatmeal. Percolating in a circular convection, it kept pulling heat and hot rock from great depths to the surface, then back down again.

It was their work in this area that prompted their heat studies at the Shock Wave Lab. These slowly rising hotspots helped create volcanoes. And Miller had long believed they could also cause enough deformity in the crust to trigger earthquakes at depths of well over four hundred miles.

Booker wasn't paying much attention to the discussion. Then Graves casually mentioned how inactive faults could be brought to life by a process called "lubrication." He likened it to loosening a stuck door hinge with a couple squirts of oil; by reducing friction within the locked fault, you could facilitate motion.

Fascinated, Booker put down his binoculars and listened.

"It's long been thought mineral fluids or water trapped in a fault could lubricate it enough to trigger an earthquake," said Graves. "They proved it out in Colorado back in the sixties." He described how a series of small earthquakes had rocked Denver, an area that had had virtually no seismic activity. During a nine-month period, more than seven hundred small quakes were recorded; then they mysteriously stopped for an entire year. The lull was followed by another outbreak. Eventually, geologists discovered that the Army was injecting contaminated water from weapons production at its Rocky Mountain arsenal deep into the ground.

"They were using bore holes about twelve thousand feet deep," Graves said. "There was a perfect correlation between the quakes and the injections."

Miller said, "Remember that USGS experiment in western Colorado? They went out to the oil fields around Rangely and pumped water into some of the wells at high pressure. Guess what? They started getting earthquakes. They could turn them on or off whenever they wanted just by regulating the injections. Turn on the faucet, you get quakes. Turn it off, they stop."

Graves said, "We had some lively seminar discussions out at Cal Tech about whether you could short-circuit or prevent a big earthquake from happening by setting off a series of smaller quakes. The theory was that if you relieved enough stress building on a fault maybe you could defuse a big one."

Following the conversation intently, Booker asked, "Could you use a technique like that to relieve the rock stress in this area?"

"Watch it, Ed," Miller said. "He's got that wild look in his eyes."

Booker's eyes were a dead giveaway whenever he was excited about a concept or an idea. They gave off a burning intensity as they did now. Booker was impatient. He couldn't wait to rush his two guests back into his spacious living room, so he could ask more questions. He actually nudged them along with light taps on their shoulders.

The room was book-lined and decorated with Navaho blankets and Zuni pottery collected during Booker's long years at the Nevada Test Site.

"You didn't answer my question, Ed," Booker said. He'd begun pacing the length of the room, hands in his pockets, head down. He could hardly stand still. "Could you use the technique you were just talking about to relieve rock stress?"

Graves shook his head. "Even if you were sure it might work—and that's a huge if in such a geologically unstable area—it would take too long. You'd have to drill all those bore holes and figure out how to get tremendous amounts of water down into the fault at high pressure."

"You'd also have to decide where to trigger your control

quake," Miller said. "That would be incredibly complicated. And who's to say you wouldn't actually set off the very thing you were trying to prevent."

"But it would still take too long," Graves insisted. "Granted, we don't know how much time we've got until another big quake hits, if one hits. It might not happen for another two hundred years. But say it was imminent, tomorrow. It would take months, years, and a billion dollars to get enough deep holes bored. The advantage of doing the experiment at Rangely was they were able to use existing deep oil wells."

Booker had taken out a notebook and was furiously scribbling notes. He stood there a few moments working through a series of figures. Then he slapped the notebook against his leg and said, "Boys, I know a faster way."

THE POWER WAS OUT IN THE SPENCER BUILDING. Atkins and Elizabeth used flashlights as they groped their way down a pitch-dark hallway. The ground shook again, another aftershock. The building shuddered and swayed, but the base isolation system cushioned the impact. The walls didn't buckle or collapse.

"I'm glad to see the aftershocks are finally dying out," Atkins said sarcastically. Their power and frequency continued to astound him. The ground remained incredibly active.

The building, a modern structure with a handsome, pink granite facade, had escaped serious damage, but the interior was a mess. Desks, computer terminals, and file cabinets were overturned. A bank of security monitors lay shattered on the floor. Office partitions had been knocked over. Window glass littered the carpets.

Atkins opened a door marked with a red exit light and they descended to the basement.

"There it is," Elizabeth said, playing her flashlight against the far wall. Two steel tables supported an impressive array of seismic instruments, all of them battery powered. There were two types of sensors, both state-of-the-art strong-motion sensing devices: an FBA-23 triaxial sensor and an FBA-11. The data was stored digitally on tape and computer disk. It could easily be downloaded into a laptop.

"Elizabeth, look here," Atkins said. One of the devices was equipped with a GPS-synchronized clock. The amber "on" light was lit.

"Yes!" he said, clenching his fists. "The GPS network must be back in operation." If true, it was the best news he'd had in days. They could finally run critical calculations on how much the ground surface had moved during the quake. And, more important, if it was still moving. The amount of deformation would tell them a great deal about whether seismic energy was loading up again in the fault system.

Atkins remembered that the building was also equipped with a GPS monitor. They climbed the stairwell and opened a door to the roof. The GPS antenna, a three-foot-high platform, was bolted to a corner. Its latitude and longitude positions were preset, so it could automatically lock on to the proper array of satellites. Electrical cables connected it to a receiver and modem. A battery and solar panel provided the power.

Like the seismographs, the data was stored on disk. They could format it back at the university. The receiver control panel indicated it had been operational for nearly six hours.

Elizabeth looked out at the city of Memphis as Atkins removed the data recorder. The roof offered an excellent view of the downtown district from the riverfront, extending far to the east. The devastation was much more immediate than when seen from the air. She could feel the heat from the fires, smell the smoke, taste it. Several buildings less than a block away were burning fiercely. One was a highrise bank. Already big, the fire there was growing larger as a strong wind spread the flames from floor to floor.

Elizabeth tried to count the fires, but gave it up. "No one ever expected this," she said. The drone of fire engine sirens made it hard to talk without shouting. "We had some fires in Northridge and during the San Prieto quake, but nothing like this. It reminds me of Kobe."

The fire that had swept through the Japanese seaport in 1995 had almost reached conflagration status. A lot of the construction was wood, small frame houses that went up like dry hay. Memphis was built mainly of brick and masonry, especially in the downtown district. The buildings weren't supposed to burn, but many of them were doing just that.

Elizabeth was struck by the randomness of the fires. Some blocks were untouched. Others were raging infernos.

"If I'm oriented right, the university's roughly in that direction," Atkins said, pointing toward the east with his hands folded. "We've got a nice walk ahead of us."

"How far?" Elizabeth asked.

Atkins shook his head. "Three, maybe four miles."
Getting there wasn't going to be easy. Not with so many streets blocked. They'd have to pick their way through the damage just as night was starting to fall.

"This wind is really spreading the fire," Atkins said. It worried him.

Columns of flaming embers sucked skyward were spreading to the roofs of other buildings. To the south, toward Beale Street and the old cotton warehouse district, they were burning more fiercely. Atkins later learned many of the homes in South Memphis were made of wood. It was a poorer, older section of the city, dense with dilapidated, single- and two-story houses. The wind was sweeping burning embers and sparks from those fires across the entire downtown district.

Atkins watched in amazement as a woman's burning dress drifted by high in the sky, the sleeves flung wide.

A tremendous explosion nearby rocked the building. A fireball curled into the sky behind them. A gas tank had blown up somewhere along the riverfront, a big one.

Atkins didn't like the way the fires were starting to ring them in.

"We're leaving," he said. "Now."

DURING THE FIRST HOURS OF THE CRISIS, GOVER-
nor Tad Parker had been strangely paralyzed, unable to decide what to do. That wasn't like him. He prided himself on
his ability to make quick decisions. It didn't seem possible
that only a day earlier, a lifetime ago, he'd been confidently
trying to raise money to run for president.

Parker was overwhelmed. His only decisive act was to
order a National Guard helicopter to take Paul Weston and
other staff members of the Seismic Safety Commission down
to Memphis. He'd never liked Weston and remembered his
calm assurances about Kentucky Dam when those cracks appeared in the walls after the first earthquake. He planned to
revisit that subject with him later, but right now Weston was
the most knowledgeable man in the state about earthquakes.
More than anything, Parker needed information about what
was happening in the ground. He hoped to hear from Weston soon.

There'd been so many disasters—all of them piling up at
once, each requiring immediate attention: the clouds of lethal
gas that had killed a couple hundred people near the uranium
enrichment plant at Paducah before the gas dissipated; the
dam break; the continuous reports of casualties from every
large city in the state.

In those early hours Parker had fired his chief of disaster
operations, a political hack who'd gotten the high-paying job
solely because of his connections. Parker had gone to the
disaster operations office in the state capitol building and

found the man seated at his desk, drinking straight from a bottle of scotch. Parker's bodyguard had to pull him off the man.

They didn't have enough shortwave radios and portable satellite dishes. And no one had thought what they would do if almost every large hospital in the state had to shut down because it was either destroyed or badly damaged.

They couldn't even get a reliable casualty count. Parker knew instinctively that the numbers were going to be horrendous. On the short drive from the governor's mansion to the capitol, he'd counted eleven bodies himself. Lying on the side of the road and covered with blankets, they'd been removed from damaged buildings and homes.

He ordered his driver to stop. An elderly man sat on the porch of his collapsed brick home, holding the body of his dead wife. Despite the cold, he wore a thin bathrobe. His face was bloody. Weeping softly, he clutched her to his chest as he rocked back and forth.

"What am I going to do?" he sobbed, recognizing the governor, who sat down next to him and offered his condolences.

It galvanized Parker, who'd been in mild shock ever since the quake. He stayed with the man for a couple of minutes, trying to comfort him. When the next crisis came, and it came soon, he was able to make decisions.

A shortwave transmission came in from the director of the state prison at Eddyville, 180 miles south of Lexington. The quake had knocked down one of the dormitories, which dated to the turn of the century. Some of the crenellated walls had collapsed. Another prisoners' building was badly damaged.

"We've got a dangerous situation here, governor," the warden said excitedly. "Most of the guard towers are down. We've got prisoners getting away. Half my people are dead or injured."

The man started to ramble.

Parker shut him up.

"I want you to do just what I tell you," he said. "You march twenty men with shotguns into that mob and shoot over their heads. If that doesn't work, open up again, and this time tell your people to shoot to kill. That ought to quiet them down until I can get some National Guard troops over there to help out. You got that, warden?''

''Governor, I can't do—''

Shouting into the radio, Parker said, ''I'm not going to lose control of that prison. I don't care how many people you've got to shoot. You just carry out those orders. If you don't, I'll get somebody else up there who will.''

ATKINS AND ELIZABETH WENT OUT A FIRE DOOR ON
the side of the building and were soon on Exchange Avenue,
heading east through downtown Memphis. For the next hour
they took whatever unobstructed road or alley they could
find. Sometimes they managed only half a block before they
ran into a collapsed wall or building and had to change
course.

More people were out. Many had come from their homes
in other parts of Memphis to try to rescue papers and docu-
ments from their downtown offices only to get trapped. Their
stalled cars and vans added to the congestion and confusion.
The streets were hopelessly jammed.

The sound of sirens, exploding glass and the frequent crash
of falling bricks made talking difficult. Atkins and Elizabeth
often had to shout in gusting smoke that was getting thicker.
For the first time, Atkins began to wonder if they were going
to get clear of the flames.

They were on Poplar Avenue. He vaguely remembered
Walt Jacobs telling him that Poplar was one of the city's
main east-west arteries. They headed east but the smoke suddenly shifted direction and was in front of them again. Somehow, the fires had moved around them.

Through drifting smoke they saw a yellow fire-pumper
pulled to a curb. A team of firefighters stood next to it,
pouring a single stream of water into what looked like a new
building. Their hoses weren't attached to hydrants. They
were using the pumper's water supply.

Atkins knew what that meant. The quake had knocked out the city's water mains. When their pumper ran dry, they'd have to pull back. It looked like the fire hadn't taken hold yet in the three-story building. Thinking it could be saved, the firemen were sticking it out as long as possible.

The building suddenly burst into flames. The fire blew out the windows and doors with a shuddering, explosive roar. A sheet of flame swept across the street.

Atkins felt the heat from the blast. He lost sight of the firemen and pulled Elizabeth around a corner. They ran down another smoke-filled street. It was no good. The flames were ahead of them again. They turned up a street, then another, and realized they'd gone in a full circle. They were back at the exact spot where they'd first seen the firemen battling the fire.

The pumper was just down the street. They headed in that direction, coughing in the smoke, holding handkerchiefs over their mouths and noses. It was difficult to see, but Atkins thought something looked wrong. Then he saw that the front wall of the building had collapsed into the street, an avalanche of bricks and glass that had just missed the pumper.

The truck's red lights were still flashing. But there was no sign of the crew.

The wind had shifted again. The heat from the burning building had slackened. Believing they could get by it and keep moving east, Atkins headed down the street. He noticed the yellow paint on the fire engine was scorched black on the side that faced the building.

"Oh, God!" Elizabeth said. She'd found the firefighters.

The four men lay crumpled in the street behind the pumper. All were dead, apparently killed instantly when the building exploded. The flames must have rolled over them before they had a chance to pull back. Two of them still had their gloved hands around the heavy brass nozzle of the fire hose.

There was a strong uplift of hot air. The flames were being sucked skyward in ferocious wind gusts created by the fires. The velocity was peaking. Burning embers dipped and swirled over their heads.

"We've got to find shelter," Atkins shouted. "It's going to overrun us."

"YOU FEEL OKAY?" LAUREN ASKED.

"I guess so," her grandson said. They'd just finished dinner—canned stew heated on a butane camping stove. Lauren was worried about Bobby's appetite. He hadn't been eating.

His forehead was cool to the touch. No sign of fever. But the boy wasn't himself.

They'd arrived at their secluded home a few miles from Kentucky Lake to find out they'd been incredibly lucky. Except for broken windows and some cracks in the foundation, the house appeared structurally sound. Fresh water was a problem, but they still had about twenty gallons left in their water heater. They had plenty of wood for the fireplace and a good supply of canned goods. They were better off than she'd expected. A lot better off than many others who lived at the lake year-round. Many of the homes, especially those made of brick, had been shaken to pieces.

"How long do you think we'll keep having these aftershocks?" Bobby asked. That's what was bothering him. Lauren knew the kid was strung out. Every time the ground trembled, she saw him grip a chair or table.

She didn't know what to tell him, how to make him feel better. She was doing the best she could, but it was hard. She hated the continual aftershocks. Even more, she hated how much they frightened her.

The two of them slept in sleeping bags near the wood-burning stove in the family room. Before they went to bed, she made sure her husband's .410 shotgun was close by. She also had the loaded .357 Magnum.

She remembered Vern Goode and his wife. That scared her a lot more than the repeated tremors. The people who'd shot the Goodes were probably still in the area. Her guess was they were locals who knew the couple sold guns and ammunition.

Lauren had tried to conceal her feelings from her grandson, but she almost couldn't handle knowing cold-blooded killers were on the loose with no one to hunt them down. She felt vulnerable and alone, and it terrified her.

She turned on a portable radio. Trying to conserve her supply of batteries, she listened only sparingly, just before they went to bed.

The local station had been knocked off the air, but late at r ght she could pick up the big stations in Chicago and Philadelphia. The national news focused entirely on the earthquake. It had been felt in thirty-nine states—every one east of the Rockies except Maine. The hardest hit were Tennessee, Kentucky, Missouri, Arkansas, Ohio, illinois, and parts of Mississippi and Alabama.

The president had declared the entire Mississippi Valley a disaster area. The latest newscast said he was soon expected to tour the damage zone.

A civil defense station broadcasting from Louisville warned people to stay home. There were reports throughout the quake zone of widespread lawlessness. In Memphis, St. Louis, and Little Rock—three of the most heavily damaged cities—law and order had completely broken down. Police were overwhelmed. With so much physical damage to streets, bridges, and overpasses, it was virtually impossible to patrol in a car, or even on foot. In all three cities, National Guard troops had fired on looters, who sometimes fired back.

The reports left Lauren numb. If it was bad in the city, it was even worse out here in the country. When Bobby was asleep, she got a bottle of bourbon from a kitchen cupboard and filled half a glass. The warmth of the whiskey helped steady her nerves, if only temporarily. She let herself cry softly, then went into the cold back bedroom for a real cry so she wouldn't wake her grandson.

God, how she missed her husband. Missed him to death.

And her parents. Not knowing what had happened to them back in Heath was unbearable. She wondered if they were still alive, whether they'd escaped that cloud of poison gas. She'd heard nothing.

Unable to sleep, Lauren was still awake at two in the morning when she heard footsteps outside, the sound of gravel crunching on the driveway.

She got the shotgun and pistol and crawled to a window. Outlined in the moonlight, two men were approaching the house. They both had rifles.

"Bobby, wake up." She gently nudged her grandson awake. "Get down to the basement."

They'd already gone over this. If there was trouble, he was to get to the basement and hide beneath an old desk.

Lauren hugged the boy tightly. "I love you so much," she said. "You stay down there until you hear from me."

Bobby obeyed instantly and crawled for the doorway to the basement stairs.

Lauen waited in the family room, where she could see both the front and rear doors. Whoever was out there had to know the house was occupied. They would have smelled the wood smoke. The house was a quarter mile off the blacktop and hidden by trees. Not easy to find.

Hell, they probably know who I am, Lauren thought. That's why they're here. A single woman living alone with her grandson. The lady who owned the boat dock. An easy target.

Peeking out the window again, Lauren saw that the men had split up. One had moved around to the back.

Suddenly, she flinched. Someone was knocking hard at the front door.

"Let's make this easy," a loud voice said. "Either you open up, or we set fire to the place. You got a minute to make up your mind."

Lauren's heart pounded. She moved to a window and tried to see who was out there.

"We'll burn it to the ground with you in there," the man said. "Open the damn door."

Moving in a crouch, Lauren went down the steps to the basement.

"Bobby, stay here," she said. The boy was under the desk and hadn't budged.

Lauren opened a trap door to a crawl space that ran under the family room and pulled herself up on the cold ground. The man out front shouted something, which she couldn't understand. Clutching the shotgun, she moved forward on her hands and knees until she was at the end of the crawl space. A car door opened. She saw one of the men looking in the Impala. He was on the far side of the house.

Lauren slipped out of the crawl space and ran across the backyard to a row of blue spruce trees that offered good cover. Staying close to the trees, she worked her way around to the front of the house, trying not to make a sound, trying not to breathe.

Two of them were out there. Not one. Counting the man at the car, that meant three in all.

"Last chance," one of them shouted.

Even before she knew what she was doing, Lauren had left the trees. Walking quietly, quickly, she approached the men from behind. She wanted to get closer. So close she couldn't miss with the .410.

She silently counted off the paces. One . . . two . . . three . . . four.

She raised the shotgun to her shoulder. It was already pumped.

"Matt, behind you!"

The man who'd been checking out the car had come around the side of the house and seen her.

Lauren took two quick steps and fired from about twenty yards. She pulled the trigger twice, the shots booming in the cold, brittle air. One of the men staggered and clutched his side, but his friend grabbed him around the waist. They kept going, lurching into the woods. The other man also disappeared into the trees.

"You come back here, I'll kill you," Lauren screamed. She didn't want to go after them alone.

Lauren figured they'd parked on her driveway near the blacktop. When she heard an engine kick over and the squeal of tires, she lowered the gun.

She stood there, breathing heavily. There was a streak of

blood on the gravel. Lauren let the feeling pass. It had taken possession of her. As she started to come out of it, she realized she would have done anything to keep them from her grandson. The boy was all she had, the only reason her life was worth living. The murderous feeling she'd experienced was overwhelming. She'd wanted to kill them all.

THE FLAMES SEEMED TO LEAPFROG DOWN THE
street. Atkins and Elizabeth had taken cover behind a low
brick wall that extended from the side of a building. They
felt a hot wind blast over them, a gale pulled along by the
fire.

All the buildings that lined the street were burning. Flames
poured from windows and shot through roofs. These were
mainly commercial buildings in this part of town. They were
going to burn for a long time.

Atkins could only shake his head in disbelief and gratitude.
He grabbed Elizabeth and hugged her. It had been her idea
to use the brick wall as a shield. It had saved their lives—
and their equipment. He'd cradled the laptop and seismograph they'd used in Blytheville. Elizabeth had the computer
disks and tapes from the building they'd just left.

"I wasn't sure it would work," she said.

"I wasn't worried for a minute," Atkins said, grinning.

Fortunately, the flames hadn't coalesced into a firestorm
that would have kept burning until it consumed every scrap
of combustible material. If it had, both of them knew they
wouldn't be having this conversation.

They quickly retraced their steps and were soon out of the
worst of the smoke. It was easier to breathe. Atkins saw a
street sign. Poplar Avenue. Somehow they'd worked their
way back to the street that he hoped would take them near
the University of Memphis.

The streets were completely blocked with stranded cars.

Many of the drivers had simply walked away, often leaving their keys in the ignition.

Atkins and Elizabeth reached Overton Park. A large sign said: MEMPHIS ZOO AND AQUARIUM.

"Listen," Elizabeth said.

They heard the howls of terrified animals trapped in their cages. Some of the trees in the park had ignited in the fire.

An olive-colored Humvee with Tennessee National Guard markings pulled up next to them.

"Better watch it around here," the driver called out. "We're using explosives." Two soldiers had walked around to the rear of the vehicle and removed what looked like backpacks. Each man slung one of the packs over a shoulder and moved off into the neighborhood.

Atkins and Elizabeth kept walking. They'd gone a couple more blocks when an explosion jarred them. It was followed in rapid succession by three more.

They saw flames spurting into the sky.

Elizabeth knew immediately what they were doing. She'd seen it once before in California when fires raced through the scrub hills surrounding Los Angeles and threatened to get out of control.

"They're dynamiting homes, trying to set up firebreaks," she said. "Those fires must still be spreading."

Another military vehicle with a loudspeaker moved slowly down the street, often driving up on the sidewalk to get around the abandoned cars and trucks. A soldier warned residents to evacuate.

This was an exclusive residential area with fine, old homes. Almost all of them appeared to have sustained major damage. Many had already been abandoned. Some people had pitched tents in their yards.

The explosions continued. They were blasting the firebreak right along Poplar, hoping they could stop the fire before it spread too far into the mid-city area. People were rushing up to the soldiers, begging them not to destroy their houses, young and old, some of them in tears. Atkins saw a sergeant grab a man who'd swung at him and throw him to the ground.

Elizabeth remembered reading accounts of how soldiers had fired on residents in San Francisco who tried to stop them from blowing up homes after the 1906 earthquake. They'd also used their bayonets on looters. Thieves had been shot on sight.

The wind had changed again. Atkins noticed that it was blowing hard in their direction. The sky had the same reddish cast.

"Do you smell that?" he asked Elizabeth.

"Gas," she said. The odor was very strong.

"Think you can run?"

Elizabeth nodded.

The smell of gas was almost overpowering. A single spark could ignite it, Atkins thought. Even one from a flashlight being turned on.

They'd run about two hundred yards when the explosion ripped through the neighborhood. They'd managed to get about three blocks away from Poplar. Looking back, they saw flames shooting out of the sewers. A row of fine, half-timbered homes Atkins had admired moments earlier no longer existed.

"I'D GENERATE A SMALL QUAKE BY DETONATING A nuclear explosion," Booker said. In his increasing excitement to show exactly what he had in mind, he rolled a green blackboard out of a closet and set it up in the center of the room. Booker often worked at a blackboard. It helped him think to see the ideas and calculations spread out in front of him in large letters and numbers.

Ever since he'd heard Graves and Miller theorize about "defusing" an earthquake by setting off a series of smaller quakes, Booker had been thinking about his experiences at the Nevada Test Site back in the 1960s. An idea had quickly taken shape. It wouldn't let go of him.

"I can recall two shots that triggered pretty good quakes," Booker said. Miller and Graves sat near the wood-burning stove in the living room of Booker's spacious A-frame. Through the windows, they could see the distant smoke of the few fires still burning at the Oak Ridge National Laboratory's Y-12 plant. They'd both noticed how animated and excited Booker had become. He was normally more laid-back, professorial. Not now. It was almost a personality change.

"Both were part of the Plowshare series," Booker said as he began to sketch out the design of a nuclear weapon on the blackboard. "You remember those? It was back when we were trying to come up with peaceful uses for nuclear fission. One of the shots was called Benham. Don't ask me why. We did them out in the Yucca Flats. I think the Benham shot triggered a Richter 4 or 5.''

Miller and Graves stared at him. They knew Booker had spent nearly ten years as a control engineer at the NTS, the 1,350-square-mile area in southern Nevada where the United States and United Kingdom had done their primary nuclear testing. Before the test ban treaty shut it down, 828 nuclear explosions were detonated there, over half of them underground. Most of these took place in the Yucca Flats, a wide, twenty-mile-long valley that was the most bombed place on earth.

Booker's job was to supervise the firing sequence. He'd never talked much about his experiences in Nevada. And for a man who liked to talk, loved it, it was a noticeable omission that Miller and Graves assumed had to do with security issues.

''But how would you control it?'' Graves asked. He'd never considered the idea of deliberately using a nuclear bomb to trigger an earthquake.

''Seems to me you could control it better than you could by injecting millions of gallons of contaminated water at depth like the Army did out there near Denver in the sixties,'' Booker said. He slapped a hand on the blackboard. ''Talk about playing cowboy. You got some poison you want to get rid of? No problem. You just shoot it deep into the ground and don't worry if it starts setting off a whole flock of magnitude 5 earthquakes.''

Booker shook his head derisively. ''We can do better, a lot better. I know we can. I've never been so sure of anything in my life.'' It was as if his entire career, all of his professional experience designing and exploding weapons, suddenly made a difference that he could feel. He absolutely knew he was right about this. Understood it completely. Understood that he was the one person trained to do it and make it work. ''You sink a drill shaft two or three thousand feet, set a bogey tower over it, and lower your bomb.'' He smiled. ''Then bingo! You explode it.'' At the NTS, the six-story movable ''bogey'' tower was used to lower the bomb into place and to conduct preliminary tests of the firing and recording systems.

Booker rapidly sketched out the shaft and bomb configuration on the blackboard. He wanted the other two men to follow him exactly.

"What size would you use, how many kilotons?" Graves asked.

"That would depend on the size of the quake you wanted. Benham was in the 2-or 3-megaton range. It was a beautiful shot."

"And how much radioactive debris did you blow into the atmosphere?" Miller asked, an edge of derision in his voice.

Booker frowned. "I was there for maybe two hundred shots in the sixties. We never had any venting. Not once. After I left, they messed up the Baneberry shot. It was a 10-kiloton bomb. Two days after the detonation the pent-up gases blew a hole in the ground. Sent three million curies ten thousand feet into the sky."

"Hell, man. That's what I was talking about," Miller said.

"That wasn't much radiation at all. You should know that, Les," Booker said. "It pretty well dissipated within twenty-four hours. But I'll agree it shouldn't have happened." Venting was the most serious risk of exploding nuclear bombs underground. It happened when the blast produced more energy than expected and created a kind of chimney in the earth that literally blew its stack, spewing radioactive debris into the atmosphere. Ventings had been exceedingly rare.

"They never found out what went wrong," Booker said.

"My guess is the earth probably shifted after the initial blast," Graves said. "When the pressure built up sufficiently, it ruptured."

"There was one other major venting, but I almost hesitate to include it because it was such an inexcusable screwup," Booker said. "Remember the Sedan shot?"

The two geophysicists shook their heads.

"Back in 1962, some folks set off a 100-kilo device and only buried it 635 feet. When it went off, the dust cloud hit 12,000 feet. Dug a crater 1,200 feet wide and 320 feet deep. The hole's still there. It's become a major NTS tourist attraction."

Booker remembered the sight of that explosion. He'd watched videos of it dozens of times. The towering columns of radioactive dirt and stone arching out of the ground like rockets. Spectacular and so very stupid.

"We used a bigger device—1.2 megatons—for the Boxcar shot in 1968," he continued. "We didn't have any venting at all. Just the usual subsidence. You ever get a chance to fly over Yucca Flats? Looks like the moon. There are hundreds of craters, depressions that formed after the shots. Some of them are a couple thousand feet in diameter."

Miller grinned. "Fred, we're talking about a major fault up here. You explode a bomb on it, there's no telling what would happen." The smile and tone were playful. He wasn't taking Booker's idea seriously.

"You'd get an earthquake and that's what you want, right?" Booker said, working out the possibilities in his head even as he described them. "A small earthquake that could turn off a bigger one. Isn't that the idea? Or am I missing something important here? You set off a smaller earthquake to turn off a larger one. I think that's an idea we damn well better put on the table and discuss."

"It's only a theory," Miller said. "No one would ever seriously consider doing it. It's too damn dangerous. You might set off the very thing you were trying to avoid."

"Or you might stop it," Booker said. "We're starting to get hit with some heavy aftershocks. I know enough seismology to know that a big quake can keep resonating in the ground for weeks, months, sending out hundreds of aftershocks. Do either of you think we've got that kind of time? There won't be anything left of the Mississippi Valley." He was pushing hard to make them see it his way. He realized how much was at stake and he thought he'd come up with a valid approach, at least one that had to be brought to the proper authorities for discussion. He could see it with a sharp, hard-edged clarity that was almost prescient. He'd never felt that way before in his life. He'd never been so certain of anything.

"You two were just talking about lubricating a fault. Well, what do you think happens underground when you detonate a nuclear weapon? For starters, you get a hot ball of gas that completely vaporizes the rock. Hollows it out and forms a cavern. Just like water would, dripping through the limestone for, say, a couple million years. You want to lubricate a fault? Reduce the friction on the rock and maybe cause some movement? All that hot gas might do the job for you. It's just a matter of crunching some numbers, running a few algorithms. Then you'd know how large a device you'd need to get the size earthquake you wanted.''

''How long would it take to reach the kind of depth you'd need?'' Graves asked.

''I'm not sure how far down you'd have to go. That's up to you seismologists to figure out. I can tell you this. You get fifty men who know what they're doing on a drill and you could hit five thousand feet in a couple weeks. I wouldn't want to do it much above two thousand feet for fear of venting.''

He continued walking back and forth across the wide living room as he talked, stopping only to make more notes and calculations on the blackboard. Another thought occurred to him.

''An interesting side issue here would be to assign a hierarchy of risks,'' Booker said. He'd come alive in a way the other two had never seen him. ''People might be willing to accept some radiation in the atmosphere if they thought they could avoid another earthquake like the one we just had. The one that doesn't show any signs of going away.''

It was a radical thought. In the antinuclear era, the idea that the risk of radiation might actually be worth it if you could avert an even greater disaster was an extreme position.

''That's an entirely hypothetical question,'' Miller said. ''The issue had never been examined in any meaningful way.''

''But what if it wasn't hypothetical?'' Booker wondered aloud. What if it's a matter of life or death as it is now? ''We've got people dying in six states and the aftershocks are showing no indication of abating. Many of these have been very strong. A high enough body count would radically alter the risk assessment.''

Booker sketched out a fault and where he'd position the bomb underground, the two lines practically intersecting. He was doing everything he could to connect with these two younger scientists, to make them see the possibility that was burning inside him. The idea had literally taken possession of him.

Graves seemed moderately interested. ''How far away would you need to place the bomb from the fault?''

Miller kept shaking his head. He'd walked over to the window, which offered a sweeping view of the Clinch River and, in the distance, the Y-12 plant. "I think this is insane," he said.

"Ed, you'd have to run some numbers to figure that out," Booker said. He walked to the large picture window and stared out at the burning ORNL. "My guess is you've got people down in Memphis who could do it. Based on what I saw happen at the NTS, you can't achieve maximum seismic effect much beyond thirty miles of the detonation site. But anywhere within that range you could really make the ground rattle."

WITHIN MINUTES OF ELIZABETH HOLLERAN AND
Atkins' arrival at the earthquake center, Guy Thompson had
started an analysis of the seismic data they'd brought back
from the epicenter near Blytheville. Two hours later, Thompson's team of USGS computer specialists had completed
some preliminary modeling on deformation—how much the
earth's crust had been pushed up or down by the tremendous
quakes and their aftershocks.

The GPS data Atkins and Holleran had retrieved from the
building on the city's riverfront was combined with several
other GPS sites in the Mississippi Valley. Two of them—
one near Louisville, the other just north of Jackson, Mississippi—were able to transmit their raw data by radio signal
to receiver towers that had survived the quake. This information, along with radar interferometry readings taken by the
SIDUSS satellite system, had been relayed to the USGS
Earthquake Information Center in Boulder, then back to
Thompson's computer through a satellite hookup.

A little before midnight, the weary seismologists gathered
in the library annex building. There were ten people, including Atkins and Holleran. A gas-driven emergency generator
provided the electricity. Paul Weston, chairman of the Seismic Safety Commission, ran the session. He was accompanied by his two assistants, Stan Marshal and Mark Wren.
Whenever he saw him, Atkins was struck by Marshal's size.
The guy looked like a professional boxer who'd hit fifty and
spread out. Not a geologist. He had a blocky, heavy build

that stretched his jacket at the seams. He never smiled. Never.

Wren was younger, easygoing. He was always carrying a laptop.

Atkins wasn't pleased to see Weston, who was always fidgeting with his clothes, pulling lint from his trousers, or trying to straighten a crease. His hands were always moving, always fluttering around his clothing. It made Atkins nervous just to watch him. He didn't trust the man and wanted to talk to him about the cracks at Kentucky Dam. Based on what he'd seen inside the wall of the dam with Holleran, Weston had been deliberately misleading about their size and severity during that public meeting in Mayfield. Atkins was eager to pursue the matter, but knew this wasn't the time or place.

Guy Thompson was the first to speak. By then he'd been working more than fifty hours with very little sleep. He'd changed into a fresh Western shirt and jeans. This time he wore a buckskin shirt with tassels that hung from the sleeves. His face was haggard. He hadn't shaved and was rapidly growing a thick black beard that matched his long, jet-black hair. In the few hours since Atkins had given him the seismic data he and Holleran had collected, Thompson's whole demeanor had changed. His engaging smile and forceful voice had vanished. Usually the picture of buoyant self-confidence, he was unusually subdued.

As soon as Thompson cleared his throat and began to talk, Atkins realized what was wrong with him: the man was scared.

"We'll go over the GPS and interferometry data first," Thompson said. He started with a matter-of-fact description of how the data were transmitted.

"We began downloading at 4:00 P.M. local time. The GPS data was from the Block II constellation. The interferometry images came from SIDUSS." The Synthetic Aperture Radar dual satellite system provided real-time images from two satellites operated in tandem in the same orbit.

"The data were transmitted on two L-band frequencies. The Y-code was in effect for antispoofing control," Thompson said, explaining that antispoofing guarded against any fake transmissions of satellite data. The use was justified, he said, based on the extreme importance of the information.

Weston interrupted. "Let's get to the summary, please. What kind of deformation do we have?"

Atkins sensed that Thompson was proceeding slowly for a reason.

"The GPS Master Control Station at Falcon Air Force Base in Colorado affirms the transmission," Thompson said, ignoring Weston. "We're concerned with two orbital planes, both focused on North America, specifically on the Mississippi River Valley." He paused to check some notes. It looked to Atkins as though he was holding on to the desk for dear life.

"You asked about deformation. The surface deformation is phenomenal. Based on GPS data of six months ago, the satellite measurements show the ground was pushed up as much as seven feet across wide areas in the fault zone."

Atkins was dumbfounded. There were murmurs of disbelief, gasps. That kind of uplift was unheard of. During the Armenian quake in 1988, uplifts of just over two feet had occurred across a 200-square-mile area and that was considered severe.

"With a deformation like that, you've got to wonder how much energy is still locked in the fault system," Holleran said.

That had always been the key question for Atkins. They were finally getting at the answer. The deformation was staggering. For the first time since the 8.4 earthquake, he realized that Holleran had been totally right in wondering whether they were experiencing a pattern of foreshocks, not aftershocks. He looked at her and caught her glance, a nervous half smile. They had to consider the possibility they were well into a cycle leading up to yet another powerful earthquake.

"It's quite possible there's very little energy left in the ground," Weston said, jotting notes on a piece of graph paper. "The elasticity in the rock may actually have decreased."

"And deformation isn't a foolproof indicator that we've got huge amounts of strain energy building up," said Stan Marshal.

"But how do you explain the phenomenal number of aftershocks we're having?" Holleran said. Like everyone else in the room, she knew the real test would come with the next set of GPS and interferometry readings. If they showed any additional rise in topography, it would mean seismic energy was still loading up in the fault.

"After a great earthquake, that's entirely routine," Weston said. "The aftershocks lasted for weeks after the Northridge quake."

"That was a magnitude 6.7 event. This one was 8.4," Holleran said. "I don't think you can compare the two. It's like comparing a one-story building with a 350-story skyscraper."

"We're getting ahead of ourselves," Thompson said. "The deformation zone covers roughly 340,000 square miles. It runs east on a line extending from Blytheville, Arkansas, into portions of Kentucky, Tennessee, extreme southern Missouri, Illinois, and Ohio." He darkened the lights and turned on a laptop, which projected a map of the Mississippi Valley on a movie screen.

"We've done some two-dimensional modeling of the deformed sections of the crust," he said.

The images were overlaid on the map. The first in the series showed the epicenter at Blytheville, which appeared as a pronounced bulge.

"You can see the asymmetric dome-shaped uplift there," said Thompson. The sharply defined upthrust of the earth spread out around the epicenter for a hundred-mile radius.

Atkins suspected he had another bombshell to announce.

"We've got a lot more to consider here," Thompson went on, still taking it slowly and methodically. "The seismic data John and Doctor Holleran brought back from Blytheville corresponds with other reporting stations. We know the quake opened another fault in the New Madrid Seismic Zone. We're still analyzing it, but this branch appears to run from just north of Caruthersville, Missouri, into northeast Tennessee and then up into Kentucky. It covers roughly 170 miles."

If Thompson's data held up, it meant the New madrid Seismic Zone had effectively doubled in size. No one spoke. Everyone was too shocked to respond.

Thompson showed the new fault on a map projected on

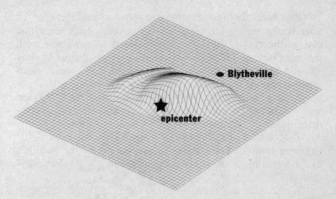

the wall. It appeared to intersect with another major fault segment, the hatchet-shaped top of the NMSZ.

Thompson's voice had become calmer, almost detached. "The New Madrid Seismic Zone has increased from a series of connected faults roughly 125 miles long to a more complex system that extends for over 400 miles."

Holleran looked at Atkins. Neither of them had experience with anything like this.

Thompson displayed another image, a map of southwestern Kentucky dappled with a series of dots. Each represented the location of major aftershocks along what Thompson had begun to call the "Caruthersville Fault." Some were in the magnitude 6 range.

The aftershocks had been recorded by USGS seismic stations at Golden, Colorado; Reston, Virginia; and other locations. Seismographs as far away as Tokyo had also monitored them.

Thompson said, "We've been averaging about six hundred aftershocks a day. Most can't be detected physically. The bigger ones have been bunched along the Caruthersville Fault."

Holleran knew that Northridge, California, had experienced more than a thousand aftershocks a day for about a month, but they weren't as strong as these, nowhere near it.

"You'll note the bigger dots represent the magnitude 6 quakes," Thompson said.

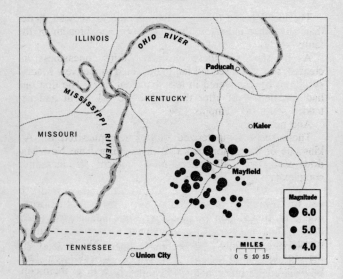

Holleran counted at least six of them.

Thompson wasn't finished with his disturbing sound-and-light show. He punched some keys on the laptop and projected a series of thirty color-enhanced images. The sequence showed how the slippage had radiated out from the quake's epicenter near Blytheville. Each image represented a second of time.

"You'll see that the rupture didn't occur instantaneously or proceed uniformly across the entire fault plane," Thompson said. "It traveled in a northeasterly direction at about four kilometers a second. Some parts of the plane showed major slippage. Other parts little or none."

The areas where the most slippage had occurred were called "asperities." Seismologists had long paid close attention to asperities as the source of energy pulses that reached the surface at different times and places as the earthquake progressed. More specifically, they were areas in a fault that contained the most slippage. The direction and manner in which a big quake ruptured across the fault greatly affected the intensity of the ground motion. The movement was never uniform or instantaneous.

The location and timing of the aftershocks showed, better than any other indicator, the true scope and breadth of the fault.

As he stared at these clusters, Atkins' uneasiness increased. It was the second fault connected to the New Madrid system to be discovered in less than four days. The first one had revealed itself after the magnitude 7.1 event and extended south of Memphis.

And now this.

Thompson's computerized images reemphasized for Atkins one of the major facts that distinguished the New Madrid zone from all others he'd studied: its incredible complexity.

"We're talking about a multiple event," Atkins said. "If you try to break it down, you've got a seven-foot deformation. My God, I don't think even Chile had anything like that." The 1960 quake, the largest one in modern times, registered a magnitude 8.6 on the Richter. "Then you've got the dip slip and strike slip subevents on two different fault segments, both previously unknown. And both of them connected to the major fault system. I've never encountered that before."

Thompson displayed an image that illustrated the kind of faults Atkins was talking about. Strike slip faults were primarily horizontal in their shearing movement. Dip slip faults moved down or upward. One of the images showed the distinctive horst and graben effect produced by the faulting process. A graben was a fault block that subsided or dropped down. A horst was one driven upward.

One detail continued to worry Atkins the most: the possibility that the big quakes were forming new faults deep in the earth or bringing old ones back to life.

"It's not just the complexity and enigma of the events that scares me," he said. "It's the way these new faults have opened up. If there's enough seismic energy left in the ground and one of them goes off, there's no telling how far the damage will spread." He reminded everyone of the duration of the 8.4 mainshock. "Over three minutes . . . I still have to take a deep swallow whenever I think about exactly how long that was."

Thompson showed another slide, a map of the two new

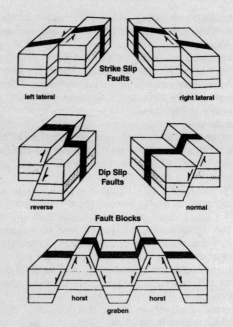

Types of Faults

faults that had appeared during the magnitude 7.1 and 8.4 earthquakes and several other major faults that extended across portions of the Mississippi Valley.

"Notice how the 8.4 fault line extends up to the Shawneetown–Rough Creek System," he said. The image showed how that fault, in turn, abutted two others—the Cottage Grove system, which cut across the bottom of southern Illinois, and the Wabash Valley Fault, running up along the Indiana–Illinois border. Branching off Cottage Grove was the long arm of the Ste. Genevieve Fault System, which started in eastern Missouri and followed the course of the Mississippi River down roughly to its juncture with the Ohio River.

"There it is, ladies and gentlemen," Thompson said, stepping back to look at the screen. "I hope that worries you half as much as it does me."

Stan Marshal immediately objected. "We don't have any physical evidence that these faults are connected," he said. "And we're in no position to suggest that an earthquake on one would trigger one on another. That's way too speculative."

"The real issue is how much crustal shear strain is left in the ground," said Mark Wren. "We don't have enough data yet to run those kinds of projections."

Wren seldom spoke at these sessions. He seemed like a competent geologist but was overly deferential to Weston, Atkins thought. He had to admit Wren was right. It all came back to getting more satellite readings to measure any new deformation.

Still, the data made him nervous. The new fault line was incredibly active.

Walt Jacobs had been largely silent up to then. It looked as if he hadn't changed his denim shirt in days. He was withdrawn, moody, which wasn't like him. Atkins was starting to worry about him. He knew Jacobs was sick with fear about his wife and daughter. He'd heard nothing from them since the quake, and he was still waiting for word from the two graduate students he'd sent to look for them.

"We need to consider the possibility we may be having a repetition of the 1811–1812 events," Jacobs said. He spoke slowly, deliberately, and immediately drew a sharp response from Weston.

"We don't have the data to support that even as a serious hypothesis," Weston said with a flash of anger. He was supported immediately by several other seismologists. They knew he was right, and all were uncomfortable with raising the specter of the big quakes from the last century. There were shouts that Jacobs was out of line.

Continuing as though unaware of the interruption, Jacobs said, "It all happened before—the sudden emergence of new faults, lingering, violent aftershocks, a huge deformation over a vast region. The complicated pattern of ruptures, main shocks, and after shocks. The same thing that's happening right now."

"The mainshock must have created the waterfall on the Mississippi," Holleran said.

"It's still there," Jacobs said. "We just downloaded some

aerial footage from one of the television networks. The scarp looks thirty feet high."

"It was closer to forty the night before last," Atkins said.

"It could be eroding," Jacobs said. "It happened in the 1811–1812 sequence." He turned on the lights and pulled down a wall map that showed the Mississippi River, twisting like a snake with a dark line drawn across it just below New Madrid, Missouri.

"That's where the waterfall was reported after the 1811–1812 earthquakes. You'll notice Caruthersville, where John and Elizabeth crossed the river. It's about fifty miles downstream, the place where the new fault breaks off into Tennessee. The waterfall in 1812 was created by a thrust fault. It was probably the greatest mid-plate thrust earthquake we've ever had—until the one yesterday."

Holleran had never been so tired in her life. And yet she found herself wide awake, totally focused on the discussion. "What if that magnitude 7.1 event we had a few days ago wasn't the first earthquake in the sequence?" she asked. "What if it was just a foreshock?"

Atkins remembered they'd argued over that very point when they were huddled in the Explorer near Blytheville. He wasn't about to argue with her this time. The GPS data had convinced him that what she was suggesting was a real possibility.

Jacobs had already considered it. "I don't think that's likely," he said, becoming more animated. "A magnitude 7.1 earthquake is one hell of a foreshock."

Unwilling to let go of the idea, Holleran said, "One of the toughest issues we deal with is trying to figure out if an earthquake is a foreshock or an aftershock. We don't really know for sure until you get a major earthquake. The magnitude 7.1 event, it seems to me, could easily have been a foreshock to the big quake we had yesterday. But say I'm wrong and you're right, Walt. It could mean we're in for one more big one instead of two. Either way, it's a disaster."

"I don't want any more talk about a triple," Weston said angrily. "You're both bordering on irresponsibility."

Again, there were loud murmurs of support. Most of the seismologists in the room, like Weston, were convinced that definitive data was still lacking, that it would be folly to try to predict another massive quake. Weston was voicing the majority opinion. He'd done so with increasing support since the crisis had started.

Holleran went on. "From what I've read, triples aren't all that unusual in intraplate settings like the one here. There were triples as recently as 1990 in the Sudan. The largest was a magnitude 7.3. The smallest a 6.7. They hit over a five-day period. In 1988, a rural area in Australia recorded three in the magnitude 6 range over a twelve-hour period."

"We'll have a panic on our hands if it leaks out we were even having this discussion," Weston said. "We don't need mass hysteria."

"I'd say we already have it," said Holleran. "How can we scare people any more than they already are?"

PRESIDENT NATHAN ROSS STARED AT HIMSELF IN the mirror in the closet-sized galley of Big Green, the VH-3D Sikorsky based at Camp David. He was a depressing sight. The dark puffy rings under his eyes had been there for days and seemed to get deeper with every additional hour he went without sleep.

He'd never liked his five-o'clock shadow. It was too heavy, too much like Richard Nixon's. And well into his second term, he sometimes thought he was almost as unpopular. His administration had been plagued by a series of domestic difficulties—worsening race relations, the increasing bipartisan sniping over affirmative action programs, yet another Medicare crisis, and the everpresent budget deficit. Very little of substance had been accomplished. Unable to find sound bites in the mire of such complex issues, the media had inevitably turned to his personal life. Much of the recent news coverage had dealt with the few women he'd invited to the White House for dinner or taken out for an evening to the National Gallery. A widower, he hadn't dated for years and suddenly found himself fair game for the tabloids.

The youngest governor in the history of Illinois, Ross was also the youngest president. He was fifty-two with two years to go in his second term. In some respects he'd been lucky, damn lucky. The economy had been robust for most of his presidency. There'd been no major international crises and his party still controlled Congress.

No major problems—until this one.

His national security adviser had called the disaster the gravest crisis the country had faced since the Civil War. Ross hadn't believed him. Not even when he sat in the NSC operations office in the basement of the East Wing and watched the early television reports from the cities hardest hit. Filmed at night, the footage mainly showed fires burning. After a while, it all looked the same. There was no perspective, no focus.

But after visiting these cities in daylight, Ross thought his adviser, a vituperative former marine, had nailed it with his Civil War analogy.

They'd made three stops the day before: Cincinnati, Louisville, and St. Louis. He'd spent a couple of hours on the ground in each city. The extent of the devastation had made him physically sick, in St. Louis especially. He'd been there several times on fund-raisers. The famous Gateway Arch, the monument to westward expansion that had towered 660 feet over the Mississippi River, was twisted sideways and leaned toward the river at a forty-five-degree angle. Three of the city's largest hospitals had been demolished. Forest Park and Tower Grove Park were being used as tent cities for the thousands who'd had to move out of their damaged homes.

Ross remembered the bodies they'd removed from one of the hospitals. More than two hundred of them lined up along a sidewalk under blankets, sheets, newspapers—any covering the rescuers could find. Again, he thought of the Civil War. A photograph of the dead piled up at Gettysburg, lying shoulder to shoulder in the grass, blue and gray alike. There was no way they could reach all of the dead, much less the injured.

The heart had been ripped out of the Mississippi Valley. Eleven major pipelines that carried oil and natural gas from the Texas and Oklahoma fields to the East Coast had been shattered. Nine of them crossed the Mississippi at Memphis or just south of it. Some of the pipes were still burning. The whole waterfront was on fire.

The East Coast and frigid New England had enough petroleum reserves to last barely a week. Temperatures were well below freezing. In a few days, millions of people were going to be hurting in ways that couldn't be imagined.

There were other problems, all of them grievous:

Grain shipments couldn't flow down the Mississippi. Fallen bridges had closed the river to barge traffic in eight places.

The financial and bond markets were a shambles. Wall Street had suspended trading indefinitely.

The insurance industry had been all but wiped out. There was no way they could cover all the losses from the earthquake and related damage. They'd started calling in their bonds, which of course wiped out the bond market, which in turn financially ruined hundreds of municipalities that depended on bonds to fund all manner of public works.

And yet all of these problems paled when Ross remembered those mangled bodies in St. Louis.

He wondered what it would be like in Memphis. He'd been told to prepare for the worst.

Ross splashed water on his face. He was a handsome man with light gray eyes, a strong jawline, and black hair graying at the temples. He was just over six feet tall, a little overweight, and prone to overeating. He'd swum thousands of laps in the White House pool to hold the line at a thirty-eight-inch waist. He had to admit, staring at himself one last time in the mirror, that he looked like hell.

In a couple of minutes the chopper would be putting down in Memphis. He wanted to meet with the USGS and university people there. He'd brought along his national science adviser, Steve Draper.

As Ross stepped out of the galley, he was confronted by his chief of security, Phil Belleau. Belleau had been with the Secret Service for twenty years. Ross liked to tell him he was the only man he'd ever met who didn't have a neck, absolutely didn't have one. The big head seemed to balance like a ball on his shoulders. He looked like an all-pro defensive back.

Belleau was angry. Ross knew why.

"Mister President, for the last time. We can't guarantee your safety. We've got ten men with you and another fifteen already on the ground. It's total chaos down there. Anybody could take a shot at you. There's no police force to speak of. No security. You were a fool the way you walked into those crowds in St. Louis."

Ross let him get it out of his system. He probably deserved it. And Belleau was about the only man he'd let talk to him that way.

"Better get used to it, Phil," Ross said when the agent had finished venting. "I . . . have . . . got . . . to . . . be . . . seen. These people have got to know they've still got a federal government to turn to. It's about all they do have right now."

Belleau, an emotional, spontaneous man, took a deep breath and exhaled slowly. He had to make him understand. "Mister President, a lot of people are damned mad," he said, softening his tone. "Out of their heads with anger. They've lost everything. Some have lost their families. A lot of them have lost homes, their businesses, jobs. Some of them are going to blame the government, blame you personally. Blame you for not giving them any warning. Blame you for not having enough emergency supplies ready or for not getting their homes rebuilt overnight. Blame you for whatever the fuck they can think of. Any one of them could try to kill you. So for the record, I'm asking you again to meet with the people you've got to meet with in Memphis. Do it in private, not out in the open. Then get the hell out. Memphis isn't a city anymore."

"I read you loud and clear, Phil," Ross said. He put a hand on the agent's shoulder. "Just do your best. And hell, you know anybody wants to shoot me, they ought to go for my ass. It's a bigger target."

Belleau grinned in spite of himself. "We better get belted in," he said, glancing at his watch. "We'll be landing in less than a minute."

The Sikorsky circled the University of Memphis campus, banking so the president could get a look at the damage. Hundreds of people were on the ground, digging through the rubble. He saw the rows of dead bodies lined up along a sidewalk and closed his eyes. It was St. Louis all over again.

Rage hammered at him, a blind rage directed against a natural force that he hated with every ounce of his being.

He knew it was a foolish, draining expenditure of emotion, but couldn't help himself. He needed to direct his anger at something, his sense of hopelessness.

Then, suddenly, they were on the ground. Ross zipped up the brown leather bomber jacket that bore the presidential seal and stepped into the cold air.

JOHN ATKINS AND ELIZABETH HOLLERAN WATCHED
the big helicopter slowly touch down, nose up, on the lawn
of the earthquake center. Every geologist there had gathered
along with a contingent of Memphis officials, including the
mayor, a short, middle-aged man in a mud-splattered overcoat, who looked completely devastated. A squad of National
Guard soldiers and Secret Service agents had fanned out
around the perimeter of the landing zone.

It was the first time Atkins had seen the president in person. He was a bigger man than he'd expected and looked
deadly serious as he stepped off the helicopter.

He recognized the president's national science adviser,
Steve Draper. He knew Draper, a physicist, by reputation—
a solid researcher, who'd written one of the definitive college
texts on physics. He'd hosted a well-received PBS documen-
tary on recent scientific breakthroughs.

Draper broke away from the presidential entourage and
approached Atkins and Elizabeth Holleran. He had longish
sandy hair and looked younger than his age. He was nearly
sixty and wore a thick parka with a hood.

"Are you John Atkins?" he asked.

Atkins nodded and introduced Holleran.

"Bob Holly at USGS said I should look you up when I
got here," Draper said. Holly was Atkins' boss, one of the
agency's top men.

Draper asked Atkins whether they could talk privately for

a few moments. He led him to the side of the library annex. He looked and sounded impatient.

"Just how bad is it?"

Atkins had anticipated the question as soon as he saw Draper start to head in his direction. He'd thought about how he should answer. In a matter-of-fact voice that surprised him, he heard himself say, "We could be heading for another big quake."

Draper looked at him hard. "You're willing to say that for the record?"

Atkins nodded. "At the very least, we've got to consider it as a possibility and run some scenarios." He quickly briefed Draper on the new fault that had appeared in western Tennessee and Kentucky and the unusually strong aftershocks they were experiencing. "The way these new faults have opened up worries the hell out of me," he said. "There's got to be a lot of energy piled up down there."

"Good Lord," Draper said slowly, trying to comprehend what he'd just been told. It was much worse than he'd imagined. "Would you tell that to the president?"

"Yes," Atkins said, knowing what he was doing, what he was risking.

Draper, understanding, squeezed Atkins by both shoulders. Then he walked off quickly, clutching a battered leather briefcase as he hurried after Nathan Ross.

Atkins explained to Holleran what had happened.

"I'll support you," she said. She'd guessed what they'd been talking about and had noticed at one point in the brief conversation how Draper's face had suddenly tightened. She knew what had happened: he'd just been told what they were up against.

"Thanks, but no sense both of us sticking our necks out," Atkins said, smiling gratefully. "Let's just see how it goes."

They joined the other scientists in the annex library. There were no preliminaries. Everyone was seated around tables that had been shoved together to form a U. The president sat near the front. Someone had given him a paper cup with steaming coffee.

Atkins got his first up-close look at Nathan Ross. The man's eyes were red, dark-rimmed, the cheeks sallow. He was slumped back, holding the cup with both hands. He appeared utterly exhausted.

Paul Weston summarized what they knew—and what they didn't. "We still need to gather a lot more data," he said, concluding his brief presentation.

The president, who'd listened quietly, asked a single question. "Do you think we're going to have another major earthquake down here any time soon?"

Taken aback by the president's bluntness, Weston stammered, "That's hard to say, Mister President. "We're only starting to get—"

Ross impatiently raised a hand to cut him off. "I want your personal opinion, doctor. Your best guess as an expert. What do you think's going to happen on the New Madrid Seismic Zone?"

Weston tried to hedge, but again Ross pressed him hard for his opinion. He was insistent and totally focused. Cornered, Weston finally said, "Mister President, I'm sorry. I can't answer that. I don't want to guess or speculate on something like this. I want to deal with facts, and we just don't have enough of them to answer your question."

When the president pressed them for their views, most of the other seismologists agreed with Weston's assessment. They were professionally loath to make any predictions. Several bluntly told the president it would be unethical for them to try to do so. Like Weston, they insisted they needed more data.

Weston's assistant, Stan Marshal, spoke about the need to set up more seismic instruments along the fault that had been discovered near Caruthersville, Missouri.

Atkins noticed how the big man glanced at Weston as if looking for guidance.

As he had with Weston, Ross interrupted Marshal in midsentence. "Let me ask you the same question I just put to Doctor Weston. Do you think we're going to have another earthquake?"

Marshal shook his head. "I don't know, sir."

"I didn't ask what you know, doctor," Ross snapped. He had a sharp, lashing voice and looked increasingly angry. "I asked you what you think, your opinion. There's a difference."

Marshal didn't respond. He sat back in his chair and shook his head.

Atkins was struck again by how physically exhausted Ross looked. Only the eyes showed any life. They were animated, boring, intense.

The president slowly surveyed the faces of those seated around him. "We've had one magnitude 8.4 earthquake and the ground, forgive me in this shrine to Elvis, keeps rocking and rolling. I've been informed about the three big quakes that occurred early in the last century. Does anyone here think we're in for a repeat performance? Yes or no? I'll settle for your best guess, anything."

No one raised a hand. Atkins wasn't surprised. He understood that Weston wasn't being an obstructionist on this issue. He was merely voicing the real concerns of the scientific majority. Offering an opinion that proved wrong in such dire circumstances would be a professional death sentence. You simply didn't risk such a thing without a lot of careful thought and soul searching. But there was no time for any of that. The president wanted an answer. Now.

Ross crumpled his empty coffee cup and angrily threw it against the wall. "You're the goddamned experts. You're supposed to weigh the pros and cons and offer an opinion. I need some kind of prediction, and if you don't like that word, call it a risk assessment. The people who live here need it, deserve it. Is that too much to ask? Are we going to have another major earthquake?"

Draper spoke up. He was standing behind the president taking detailed notes.

"Doctor Atkins, what do you think?"

It had been much easier to offer an opinion outside. Atkins decided to keep it short and simple. "From the data I've seen, the way the fault keeps expanding, yes, I think we've got to consider the likelihood of another high-magnitude earthquake. It would be negligence on our part not to."

Ross shot a glance at Steve Draper. Staring straight at Atkins, the president said, "Do you think another major quake is likely?"

"I think we should assume so and try to prepare accordingly," Atkins said. "My personal opinion is that the chances of a big quake sometime soon are a little better than fifty percent. And that's just an opinion."

Weston and several other seismologists in the overheated room spoke up at once, objecting. As sweat rolled down his cheeks and soaked his shirt, Atkins knew what was happening. Now that he'd stuck his neck out, his esteemed colleagues were going to chop it off.

"I've got to disagree with Doctor Atkins," Weston said coolly. "I've seen nothing in the data we've been able to collect that shows conclusively another 8.4 event is likely. The issue of how much strain energy remains locked in the ground after an earthquake is fraught with difficulties of interpretation. No adequate measurement tool exists. We can check for strain in any number of ways. We can measure dilatancy, the degree of cracking, uplift. We're trying to get some of that information by satellite. But the problem is you could get seismic measurements right now along certain gaps or segments of the San Andreas Fault that would indicate a big quake is imminent. There's plenty of deformation, plenty of seismic energy in the ground, but nothing's happening there. Everything's been quiet for over a century. Mr. President, the truth is we don't know what's going to happen here. If we issue a public statement suggesting we think another major quake is likely, it's my opinion we'd be criminally responsible for the panic it would cause."

"I second that," said one of the USGS geologists, who was quickly supported by Stan Marshal.

The president asked for a show of hands. Seven of the ten in attendance voted with Weston. Three highly respected USGS scientists were among the group.

With Atkins were Holleran and Walt Jacobs.

"I'd be more inclined to agree with Doctor Weston if it weren't for the power of the aftershocks we've been experiencing and their locations," Holleran said. "I'm not aware of anything comparable to what's happening here. Certainly nothing in my experience in California. We know big earthquakes kick up lots of aftershocks, but nothing like this."

"Not to mention the existence of two new fault planes," Jacobs said. "Both of them are larger than any other known segment in the New Madrid Seismic Zone. And we've also got the history, which you've already alluded to, Mister President.''

"The history is meaningless," Weston said. "All we know is that within the last two hundred years three powerful earthquakes occurred in sequence. We know nothing about the previous seismic record."

"Is there any way we could find that out?" Ross asked.

Holleran said, "We could dig for it, Mister President." She explained how they could do trenching to search for the geological record of previous earthquakes. Their imprint would be left in the layered subsoil. It was just a matter of finding the right location and going deep enough.

Ross was intrigued and asked how it could be done.

"I'd dig a trench along one of the fault segments and see if we could find any evidence of old earthquakes—things like sand blows, fissure scars. Then I'd try to find something we could radiocarbon date—peat, carbonized wood."

Weston shook his head. "That would be a costly diversion. It would take weeks to dig a trench even if we could find a suitable site and get backhoes out to it. Then more weeks to analyze the data. We don't have the time or equipment to go on an archaeological fishing expedition."

"It seems to me what we need more than anything right now is additional seismic data," Draper said. "You've said as much yourself, Doctor Weston."

Atkins had a suggestion, breaking the tense silence. "We could do some bore shaft explosions and tamping along that new fault." He explained how they could capture computer-enhanced "images" of the fault by using sound waves generated by dynamite charges. Another technique was to use gas-powered tampers that resembled jackhammers. The results provided a seismic CAT scan. They used a sonogram technique, whereby the explosions produced sound waves harvested by special receivers. Low wave speeds indicated the presence of a fault and serious fracturing of the adjoining rock. These cracks, in turn, were evidence of strain building up. All of this could be transformed into two-dimensional computer images.

It would give them a better idea of what they were dealing with—the shape and structure of the fault and how deep it extended. Atkins especially wanted to look at the place where the newly discovered Caruthersville Fault intersected with the New Madrid Seismic Zone. It was certain to be an area of severe stress.

Jacobs and some of the other seismologists liked the idea. "So tell me what I can do to help," the president asked. "Get us a helicopter," Atkins said.

MARSHAL WAITED UNTIL HE COULD APPROACH WES-
ton alone in the library annex, then quietly suggested they
take a short walk outside. The president's helicopter had just
taken off. When Weston started to object, Marshal took him
by the elbow and firmly led him toward a door.

"We've got a problem," he said when they were outside.
He looked and sounded nervous. He handed a white envelope
to Weston. They'd gone behind the annex building, where
they could talk without being overheard.

Weston opened the envelope, which contained four
photographs.

"Who gave you these?" he gasped.

"One of the construction people up at the dam," Marshal
said. "You know him. Jensen. He's lucky he's alive. He got
out about an hour before it washed out. Wanted to let us
know about this. Of course, he also wants to be paid."

"How did he get here?" Weston was still staring at the
photographs. The quality was grainy, but the images were
remarkably clear.

"Hitched a ride in an Army helicopter from Fort Campbell," Marshal said. "A squad was sent down to provide
security for the president. He pulled some strings and got
aboard. Said he had some important information about the
earthquake."

The photographs that Weston was studying so intently
showed John Atkins and Elizabeth Holleran inside the dam

at Kentucky Lake. A security camera had taken the pictures when they were on one of the catwalks.

"They know all about those cracks," Marshal said, angrily. He caught himself and lowered his voice. "They were snooping around in there after you had that meeting with all those people in Mayfield. The one where you said the cracks weren't serious."

A big man in a bulky, down-insulated overcoat, he towered over Weston. "What are we going to do?" he asked.

"Absolutely nothing," Weston said. "In case you forgot, the dam was destroyed in the quake. They can't prove anything."

"They can start asking questions," Marshal said, becoming agitated.

"Calm down and forget this," Weston said, carefully putting the photographs back in the envelope and placing it in his jacket pocket.

"No fucking way," Marshal snapped. "How many people died when that damn broke? A thousand? Two thousand?"

"Keep . . . your . . . voice . . . down," Weston said. "You need to get a grip on yourself. We're not to blame for what happened at the dam."

"We've got to do something," Marshal said, taking Weston by the arm again.

Weston pulled away, squaring back his shoulders. He quickly looked around to see if anyone was watching.

"We'll discuss this later," he hissed, turning away and striding back toward the building. "Meanwhile, doctor, you're going to do what you're told."

FRED BOOKER BOARDED THE SMALL, SINGLE ENGINE plane early in the morning. He'd been told the air was calmer at that time of day. That was important because for the first time in his life he was going to jump out of an airplane. He didn't want to fight a strong wind, which might blow him off course.

It was going to be difficult enough landing near the University of Memphis. News reports said many parts of the city were still burning. Booker didn't want to get caught in the updraft from the fires—or drift down into them.

That's why he'd paid strict attention when his good friend from the ORNL, a former Army paratrooper, had explained how to operate a parachute. The day before, the friend had outfitted Booker with a brand-new parafoil chute. "You want to go left, pull on the left cords," the friend told him. "You want to go right, pull on the right side. You want to drop straight, let up on the cords and just hang on. When you land, loosen up; take the jolt in your legs, keep them bent. You'll hit nice and easy. Just like jumping off a ten-foot wall. No problem."

No problem for a forty- or even a fifty-year-old, Booker remembered thinking. He was nearly seventy with a bum left knee that needed cartilage surgery.

The pilot looked like the recently retired air force major he was—lean, tanned, and wearing dark green aviator sunglasses. When he found out why Booker wanted to go to Memphis, he'd agreed to take him for free.

"You sure you want to do this?" he asked.

Booker nodded. He wanted to talk to some of the geologists in Memphis and explain his idea for using a nuclear explosion to try to turn off the cycle of earthquakes. The aftershocks, which had shown no evidence of slackening, were killers. His friends, the two geophysicists from the Shock Wave Lab, thought he was crazy, but had written him letters of introduction addressed to Walter Jacobs.

The flight west to Memphis was short, less than two hours in a small plane. The pilot had to keep changing altitude because of all the emergency air traffic.

"The hell of it is they can't land there," he explained. "The airport's closed. All the navigationals were knocked out. Radar, light beacons, everything. The whole damn control tower went down."

"So where's everybody going?" Booker said. They'd just dropped from ten thousand to eight thousand feet to make way for a C-140 military cargo plane. The huge gray jet seemed to move in slow motion yet rapidly pulled away from the Cessna.

"They're using Interstate 55 just north of Memphis on the Arkansas side of the river. Highway over there's in pretty good shape. They're flying in relief supplies. Cargo planes are stacked up all across the country, waiting to get in. That stretch of highway is the only place within four hundred miles where they can land. The airport in St. Louis is out of commission; so are the ones in Little Rock and Louisville."

The time to jump came with dramatic suddenness.

"There's Memphis and look at her burn!" the pilot said. "I don't believe it."

Booker saw the smoke long before he saw the flames, so much smoke it was almost impossible to pick out any landmarks.

The pilot dropped lower. He found an opening in the clouds of smoke and thought they were over the eastern part of the city. "This is as good as it's gonna get," he shouted to Booker, who'd worked up the nerve to move to the open doorway. "You ready?"

Booker nodded. He was holding tightly to the doorframe, then he let go and leaned forward, closing his eyes as he fell into space. The wind slashed at his face and howled in

his ears. It was incredibly loud and pulled at his trousers so
hard he thought he was going to lose them.

Pull the ring, he told himself. Pull the ring.

Groping, eyes still closed, he clenched the metal ring and
gave it a strong downward tug just as he'd been instructed.

He immediately shot upward, a bone-jarring ascent, and
felt his bladder start to go. He was falling more slowly now,
swaying in his harness. He opened his eyes and stared up at
the parafoil, a brilliant yellow rectangular canopy. It was
swept back slightly along its rear edge. The puffed-out rip-
stop fabric, all that was holding him up, was much smaller
than he would have thought.

Booker took a breath and looked down. The ground was
coming up quickly. He pulled on the right cords and immediately moved right, away from a cloud of thick smoke. He
was relieved to see how easily he could steer. He pulled on
the left cords and veered in that direction.

Beautiful.

Now where the hell was he?

It looked like a residential district. Through the drifting
smoke he could make out the damage; many of the buildings
were down. He figured he was about a thousand feet up. He
twisted slightly in the harness, trying to pick out the university. It was impossible.

The wind was screaming in his ears, and he was coming
down a lot faster than he imagined.

He saw specks moving on the ground, clusters of people.
He was too high to make out faces. He steered straight for
them, figuring it would be a good idea to have someone
around in case he botched the landing and got hurt. A lot of
telephone and electrical lines were down there. He hadn't
thought about that.

He tugged on the right cords and heard a popping sound;
it was distant, yet distinctive. He heard it again, more clearly
this time, a series of sharp cracks. It sounded like firecrackers
going off.

They were shooting at him!

He saw three or four men with raised guns; he could see
the muzzle flashes.

Booker pulled hard on the left cords; his whole body tilted
in that direction. About seven hundred feet in the air, he

pulled away from the shooters, moving out of range. He eased up on his grip and straightened out his course again. The ground was very close.

He tried to remember what the instructor had told him about landing. Take the shock in the legs.

He glimpsed the river behind him; that meant he was facing east. Good. At least he was going in the right direction.

Power lines and trees were coming up. He was going to land in someone's backyard. Or in a tree. Some people were running in his direction, pointing up at him, shouting. He wasn't sure if they were the shooters. But he wasn't going to stick around and find out.

Booker tugged hard on the cords with his right hand, moving away from a tall tree. He was drifting through the air sideways, his body almost horizontal to the ground. A sudden gust of wind blew him up about a hundred feet. He looked down again and found himself over a large park. He saw an opening in the trees and pulled left, steering for it. He tried to prepare for the impact and then he hit. His legs bucked and he pitched forward on his stomach. The chute, still open, dragged him along the grass before he remembered to tug the harness release.

He rolled over several times and lay on his back. He stared up at a blue sky streaked with dirty trails of smoke. He tested his arms and legs. Everything moved and seemed to work. He got his bearings and started walking east, toward the university.

WITHIN THIRTY MINUTES OF THE PRESIDENT'S DEPAR-
ture, an Army UH-60 helicopter from Fort Campbell, Kentucky, landed at the University of Memphis' earthquake center. The president had personally ordered the aircraft diverted
from rescue operations. The seismologists could use it as
long as necessary.

The first order of business was to try to get a better "picture" of the new fault. Their initial data showed it started
just north of Caruthersville, Missouri, crossed the Mississippi
and a sliver of Tennessee, and extended about 150 miles
into Kentucky.

Atkins and Jacobs were particularly interested in the area
in extreme southwestern Kentucky and northwestern Tennessee where that fault intersected with one of the major segments of the New Madrid Seismic Zone. Due west of
Kentucky Lake and the town of Mayfield, it was familiar
ground for Atkins and Elizabeth Holleran.

A five-member team flew up there—Atkins, Elizabeth,
Walt Jacobs, and two of Weston's geologists—Stan Marshal
and Mark Wren.

They'd brought two hundred pounds of water-gel explosives packed in plastic sticks. The electric blasting caps that
detonated the charge were connected to a specially designed
condenser. The explosion was set off by radio wave, using
a 1,000-volt remote-control blasting machine.

They also had half a dozen portable seismographs and
geophones, which would record the ground vibrations and

convert them into electrical signals that could be captured on magnetic tape. The seismographs would measure the waves as they moved through the deep earth. Faults and other irregularities would cause the signals to slow down or speed up. This so-called "reflection" technique had been used since the 1920s to detect buried oil and gas formations.

The other equipment consisted of two German-made "vibrators," big gas-powered devices that looked like jackhammers. The machines rapidly pounded a flat metal plate against the ground, producing seismic waves. The seismographs and geophones recorded them.

The idea was to use the varying wave patterns to map out, much like a CAT scan, what the fault looked like and how much fracturing of the rock had taken place. The data would project the fault's length and breadth and help them determine how much strain energy remained in the ground; heavy fracturing and the degree to which the fractures had opened were dead giveaways that rocks were under severe strain.

The three-man Army crew, all heavily armed, served as a security detail.

When Atkins asked about the need for this, the pilot told them it was too dangerous to travel unarmed. "There's been a lot of looting," he said. "It's going to take a while before we get things under control."

There were also reports of wild dogs roaming the countryside in packs, he said.

Elizabeth felt a twinge of anxiety, remembering how close she'd come to being mauled in that creek bed near Blytheville, Arkansas. Like Atkins, she wished they had time to investigate whether the animals were reacting to something they detected in the ground. She wondered if the continued aftershocks had anything to do with their behavior.

Or did they sense another big quake was coming?

She put that troubling thought out of mind as the chopper flew right over Kentucky Lake. The water level had dropped a good thirty to forty feet, but water was still rushing through the smashed dam into the swollen Tennessee River.

It was her first good look at the dam since the earthquake. She couldn't believe how totally it had given away. The huge structure—gates, concrete walls, power station—had vanished. Only the twisted remains of the boat lock remained.

She stared at the gray water, remembering how she'd almost drowned down there. The surface was still choppy with whitecaps. They were flying across the lake from east to west, against a strong wind.

Elizabeth figured something more than the wind was responsible for all that boiling water below them. The turbulence extended as far down the wide lake as she could see.

Atkins knew what she was thinking.

"The ground is still incredibly active," he said. "The lake hasn't had time to settle down."

THE first stop was near Dexter, Kentucky, about forty miles west of the lake. Atkins remembered the countryside well. It was close to the coal mine he and Jacobs had descended to get seismic readings the morning before the earthquake.

How long ago had that been? Three days? Four? He'd lost count.

Working in teams, they operated the vibrators, moving them back and forth over sweep zones a hundred yards wide. They took readings at several sites. It was a cool day with the temperature in the mid-forties, but after ten minutes of trying to hang on to the bulky machines, Atkins and Jacobs were breathing heavily. The instrument packs they carried on their backs felt like they were filled with bricks. It was hard to take the pounding as the flat metal plate at the end of the vibrator, moving in a blur, struck the ground repeatedly. Every muscle began to ache—bones, jaws, teeth.

Elizabeth monitored the seismographs and geophones. The readings were clean and clear. After several hours, they flew to another site closer to the point where the new fault intersected with the old one in the extreme northwestern corner of Tennessee about 120 miles from Memphis.

The procedure was simple and not unduly hazardous. Using a posthole digger, they dug holes six feet deep and placed the sticks of explosive in them. The water-gel charge was as powerful as dynamite but much safer to handle.

The charge was detonated by remote control from a distance of several hundred yards. The explosions, which blasted clumps of dirt and mud a hundred feet into the air, also sent seismic waves radiating deep into the earth just like a miniature earthquake. Traveling tens of miles, these waves were recorded on seismographs placed near the blast site. The array of geophones picked up the sound waves.

They took turns, setting the explosive charges and detonating them. By three in the afternoon the sun was already low in the sky. The pilot was under strict orders from his base commander to be back in Memphis before nightfall. Too many people were shooting at aircraft in the dark. It had become a popular post-earthquake pastime. Several planes had been hit by automatic rifle fire in rural Tennessee and Kentucky.

Before they had to leave, there was time for one more test shot. It was Atkins and Elizabeth's turn to place the charge. Jacobs helped.

As the helicopter crew watched from the safe distance, Elizabeth lowered the explosive charge gently into the hole they'd dug. She'd already wired the electric blasting cap to the condenser, which was attached to the stick of water gel. By adjusting a dial, Atkins set the condensing device to receive the radio frequency that would detonate the explosives.

As they started back from the hole, Atkins saw Wren frantically waving at them. About a hundred yards away, he was shouting something and motioning with his hands, holding them palms down.

"Hit the dirt!" Jacobs yelled, instinctively realizing something had gone wrong.

Atkins threw himself into Elizabeth, pushing her down just as the ground erupted behind them. The concussion knocked them breathless. Clods of dirt and mud rained down on them.

Still gasping for air, Atkins staggered to his feet.

Wren ran out to meet him. "It was an accident," he shouted. "Are you all right?"

"What happened?" Atkins said. He was furious.

"Something must have gone wrong with the blasting machine," Wren said. "The ready-to-fire light blinked on. That's when I started shouting to you. Then the charge went off. It just happened."

Just happened?

Atkins didn't believe it for a minute. The blasting machine wouldn't send out a radio signal unless the red "fire" switch was deliberately pressed. The machine required a precise series of steps to detonate a charge. First you had to press a green "charge" switch and hold it down until the meter showed the device was fully deflected to 1,000 volts. Then, while continuing to hold down the "charge" switch, you pressed the red "fire" switch. It was definitely a two-hand procedure, not easy to make a mistake.

Atkins shouted for Marshal, who hadn't moved from his position by the blaster.

"Why did you push the firing switch?" Atkins yelled. "You could see we weren't clear of the blast site."

"I didn't touch it," Marshal said. "It was your job to set the frequency on the condenser. You must have screwed up."

Marshal was almost a head taller than Atkins and heavier through the shoulders and chest. Moving straight at him, Atkins ducked under a right upper cut and hit him in the chest. He hit him twice in the face, but Marshal didn't go down. He fought back, throwing hard punches that Atkins deflected.

Jacobs and the soldiers ran over and separated them.

"You stupid sonofabitch!" Atkins shouted. "You could have killed us."

Marshal, bleeding from the nose, roughly pulled away from two soldiers who were trying to hold him.

"I'll sue your ass for slander you keep that up. You were careless. That's all."

Atkins lunged for Marshal again and had to be held back.

When Atkins had calmed down, the pilot took him aside. "I don't much like that bastard any more than you do. I don't know what happened," he said. "Or who's to blame. And I don't much care. We've got to get back to Memphis. I don't want to be flying in the dark and get my ass shot out of the sky by some hillbilly who's pissed because he lost his cabin in the earthquake."

BOOKER REACHED THE UNIVERSITY EARLY IN THE
afternoon. He'd come with a companion, a small gray monkey that had started following him soon after he'd landed in
Overton Park. Booker knew the Memphis Zoo was located
there and figured the animal must have escaped from its cage
during the earthquake. The monkey was shivering in the cold
and Booker had given him one of the apples he'd brought
with him. From that moment, the monkey stayed about ten
feet behind Booker at all times and had trailed him to the
university.

It took him a while to locate the earthquake center. The
campus was a mess. The damage was worse than anything
he'd seen at Oak Ridge, which was bad enough. The front
of the new library had fallen off. Buildings were down wher-
ever he looked, and even though it was cool, he smelled the
sickly sweet odor of bodies that hadn't been pulled from the
wreckage and were starting to decay. If they didn't take care
of that soon, he knew they were going to have an epidemic
on their hands.

When Booker finally found the earthquake center, he was
told Walt Jacobs was in the field running tests and wouldn't
be back until later that evening. An armed guard also told
him all the other seismologists were too busy to talk to him
and denied him entrance to the building.

Booker showed the guard his ID from the Oak Ridge National Laboratory. "I jumped out of a goddamned airplane

to get here," he said angrily. "You've got to let me in there to talk to someone."

The Army corporal shook his head. "Sorry, sir. I can't do that."

One of the seismologists stepped outside to smoke a cigarette. In an instant, the monkey shot from behind Booker and scurried through the open door. Feeling the annex's warm air, it was trying to get out of the cold.

"Dammit," the guard said, turning to give chase.

Booker entered the building right on the soldier's heels. He was still wearing his bright-red jumpsuit and boots. He carried a small backpack. A pair of goggles were suspended from his neck. He made quite an impression.

As it ran about the library annex, the monkey kept up a frantic ear-splitting screech.

Steve Draper, the president's science adviser, stepped into the hallway to see what was the matter. He'd stayed behind to monitor the situation after the president left.

"I want to talk to someone about the aftershocks," Booker said, walking right up to him. He didn't recognize Draper and assumed he was one of the seismologists. "Promise me, you'll just hear me out." He quickly explained who he was and why he was there.

"I've brought some notes," he said, rushing along with his description. "I'm fairly sure the best depth would be at a minimum of two thousand feet. The deeper the better. I did a little research before I left. I've been playing with a graph that plots the magnitude of an earthquake with energy released in ergs. The energy released by a magnitude 5.5 quake has an energy equivalent of about 10 ergs to the twentieth power. A nuclear bomb, a small one, say 2 or 3 kilotons, would release about the same amount of energy. The trick here will be to release enough energy along the fault so you get a modest earthquake. But not enough to set off a big one. I can make that happen. The geologists need to tell me how big a bomb is required to do the job and where to place it. That should be pretty straightforward number crunching. I'd do it myself, but I'm getting a little rusty."

Draper stared at him. He didn't say a word.

EVERYONE IN THE EARTHQUAKE CENTER WAITED NER-
vously for Guy Thompson to begin. He and his small team
of computer imagers had worked hours analyzing the seismic
wave data generated by the many aftershocks as well as
by the vibration and explosion tests Walt Jacobs' team had
carried out.

Weston, as usual, sat with Marshal and Wren. They were
armed with stacks of technical papers on the New Madrid
Seismic Zone.

Atkins had taken a seat as far as possible from Marshal.
He still didn't know what to make of that screwup with the
explosives. It seemed impossible that Marshal could have
accidentally fired the blasting machine. But he didn't like
thinking about the only other option. Until he had time to
sort it out, he resolved to keep a close watch on Marshal.

Thompson, CD headphones draped around his neck, asked
for the lights to be dimmed. He wore a pair of beautifully
stitched blue and black cowboy boots and a green Western
shirt with a white yoke. He'd let his raven hair hang down
to his shoulders.

His first image was a two-dimensional view of what everyone was calling the Caruthersville Fault where it intersected
with a previously known segment of the New Madrid Seismic Zone.

The fault appeared on the screen as if suspended on the
grid—beautiful computer graphics.

The rupture was thirty kilometers deep and extended on a

northeasterly line into western Kentucky. It started roughly at Caruthersville, ran across the western edge of Tennessee and up into Kentucky. The fault line ended near Elizabethtown, about thirty miles from Louisville. Lexington was sixty miles away; Cincinnati, 105.

"The total length appears to be about 180 miles," Thompson said.

Atkins glanced at Elizabeth. That was longer than the original estimate.

When combined with the New Madrid Seismic Zone, the combined fault system reached into six states.

"This is huge," Thompson observed. "Nothing in North America compares. Not San Andreas. Nothing. The seismic data from other stations in the upper Mississippi Valley indicate aftershock activity on almost every segment of the New Madrid system. Most of it remains concentrated along the Caruthersville Fault."

A pall of silence followed. The scientists in the room were tired, wrung out. They'd been working for days in a city devastated by the earthquake, where the damage was all around them. Where dead bodies still lay in the streets. They were emotionally drained. It was hard for them to summon up the energy to respond to Thompson's chilling data.

Atkins thought it might be among the largest intraplate fault systems in the world. Several in Asia were longer. He never would have considered anything like this possible in the continental United States. And all those fault lines were quivering with seismic energy.

It got worse.

Thompson's next image was another two-dimensional close-up of the Caruthersville Fault, the point where it intersected with one of the older New Madrid segments. Radiating from both lines were literally hundreds of smaller ones, so many they looked like veins connected to major arteries.

"Those are stress fractures," Thompson said. "In some places, they extend twenty miles or more. I've never seen such clear delineations. The seismic waves produced by the explosions slowed dramatically every time they hit one of these fractures."

Another image, one of the most dramatic of all, showed a series of sharp peaks that rose up like a mountain chain

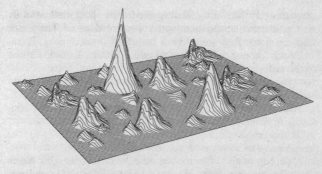

**Cumulative Aftershock Activity in a Twenty-Square-Mile Area
Near Mayfield, Kentucky**

from the new fault zone. The peaks illustrated cumulative
aftershock activity in that area. Each of the taller peaks represented a minimum of twenty aftershocks that had occurred
in roughly the same twenty-square-mile area. The proportional ratio was less for the smaller peaks.

As she listened, an oppressive gloom settled over Elizabeth. The complex network of faults and fractures indicated
a large amount of strain energy was still in the ground.

"Can you tell us, estimate, how much energy's been released?" she asked.

Thompson had been waiting for that question. He knew
the answer was going to hit hard.

"Our analysis suggests the release of slightly less than 10
ergs of energy to the twenty-fourth power." An erg was a
standard unit of energy.

"Impossible!" Weston exploded.

It meant the 8.4 event had released about as much energy
as the daily consumption rate for the entire United States or
about as much as the stupendous volcanic eruption at Kraka-
tau in 1883, which darkened the earth's atmosphere for years
with ash and dirt. Only the 1960 Chilean earthquake, a magnitude 8.6, had released more energy, but its range was much
smaller. Several hundred miles compared with more than a
thousand for New Madrid's 8.4.

Thompson put it in perspective with another image he

projected on the wall. "If the amount of energy released in a magnitude 3 earthquake were represented as a marble, the quake we just had would be a hot air balloon."

"And the ground's still shaking," Elizabeth said, almost to herself. It was hard to understand how any energy could remain after such a massive earthquake and the chain of strong aftershocks.

Walt Jacobs pulled down a wall chart he'd used for lectures. It described, step by step, the chronology of the three great quakes of 1811–1812.

Atkins was distressed to see how much his friend had slipped physically. He looked like he'd lost weight, especially in his thin face. He hadn't shaved for days, and the beard and dark, sunken eyes gave him a wild, unkempt look. He seemed to be moving in a fog. Just before the meeting, Atkins had found him sitting at a desk, staring into space. He asked whether he'd heard from his wife. Jacobs shook his head. He looked scared. Atkins knew he'd been waiting to hear. There was still no word.

"The first event, the one of December 16, 1811, was conservatively estimated to be in the magnitude 8.1 to 8.3 range," Jacobs said. As soon as he began to talk, the fatigue seemed to fall off him. He was animated, well spoken. "We've estimated that single quake and related aftershocks released only half of the strain energy stored in the fault zone. Only half, ladies and gentlemen."

Elizabeth whispered to Atkins, "I don't know if I want to hear the rest of this."

"Then the second big quake hit on January 23, 1812," Jacobs continued. "Research indicates it was another magnitude 8-plus event. Like the first one, the shock waves were felt from the Rockies to the East Coast. We believe it released about sixteen percent of the available strain energy."

So there was still a ton left in the ground, Atkins thought. It was almost unbelievable.

"Again, there was another flurry of severe aftershocks," Jacobs said. "Then another big one hit. The last in the sequence. It struck at 3:45 on the morning of February 7. A dip slip rupture that radiated over the entire Reelfoot Rift. It's been variously estimated as high as a magnitude 8.6 and as low as an 8.1."

Jacobs looked out at the assembled faces. They were hanging on his every word. "The only point I'm trying to make is that plenty of seismic energy remained locked in the ground after the first quake in the sequence."

Weston stood, shaking his head. "That's very interesting, Walt. But the fact that we've got a lot of elastic strain energy stored in the ground isn't proof we're going to have another magnitude 8 earthquake. And that's what you're suggesting. Statistically, it's a virtual impossibility. For all we know, there are structural barriers that will halt the progression no matter how much strain energy remains. There are too many variables. Too many unknowns. I'm not going to approve any public statement to the contrary."

"You don't think we should even warn people of the possibility of another major earthquake?" Atkins asked. They'd had this argument a few days earlier, without result.

"That wouldn't be responsible," Weston said. He wasn't alone in his opinion. Other seismologists, including several prominent members of the USGS, supported him loudly. The atmosphere was tense as Weston argued for restraint.

"But Goddammit, you're not answering the question. Give me a yes or no answer here, Paul."

Steve Draper, who'd sat in the back of the room, taking copious notes, suggested they temporarily adjourn the meeting.

"Why don't we all get something to eat. Try to rest, then get back here in, say, one hour. We'll go over the numbers again. And our options—if we have any. The president's eager to get your thinking on further seismic activity." He studiously avoided the word "prediction."

Draper took Atkins and Elizabeth aside. "I'd like you to meet someone. He's got some thoughts on the situation. You might find them provocative."

He led them to a small conference room in the back of the building. "Atkins, Elizabeth, this is Fred Booker," Draper said.

LAUREN MITCHELL WAS WORRIED. HER GRANDSON had been gone nearly five hours. He'd left with the shotgun to go hunting. They needed meat, and the boy was a good shot. He'd often killed rabbits and squirrels for the table. The year before, he'd shot his first deer, a two-point buck.

Lauren had made him promise to stay away from any roads. If he heard any cars or trucks coming, she told him to take cover. The roads weren't safe. Too many bushwhackers were traveling the countryside. In the quake zone, law enforcement had become largely a personal matter. Residents had been urged to do whatever they thought necessary to protect themselves and their property.

Almost as troubling were the reports of unusual animal behavior—stories about wild dogs, cattle, and horses that had gone out of their heads. Lauren still remembered her great-grandfather telling her about the New Madrid quake of 1895. How two days before it hit, all the chickens and dairy cattle on their farm had become frantic. A big Rhode Island red that had never shown any hostility had suddenly attacked him in the hen shed, slashing him with a talon. She remembered how he'd rolled up his shirtsleeve to show her the white scar that ran from his elbow to his wrist.

Lauren thought about that story and about what could happen to Bobby. She was angry with herself for letting him go out alone. They had enough food to last for several more weeks. She never should have let him talk her into going hunting by himself.

She was getting ready to put on a coat and go looking for him when she heard him shouting.

He was running through corn stubble in the field behind their house. He was panting, his breath forming white clouds as he jogged up a low hill. Three large rabbits dangled from his belt. He wore a blue stocking cap and carried the .410 shotgun.

When she stepped out on the back porch, he waved and shouted: "It's like . . . a . . . canyon!"

Struggling to get the words out, he doubled over at the waist and tried to fill his lungs. He dropped his shotgun and the rabbits.

"It's down by Millet Creek," he said, still gasping for air.

"What's down at the creek?" Lauren asked. He'd gone farther than she'd thought. The creek was almost five miles away. It meandered on a crooked line into Clark's River, which emptied into the Tennessee near Paducah.

"A deep crack in the ground," Bobby said. "It must have opened up in the quake. You've got to come look. It must be a mile long. I couldn't see the bottom."

WALT JACOBS SAT BACK IN HIS CHAIR, EYES FIXED straight ahead and shook his head.

"I don't want to hear any more of this," he said. "It's lunacy."

Steve Draper had asked him to join Atkins and Elizabeth Holleran in an equipment room for a private conversation. It was hard enough for him to focus; he was still waiting for word on his wife and daughter. The two graduate students who'd volunteered to go to his home hadn't returned, and he was very worried about them as well as about his family. He'd been sleeping less than four hours a day, and his jittery nerves were ready to snap. He had no patience for crazy ideas.

Jacobs rarely lost his temper, but he was as angry as Atkins had ever seen him.

They'd just listened to Fred Booker explain his theory about using a nuclear charge to defuse the earthquake sequence.

Booker was hardly aware of Jacobs' increasing hostility. Deep in thought, he was standing at a blackboard, using a piece of broken chalk to sketch the fault zone Guy Thompson had displayed graphically. He was working rapidly, making quick, sharp strokes on the board. Chalk fragments were flying.

"If this is the most seismically active segment, I'd make it my target." He circled the area then drew a horizontal line right through it. "That's where I'd sink the shaft. We put the bomb down as deep as we can go. As deep as we have time for. The size and location, of course, would all have to be precisely calculated. I'd let you people—''

Jacobs had had enough. ''We're in the middle of a catastrophe, and you're wasting our time with this,'' he said, knocking over a chair as he stood up. ''We are not going to set off a nuclear explosion. It's not even worth discussing.''

Atkins said, ''How would we know a nuclear charge wouldn't actually precipitate another big quake? Push it over the edge.'' That was the very thing they wanted to avoid and to his way of thinking was the most dangerous element of Booker's startling proposal. They had absolutely no empirical evidence to fall back on. The thing had never been done. He couldn't buy this at all.

Booker said, ''I can't answer that. There's going to be a risk. And I don't underestimate that. All I'm saying is that if you people can tell me how much energy needs to be released along the fault to reduce the strain energy, I can design and fire a charge that might do the job.'' He looked at Jacobs. ''Throwing chairs around isn't going to solve our problem. It never did out at the Nevada Test Site.''

''To hell with you,'' Jacobs said. ''So you know how to blow big holes in the ground. Goddammit, what's the point?''

Booker stood right in front of Jacobs and stared at him. ''The point is we can do something,'' he said in a loud, frustrated voice. ''We can try to do something. We don't have to sit here and look at our precious data and get clobbered again.'' Booker took off his goggles and threw them across the room.

Draper ordered Jacobs and Booker to cool off.

There had long been speculation that a nuclear blast, properly located, might be able to defuse an earthquake. Atkins was aware of it, but that's all it was. Speculation. No reputable geologist had ever seriously suggested such a thing beyond raising it as a hypothetical. It was a fringe issue—too far-out to be seriously debated, too far-fetched. On the other hand, no one doubted a nuclear bomb could trigger an earthquake. There'd been too many examples. Some of the quakes had been fairly substantial, in the magnitude 5 range, perhaps even a little larger.

Elizabeth said, "Wasn't there discussion that a Soviet underground test may have set off a mag 7 quake in Iran back in the late seventies?"

"I'm familiar with that earthquake," Atkins said. He'd visited Tabas, a city in remote western Iran, where at least 25,000 people had been killed. "The Soviets had set off a 10-megaton blast at Semipalitinsk about thirty-six hours before the quake. But no one has ever established a definitive cause-and-effect link between the two events. And that's the problem with all the antibomb people who worry that underground tests have made the earth more vulnerable to major earthquakes. There's no hard evidence. It's an emotional argument without any scientific basis in fact."

"There are maybe a couple million people living within a three-or four-hour drive of any place you'd put a bomb along that fault," Jacobs said in a voice that had lost none of its anger. "What happens if something goes wrong and all that radioactivity is vented into the air or leaches into the ground?" He was furious and was making no effort to conceal how he felt.

Booker said, "I'm reasonably sure we can prevent any venting and that if we—"

"Reasonably?" Jacobs sneered, interrupting him.

"Exposing a lot of people to radioactivity is an issue," Booker said angrily. "No doubt about it. But an equally important question you have to answer is what happens if you get another magnitude 8 quake? What if it triggers seismic activity on those other faults Doctor Thompson was talking about a few minutes ago?" He was as mad as he'd ever been in his life. He'd dealt with stubborn fools all his life. Stubborn fools with Ph.D.'s. He stormed over to where Jacobs was sitting and slammed his fist on the table. "If you think that's a serious possibility, my question to you is this: Do you try to come up with a way to stop it, or do you just shrug and say, sorry, there's nothing we can do. It's an act of nature."

Booker turned to Atkins, who stood with his back to him, staring holes in the blackboard. "What if you get another triple here? Isn't that what's got everyone worried? It's sure as hell got me worried. I wouldn't want to see another mag

8 earthquake rip through the valley. It couldn't survive it, and I'm not sure the country could."

"We still don't know how much energy is locked down there," Atkins said. "There aren't any adequate ways to measure it."

"Excuse me, excuse me," Booker said, clenching his fists and lowering his head in frustration. "But didn't I just hear a discussion of multiple fractures along that new fault. Isn't that evidence of elastic strain energy?"

"Yes, but the problem's always been trying to measure it," Jacobs said, his hostility unabated. "All we can say for certain is that deformations, or uplift, or the number of aftershocks can indicate a serious buildup of tectonic stress. But we don't know how much stress has actually loaded up there, or how much it would take to trigger an earthquake."

Booker took a deep breath. He wondered if the man was even listening to him. "Let me put it as simply as I can," he said. "Do you think there's going to be another big earthquake? That's the question, isn't it? Is another big earthquake possible?"

For a long time, no one spoke. Then Jacobs said, "Yes, it's possible."

THE NEWS ABOUT THE DEEP FISSURE CAME FROM
Lauren Mitchell, who'd managed to find a Red Cross unit
near Mayfield with a shortwave radio. Shortly after first light,
a team from the earthquake center in Memphis flew directly
to the site aboard an Army UH-60 helicopter.

Elizabeth Holleran had never seen anything like it: a fissure running nearly a mile long at depths varying from two
hundred to six hundred feet. The deep tear in the ground had
been much larger at one point. Visible from the air, the scar
that marked where it had already closed extended nearly two
miles through the hilly, forested west Kentucky countryside.

It was just after eight in the morning. Powerful spotlights
hooked to portable generators illuminated the depths of the
crevasse. After spending an hour inspecting it and helping
to set up the lights, Elizabeth was ready to make a descent.

Atkins took her aside. "You're sure about this?" he asked.
He didn't like anything about the plan, but he realized there
was no stopping her. The fissure provided an unprecedented
opportunity to look for evidence of previous earthquakes.
Elizabeth was determined to make the most of it.

"I couldn't get a trench this good in California if I had a
dozen backhoes working overtime for a decade," she said.
She'd spent three years digging two trenches on the San
Andreas that were ten feet deep and barely fifty yards long.
They didn't compare.

Elizabeth, Atkins, and a small team from the earthquake
center had made the hurried trip to Millet Creek. Paul Wes-

ton had wanted to send along Stan Marshal, but had to back off when Atkins and Elizabeth refused to go if he was in the party. Weston chose not to force the issue, realizing he didn't have a choice. They needed Elizabeth because of her expertise.

The accident with the explosive charge still nagged at Atkins. He wanted to believe it was an accident and yet it bothered him. A man with Marshal's background and field expertise didn't make a nearly lethal mistake like that. It just didn't happen. He needed to think it through. So far he had only a troubling suspicion and enough lingering anger to keep Marshal as far away from him as possible.

He'd hoped Walt Jacobs would make the trip, but Jacobs had been unusually subdued since their conversation with Draper and Booker. Jacobs had begged off looking at the crevasse, saying he needed to stay at the earthquake center.

Atkins guessed there was more to it than his friend's negative reaction to Booker's provocative suggestion about using a nuclear explosion. Atkins wasn't ready to take the idea seriously either. It worried him that an eminent scientist like Steve Draper seemed so interested. After the meeting with Booker, Draper had peppered all of them with pointed, often unanswerable questions. Jacobs had looked distracted, even uninterested, which wasn't like him. Atkins figured it had to do with his wife and daughter. He still hadn't had any word on their safety.

Elizabeth wore coveralls, leather gloves, and a hard hat equipped with a powerful spotlight. She also carried a small 35-mm camera from a strap around her neck. They were going to lower her by rope into the fissure, using the helicopter's electric-powered hoist and air rescue seat.

Atkins didn't want her to be down there any longer than necessary. Several mild tremors had shaken the region since their arrival and parts of the trench were showing signs of collapse. Pieces of the edge kept breaking away and falling into the chasm.

Atkins had wanted to make the descent with her, but knew he'd only get in the way.

Elizabeth planned to descend as far as possible, looking for evidence of sand blows or offsets, thin cracks in the soil, some of them no more visible than a hairline fracture. Buried in the various strata, they were telltale signs of earthquakes and her trained eye, sharpened by years of trenching in the San Andreas fault, was expert at picking them out. The recent earthquake had laid them all bare, creating a mural of the past.

She'd look for bits of carbon—fragments of leaves, peat, or twigs deposited in the soil about the time the offset or sand blows had occurred.

By radiocarbon dating these fragments, she could develop a stratigraphic map of the history of the fault's previous earthquakes. Another Army helicopter—it was already heading their way—would take the samples to the University of Illinois at Champaign-Urbana where they could be carbon-dated. It was the closest accelerator mass spectrometer, a device that could get precise dates from even minute bits of carbon and, in so doing, date the earthquake that had produced the offsets, sand blows, and other formations Elizabeth might find.

Elizabeth didn't need much carbon, just a few grains. The technology was based on burning the fragments and converting them to carbon dioxide. The carbon dioxide was then heated and converted to graphite. The graphite was inserted into the spectrometer, which could analyze the carbon-14 atoms in the sample and determine its age, give or take thirty years.

"I know it's your call, but I'd recommend against this," the crew chief said as he expertly looped a rope under Elizabeth's arms and fashioned a bowline knot that wouldn't slip. "This ground's jumping. This trench could slam shut any time now."

Atkins couldn't have agreed more. The recent tremors had been unusually sharp. "Try to make it quick, Liz," he said. He took her hands in his. This was a fine, brave woman. During the last few days, he'd come to realize how extraordinary she was and how much she meant to him. He wanted to talk to her. They hadn't had many chances since the quake. Atkins sensed she felt the same way but wasn't sure. He hoped so at least.

"Don't press it," he said.

"Don't worry about that," Elizabeth said, smiling. "I flunked rapelling when I was a Girl Scout."

Elizabeth's helmet was fitted with a headset microphone so she could talk with the team on the surface. She rechecked all the knots and buckles in her seat harness and signaled to the men to lower her over the side.

"Take me down ten feet," she said. Her back to the trench, she pushed away from the wall with her feet, letting the rope glide through her fingers. She'd already picked out several places to check that were close to the surface.

In a few minutes, she shouted: "Bull's-eye! There's multiple scarring here. Sand boils, a big lateral offset. This might have been made by the 1811–1812 quakes." Using a trowel, she gently scraped away at the side of the cliff. "There's plenty of peat down here." She put the samples into cellophane packs that she carried in a waist pouch.

Atkins hoped that would be enough, but he knew better. He heard Elizabeth say, "Let's try another fifteen feet down."

A helicopter crewman carefully played out more rope.

"I see some evidence of scorching," Elizabeth said. "They may have been caused by lightning strikes that burned away some of the hillside." She deposited a few more fragments of charcoal into her sample bag and asked to be lowered ten feet.

It was a gray, gloomy morning with a sharp wind. Not much light filtered down into the crevasse. Atkins and the others had safety ropes tied around their waists so they wouldn't fall in if the ground suddenly gave way. From what he could see from above, the exposed wall of layered sediment would probably be measured in the thousands of years, not tens of thousands.

That was fine, he thought. They were more interested in the recent record of big quakes—those that had happened one or two thousand years before the cataclysms of the last century. That would be long enough to show a pattern—if one existed.

"It's like a layer cake down here," Elizabeth said. "Let out another fifteen feet."

Playing her light on the uneven walls of the trench, Elizabeth zeroed in on another big scar, which appeared to have been made by an explosion crater.

"This sand blow . . . is . . . a . . . monster!" she cried

out. She was down about eighty feet. The vertical offsets were even more impressive—and equally troubling. She examined two of these zigzag tears, scraping samples from each. One of them appeared to have severed an ancient streambed. The slightly coarser, darker sand might have been easy to overlook, but not for Elizabeth's practiced eyes.

"It took a pretty good-sized quake to break through this streambed," she said. "I'm going to do a little measuring."

She used a steel tape measure to get the exact dimensions of the offsets, requesting several times to be raised or lowered a few feet. She also took photographs with the camera, which had an automatic flash.

"How long's she been down?" the crew chief asked.

Atkins glanced at his watch. "Nearly forty minutes."

The soldier shook his head. "We're pushing our luck."

Atkins wanted to bring her up. Then he heard Elizabeth's excited voice over his headset.

"Here's another slam dunk! That offset was bigger than I thought. At least twelve meters." Caused by the fracturing waves of an earthquake, an offset was a clear break or crack in a layer of sediment or rock.

The news startled Atkins. An offset of that size could only have been made by an exceptionally strong earthquake. It was evidence the fault had already produced several large quakes long before the triple play in 1811–1812. The deep tear in the earth's crust had remained dangerous for a long time.

"Liz, did you find any carbon on the offset?" he asked.

"You bet," she said. "Some good pieces."

A strong northerly wind stung their faces and made it feel much colder. Atkins had just put his hands in his pockets to warm them when the earth moved. A minor tremor.

"Hey, look over there!" one of the geologists shouted. About thirty yards away, a twenty-foot-long strip of earth had peeled away from the edge and fallen into the fissure.

"Elizabeth, are you all right?" Atkins said into his radio. Dust clouds were rolling out of the crevasse.

He heard her say, "Bring me up!"

The lift began, but the rope hit a snag and wouldn't budge. The hoist started to smoke from the friction.

"Shut it down!" the crew chief shouted to the operator.

After pulling Elizabeth up about ten feet, the rope had stuck on something.

"I'm hung up," Elizabeth said.

A shower of dirt and clay had fallen on her. Her shoulder throbbed where one of the larger pieces had struck her. She tried to see in the choking dust, covering her mouth and nose with a handkerchief. It was like groping in fog. She couldn't see her hands in front of her face.

The ground lurched again, rocking her harness. A block of sediment broke away from the wall of the fissure somewhere below her and smashed into the bottom, throwing up more thick dust. From the sound it made, it was a big, heavy chunk of earth.

Elizabeth figured she was down about 150 feet. Keeping one hand on the harness, she reached up with the other and felt something overhead. The rope was twisted around it.

The next jolt was even stronger. The upper walls of the crevice seemed to move closer together. But maybe that was just her imagination.

Elizabeth smelled something coming up from the depths. Sulfur.

As the dirt settled, she saw what had fouled her rope—the root system of a tree. Long buried and completely carbonized, part of the trunk had broken through the wall during the last tremor. The rope was caught between several gnarled roots, each as thick as a man's arm.

"I've got a problem here," she said. "Give me a little slack." Pulling herself up in her seat, she was able to clear the tangle, using her feet for leverage, pushing out against the wall.

"I'm free. Get me out."

The hoist started pulling her toward the surface again. Grit and clay kept pouring down on her from the sides of the crevasse. A couple of pieces grazed her helmet. In minutes she was back at the surface.

Someone estimated that the fissure had closed about a foot. There was no telling how long it would remain open.

"How are you doing?" Atkins asked Elizabeth after he helped pull her out of the trench. Her face and hands were covered with mud.

Elizabeth managed a smile. "I've got a whole sackful of samples," she said. "The fissure is like a road map. There've been a lot of quakes here. They've left marks everywhere. I counted at least fourteen of them." She looked at Atkins. "They're big, and they come in clusters."

WHEN THEY RETURNED TO MEMPHIS, ATKINS AND
Elizabeth were exhausted. Nursing a headache, Elizabeth
took some aspirin and went to lie down. Meanwhile, the
earthquake command center was rolling in high gear. Another round of GPS data was due by satellite transmission
within an hour. And Guy Thompson's people were running
computer simulations of the latest aftershock activity along
the greatly expanded seismic zone. Each pass helped them
scope out in sharper, ever clearer detail the length and
breadth of the new fault.

Using Elizabeth's samples from the fissure, a team of scientists at the University of Illinois at Champaign-Urbana
were already working on the radiocarbon analysis. The results weren't expected for another five hours.

Elizabeth unrolled a sleeping bag in one of the equipment
rooms in the library annex. A long worktable was piled with
spare parts for seismographs—starters, timing circuits, pen-
dulums. The room was poorly heated but had the luxury of
privacy. The men slept between the stacks on the floor of
the library, grabbing a few hours whenever they could. Elizabeth rated her own space.

She'd just slipped into her sleeping bag when someone
rapped lightly on the door. It was John Atkins. He'd
scrounged a cup of milk, which he'd heated on a butane
stove.

"This might help you sleep," he said. "It works with
me—especially when I mix in a good shot of bourbon. Un-

fortunately, we're fresh out of bourbon." He grinned. "You'd think something like that would be illegal in Tennessee."

Elizabeth took a few sips, holding the warm cup with both hands. "That's nice," she said, smiling. "Sit with me for a few minutes. I'd like the company."

Atkins sat next to her, his back against the wall. She curled into the crook of his arm. She felt sleep coming.

"Thank you for today," she said, looking up at him.

He kissed her, gently. Then she put her hand against the side of his face, and they embraced.

"Hold me," she said.

"Go to sleep," he said softly. All the old emotions were rushing back, the wonderful sensation of just being close to a woman. And he did care for Elizabeth Holleran. He'd known that since their wild trip across the Mississippi. She was cool under pressure, caring, and incredibly bright. She'd shown nothing but courage and conviction since she'd arrived in Memphis.

There was something else, too. He loved to look at her. She was a beautiful woman.

Snuggling closer to him, she said, "I'll be awake the next time. Promise you'll be there when I wake up."

He kissed her on the lips. Then she was quiet. He felt her go to sleep in his arms and must have dozed off himself, sliding down next to her on the warm sleeping bag.

He hadn't planned on that. It happened so quickly he was asleep before he knew it. Awakened, he had no idea how long he'd been out. Elizabeth was sitting next to him. She was slowly, gently unbuttoning his shirt.

He touched her and felt her breasts against his chest. She'd already opened her shirt and slipped off her bra. He glimpsed the long, wonderful legs as she straddled him. He twisted slightly so that he could unbuckle his trousers. Elizabeth pulled the sleeping bag over them and lay on top of him, touching him ever lower with her hands as they embraced.

He started to say something, to tell her that he loved her. There was so much to say, and he was still groggy with sleep. He hadn't said enough the last time he loved someone. This was a second chance. A gift. He wanted Elizabeth to know how much he cared for her.

"I love you," he said.

She touched his lips. "Keep saying that. I won't ever get tired of hearing it."

He kissed her deeply, clasping his hands around her waist, afraid even then of losing her. He'd take her as far as she wanted. As far as she'd let him.

PRESIDENT ROSS HAD CALLED THE EVENING MEET-
ing in the national security adviser's conference room in the
basement of the White House's West Wing. He'd flown in
a handful of scientists from the Memphis earthquake center
and the USGS. They'd taken an Army helicopter to Fort
Campbell, Kentucky, where Air Force One picked them up
for the one-hour flight to Dulles.

Ross had deliberately kept the group small. In addition to
the seismologists, he'd limited attendance to Margaret Greenland, his national security adviser; the speaker of the House
and Senate majority leader; and his science adviser, Steve
Draper.

The president had already been warned that the news was
bad, but he hadn't realized its true gravity until Elizabeth
Holleran began to speak. As she described the carbon-14
dating tests and their implications, he struggled to keep his
composure.

In a concise, factual delivery, Holleran laid out the key
point: the radiocarbon dating of fossil chips she'd scraped
from the walls of the deep trench showed unmistakable evidence that massive earthquakes had ruptured the fault no
less than six times during the last fifteen hundred years. The
horizontal layers of clay, sand, silt, and gravel were riddled
with the trace marks of those disturbances. The sequence
was striking. The shortest period between quakes was
roughly two hundred years. Most occurred at intervals of
anywhere from five hundred to eight hundred years.

The zone had been incredibly active over the centuries. The vertical displacements varied from several inches to as much as forty feet.

"They're textbook examples of severe faulting," Holleran said. She showed a blowup of a photograph she'd taken about a hundred feet down into the fissure.

Even to the president's untrained eye, the thick scarring and darkening of the soil stood out clearly.

Using a pointer, Holleran outlined the telltale signs of repeated faulting. The small room was stuffy and crowded, but no one moved or fidgeted. They were all listening intently, jotting down notes.

"The quake that left those footprints dates from just after the time of Columbus' voyage of discovery," she said.

The jagged crack in the exposed soil was striking. But the most distinctive aspect was the clear indication that the fault had repeatedly produced great earthquakes. The evidence appeared in each of the different strata, which were separated by bands of lighter-colored soil.

"I take it this wasn't caused by just one earthquake," Ross said.

Here it comes, Atkins thought.

"As best we can tell, there were at least four major earthquakes," Holleran said, outlining their tracings. "They were probably concentrated over a very short span of time."

"How short?" Ross asked.

"That's difficult to say," Holleran said.

"Give me a range."

"At the longest end, months."

"And at the shortest?"

Holleran's reply was quietly stated: "Weeks."

With a possible error of no more than thirty years, the carbon-14 tests had shown major earthquakes around A.D. 200 then again in 631, about the time of Mohammed. Mega quakes had also occurred when the ancestors of the American Indian were migrating to North America in the 1100s and, again, during the Black Death that depopulated much of Europe in the 1650s.

The sedimentary patterns Holleran had found in the deep fissure indicated that the big quakes often came in groups of three, but at least one sequence had four, possibly five major earthquakes. The best evidence of a huge earthquake was a sharp, twenty-five-foot offset that dated roughly to the mid-1600s.

Only an extraordinary quake could have done that, Atkins thought. The growing body of data increasingly indicated that the American heartland was prime earthquake country to a degree no one had ever imagined before. And much of the credit for nailing this definitively had to go to Holleran. He had no doubt, none, that she was right in her analysis. It was highly likely they were going to get rocked again.

"So we could be looking at maybe two or three more major quakes?" Ross asked. Casually dressed in jeans and a blue pullover, he was taking notes on a yellow legal pad.

"It's possible, Mister President," Holleran said. "If the fault follows the usual pattern."

"How possible?" Ross persisted.

Holleran said, "I can't give a percentage. I'd say at least one more big quake in the magnitude 8 range is likely."

Weston, who'd been biding his time, objected. He'd managed to find a clean suit and tie for the trip to the White House, even a set of cufflinks. He launched into an attack on the whole field of paleoseismology. He wasn't alone in his argument. Several of the USGS scientists were also leery of basing seismic projections on the physical evidence of past quakes. There were simply too many exceptions, too many gaps in the chain, too many inconsistencies.

"At best it's interesting data that needs more interpretation," one of them said. "It would be a mistake to use it now to try to project for future earthquakes, especially under present circumstances."

Atkins had expected their objections, which echoed Weston's. He had a serious problem with Weston over the cracks at Kentucky Dam, a problem they still needed to resolve. But he understood that Weston expressed what most of the seismologists working on the crisis were thinking. Weston had been an effective spokesman for their viewpoints. Argumentative and opinionated, he had history on his side. Back-to-back earthquakes of magnitude 8 or greater were incredibly rare.

Holleran let the remark pass without comment. She knew she had the support of most of the seismologists in the room.

But on another level, she no longer cared what others thought. Her job, as she understood it, was to examine the physical evidence and try to draw meaningful conclusions while keeping speculation to a minimum. She'd done just that. The evidence was rich. The clues, buried deep in the ground, told them a great deal about the area's violent seismic history.

Walt Jacobs had information to report—if not as dramatic, equally as troubling.

The man looked awful, Atkins thought. The bags under his eyes were dark and puffy. He hadn't shaved or changed clothes in days. Atkins noticed his old friend was still wearing the rumpled blue denim shirt he'd had on two days earlier. He resolved to talk to him, see if he could help him pull out of it.

"The latest GPS sweep shows continued deformation along a line running roughly northeast of the Caruthersville Fault about two hundred miles into Kentucky."

The satellite data had just been harvested by the GPS Master Control Station near Colorado Springs. It had been analyzed and enhanced at the Jet Propulsion Laboratory at Cal Tech before it was relayed by satellite to Memphis. The data was projected on a map.

"How much uplift are we getting?" Weston asked. Like the others, he was seeing the data for the first time. Thompson had only recently processed it.

"Twenty inches along most of the fault. A little more than that at the point of axis with the main New Madrid segment. It's roughly thirty inches there."

Even Ross knew enough geology by then to realize an uplift of that magnitude was serious, an unmistakable signal that tremendous amounts of seismic energy continued to build along the fault lines.

Jacobs had another satellite-generated detail to add to the analytical mix.

Earthquakes were known to produce strong energy currents or pressure waves in the earth's upper atmosphere, the ionosphere. This connection had been first noticed after the Northridge quake of 1994.

Jacobs said, "We saw then that for two days before the earthquake, the GPS 10-3mn frequency band began to pick up a train of strong pressure waves. The waves were generated by a change in electrons. The greatest waves appeared within minutes after the first strong tremors.''

"What's your point?'' snapped the president, exasperated by the unrelenting complexity of the science.

"We're starting to see some significant electronic disturbances in the atmosphere at distances of five hundred to six hundred kilometers above the fault line,'' Jacobs said. "The waves are intensifying in strength.''

Guy Thompson hadn't changed his Western look for the visit to the White House. He wore his usual attire—jeans, expensive cowboy boots, and a gaudy Western shirt. He'd braided his black hair in the back.

"I'd like to talk about the P velocity data.'' Thompson explained that the velocities of the P waves had dropped by about 10 percent since that magnitude 8.4 event. "In the last twenty-four hours those velocities have started climbing again,'' he said.

Ross asked him to explain.

"The theory was developed from observations in Russia,'' Thompson said. "It holds that P velocities decrease after a precursor quake, then start to return to more normal levels just before a major event.''

"That's only a theory,'' Weston said, making no effort to conceal his anger. His view was shared by several others.

"I want to hear this,'' Ross said, silencing Weston.

Thompson explained that his team had prepared a map of the entire seismic zone based on geomagnetic data gathered by satellite. Shifts in magnetic fields were recognized indicators of seismic activity. The recent readings showed a major change in the zone's magnetic field.

On Thompson's map, projected on the screen, areas of high magnetic intensity showed up as hills. Low intensity as valleys. The hills, which were colored red, dominated the image.

Atkins was interested in these geomagnetic readings. He continued to wonder whether magnetic fields were responsible for the strange, green glow that had shimmered deep in Kentucky Lake.

There was another possible source. All that fracturing of the rock deep in the ground generated heat. The role of heat in earthquakes was little understood. Some laboratory experiments had demonstrated that rocks would melt under the extreme pressures of a major earthquake. Other tests showed this didn't always happen. Scientists were nowhere near an explanation of the heat dilemma.

Atkins wondered if New Madrid was showing a phenomenon never seen before in earthquake country—the visible discharge of tremendous amounts of heat up through the crust. An action that was almost volcanic in power.

Ross interrupted Atkins' train of thought. The president asked his national security adviser for a damage assessment.

Margaret Greenland stood and smoothed the hem of her rumpled skirt. She was a heavyset woman who didn't care much about her appearance. She'd received her doctorate from the University of Chicago. Her rise through the ranks of the Central Intelligence Agency was the result of talent, grit, and hard work. Ross liked and respected her.

"This is based on our most recent damage assessments," she said, switching off the room's overhead lights. "We'll start first with cities on the periphery of the damage zone."

She began with footage of Chicago. The towering skyline was unmistakable.

"That's Lake Shore Drive," Greenland said with her slow, Southern drawl. "Most of the buildings along the Magnificent Mile sustained moderate damage. Every aftershock sends more glass falling down on the streets." Some of the shards were found embedded like daggers in the walls of buildings.

"Pittsburgh and Philadelphia have also reported damage," Greenland said. "Some underground pipes have snapped."

A map on the wall showed the Mercalli damage zones rippling out from the epicenter like rings on a bull's-eye. The Modified Mercalli Intensity Scale ranked earthquakes on the basis of observed physical destruction.

The film switched to Columbus, Ohio—the area around the State Fair Grounds and German Village. Both had been hard hit.

Greenland followed with photos of the collapsed Hoosier Dome and the devastated White River Park district in Indianapolis. Both cities were closer to the epicenter. The images were always the same. Buildings in various stages of collapse, the flashing lights of emergency vehicles, crowds of people with dazed, shell-shocked expressions, weeping children.

"The total death toll in the country stands at 130,000 and climbing, but no one really knows," Greenland said. "Disaster officials are sure of only one thing—that the numbers will go much higher. A big problem right now is finding the bodies."

As he listened, Ross slowly massaged his temples, trying to alleviate a crushing headache. He knew there was no way to put human losses like that in perspective. They were unprecedented in the United States.

Continuing her grim assessment, Greenland said, "We've already talked about command and control in the damage zone. For all practical purposes, civil authority has collapsed. Army and National Guard units are providing what security exists under your previous declaration of martial law."

Ross nodded. He'd recently boned up on President Lincoln's decision to impose martial law during the Civil War and wondered if the man he considered the country's greatest president had gone through as much agony before he sent federal troops into so many American cities. Ross had hated to do it, but felt he had no choice. Killing and looting had broken out on a mammoth scale. In a single neighborhood in Little Rock—Geyer Springs—federal troops had shot and killed nearly thirty people who'd been caught stealing items from smashed homes and stores. That's what a shoot-to-kill order meant. And that awful body count was from just a single neighborhood.

Less than an hour earlier, Greenland had told Ross privately that the military, stretched dangerously thin, wouldn't be able to respond to even a moderate international challenge.

Every available soldier on the East Coast and in the South had been pressed into earthquake duty. Unless the situation improved—and that appeared unlikely—they'd have to call in troops from the far West. They'd start with Fort Riley in Kansas. The 1st Infantry Division there had already been put on full alert. They could also bring in Marine units from Camp Pendleton.

"The basic necessities—food, water, medical care—are virtually nonexistent in the quake zones," Greenland said.

The images from the cities that had sustained the heaviest damage all seemed to merge together into one overwhelming tableau of grief and destruction.

And you're in charge, Ross kept telling himself. You're supposed to know how to handle this. Tell people what to do. Suggest options. Keep their spirits up.

He knew he was failing badly on every front.

His national security adviser was talking about hospitals. In the heart of the earthquake zone, most of them had been destroyed. Ross looked at a close-up of Central Hospital in Little Rock and closed his eyes. It had the largest neonatal unit in the state. The building had split in two.

"Heating and fuel oil are already being rationed throughout the East Coast," Greenland continued. "The situation there will be critical in three or four more days."

Ross stopped her. "That's enough, Margaret," he said, gently touching her on the shoulder. She nodded and turned off the machine. She looked grateful to sit back down.

The president faced the gathered seismologists. "We're going to have another quake, aren't we?"

"Almost certainly," Elizabeth Holleran said. The evidence she'd found in the fissure had removed any of her lingering doubts. "The only question is when and how big."

"Anyone here agree with Doctor Holleran?"

John Atkins and Walt Jacobs raised their hands. Holleran had uncovered irrefutable evidence that couldn't be denied. And Atkins was proud to go on record supporting her. They were taking a huge professional risk. He had few doubts they'd be proven right. But at what incredible cost?

It was an overpowering feeling of both intense excitement and fear. They were way out in front on this.

The five other seismologists in the room were hesitant to offer an opinion, much less a definite yes or no.

"What about you, Doctor Weston?" Ross asked.

"I'm sorry, Mister President," Weston said, shaking his head. "I refuse to speculate."

"After what you've just seen and heard, you're not convinced?"

"No, sir. I'm not," Weston said. "I'm still not sure the

quakes we're having aren't part of a normal aftershock pattern.''

Ross was trying to be agreeable as he kept probing, pushing. "Then let me ask you this: what do you think will happen if we get another magnitude 8 quake on the New Madrid Fault?''

He read the look in Weston's eyes and in the eyes of the others. He'd seen it often enough, the fear and uncertainty. He'd seen it in his wife's eyes when the doctor met them in his office on that bright spring afternoon seven years ago and told them what they already knew. The tests were positive. She had breast cancer. He'd seen it in his own eyes earlier that morning when he looked at himself in the mirror.

"I'll tell you what I think," Ross said, giving way to the nightmare that had kept him awake every night for the last four. "Another quake would pretty much finish the Mississippi Valley. It would push us back to World War II productivity levels. Our economy would be in shambles. In many ways that's already happened. Millions of Americans would be left totally on their own, without schools, medical care, even food or water. Without police protection." He leaned over the broad conference table, supporting himself heavily with both hands.

Up close, Atkins was struck again by how tired the man looked. And yet his voice remained firm, decisive.

"This is a great country," Ross said. "Our people have courage and resiliency. They'll bounce back eventually. But we wouldn't be the same United States.''

He looked at everyone in the room, locking in on their eyes, staring hard.

Atkins felt the power of the president's gaze. He was exposing them to his deepest, most intimate fears.

Ross held them like that for a long time before he said, "Is there anything we can do to prevent that from happening?''

IT was late in the evening. Everyone was dragging. The president suggested they take a fifteen-minute break. He had a big urn of coffee and a platter of fruit and sweet rolls sent down from the White House kitchen.

Walt Jacobs took Atkins aside and whispered that he had

something he wanted to tell him in private. They went into the hallway. Secret service agents and military aides watched them carefully as they walked down the long, brightly lit corridor and sat on an upholstered bench seat under a wall map of the Louisiana Purchase.

"My wife and daughter are dead," Jacobs said. "They were trapped in our house. I found out yesterday." He looked at Atkins and shook his head. "I've studied earthquakes since I was eighteen years old. I thought I understood them pretty well. I never thought one of them would kill my family."

"Walt, my God, I'm so sorry," Atkins said, putting his arm around his friend's shoulder. "I had no idea. None of us did." He couldn't believe it. Jacobs had just kept on working as if nothing had happened. Atkins had suspected something was bothering him. His usually buoyant friend had seemed uncharacteristically moody, remote.

Jacobs suddenly got up and pounded his fists against the wall. The map print crashed to the floor, the glass dust cover shattering. He knocked over a lamp and staggered away sobbing.

Two Secret Service agents ran toward them. Atkins pushed one of them back as the agent reached out to grab Jacobs.

"No, let him go!" he shouted. He put an arm around his friend's waist.

"I can't do this anymore. . . . Can't go on," Jacobs said. "My wife's dead, John. My daughter. I don't give a fuck about another earthquake. I don't care. . . ."

He stood there with tears in his eyes. Atkins helped him sit down. Jacobs started to regain his composure.

"I had a feeling after that first good aftershock," he said, staring at his folded hands. He was calming down and needed to talk, the words coming quickly. He mentioned the two grad students he'd asked to go out to his house to check on things. He glanced sideways at Atkins. "The kids got back yesterday. They had a hell of a trip. They had to go about ten miles out of their way because of fire and fallen buildings. When they finally got to my home, a neighbor who lives across the street told them what had happened. The guy had dug through the rubble and gotten to the back bedroom, or what was left of it. He found them just where I told them to go in a bad quake. They were in the bathroom right under the main floor joists. The strongest part of the house. The thing I never counted on was the entire brick wall caving in.''

THE PRESIDENT SUMMONED THE GROUP TO ORDER.
He was in shirtsleeves, collar open wide, his eyes bleary
with fatigue. He nodded to Steve Draper.

Stepping into the hallway, his national science adviser returned moments later with Fred Booker. The physicist carried
the same blue backpack and wore the same red jumpsuit
he'd had on when he parachuted into Memphis. He hadn't
changed clothes. There hadn't been time. He'd flown to
Washington on a military plane.

Introducing him to the group, Draper said, "Some of you
have already met Doctor Booker. For those who haven't,
Fred's a nuclear physicist at the Oak Ridge National Laboratory. He's got some thoughts about the earthquakes."

Atkins, Holleran, and the others were startled to see
Booker. They hadn't been told he'd been invited. Atkins
glanced at Walt Jacobs, whose face had gone hard the moment Booker had entered the room. Atkins was already worried about his friend's ability to cope with his tremendous
personal grief and his responsibility as the lead seismologist
at Memphis. He didn't like the way he looked, especially
now, seeing Booker standing in front of them.

Draper said, "Doctor Booker, why don't you describe
what you've got in mind."

Obviously, Draper had already briefed the president on
Booker's ideas, Atkins realized. This was more than a cour-
tesy call. His presence meant the president and Draper were

seriously considering the physicist's proposal to use a nuclear device to try to head off another big quake.

Booker quickly sketched out his thoughts. He'd lost nothing of his zeal. There'd been no major change since he'd described the procedure to them a few days earlier in Memphis. If anything, he'd become even more insistent.

"I believe a nuclear explosion, properly designed and positioned underground, can reduce the dangerous levels of seismic energy that have built on the fault," he said.

"Where would you suggest detonating it?" the president asked.

"That depends on what the seismologists say," Booker said. "From what I've heard, a plausible location might be near the point where your new fault, the one that starts around Caruthersville, Missouri, intersects with the previously known fault segment in western Kentucky. I'm told seismic stress generally builds at the ends of a fault. I'd suggest it might make a good target."

"Mister President, this is insane," said Paul Weston, who'd almost come out of his chair as soon as he realized what Booker was suggesting. "A nuclear explosion anywhere near that fault could be catastrophic." Other seismologists in the room also objected. There were angry shouts as several tried to speak at once.

The president silenced them, slamming the flat of his hand on a desktop. "I don't give a damn if you think it's insane. I just want to know if it has the slightest chance in hell of working. Because right now, I don't see any other options. If you have one, any of you, I want to hear it."

Ross knew he'd almost lost it. That wouldn't do. Would never do. Not even a momentary lapse. If he was going to make this work, he had to be absolutely in control of his emotions.

Still tense, but in control of his voice, Ross said, "After listening to Doctor Holleran, it's obvious to me—and it should be to you—that we're probably going to have at least one major earthquake, maybe more, sometime in the near future. I want to do anything I can to prevent that. So I'll listen to anybody who puts a serious proposal on the table. And I've got to tell you this—I'd consider setting off a hun-

dred nuclear weapons if I thought it would spare the country
from going through this nightmare twice.''

"It might work," said Guy Thompson. He looked genuinely intrigued by Booker's idea. "It's conceivable that we
could selectively reduce some of the strain energy. And I'd
agree with the Caruthersville fault as a target. That's the
critical point, the segment that's showing the greatest concentration of stress. We can run some projections to see if
the data supports that location.''

"The idea is to see if we can get a moderate quake without
triggering a big one," Booker said. "I can guarantee I can
produce an earthquake. It's up to you people to tell me how
big you want it.''

"So you can explode a bomb, and that means we should
listen to you on something this incredibly complex," Weston
said. He looked furious.

"Doctor Weston, I think you better listen to somebody
because we're way out of options, and we could be out of
time," Booker snapped. He knew better, but couldn't help
himself. He was starting to get in a fighting mood.

"What about you, John?" Draper asked, choosing to ignore the exchange. "You've had some time to think about
this.''

Atkins had anticipated the question as soon as he saw
Booker enter the room. The president was right. They had
to try something. They couldn't just sit there and take all
the horrible consequences of another magnitude 8 earthquake
if there was even the slightest chance it could be averted.
He also knew that Thompson was entirely correct. Stress
would be concentrated at the end, or tip, of the fault and
would continue to build there until it loaded up the adjoining
fault segments with stress. A kind of seismic fusebox, it was
the only logical target.

"We'll need to run some numbers before we settle on the
exact location and depth for an explosion," Atkins said.
"And I'd want to find out as much as I could about the
kinds of seismic waves nuclear explosions produce.''

Holleran agreed. The location was critical. So was the size
of the nuclear device. If they used one too big, it would be
a disaster. "If we make a mistake, we could wind up over-
loading the fault with stress energy and possibly trigger a

chain reaction,'' she said. ''I've never seen a fault system that's so tightly interlocked.''

''But you think it might work?'' the president asked.

Holleran paused, carefully weighing her response. ''It might, in theory,'' she said.

''But what about here and now?'' Ross persisted.

''I'm not sure,'' Holleran said. ''There are so many variables, so many unknowns. But even taking that into consideration, I can't see that we have any choice. If we're in a multiple quake pattern—and I think we are—there aren't many alternatives.'' At least she couldn't think of any, and with all her heart, she wished she could. Booker was proposing a huge gamble, rolling the dice with the most powerful natural forces known to man. Still.

''If we do nothing, we're going to get hit again,'' she said. ''Possibly harder than any of us can imagine. We have to try something.''

''But what if it doesn't work?'' Weston said, refusing to be cowed. ''What if it sets off Armageddon?'' There were immediate loud shouts of agreement. Most of the people in the room were shocked by what had been proposed, outraged that it was even being discussed.

Ross said, ''I totally agree with your choice of words, Doctor Weston. We could have an Armageddon. And in a matter of weeks, maybe days. The evidence Doctor Holleran found in that fissure in Kentucky reads like a damn road map. Even a nonexpert like me can understand what all those cracks mean.''

''I'm not sure that a nuclear detonation wouldn't violate the test ban treaty,'' said Margaret Greenland.

''This wouldn't be a test,'' Ross snapped. ''This will be for real. An attempt to avert a national calamity. I'll personally call the Russian ambassador. Talk it over with him. Tell him what we're up against.''

Ross wanted data run on where the shot should be made and its likely energy discharge. He wanted the answers—or best guesses—by tomorrow at the latest.

''That could be a problem,'' Thompson said. ''My concern is the time it'll take to run the computations. Our computers are maxed out right now.''

''Tell me what you need,'' Ross said.

Thompson didn't hesitate. "Two Sun Sparc 10s. And enough disk storage space to handle two or three G-bytes. The programming codes we use are real space-eaters. Just to run good P- and S-wave velocities, you're talking roughly sixteen thousand lines of computer coding."

The president turned to Draper. "See that he gets whatever he needs. I want that equipment loaded on Air Force One within an hour."

Booker had been fiddling with a pocket calculator, working on some rough critical mass projections.

"Where would you get the nuclear device you need?" Ross asked.

"The Pantex plant, Mister President."

Ross was aware of the Department of Energy facility in east Texas. The huge complex where thousands of America's nuclear weapons were kept in cold storage was just outside Amarillo.

"You'd use one of our stockpiled warheads?"

Booker nodded. "Depending on the requirements, I might customize one." Fusion or fission. He wasn't sure. As he worked out the pros and cons of each, he thought they might go either way. Fission had the advantage of being a cleaner bomb, but not as powerful as a thermonuclear fusion device. Depending on the design, however, a fission warhead could generate nearly as many kilotons as a thermo. He'd designed one himself back in the early 1960s, a fission bomb that produced a 500-kiloton yield without using the customary fusion boost of injecting heavy hydrogen into the core.

"I want you to go to Pantex and get what you need," Ross said. "Meg, make sure he gets the necessary clearances. The highest priority. I'll make the calls myself if necessary."

"It might be a help to have a seismologist go with me," Booker said. "I'll need some advice."

Draper looked at Atkins. "John, are you up for a trip to Texas?" he asked.

"Sure, I've always wanted to see Amarillo," Atkins said. His smile belied his fear. He knew that he was in this up to his neck. Once they got started, there'd be no turning back. The clock was running. He instinctively realized he needed to commit himself totally. He glanced at Holleran and understood she felt exactly as he did. He could read it in her eyes. He experienced another strong twinge of excitement, a strange mingling of anxiety and elation. They were about to embark on something that had never been tried before. He wanted it to work, knew that it had to work.

Walt Jacobs had been conspicuously silent. Atkins felt his friend's eyes boring right through him.

Ross asked for his opinion. Jacobs shifted in his seat and glanced at some notes he'd scribbled. He spoke with a force that startled Atkins. "Mister President, I think we'd make a tragic mistake if we detonated a nuclear bomb anywhere near the fault. Right now, we have a chance, a slight one, but a chance that the New Madrid system won't fire, won't produce another series of earthquakes. I admit that Doctor Holleran's data scares me stiff. But if we try to set off a controlled quake on that fault system, we might get something that can't even be described. The Reelfoot Rift, which contains much of the New Madrid Seismic Zone, is at the middle of the North American plate. It's a weak spot deep in the earth, a giant scar in the rock at the precise place where 400 million years ago the continent tried to split apart. I worry that we'd be driving a wedge deep into a place of critical weakness."

"Kind of like using a peg to split a log," the president said.

Jacobs nodded. "Exactly, Mister President. What if we split the plate? Make it crack wide open. The deep fissures are already there. If a bomb somehow unlocked them, how do we know it wouldn't restart a geological process that ground to a halt millions of years ago?"

"What could happen?" the president asked.

Jacobs didn't answer. It was as if he was afraid to say more.

Atkins said, "It would mean you might have the Gulf of Mexico in Memphis."

A KENTUCKY STATE TROOPER KNOCKED ON GOVERnor Tad Parker's bedroom door, waited a respectful ten count, then knocked again. There was a deep cough, then the sound of footsteps. Parker opened the door.

The governor, hair tousled and wearing a baggy terry-cloth robe, rubbed his eyes. He'd just gone to sleep, thanks to two large glasses of red wine. He hadn't had more than a few hours of sleep a night since the earthquake five days earlier.

"We've got a satellite transmission from Washington, sir," the trooper said. "It's Doctor Weston. He said it's urgent."

"I'll be right there," Parker said.

It was a short walk, just up a flight of steps, to the state disaster operations office.

The governor's mansion, an early twentieth-century Beaux Arts building with a granite facade and beautiful English gardens, had been heavily damaged during the quake. Parker and his wife had moved across Capital Drive into the Executive Office Building, where they'd taken up makeshift quarters in the basement.

They were doing better than most residents of the Bluegrass State. At least they had portable toilets and bottled water. Critical shortages of drinking water were widespread. Telephone service was nonexistent. With virtually all of the relay towers knocked down or badly damaged, the cell phone system had also collapsed. For long distance communications, disaster officials continued to rely on shortwave, packet radio, and infrequent satellite transmissions.

Frankfort was roughly halfway between Louisville and Lexington, and all three cities were in bad shape. For that matter, so was virtually every other city, town, and village in Kentucky. Bowling Green was probably the hardest hit. Two hospitals had been destroyed. There'd been a bloody riot over food. Shooting had broken out along the Old Morgantown Road as people tried to force their way into a grocery store that had managed to reopen. The day before, a relief convoy was attacked on the Green River Parkway just outside the city limits. Four National Guard soldiers had been shot dead, the trucks looted by a large group of armed civilians.

Parker's people still hadn't been able to get him a detailed damage estimate. With the exception of limited shortwave transmissions, most towns were cut off from the outside. The earthquakes had shattered the interstates and local highways; bridges were down, over two hundred at last count. The rural folks were in the best shape; most of them had horses to ride and food to eat. They also had well water.

From the front door of the Executive Office Building, Parker could look south, toward shattered Interstate 64. Just beyond it, on a granite bluff, stood the tomb where Daniel Boone was buried. Parker appreciated the grim irony that Kentucky was just about as cut off and inaccessible as it had been when Boone made the first of his long hunts through the state more than 200 years earlier. The Indian name for the area was more haunting than ever—Dark and Bloody Ground.

When the governor arrived at the emergency communications office ten minutes later, they'd lost the satellite link with Washington. It took over an hour to reestablish one. Like everything else, the satellite system was overloaded. The Intelsat network was struggling just with priority traffic.

Weston finally got an uplink.

"This isn't a secure line," an aide warned the governor.

"Let's go with it," Parker said.

Weston appeared on screen. He looked haggard, upset. He told the governor about the discussion in the White House.

Swallowing hard, he said the president was considering exploding a nuclear device in Kentucky.

Parker gasped. He held on to the table to keep from staggering. He was aware that people were staring at him, all of them trying to hide their emotions. His head was throbbing.

"He can't do that," Parker said hoarsely. Then more strongly. "The sonofabitch can't do that! I won't let him do that! Not in my state. Not in Kentucky!"

"I DON'T LIKE THE WAY THOSE FIRES ARE MOVING,"
the paratrooper said. He stood next to Elizabeth Holleran. A
member of the 101st Airborne, he was one of a detail of ten
soldiers the president had assigned to guard the earthquake
center at the University of Memphis. The troops were spread
out around the compound in full battle gear—helmets, camouflage, and automatic weapons.

Elizabeth watched the glowing red haze to the southeast.
A strong wind was blowing the flames in their direction.

"If that wind keeps pushing those fires, we're gonna have
some trouble," said the soldier, a corporal.

The threat of fire overrunning them had been a constant
worry. The multiple fires that had broken out after the earthquakes were proving incredibly resilient. Without water to
fight them, there was nothing to do but let them burn out.

For Elizabeth, the number of fires and their intensity was
a big surprise. Fire had always been considered one of the
major hazards following a quake, but nothing like what was
happening in Memphis had been anticipated, especially in a
city with so many brick and masonry buildings.

It was nearly midnight. An hour earlier, Atkins and Fred
Booker had left for Texas aboard an Army helicopter that
ferried them across the Mississippi to a makeshift runway
on Interstate 55 twenty miles north of Memphis. A military
jet was waiting there to fly them to Amarillo.

Missing Atkins and exhausted after a day that had started
nearly twenty-four hours earlier in Washington, Elizabeth de-

cided to turn in. She walked back to the library annex and was heading for the equipment room when the lights blinked once and went out. The building was instantly plunged into darkness.

"Goddammit!" someone shouted from the computer room. "The generator stopped."

It sounded like Guy Thompson. All of his people were still at work. There were groans, shouts of rage. A power failure could mean a loss of crucial data as they continued to monitor seismic activity along the new faults.

Elizabeth saw flashlights come on, the shafts of light criss-crossing in the darkness. Thompson and another geologist hurried past her as they headed outside to check the emergency generators that supplied the annex and its elaborate bank of computers with electricity. It was imperative that they get back on-line as quickly as possible.

Elizabeth started to follow them, then decided against it. She didn't know anything about power generators and was afraid she'd only get in the way.

Slowly groping her way down the pitch-dark corridors, she found the equipment room and opened the door. She was upset with herself for not remembering to carry her pocket flashlight. She'd left it in her sleeping bag.

Moving carefully, one step at a time, between the rows of tall shelves, she found the bag, which lay unzipped on an insulated sleeping pad. Kneeling down, she started to feel around for her flashlight.

She heard something, a footstep or maybe a sleeve brushing against a shelf or wall. She wasn't sure.

"Who's there?" she said.

Someone was in the room. She got to her feet and stood perfectly still, trying to listen.

"I know you're in here," she said, straining to see.

She heard the sound again at the far end of the room, near the door. Definitely footsteps.

"Who is it?" she shouted.

In the darkness, she glimpsed a shape moving against the back wall. She saw a glint of pale green light. A faint blur of color. Then the door opened and quickly closed. Whoever it was had left.

Elizabeth hurried for the door, banging into a chair and

bruising a knee. She looked into the dark hallway, but saw no one. Whoever it was had disappeared around a corner. A gasoline engine sputtered outside and the lights came back on. They'd gotten the generator running again. Elizabeth guessed they'd been without power for no more than seven or eight minutes.

"Someone switched it off," Thompson said angrily, storming back into the annex. He hurried past her on his way to the computer room. "We've got to get everything booted up again. I don't know how much data we lost. I don't believe this. It was done deliberately. There's no other explanation. Fucking sabotage."

Elizabeth went back into the equipment room. Her nerves on edge, she locked the door, something she hadn't done before. She wasn't sure if she should tell someone about the intruder, especially with everyone hustling to get the computers operational again.

She found her flashlight rolled up in the foot of her sleeping bag and sat down, trying to think it through. It didn't make sense until she glanced at the worktable near her sleeping bag.

She suddenly realized why someone had come into the equipment room. She'd left her laptop on the table plugged into an outlet. It was missing.

THE BIG C-135B STRATOLIFTER SWUNG LOW OVER the Pantex plant on its approach to the Amarillo airport. It was just after dawn and overcast, but there was enough hazy light for Atkins to make out the looming storage bunkers that housed the plutonium "pits" of nearly 10,000 nuclear weapons. There were more than sixty such bunkers at the huge facility that spread over 16,000 wind-blown acres in the Texas panhandle.

"They call them 'igloos,'" Booker said. He pointed out a row of odd-looking, dome-shaped structures. "And those are the 'Gravel Gerties.'" Some of the most powerful weapons in the nation's nuclear arsenal had been assembled in them, he explained. But with the end of the Cold War, thousands of bombs had been dismantled there, the nuclear components put in cold storage. It remained a full-time job.

The distinctive name came from the twenty-foot mound of compacted gravel heaped over the blast-resistant concrete roofs.

"They're designed that way so, in case of an accident, they'll blow straight up and absorb the energy," Booker said. He noticed Atkins' subdued expression. Grinning, he said, "Don't sweat it. There's no danger of a nuclear explosion, but if you screw up with the high explosives that detonate the nuclear primary, you're going to have trouble."

"What about radioactivity?" Atkins asked.

"Only if you puncture the shielding in one of the pits or accidentally release some of the tritium gas," he said. Used in combination with plutonium, tritium was a booster that increased the bomb's explosive yield.

During the short flight to Texas, Booker had given Atkins a crash course in the fundamentals of nuclear fusion. Boosting was one of the keys to getting highly explosive yields from relatively small quantities of fissile material. It involved injecting a mixture of tritium and deuterium gas directly into the pit, the weapon's explosive core.

Booker, Atkins soon realized, was a gifted practitioner of the bombmaker's art.

Within an hour of their arrival—their plane was met on the runway—they'd already checked into Building 16-12 at the Pantex plant, where they received picture IDs, badges, name tags, and dosimeters to register any exposure to radiation. Armed guards went over their clothing and shoes with hand-held metal detectors.

Security was formidable. Atkins noticed there was even a guard on the roof of the building, manning an M-60 machine gun. The roads that crisscrossed the complex were lined with fourteen-foot-high fences topped with barbed wire. As at the Oak Ridge Y-12 plant, guard towers were plentiful.

Booker and Atkins were ushered into a small office, where the plant manager—his name was Carson—met them. A somber-looking man in a blue suit, he kept dabbing at his chin with a bloody handkerchief. He'd cut himself shaving as he hurried to meet them at the plant.

"You have presidential clearance to remove any weapon you need," Carson said irritably. "I've got to tell you I don't approve of this."

Booker asked whether they'd felt the quake here in Texas.

The plant manager nodded. "We had some light damage. Nothing serious."

Booker said, "You're nearly a thousand miles from the epicenter." He shook his head in wonderment. The main seismic wave energy had traveled in the opposite direction and yet they'd still felt it out here in Texas. Amazing. "We're looking at another quake, maybe even larger," he said. "So make me feel good. Tell me I'm going to have your full cooperation and support."

"Whatever you need will be made available," Carson said tersely. He asked what kind of weapon they wanted.

"One of the MK/B-61s," Booker said. "It's a superb warhead. Many of them are still in service. The cruise missiles use your basic MK/B-61. Excellent safing components and a superb hard case." One of the larger weapons still in use, the bomb came in four configurations, ranging from a 500-kiloton yield up to one megaton. It was designed so that the yield and fusing could be programmed in flight.

Carson sat down at his desk and tapped a few keys on a computer terminal. "We have more than a hundred of those warheads in storage in Building 12-11." He printed out a sheet of paper and handed it to Booker. "The manifest lists the dates of disassembly. May I ask what yield we're talking about?"

"One megaton, maybe a little more if we have to boost it," Booker said. "Right now we're not sure."

The debate on what size weapon to use was still raging in Memphis. Atkins hoped to hear soon from Guy Thompson, whose team had been crunching numbers around the clock, trying to calculate the maximum yield and where to place the weapon. They were playing a deadly balancing act. Atkins wasn't sure that clear-cut, definitive answers existed. No matter what they did, it was going to be a huge gamble. At times he thought the only thing that came close to explaining what they were up against was Chaos Theory, the notion of the importance of randomness in the universe.

Carson drove them to one of the igloos. A truck-sized forklift rolled away the twenty-five-ton concrete barrier that blocked the entrance. Punching a code into a keypad, he unlocked a pair of steel blast doors that opened automatically. They entered a bunker that roughly resembled a Quonset hut in shape. The arched roof was fifteen feet high. A pair of tracks ran down the middle of the floor.

"The walls are made of corrugated steel two inches thick," Carson said. "On the outside, they're banked with six feet of dirt."

Fascinated, Atkins watched as a tractor operated by remote control rolled down the tracks and removed one of two dozen stainless steel drums stored on a metal rack that ran the length of the wall. The drum contained the "pit" or nuclear package of an MK/B-61 weapon that had been retired five years earlier.

Carson placed a small handheld instrument that resembled a photographer's light meter next to the steel canister. "This is a spectrograph," he explained for Atkins' benefit. "Each one of these bombs has its own electronic fingerprint. This tells me we've got the right one."

The tractor loaded the canister on the forklift. Within minutes they were headed to Building 12-11, one of the Gravel Gerties. After Carson opened the double doors, again with a special keypad, Atkins stepped into a tunnel that intersected with a labyrinth of other long passageways.

"Where to now?" he asked Booker, who was striding ahead of him. The physicist looked completely at home.

"The X-ray cell."

A guard had them place their right hands on a glass-surfaced scanner. The reading was automatically compared with a similar scan taken when they'd first arrived at the plant. They were ushered through a steel door into a wedge-shaped space outfitted with a turntable and CAT scanner. The weapon's nuclear package had already been removed from the stainless steel canister and placed on the turntable.

"That's all there is to it?" Atkins asked, staring incredulously at the cylindrical device. About four feet long, it was barely a foot and a half in diameter.

Booker grinned. "That may not look like much, but it makes a hell of a bang. Its compact size makes it perfect for an underground explosion. When I'm finished, we'll put it back in its hard case. It's got one of the best subassembly designs I've ever seen. A series of polyurethane spacers absorb shock and support all the internal components. It was designed to slam into the ground and still go off."

Seated at a computer terminal above the turntable, Booker carefully examined the CAT-scan images of the pit. The X rays showed diagonal slices of the weapon. For security reasons, Atkins wasn't allowed to watch. He knew that Booker was inspecting the weapon's nuclear components, namely the plutonium-239 in the primary and the lithium deuteride uranium in the secondary.

Booker had explained the physics. When the secondary

implodes, the lithium converts to tritium, which, in turn, undergoes fusion with the deuterium to create the thermonuclear blast.

After nearly an hour hunched over the computer screen, Booker pronounced the nuclear package fit.

"Now comes the tricky part," he said.

Atkins understood. Booker had to install the double layer of high explosives that were bonded with plastic so they could be shaped. The explosives and detonators surrounded the weapon's pit. When this material exploded, it started the implosion process, compressing the plutonium to a supercritical mass. The amount and type of high explosives used in the weapon was a carefully guarded secret.

They took an elevator to a lower level, where Booker would work alone on the explosives in a space that reminded Atkins of an operating room—all bright lights, gleaming tile, and stainless steel. Booker put on a heavy lead apron, gloves, and a face mask to protect himself from any radioactive emissions from the pit. He also wore antistatic booties.

"I helped develop the explosive," he said. "I wish I could tell you about it. Wonderful stuff. A mixture of PETN, C4, and some other goodies."

Atkins knew that C4 consisted of TNT plus a plasticizer and had the consistency of putty. It was fashioned into precisely cut "lenses" and carefully fitted around the plutonium pit. The lens design, one of the great breakthroughs of the Manhattan Project, controlled the explosion, shaping the blast to flow inward and set off the required implosion. The explosives were already cut and available. But it would take Booker several hours to position them and install the detonators and fuses.

"Come back in two hours," he said. "If my legs don't give out, I ought to be finished by then." He entered the operating room through another pair of air-locked steel doors.

At the plant manager's invitation, Atkins rode with him to his office.

There was news from Memphis.

Guy Thompson was calling on a satellite hookup.

"We've got it pretty well nailed," Thompson said. In his excitement, he spoke too fast and Atkins had to slow him down. "A one-megaton underground explosion would approximately equal an earthquake in the magnitude 6.5 range, maybe a little less.''

"What distance are we talking about?'' Atkins asked.

"Maximum intensity up to twenty-six to thirty miles,'' Thompson said. "We've done some wave-form modeling that suggests a one-megaton explosion would release large amounts of tectonic strain energy.''

The estimate, he explained, was based on the results of the 1969 Milrow shot, the second of three underground explosions conducted in the late 1960s and early 1970s near Alaska in the Aleutians. One of the key indicators was the amplitude of Love waves such a blast produced. Love waves—seismic surface waves with a horizontal shear motion—were evidence of the release of tectonic strain energy. The more waves picked up by seismographs, the greater the tectonic release.

"The Love waves from Milrow were incredible,'' Thompson said. "It produced a main earthquake of magnitude 6.5 and dozens of aftershocks in the magnitude 3 and 4 range.''

"How deep did they set it off?''

"Thirteen hundred meters,'' Thompson said. "And there was absolutely no triggering of large earthquakes along other faults in the area.'' That had been a major worry because it was one of the world's most active plate boundaries. The seismic behavior was virtually identical on the other Aleutian blasts—Longshot in 1965 and Cannikin in late 1971.

Atkins almost shouted out loud. That was good, good news. The fear that a nuclear shot in the New Madrid Seismic Zone would trigger quakes on other faults was everyone's nightmare. Here was solid evidence that it hadn't happened before.

His fear all along had been that a nuclear explosion might set off a chain reaction on other faults. There was no question in his mind they had to try something. The stakes were too horrendously high. A big quake was a virtual certainty. He was resigned to Booker's nuclear explosion, but he'd been worried sick about the risks.

Now some of that fear had been lifted. He began to think that they might be able to stop the earthquake cycle, or at least slow it down.

"The only problem is the depth of the shot," Thompson said.

All right, here it comes, Atkins told himself. He was saving the bad news for last.

"Everyone agrees we've got to get lower than thirteen hundred meters for maximum effect," Thompson said. "The Caruthersville Fault is about eighteen miles down. The closer we can get to it, the better."

That sure as hell eliminates boreholes, Atkins thought. It would take weeks to drill down that far. They didn't have that kind of time.

"We've got one option," Thompson said. "There's an abandoned coal mine within five miles of the place where the Caruthersville Fault intersects with the New Madrid Seismic Zone and the fault that opened up after the 7.1 earthquake. It's two thousand feet deep."

Atkins understood why the mine was perfectly located for their purposes. Seismic stress was most likely concentrated at the ends of a fault or at the point where one intersected with another. The two newly discovered faults and the eastern edge of the New Madrid system all came together in roughly the same area.

The mine was near that bull's-eye.

"We're trying to get a team there to scout it out. Right now it looks like the best site. Walt Jacobs tells me you've already been there. It's called the Golden Orient."

Atkins remembered their trip to the mine—how frightened he'd been from start to finish.

"John, are you all right?"

Atkins was aware of Guy Thompson's voice on the other end of the line. He noticed how the plant manager was watching him.

"I'm fine," he said. He was lying. He didn't want to have anything to do with that mine. But the issue was already settled. They had to explode the bomb at depth. The mine was their only option.

He was going to have to go down there again.

At the mention of Jacobs' name, he wondered how his old friend was doing. He continued to worry about Jacobs and his ability to cope with the loss of his wife and daughter and still do his job. The man needed professional help.

Atkins quietly asked about Elizabeth Holleran. He'd had no idea when he left for Texas how much he'd miss her, or how often he'd find himself thinking about her.

It was Guy Thompson's turn to fall silent. He hesitated before he said, "Something's happened, John. She's all right. We'll talk about it when you get back. We had some trouble with our equipment."

ELIZABETH WASN'T SURE HE UNDERSTOOD HER, OR that he was even listening.

"Walt, did you hear what I just said? Someone stole my laptop. It had to be the same person who turned off the emergency generator. It happened at the same time."

Elizabeth Holleran had gone to Walt Jacobs' partitioned work space after catching several hours of sleep in the equipment room. This time she'd kept the door locked. The sun had just come up. She'd found Jacobs sitting at his desk, staring at printouts of seismograms from aftershocks that continued to occur along the new Caruthersville Fault. The activity hadn't slowed.

Jacobs looked up as if hearing her for the first time.

"Someone . . . stole your computer?" He sounded incredulous.

"In the equipment room. When the power was out."

Elizabeth spoke softly. They were in the library annex. Across a hallway, Guy Thompson and some of his people were feverishly working at an array of computer terminals, trying to calculate the seismic effects of underground nuclear explosions. They'd worked right through the night. Thanks to the president, Thompson had four new high-speed computers to help them crunch numbers. He'd brought the machines back from Washington. Fortunately, they hadn't sustained any irreparable harm when the generator went out. They'd lost some real-time seismic data on the aftershocks but had arranged to have it retransmitted.

Anger had replaced Elizabeth's shock. She regretted she

hadn't gotten a good look at the thief. She couldn't even guess his size or weight and was upset with herself for not reacting more quickly. She'd let him get away.

Elizabeth had already told Thompson, someone she knew she could trust completely. Then she'd gone to Jacobs, who listened quietly as she described what had happened. He seemed distracted.

Before leaving for Texas, Atkins had told Elizabeth about Jacobs' wife and daughter.

She wanted to respect the man's need for privacy to deal with his grief and would have preferred not bothering him at all. That's why she'd initially gone to Thompson, but Jacobs was in charge of the lab. He had to know.

She wished Atkins were back. She needed to talk to him, to be close to him. She admitted to herself for the first time that she was falling in love with him. It was a strong, warm feeling and one she didn't want to lose.

A single fact haunted her. The man who'd entered her room had to be someone who worked at the annex and knew she slept alone, someone she'd seen before. One of the scientists. Someone who knew her movements and was probably still in the building, keeping an eye on her.

Guy Thompson was sure that it was deliberate sabotage by the same person who'd turned off the generators. In his opinion, someone wanted to shut down or steal as many computers as possible to create confusion.

"It's got to be someone who doesn't want us to set off that bomb," he'd said. "What other motive could there be?"

Elizabeth wasn't convinced, if only because she found it almost impossible to believe any of the scientists at the center would go to such lengths. And even if they had, most of them, Jacobs included, had expressed serious doubts about setting off a nuclear bomb underground. So who was it?

She repeated Thompson's comments to Jacobs, who kept staring through her. It was creepy. As if she weren't there.

Finally, he seemed to snap out of it. But when he spoke, it wasn't about what she'd just told him.

"We can't do it," he said, fixing his deep-set eyes on her. "We can't set off a nuclear bomb near an active fault."

IT TOOK BOOKER NEARLY THREE HOURS TO COM-
plete the delicate task of affixing the bonded outer layer of
high explosives and detonators to the MK/B-61's nuclear
package. Working alone in the "operating room" cell deep
in one of the Pantex plant's Gravel Gerties, he was halfway
through the procedure when Atkins told him by telephone
hookup that they'd decided to go for a one-megaton shot.

"Consider it done," the physicist said.

Compared with layering the high explosives, setting the
yield was a simple procedure. By injecting a sufficient quantity of tritium-deuterium gas into the plutonium pit, Booker
was able to boost the bomb's yield from 500 kilotons to just
over one megaton. The implosion process would heat the gas
to the point where its atoms underwent fusion. The result was
a jolt of high energy neutrons that produced the extra bang.

Booker finished up by using an overhead hoist to slip the
nuclear package back into the missile's center subassembly,
its "hard case." The unit contained an array of timers, electronic fusing, and firing circuitry. Weighing less than four
hundred pounds, the bomb resembled an elongated, slimmed-
down trash can made of gleaming stainless steel.

Booker was drenched with sweat when he took off the
lead apron and stepped into the hallway. The steel blast door
clicked shut behind him. Atkins told him that Guy Thompson
and other seismologists back in Memphis had recommended
detonating the bomb in an abandoned coal mine.

"How deep?" Booker asked.

"About two thousand feet. I've been there. It's a vertical shaft mine with two air vents."

"Good. I can work with that," Booker said. "But we'll have to worry about venting."

Atkins knew that was one of the main risks of an underground explosion, the possibility that radioactive debris and gases would escape into the atmosphere, venting from cracks that blew open in the ground.

It had happened before—sometimes with disastrous consequences. Massive amounts of "hot" dust, soot, and gas had contaminated the earth's atmosphere.

One of the worst accidents, Booker explained, happened during a test code-named "Baneberry." The device was detonated in December 1970 at the Nevada Test Site sixty-five miles northwest of Las Vegas. Booker had been there.

It was a relatively small shot—ten kilotons. At zero hour, the moment they fired the weapon, Booker had been sitting in the "red shack," the control room three miles from the test site.

"The hole was too shallow. Only about five hundred feet deep. We'd stemmed it with sand and gravel after wiring the bomb. When it went off, I was watching the television monitors. You could see the ground ripple up and down as the shock wave moved toward us. It pitched us up in our chairs. Then all hell broke loose."

The explosion ripped a gaping hole in the desert floor and sent a cloud of radioactive gas eight thousand feet into the sky. The cloud drifted as far as North Dakota.

"We'll have to figure out how to collapse those air tunnels and the elevator shaft," Booker said. "We won't have time to backfill them." He looked at Atkins. "This is going to be tricky."

"How will you detonate the bomb?" Atkins asked.

"We used cable with all of our underground shots at the NTS," Booker said. "That's out of the question. The ground's too active. One good earthquake, and the cable could snap." He considered the options. "We might try a radio signal, but I'd worry about all the deflection—bouncing the microwave beam down a mine shaft." He thought some more. "I'd opt for a timed charge."

"Where would you set it?"

"As deep in the mine as I could go. I'd use a capacitor bank to produce the electrical charge that would start the firing sequence."

"What happens after you set the timer?"

"You get the hell out of there as fast as you can," Booker said. He didn't smile. "The advantage of a timer is that it's virtually foolproof. The disadvantage is that once it's set and the bomb is armed, you can't easily stop the process."

Their immediate job finished, Booker and Atkins took the elevator up from the lower cell to the bunker's main level. Carson, the plant manager, was waiting for them.

Atkins knew something was wrong as soon as he saw him. The man was holding several sheets of yellow paper with shaking hands. He looked like he'd just been given terrible news. He nervously pushed his reading glasses higher up on his nose.

"The president's national security chief just called," he said, his voice faltering. "Fighting has broken out between units of the Kentucky National Guard and the regular Army."

"What!" Booker said.

Atkins felt like sitting down. He was numb. To his knowledge nothing like that had happened since the Civil War, American troops fighting other American soldiers. He couldn't even begin to comprehend the horror of what that meant.

Looking at his scribbled notes, Carson said, "The governor of Kentucky has ordered National Guard units to oppose any attempt to explode a nuclear device in his state. They've been instructed to use deadly force if necessary. There's been shooting in western Kentucky between guardsmen and units of the 101st Airborne. The fighting is continuing sporadically."

"Any casualties?" Atkins asked.

The plant manager nodded. "On both sides. I don't have any numbers."

All this meant a drastic change in plans. Instead of waiting until morning to leave, Booker and Atkins had been ordered to depart immediately. Originally, they'd planned to fly. Now they were going to ride back with the bomb in a tractor trailer.

"Why don't we fly?" Atkins asked. "It'll take another half day to drive back to Kentucky."

"They're worried about a rocket attack when the plane lands," Carson said. "There aren't that many landing places and they're probably under surveillance. Apparently some of the guard units in Kentucky are equipped with shoulder-fired SAM rockets. The fear is a plane would be too good a target. They'll know what it's carrying, and they'll be watching for it."

"When do we leave?" Booker asked.

"In fifteen minutes," the plant manager said. "We've already sent out two decoy convoys. I'd suggest you get something to eat."

The gray eighteen-wheeler was already waiting for them outside the Gravel Gertie, its engine running. Guards in military fatigues were lined on both sides of the vehicle, weapons at the ready. The big rig looked as though it had logged a lot of miles. The fenders were coated with red, Texas dust.

"The truck is armored," Carson said. "Its communication system allows it to be tracked continuously by satellite." The convoy would also include two vans. "These vehicles will be operated by DOE couriers who have authority to shoot to kill."

At exactly 1:30 in the afternoon, they rolled through a back gate at the Pantex plant. A cold wind knifed across the east Texas prairie, blowing rain against the windshield. Atkins and Booker sat behind the driver and a guard who had an automatic rifle nestled between his legs. The semi was flanked by two beige vans. They'd also have an air escort— Air Force helicopters and fixed wing aircraft that patrolled the highway along their route, all 780 miles of it.

Within twenty minutes, the truck was on Interstate 40, skirting Amarillo. The Oklahoma border was a one-hour drive to the east.

The bomb was in a padded container in the back of the trailer. It was strapped down, the container bolted to the floor and padlocked. Three armed guards rode with it.

"It's going to be a fast ride," the driver said, glancing over his shoulder at his two passengers. "We want to be across the Missouri line in five hours. As soon as we get out of the Amarillo traffic, we're gonna open it up. You might want to try to catch a few winks. It's a long drive."

Atkins settled back into his seat. The compartment behind the driver was equipped with a bunk bed, a tiny bathroom, and a television console. He watched the rain and sleet beat on the windshield and listened to the wipers click back and forth. During the last twenty-four hours, he'd only managed a couple of catnaps. Normally the sound of the rain would have been enough to help him drift off. Not this time.

He knew he wasn't going to sleep.

CHANDLER. Bristow. Sapulpa.

The driver was as good as his word, blasting by the small Oklahoma towns that lined the highway at more than eighty miles an hour. He picked up Interstate 44 just east of Oklahoma City. Three hours later, they were approaching the Missouri line.

The guard seated next to the driver occasionally spoke by radio to the helicopters and other aircraft shadowing the small convoy. They'd also picked up several more vehicles near Oklahoma City, four vans that had driven up from Fort Sill.

"They're carrying two teams of Special Forces troops," the driver said. "They're gonna hang with us until we get to the Mississippi."

Unable to relax or get his mind off Thompson's cryptic message about Elizabeth, Atkins asked Booker about some of the nuclear test shots he'd witnessed. More than an attempt to make conversation, he was genuinely curious.

"The first was Mike out on Elugelab Island in 1952," Booker said, rousing himself from a catnap. "It had a couple of firsts. The first hydrogen bomb, the first yield over one megaton. It was way over. Mike yielded 10.4 megatons. Only one other shot since then has even come close. When we got the primary and secondary all set up, I swear the thing looked more like a small oil refinery than a bomb. It completely vaporized the island."

The fireball left a crater two hundred feet deep and a mile across, a blue hole punched into what had once been an atoll lagoon. Birds turned to cinders in midair. An island fourteen miles to the south was incinerated. Trees were stripped of bark. Animals of their skin.

"It was an incredibly dirty bomb," Booker said. "No one really knew how big it was going to be. No one could have imagined . . . The cloud reached 57,000 feet in two minutes. The stem was thirty miles high. The top eventually billowed out like a huge umbrella one hundred miles wide. Mike scared the bloody shit out of us."

"Where were you at zero hour?" Atkins asked.

"On an old World War Two minesweeper thirty miles away. I was up on deck and had dark glasses on. The heat felt like someone had opened an oven door in my face. The shock wave was spectacular, a long, loud clap of thunder. I waited a couple minutes until I thought it was safe and whipped off my glasses. I had no idea . . . You can't imagine how big it was. The enormousness of the fireball. It blotted out the sun. The cloud looked like it was going to roll right over us."

Booker reclined in his seat. The soft glow of a reading light in the overhead console left his face in shadows. "I got my first dose of radioactivity on the Mike shot," he said. "You think I would have learned my lesson, but I let it happen again ten years later. That time I really did it up good."

When Atkins asked what had happened, Booker folded his hands on his chest. He sat there a few moments before he began. "It was at the NTS in 1962. The Sedan shot. We set off a 104-kiloton device at a depth of 635 feet. We must have been out of our minds to do it so shallow. It was part of the Plowshare Program to show that nuclear explosions could be used for such peaceful purposes as digging canals and God knows what else. The bomb blew a 320-foot-deep crater a quarter-mile wide and sent columns of dirt, stone, and highly radioactive dust 12,000 feet into the air. Seven and a half million cubic yards of debris went up. All of it red hot. The ceiling was twice what we'd predicted."

Booker described how they'd penned up thirty beagles in wire cages at distances between twelve and forty miles from ground zero. Their mouths were taped shut so they wouldn't ingest the fallout.

"All but two of those dogs died," Booker said.

The bomb team waited out the explosion in the red shack several miles away. "I went back to the blast site way too soon," Booker said. "The place was a lot hotter than I'd been told."

Booker stared at Atkins, blinking in the dim light. Then he said, "They told me I'd gotten about two hundred roentgens. I found out a couple years later through back channels that I'd actually received a whole-body dose of nearly four hundred roentgens."

Atkins knew that a roentgen measured the amount of exposure to gamma rays. Four hundred roentgens was a lot of radiation.

Guessing his thoughts, Booker said, "Six hundred is usually lethal."

"Doesn't it affect bone marrow?" Atkins said.

There was a strange look on Booker's face. "It can cause leukemia," he said, turning off the overhead light. Atkins could hear his deep, regular breaths in the darkness.

"I've been in remission for two years, but it's starting to come back," Booker said. "My white blood cells are a mess. Most of the time, like right now, I feel fine, but I can tell I'm slipping, losing energy in bits and pieces. The doctors say I could live another three to five years. Or maybe a lot less."

"Why are you doing all this?" Atkins asked. He didn't know what else to say.

Booker leaned closer and spoke in a whisper so the two men in the front of the cab couldn't overhear him.

"They lied to me," he said. "The government, my superiors. They all lied, and I'm going to die because of it. They've lied to the American public for years about the effects of the radiation clouds that blew across the country in the fifties and sixties. They lied about the high rates of leukemia and sterility and cancer in Nevada, New Mexico, and Wyoming. Lied about what caused it. I made my peace with myself over that a long time ago. Had to or I would have gone crazy. But I swear to God, whatever happens in the next few days, I'm not going to let anybody lie about it."

THE PRESIDENT STARED IN GRIM SILENCE AT THE
aerial photographs arrayed on his desk. One showed the
wreckage of an Army Huey burning in a field in western
Kentucky. Others were tight close-ups of Kentucky National
Guard tanks dug into position at key intersections in that
part of the state.

"How many units have declared loyalty to Governor Parker?" he asked.

"We think no more than five," said Meg Greenland, his
national security adviser. "About seven hundred men in all.
They control twenty-five heavy tanks and two helicopter
squadrons. They've also attracted some paramilitary types."
She looked hard at the president, who was studying the enlarged photographs taken a few hours earlier by air reconnaissance. "Injuries are estimated at just over one hundred."

"How many killed?" Ross asked.

"At least thirty," Greenland said. "That includes about
sixteen men from the 101st Airborne and other units based
at Fort Campbell. Most have been killed in fire fights in
the far western part of the state. We expect those numbers
to increase."

President Ross had gathered his key advisers in the Oval
Office to discuss the rapidly worsening military picture in
Kentucky. The governor, interviewed in hiding by a cable
television crew, had explained his reasons for armed resistance. Ross had watched the tape five times. He had to admit
that Governor Parker had eloquently stated his opposition to

a plan to detonate a nuclear device in his state. He'd called it madness and questioned the president's sanity, pledging to the people of Kentucky that he'd do whatever was in his power to stop the blast, even if it meant armed opposition. He told them that federal troops had attacked elements of the Kentucky National Guard, who were defending themselves.

That last part wasn't true, but Ross was going to make no mention of it when he addressed the American people within the next hour.

All in all, Parker had been impressive. Just the right mixture of somber gravity and determination.

The president's science adviser, Steve Draper, had been on a special satellite hookup almost constantly with the seismologists in Memphis. He'd given Ross a list of arguments for detonating a one-megaton bomb deep in a coal mine near the town of Benton in southwestern Kentucky.

It was anything but a unanimous decision. In fact, a narrow majority of the scientists opposed the idea as too risky. Those in favor of the plan thought it had no more than a fifty-fifty chance of success.

"Are there any other options?" Ross asked. He kept coming back to that.

Draper shook his head. "They've offered none."

"Do they still think we're going to get hit with another big quake?"

"They do," Draper said. "Opinions on when vary from a couple days to months."

"Then we go ahead as planned," Ross said. The scientists were going to let him make the call. So be it. He'd known that all along. The decision—and the blame—would be his. That was as it should be. He didn't mind. As he saw it, he had no choice. It was either gamble and try to defuse the quake with a nuclear explosion, or do nothing and face unspeakable devastation.

He asked about evacuations. Soldiers were trying to remove everyone within a thirty-mile radius of the Golden Orient mine. It was a huge undertaking and there wasn't much time. The difficulties were aggravated by the lack of communications and the earthquake-damaged highways.

Fortunately, the area wasn't densely populated. Still, an estimated 200,000 people lived in the danger zone.

"Where's the convoy from Texas?"

Draper glanced at his watch. "They should be in Missouri about now, Mister President. Estimated arrival time is 10:00 P.M. So far, the trip's been uneventful."

"We've sent two companies of paratroopers to meet them on the Missouri side of the river," said General Frank Simmons, head of the Joint Chiefs of Staff. "I'm worried about the crossing. It's a damn big river down there with a lot of places to launch an attack on that pontoon bridge."

They were going to cross the Mississippi in extreme southeastern Missouri a few miles downstream from its confluence with the Ohio. The crossing was about 150 miles north of Memphis. With the flooding rivers far out of their banks, the pontoon span that stretched to the Kentucky shore was nearly three miles long.

"Do whatever needs to be done to secure the area," the president told the general. "If there's fighting, we won't be the ones who start it. But I want that bomb delivered."

BULLETINS had already flashed on radios and television screens, announcing that the president was going to address the nation at 7:00 P.M. EST "on a topic of greatest urgency."

The cameras were set up in the Oval Office. When the hour came, Ross wore a blue suit and tie. It was the first time he'd shaved in several days. He knew it would be the most important speech of his life.

"Good evening, my fellow citizens," he said, echoing the words John F. Kennedy had used when he announced his arms embargo on Cuba in 1962.

Ross began by explaining the scope of the damage from the earthquake that had struck only five days earlier. The tremors had been felt as far northeast as Montreal, as far west as Albuquerque, New Mexico, and as far south as Biloxi, Mississippi.

"It's the worst natural disaster ever to befall our country," Ross said. "I don't have to tell you that. The odds are you felt the main earthquake and continue to feel some of the aftershocks. Nearly sixty percent of the population live in areas that have experienced shaking. If you live on the East Coast, you're facing shortages of food and heating oil. If you live in middle America, the heartland, my part of the

country, you're coping every day with a horror that's hard
to imagine.

"In my own state of Illinois, more than two thousand
people have been killed. Most of them in the southern part
of the state near the quake zone. In Memphis"—he paused,
looking down at some notes—"the death count is estimated
at twelve thousand men, women, and children."

There were gasps among the assembled reporters listening
to the speech in the press room in the East Wing. These
were the first official death counts. And they were staggering.

"Some towns have been destroyed. Paducah, Kentucky,
no longer exists. Neither does Caruthersville, Missouri.
Memphis has been devastated. Little Rock, St. Louis, Louisville, Indianapolis, and Cincinnati have been hard hit. Chicago has been damaged.

"My fellow Americans, I want you to see the names of
some of the cities and towns that have suffered fatalities.
The list I'm going to show you is only partial."

The president spent the next ten minutes reading the casualty list. As he spoke, the state-by-state list was shown on
television screens.

Missouri	DEAD	INJURED	MISSING
St. Louis	7,321	22,000	12,000
Farmington	590	430	320
Perryville	158	110	129
Poplar Bluff	1,785	442	441
Dexter	240	111	224
Cape Girardeau	2,150	1,822	664
Charleston	351	335	156
Malden	288	166	123
New Madrid	156	99	78

Arkansas	DEAD	INJURED	MISSING
Blytheville	2,320	7,207	1,205
Jonesboro	3,159	9,983	986
Trumann	130	542	223
Newport	175	334	44
Wynne	59	123	65
Searcy	111	435	156

Arkansas	DEAD	INJURED	MISSING
Cabot	201	498	89
Jacksonville	394	1,288	455
Pine Bluff	1,403	7,334	337
Little Rock	1,515	12,998	567
Brinkley	607	1,232	114
Forrest City	352	4,567	495
West Memphis	1,506	8,002	653
Osceola	794	1,500	93
Stuttgart	317	2,456	253
Marianna	510	1,139	46
Paragould	651	1,988	112

Kentucky	DEAD	INJURED	MISSING
Madisonville	1,450	4,568	336
Hopkinsville	1,382	5,899	657
Central City	112	782	62
Paducah	3,115	9,201	304
Mayfield	2,469	3,998	509
Murray	876	1,674	110
Princeton	386	871	99
Owensboro	1,590	8,345	503
Bowling Green	1,699	5,877	223
Elizabethtown	1,498	4,556	321
Radcliff	1,101	4,338	403
Louisville	5,160	20,227	1,206
Frankfort	2,590	6,203	887
Lexington	4,153	17,456	1,455
Harrodsburg	1,112	7,659	348
Bardstown	943	6,865	276
Glasgow	956	2,128	318
Russellville	678	1,356	445
Henderson	1,334	8,542	1,278
Convington	873	11,237	1,452

Tennessee	DEAD	INJURED	MISSING
Union City	1,084	3,112	349
Dyersburg	1,756	5,433	874
Millington	1,802	4,621	470

Tennessee	DEAD	INJURED	MISSING
Martin	211	1,347	273
Dickson	789	7,403	728
Clarksville	2,223	13,906	1,256
Bolivar	849	2,334	448
Memphis	12,301	38,446	3,456
Savannah	498	1,236	108
Lawrenceburg	896	2,333	302
Pulaski	674	1,802	225
Nashville	1,568	19,995	1,445
Murfreesboro	982	9,332	874
Lewisburg	610	993	156
Shelbyville	1,473	3,489	347
Fayetteville	641	1,543	76
Winchester	396	885	64
Tullahoma	817	2,877	274
Oak Ridge	887	4,886	392
Cookeville	1,245	6,112	406
Knoxville	1,539	23,023	1,112
Harriman	293	1,654	402
Beckwood	21	121	12
Athens	802	2,456	294
Crossville	94	653	87

Indiana	DEAD	INJURED	MISSING
Evansville	1,826	13,459	445
New Albany	1,246	8,334	997
Boonville	348	995	16
Mount Vernon	312	887	34
Richmond	856	7,556	456
Fort Wayne	991	16,225	1,043
Muncie	1,119	7,034	761
Indianapolis	1,159	18,877	667
Anderson	1,005	6,034	774
Huntington	599	8,861	138
Kokomo	983	5,645	304
Terre Haute	1,198	5,991	802
Madison	598	7,558	760

Illinois	DEAD	INJURED	MISSING
Metropolis	650	2,039	178
Cairo	826	3,451	456
Evansville	63	224	13
Lawrenceville	632	877	145
Mount Vernon	1,529	2,344	287
East St. Louis	552	1,877	882
Belleville	1,113	5,002	446
Carbondale	2,496	6,034	332
Murphysboro	812	1,334	112
Effingham	302	986	223
Vandalia	224	882	98
Decatur	1,324	5,432	338
Bloomington	994	6,788	445
Champaign-Urbana	1,344	8,344	600
Peoria	882	1,455	551
Chicago	498	5,203	7,714
Kankakee	79	443	21

Ohio	DEAD	INJURED	MISSING
Hamilton	240	678	32
Fairfield	192	487	112
Middletown	478	1,345	334
Portsmouth	567	4,566	116
Cincinnati	1,842	8,912	223
Hillsboro	216	778	101

Mississippi	DEAD	INJURED	MISSING
Corinth	965	6,432	249
Holly Springs	217	784	83
Oxford	798	8,201	449
Booneville	551	1,203	228
New Albany	112	892	173
Clarksdale	872	2,003	445
Grenada	847	1,333	269
Columbus	903	5,777	339
Greenville	651	6,212	230

Mississippi	DEAD	INJURED	MISSING
Aberdeen	59	445	17
Vicksburg	788	1,998	107

Alabama	DEAD	INJURED	MISSING
Florence	65	445	72
Decatur	115	656	46
Huntsville	194	558	32
Normal	35	188	56
Russellville	79	358	98
Barton	22	113	11
Cherokee	105	605	22

Louisiana	DEAD	INJURED	MISSING
Lake Providence	84	334	14
Bastrop	37	267	9
Monroe	41	498	56
Ruston	65	601	18

The death toll had edged over 130,000.

As he finished reading the appalling list, Ross looked up at the cameras. He said that one, possibly two more quakes in the magnitude 8 range or greater were extremely likely.

There were more audible gasps from the news corps and from some of his own staff members who hadn't been privy to these details.

Ross announced what they were going to do. Explode a nuclear bomb underground.

And why.

Some reporters dashed out of the press room and began calling their news desks. Ross went on to describe the evacuations.

"Even as I discuss these grave issues with you, efforts are under way in the state of Kentucky. I know the thought of a nuclear explosion can be frightening. The scientists say it's the only way we can hope to defuse another earthquake, turn it off in the ground by releasing some of its energy.

"There is disagreement among the experts about whether this will work. I'd be lying to you if I said most of them supported this approach. The truth is otherwise. Most are opposed. I've decided to side with the minority who have argued—persuasively, in my opinion—that we have no other choice. There is sufficient evidence from ground surveys made by satellite that energy continues to build at a frightening rate in the New Madrid Seismic Zone, especially along a newly discovered fault, which slices through the heart of west-central Kentucky.''

He told them the kind of bomb they planned to explode and the anticipated yield. He didn't give specifics on where it would be detonated. That would remain top secret for as long as possible.

"The truth is we already have experience with a nuclear explosion in the Mississippi Valley.'' He mentioned a five-kiloton blast near the tiny Mississippi town of Salmon, about thirty-five miles from Hattiesburg. The shot in 1964 was a successful effort to hollow out a salt dome as a possible storage site for oil reserves. No radioactivity had vented from the explosion, which was done at a shallow depth of less than 400 feet.

"They barely felt it over in Hattiesburg,'' the president said. "This explosion will be considerably larger. The geologists say it will have the short-range effect of a magnitude 6.5 earthquake. I have to tell you that this will probably cause some additional damage.''

Ross paused and in his firmest voice went on: "I believe the damage will be nothing compared with the consequences of another magnitude 8 earthquake. There will be risks, but I'm convinced we have to take them. I don't think the Mississippi Valley could survive another major earthquake.''

Turning aside from his notes, Ross spoke to those who'd taken up arms against the government, quoting from President Lincoln's second inaugural address. Carefully avoiding any mention of the governor of Kentucky, he repeated Lincoln's words about people who stood on two sides of a national debate, those who "would make war rather than let the nation survive; and the other would accept war rather than let it perish.'' He asked members of the Kentucky National Guard and any others "who have joined their ranks'' to lay down their arms. He promised there would be no penalty if they did so within forty-eight hours.

Finishing, Ross said, "I want you all to know that I'll be

there when the bomb is detonated. We've got to try to turn off this monster in the ground. Kill it by whatever means possible. Then we can start the long and painful task—and it will be painful—of rebuilding our cities and our lives.

"I'm sure we'll come through this and look back upon these awful times as one of our greatest moments. May our Heavenly Father guide and help us all. Good night."

Ross sat at his desk, staring into the cameras as the television lights blinked off. He felt overwhelmed by what he'd just told the American people and was grateful his voice hadn't cracked. He'd almost lost it as he read the casualty list.

Steve Draper approached. He had news.

The convoy from Texas had made better time than expected. It was nearing the Mississippi River.

THE TRANSPORT GROUP FROM THE PANTEX PLANT
turned off Interstate 44 near St. James, Missouri, and took
two-lane blacktop that rose, plunged, and twisted through
rolling Ozark foothills. Several hours later, it picked up Interstate 55 near Sikeston, deep in the southern corner of the
state. Demolition teams were blasting away the rubble from
dozens of collapsed overpasses to open the highway, which
had become a major lifeline for the stricken Mississippi Valley. With most airports knocked out, a hundred-mile stretch
of I-55 running from the Missouri–Arkansas border to just
north of Memphis had been transformed into a series of run-
ways for cargo planes loaded with relief supplies.

Forty minutes after reaching Sikeston, the convoy arrived
at their destination, Wilson City, Missouri. It was just after
midnight.

The town had been converted into a staging area for Army
engineers who'd thrown the pontoon bridge across the swollen Mississippi. The streets were filled with Humvees, troop
trucks, earth movers, and other pieces of heavy equipment.
The earthquake-ravaged town had been evacuated. Most of
the frame and shingle homes were severely damaged, the
residents moved to a tent city near Sikeston, one of hundreds
that were being set up throughout the Mississippi Valley to
house the homeless.

They were about forty miles due west from Paducah and
fifty miles north of Caruthersville, where nearly six days

earlier, Atkins had crossed the river with Elizabeth Holleran aboard the ferry.

It was pitch-dark. Atkins could smell the river's pungent scent and felt a tingling up his back when he remembered the last time he'd had to cross it. He asked an Army major about the waterfall.

"It's still there, but subsiding," said the officer, who was with the Corps of Engineers. "The drop-off is down to about ten feet. The river's still running backward in stretches. It was a bitch throwing a pontoon across it."

"We lost two men," another officer said curtly, a colonel. Like everyone else, he wore fatigues, flak jacket, and helmet.

The plan was quickly worked out. The bomb was unloaded from the tractor trailer into the back of a Humvee for the trip across the bridge. Two squads of paratroopers from Fort Campbell were already patrolling its three-mile length. A flotilla of small boats, fighting the current with powerful motors, was in position above and below the span. So were helicopter gunships. The darkness was filled with the staccato beat of rotor blades.

"I've got to tell you, this is going to be dicey," said the colonel, the officer in charge. "We've had a couple nasty fire fights on the opposite shore. I wish we could hold this up until it was secure over there, but they want to get you across right away."

The Humvee with the bomb was the third of six identical vehicles that would cross the river at spaced intervals. After Booker made sure the weapon was securely strapped down in back, they drove out to the bridge, where they were given life jackets. The crossing was to be made in complete darkness. Only the taillights of the vehicles were lit.

"We're going to drive over that?" Booker said in shock, staring at the narrow, single-lane roadway that floated on what looked like an interlocking chain of barges. The metal couplings creaked loudly as the sections rocked and banged together in the rough water. Atkins heard the waves slapping hard against the shore.

"We've got fifty paratroopers out there," said their driver, a sergeant. "We'll get you boys across."

Accelerating slowly up the metal ramp, they drove out on the pitching span. There was less than a yard of freeboard on each side of the vehicle and no side railings to prevent a tire from slipping off.

"I guarantee this is one ride you're gonna remember," the driver said, grinning. He clenched an unlit cigar in his teeth. A soldier wearing a radio headset sat next to him. Booker and Atkins were in the backseat. The bomb was in the Humvee's cargo bay.

They were about a quarter of the way across when the first explosion sent up a spray of water to the right of them. Atkins saw a flash of light and felt the bridge rock up and down. Another rocket hit the river thirty yards upstream. The first rocket had been fired from the Kentucky side. The second from the Missouri shore.

"They've got us bracketed," said the sergeant.

Automatic weapons hammered away somewhere upstream. Two helicopters appeared suddenly, zoomed over the bridge at low altitude, and streaked upriver, their powerful spotlights angling down, probing the shoreline.

They were out about a mile. Not even to the middle of the river. Atkins saw two boats roaring upstream, leaving wakes that glistened in the misty gloom. There was another flash of light, much closer, followed by an explosion.

The driver slammed on the brakes.

"Motherfucker. They hit one of the Humvees," he shouted.

Atkins saw the yellow flames ahead of them. He leaned out of the window and watched as soldiers hurriedly pushed the burning vehicle into the river. Then the sound of rapid, heavy gunfire erupted again. Coming from the Kentucky shore, red tracers arched across the water. The soldiers on the bridge were returning fire.

Leaning forward, Atkins said, "How much farther?"

The driver started to answer when the front windshield shattered. Hit in the shoulder, he pitched to the side. There was blood everywhere.

Reaching around the wounded man, Atkins grabbed the steering wheel. The other soldier, a corporal, managed to get a boot on the brake pedal. When they stopped the Humvee, Atkins helped him get the sergeant into the back.

"Can you drive this?" the corporal shouted, sliding into the front seat. He was returning fire with an M-16, the ejected brass casings clattering on the metal floorboards. He'd braced the barrel of the rifle on the door's window frame.

Atkins inched along the side of the Humvee and slipped into the driver's seat.

There were still two Humvees in front of them, the closest fifty yards ahead, its taillights rapidly receding in the darkness.

Another rocket slammed into the bridge from the Kentucky shoreline. The span lurched up and down.

"This man's badly hurt," Booker said. The sergeant lay slumped in his arms as he held a compress over the wound.

Atkins gave the Humvee the gas. He got the speed up to twenty and held it there. They were nearing the place where the rocket had slammed into the deck.

Two soldiers were waving for them to stop. They were out in the middle of the bridge.

The pontoon section in front of them was starting to come apart.

The rocket had severed some of the cables.

Atkins pumped on the brakes and the Humvee started to slide on the wet metal surface. He saw the black gap opening between two pontoon sections. They were coming up on it fast. He pushed down on the brakes for all he was worth, downshifting into first gear.

The Humvee came to a stop several yards from the edge.

Gunfire raked the bridge. Bullets ricocheted off the Humvee's right fender. Tracers were arcing out at them from the black shoreline.

Soldiers were frantically pulling on two long chains, trying to draw the separated sections of the floating bridge back together. The opening between them was about five feet.

"Get it closer!" Atkins shouted to the soldiers. He threw the Humvee into reverse and started backing up.

"What the hell you think you're doing?" the corporal said. "You gonna try to back all the way off this thing?"

Atkins stopped suddenly. He was about one hundred yards from the gap in the deck. He told the corporal and Booker to brace themselves and check the straps of their life jackets. Then he floored the gas pedal.

"Jeeeesus!" the soldier shouted, realizing what Atkins had in mind. "We're never gonna make this."

Atkins glanced at the speedometer as he fought to hold the heavy vehicle in a straight line on the wet deck.

They were doing thirty miles an hour when they reached the gap between the sections. They were airborne less than two seconds, slamming down hard on the pontoon deck with a few feet to spare. Atkins fought to keep from losing control as the Humvee slid sideways, then straightened out.

In another minute they reached the end of the span and banged down off the metal deck onto muddy ground. Atkins pulled into a clearing in the woods and parked. Soldiers ran up to them.

The corporal slumped back in his seat. Reaching across to shake Atkins' hand, he said, "You can drive for me any time you want."

After helping a team of medics get the wounded sergeant out of the backseat, Booker examined the bomb. He made a brief but careful inspection and pronounced it undamaged.

The colonel who'd led the convoy met them. There was more trouble. National Guard troops were dug in around the route they'd planned to take to the mine. Not many, but enough to risk a bloodbath if they tried to force their way through. The road was also clogged with people trying to get out of the evacuation zone.

"The president doesn't want a confrontation," the officer said. "We've got scouts out trying to find another way to the mine."

Atkins heard gunfire in the distance, the spatting of small-arms fire. "I may know someone who could help," he said. Someone who knew this country better than anyone else.

AN ARMY UH-60 LANDED IN THE CLEARING, ITS RO-
tors kicking up dirt and fallen leaves. Coming in at low
altitude from the Missouri side of the Mississippi, the big
blue helicopter made its approach as four Cobra gunships
hovered overhead.

Atkins watched as Elizabeth Holleran, Guy Thompson,
and Walt Jacobs scrambled out, heads down, running to get
away from the strong downdraft. Two other men he didn't
get a look at followed them in the darkness.

Atkins ran over to meet Elizabeth. She put her hands on
his face and gave him a quick kiss.

"I'm fine," she whispered, smiling when he started to ask
about the "trouble" Guy Thompson had mentioned. "I'll
tell you later."

Atkins had been worried about her ever since he'd left
Texas with the bomb. Wondering what had happened, he
wanted to talk to her, but there was no privacy and too much
was happening. He was struck by the power of his emotions
when he saw her after their brief separation. Her smile and
the touch of her fingers on his face lifted his spirits. The
strength of his feelings for her continued to surprise him.

"I was hoping you'd be here," he said.

"Sorry I didn't make it until you were already across the
river," she said.

He laughed out loud, and it felt good. "You planned it
that way, right?"

"Absolutely."

He was surprised to see Walt Jacobs with her. Jacobs looked totally exhausted. His bearded face and bright eyes peered out from under his hooded parka.

Guessing what was on Atkins' mind, Jacobs put up his hands apologetically. "I know. I still think this is a bad decision and that we're taking a tremendous risk, but I had to be here, John. I want to help, and anyway, I feel like I got you into this mess in the first place." His smile was genuine. "If this works, I'll make sure you get a nice promotion."

"And if it doesn't?" Atkins asked, taking his friend's hand and shaking it hard in gratitude. It meant a lot to have Jacobs here. And it was good to see him smiling again.

"Then we'll both enjoy an early retirement."

Or a jail cell, Atkins thought, only half in jest. He wasn't sure a nuclear explosion at depth would work either, not completely, but he knew it was their only chance to stop another earthquake. He agreed with the president. He wanted to kill the beast that was growing ever stronger in the ground, kill it any way he could by whatever means. There was no way he was going to back away from this. They were going to explode that bomb. For once, they were going to fight back. They weren't just going to sit there and wait for the country to be shaken apart again. Not this time.

Atkins was convinced this was the right place to try to end the nightmare. The American heartland. The heart and soul of the Mississippi Valley. It gave him an emotional boost just being there and knowing he was with the right people. Booker, Elizabeth, and now Jacobs.

And if it worked, if they actually pulled it off? What would that mean?

He didn't want to try to think that far ahead. He tried to put those thoughts out of mind.

It was just after midnight. No stars were visible in the overcast sky. Lights were kept to a minimum. It wasn't until they'd all jammed into the back of a windowless Army trailer to work out their plans that Atkins noticed the two men who'd also gotten off the helicopter with Walt and Elizabeth—Paul Weston and Mark Wren.

Not expecting them, he looked for Weston's other assistant, Stan Marshal, the geologist who'd been operating the blaster when that unexpected explosion nearly killed Elizabeth and him a few days earlier.

He still hadn't figured out what had happened. A freak radio signal might have triggered the premature detonation just as Marshal and Wren had suggested. That kind of thing happened often enough during highway blasting, often with tragic results. And yet Atkins still had his doubts and that bothered him.

One thing remained fixed in his mind: there was no way in hell he would have gone into a mine with Marshal. Weston must have realized that.

Looking well-groomed even in a dirty jumpsuit, Weston was clean shaven, something Atkins hadn't managed for several days. He'd been wearing the same clothes for nearly a week—a pair of twill trousers, cotton sweater, and an insulated parka. He couldn't remember the last time he'd changed or had a shower.

Weston started with the announcement that the Seismic Commission had broken all ties with the governor of Kentucky. "If I could make a personal comment," he said. "I believe the course he's taken is treasonable. I also believe it's tragic. I liked the man."

He then made a stunning comment. He said he'd come to agree with the minority viewpoint, believing that a deep explosion was their only viable chance to break the lethal cycle of earthquakes. He said he'd gone on record with this in a letter to the president.

"I want to apologize to anyone who feels I was short-tempered or . . . unreasonable these last few days," he said, looking straight at Atkins and Elizabeth. "I've got to be honest. I doubt this will work, but I can't think of any other option. I keep coming back to Doctor Holleran's data about previous earthquakes. It's what finally convinced me we've got to try something. The paleoseismic record of those earthquakes was overwhelming. I couldn't ignore it."

"Wow," Elizabeth said softly to Atkins. "I knew about Walt. I wanted to let him tell you himself. But Weston's a real surprise."

It was interesting, but it didn't change anything, Atkins thought. After this crisis passed—if it passed—he still meant to call for an investigation about those cracks they'd seen in the Kentucky Dam. He figured he owed it to the people who'd drowned when the dam was swept away. Weston should have called for an evacuation. He hadn't done so, and Atkins vowed he wouldn't let the matter drop.

Atkins had already mentioned it to Weston. He'd had a brief conversation with him just before he left for the Pantex plant with Booker. He wanted to see how Weston would react when he casually told him that he'd seen the cracks himself and thought they looked pretty large. Weston hadn't even blinked. He simply told him his observations might be useful later when they did a postmortem on the disaster. Then he walked away.

The man, Atkins realized listening to him here, was incredibly smooth. It wasn't going to be easy to nail him.

A brigadier general from the 101st Airborne had begun to bring them up to date on the fighting when there was a sharp knock on the trailer's metal door.

"You people better take a look at this," said a paratrooper, whose face was streaked with black camouflage paint. He carried a machine gun.

They all poured out of the trailer into the cold, damp air. The shooting had stopped. The sound of patrolling helicopters echoed overhead.

Everyone's eyes focused on the eastern sky, where the thick cloud cover had broken open.

Bands of brilliant lights were streaking across the horizon—blue, white, pale orange. Shimmering waves of color that seemed to change in hue and vividness as they rippled in the sky. The hills were rimmed in greenish light that seemed to hover just over the ridgeline.

The spectacle was riveting. The earthquake lights were brighter, the colors more vivid than the last time Atkins had seen them.

He felt the first movement then, a slight quiver.

Elizabeth looked at him.

The ground had started to shake.

GOVERNOR TAD PARKER FELT THE TREMOR.

His command post was in southern Kentucky twenty miles north of the Tennessee border. It was one of the sharpest tremors he'd experienced since the big earthquake.

They'd taken shelter in a remote, backwoods valley near Mammoth Cave, about twenty-five miles northeast of Bowling Green. For the last few days they'd let the hills screen them as much as possible, moving mainly by jeep and all-terrain vehicles. They'd changed position repeatedly, trying to avoid a confrontation with Army troops.

The governor was with a squad of the Kentucky National Guard. Fifty men. Most of the guard units in the state had ignored his call. Only five had turned out, and he'd had no complaints about their performance. About thirty men had taken positions in the hills around the mine. They could be overrun, but it wasn't going to be easy. It was rugged country with a lot of good defensive positions. With any luck, they could delay the movement of the bomb for a long time.

And that was the best Parker could hope for. Delay.

He was under no illusions. There was little he could do to stop them.

When the latest tremor struck, Parker still hadn't fallen asleep in his tent. He hadn't been able to sleep more than a few hours in days. Getting out of his cot, he was unable to tie his boots. His hands fumbled with the knots.

Parker stepped outside his tent and saw the strange lights blazing in the sky. He stared at them for a long time. He'd heard about the eerie phenomenon. But this was the first time he'd actually seen it. He stood there, watching the bands of light swirling across the horizon. The spectacle fascinated him.

Once the ground started moving, the only thing that mattered was how long it would last. There'd been a few times during some of the earlier aftershocks when he'd almost screamed, thinking the shaking would never stop, that the earth would just go on heaving until everything on it—every building, church, home, and school was pulverized.

"THAT WAS AT LEAST A MAG 5," WALT JACOBS SAID
with a professional's cool detachment. Sitting with him in
the rear of the Humvee, neither Atkins nor Elizabeth Holleran objected. The latest in a series of strong aftershocks
that had started just before they left the river, it had snapped
them sideways in their seats.

"They're getting worse, aren't they?" said Lauren Mitchell, who sat next to the driver.

"We're getting more of them in the magnitude 4 or greater
range," Jacobs said. "The ground's working up to something."

Two hours earlier, an Army helicopter had landed in the
front yard of Lauren's home near Kentucky Lake with a
message from John Atkins, telling her about the bomb and
asking her to help them find a backroads route to the mine.
She didn't like leaving her grandson behind alone but had
climbed aboard the chopper when a soldier agreed to stay
with the boy.

After the strong tremor, she was starting to have serious
second thoughts about her decision.

Using a radio headset, Lauren was giving directions to a
convoy of ten vehicles as she led them on a cross-country
journey from the river to the Golden Orient. Booker and the
bomb were in the Humvee directly behind them. The other
seismologists, Weston and Wren, followed in another all-
terrain vehicle. They were flanked by a protective screen of
M-1 tanks, three on each side.

Lauren wasn't happy with the continued earthquakes. They scared her. So did the thought of going back to the mine, which had haunted her dreams for years. The Golden Orient had always been dangerous, deadly. A fifty-year history of methane explosions, roof cave-ins, and fires. Her husband had died there in a flash fire a decade before the mine closed, a victim of clean air regulations that made it unprofitable to produce high-sulfur-content coal.

They'd made slow progress since leaving the Mississippi, barely twenty-five miles in four hours. The backroads were muddy, washed out in places, and cut between steep hills covered with pine and scrub oak. The convoy had to make frequent stops as Army patrols fanned out in the dark looking for snipers.

During one halt, Elizabeth got out of the Humvee with Atkins. She told him what had happened the day before in the library annex, how someone had stolen her laptop computer from the equipment room.

"Any idea who it was?"

She shook her head. "I didn't see his face." She'd tried to take a discreet look at every man who worked at the earthquake center. She didn't detect anything unusual in their behavior or attitude toward her.

"It could have been anyone," she said.

"I don't think so," Atkins said softly. "For starters, maybe someone wanted to check your E-mail messages."

"But why?"

"What if they wanted to see if you've messaged anyone about those cracks we saw at the dam," Atkins said. "Find out how much you know about that and whether you've told anyone." Cracking a computer password wasn't all that difficult, especially for an expert. Atkins knew hackers who could do it in less than twenty minutes.

"Weston?"

"Or his friend Marshal," Atkins said. "I could see either of them wanting to take a look at whatever data you've got on that computer. Go on a fishing expedition. For all we know maybe they wanted to download the zipped files you got from Doctor Prable. Take a close look at his data and see if they could find something they could use against you later. Work up a case to discredit you if you try to go public with what happened at the dam.''

Atkins took Elizabeth by the shoulders, holding her tightly as he looked into her light gray eyes, which held such intelligence.

He'd lost one woman he loved. Sara. They'd gone into that building in Mexico City and gotten separated. He couldn't allow that to happen again.

''I want you to stay close to me when we go into that mine,'' he said. ''No matter what happens, stay close to me.''

AS HE'D PROMISED, PRESIDENT NATHAN ROSS WAS
already there when the convoy arrived at the Golden Orient.
Atkins saw him standing near the main entrance, talking to
a rugged-looking man wearing white coveralls and a yellow
hard hat. The two were surrounded by Secret Service agents
and paratroopers, who were nervously scanning the surrounding hills with binoculars and spotter scopes.

Helicopter gunships circled the ridges, swooping low, then
pulling up and swinging around for another pass. Army patrols had spread out in force, looking for snipers. The mine
was about thirty miles from the Tennessee border, 140 miles
north of Memphis.

Steve Draper, the president's science adviser, hustled over
when he saw Atkins and Holleran get out of the Humvee.
He looked grim.

"You'll want to hear this," he said. "It's not good."

The mine was just as Atkins remembered it. The large,
gray metal building that housed the entrance didn't appear
damaged. It was a different story with the wooden tower that
supported the massive wheel and counter weight that lowered
the miners' cage into the shaft. Leaning at a precarious angle,
several of its support timbers had snapped in two. The adjoining tower and fly wheel, also badly damaged, operated
the "skip shaft," which powered the conveyor belt that
brought out the coal.

With the towers out of service, two diesel engines had

been flown in a day earlier to operate the elevator and power two huge fans that pushed fresh air into the shafts.

Atkins couldn't shake the foreboding that had been building in him ever since the towers had first come into view over a rise in the hills. Ten stories tall, they stood there like dark monoliths. His eagerness to go on the offensive notwithstanding, descending into that mine would be the hardest thing he'd ever done. The risks of taking a nuclear weapon to its depths were secondary. Now that he was actually there, the thought of going underground was enough to trigger in him an overwhelming sense of claustrophobia, of being buried alive.

"John, what's wrong?" said Elizabeth, staring at him. He looked white, faint. "Are you sick?"

"I just forgot how much I like this place," he said. He tried to smile, but his dry lips felt like they'd split open. His morale wasn't helped after he met the man who'd been brought in to lead the party into the Golden Orient.

Glen "Doc" Murray had arrived four hours earlier on a military flight from the Mine Safety Academy in Beckley, West Virginia, where he was chief instructor. He'd just returned from inspecting the mine with two other disaster specialists from the academy.

Murray was a big man, over six-foot-three, with a gaunt, sunburned face and a short white beard. He wore "bunker gear," the heavy protective clothing of a firefighter. He took off his thick leather gloves and helmet and used a towel to wipe his face, which was caked with sweat and coal dust.

Murray nodded to the new arrivals and for a moment seemed to be sizing them up. He didn't look impressed or reassured by what he saw.

"The earthquake broke things up pretty bad down there," Murray said in a low-pitched Appalachian drawl. "Part of the man shaft has collapsed. Other sections run clear for a couple hundred feet, then break off where the earth shifted. The main air shaft is blocked in places."

It was what Atkins had feared all along. The big quake had knocked the hell out of the mine. This was going to be more difficult than any of them had imagined.

Murray went on, "We got down about eight hundred feet and had to leave the man shaft and move over to one of the air shafts. We got down another five levels and cut back over to the skip shaft.''

Murray took out a small, spiral notebook and sketched what he was talking about. The mine descended twenty levels. Each level, separated by about one hundred feet, consisted of a series of three or four parallel tunnels, each about a thousand feet long. These were connected by intersecting or crosscut tunnels, forming a gridwork pattern on each level. The long tunnels provided access to the coal seams.

The coal was removed by the "room-and-pillar" technique. Miners cut or blasted it out of the seams, forming rooms that opened onto the tunnels. The crews left behind sufficient pillars to support the overlying rock, or "hanging wall."

Murray drew four shafts. The first of these, the miners' elevator, or "man shaft," ran down the center of the mine and carried the work crews to and from the different levels. The coal conveyor, or "skip shaft," was a tunnel that once housed a conveyor belt for carrying the cut coal up to the surface. The skip shaft tunnel slanted at a forty-degree incline and was about five feet high and six feet wide. The conveyor had long since been dismantled and removed. Like the rungs of a ladder, the coal tunnels ran between the skip shaft on one end and the main air shaft on the other.

There were two air shafts, which Murray drew in the notebook. The main one was virtually identical to the skip shaft in its dimensions and angle of incline. It was used to circulate air throughout the mine and also made a good escape route in an emergency. The secondary air shaft ran up vertically through the mine, roughly paralleling the elevator shaft. Carved out of the rock, the shaft was four feet wide.

"We took the skip shaft down to the eighteen-hundred-foot level," Murray said, drawing the position where they'd halted and turned back. "The man shaft is completely gone, caved in. But there's a deep crack that's opened up at that level. A fissure. I couldn't tell how far down it goes. We started picking up a little methane and decided to pull out. My hope is we can ventilate the shafts awhile longer and clear out some of that gas." He closed the notebook and put it back into a pocket in his bib coveralls.

"The bottom line here is I think I can get you down

eighteen hundred feet—if we're lucky and nothing else collapses. Is that deep enough for what you've got in mind?''

''It'll have to be,'' Booker said. He'd gone over the numbers several times with Thompson and Atkins. Based on the record of previous underground shots, a depth of two thousand feet would provide maximum seismic impact on the fault.

''How big is that bomb?'' Murray asked.

''Approximately four feet by two and a half. It weighs 420 pounds,'' Booker said.

Murray whistled between his teeth. ''We'll talk about that later,'' he said. ''I've got to tell you people there are a lot of ways to die in this old mine. And I'm not even including the methane, which is worry enough. Some of the roofs and wall ribs have caved in. I'm not telling you anything you don't already know, but whenever the ground moves, we've got more problems.''

Murray leaned over and spat. A wad of chewing tobacco bulged out his left cheek. ''You got any other place to explode this bomb?''

''It's got to be here,'' said Steve Draper. ''We don't have any other options.''

Arms folded across his chest, Murray nodded as if to say he'd expected that answer. He seemed to be contemplating his boots, which were crusted with white powder.

Atkins noticed the president's furrowed brow. He was following Murray's description intently.

''Let's talk about the methane,'' Murray said. ''You get a methane concentration of five to fifteen percent, you're gonna risk an explosion. When we got down to eighteen hundred feet, we were reading three percent methane and it was starting to nudge up a little. That can be bad news.'' He had a question for them. ''You know what it's like if you're in one of those shafts and methane explodes below you?''

No one answered.

Murray said, ''It's like sitting inside a shotgun barrel.'' He let his words hang there a moment, then asked how many were going.

''Six,'' Atkins said. It was the absolute minimum. If anything happened to some of them, the others might still be able to get the job done. Booker was the only absolutely essential member of the group. Atkins wasn't excited at the prospect of making the descent with Weston, but he had to admit that Weston had been acting with unusual restraint. He was listening attentively and was not trying to run the show.

"Make that seven," Booker said. "I want to take a robot with us. It can carry the weapon and other supplies." He'd already made arrangements with the Oak Ridge National Laboratory to have the robot and other equipment sent to the mine. The president himself had ordered the transportation. The helicopter was expected any minute.

"Can it maneuver?" Murray asked. He looked skeptical.

"On a dime," Booker said. "It can go anywhere we can. It's forty inches tall. The arms are retractable."

"Does this robot of yours have a name?" Murray said. His crinkled face broke into a frown.

"Neutron," said Booker.

"That's perfect," Murray said, still frowning. "I don't like it, but as long as I don't have to tell it what to do, I don't have a problem." He spat again and cleared his throat. "In a couple minutes, I'll give you some instructions on the breathing apparatus and other equipment you'll be carrying. Listen hard and pay attention. Your life could depend on what I'm going to tell you."

Murray looked at his watch. His arms, hands, and wrists were thick-boned, the forearms wrapped with coils of muscle. "If you still want to do this, we'll start down in another hour."

"JEFF, great to see you."

Booker had hurried over to a helicopter as it landed on the mine's gravel parking lot. It took off quickly as soon as Jeff Burke was on the ground and his equipment unloaded. Booker pumped his friend's hand.

Burke had arrived straight from the ORNL. He came bearing gifts. "I've got Neutron," he said. "Everything you asked for."

The small robot was covered in plastic sheeting. So were the two boxes of explosive charges that had also been shipped from Oak Ridge. Booker planned to use them to seal up the mine before the bomb was detonated.

Booker couldn't help smiling. Burke had fitted Neutron with an oversized football helmet. It was bright orange, the color of his favorite college team, the University of Tennessee. His alma mater. It even had a big UT logo on the side.

"I couldn't find a miner's helmet big enough to go over the actuator housing," Burke said. "I wanted to protect it. This was the best I could come up with."

"And so you just happened to find that helmet," Booker said.

"What can I say. It fit," Burke said, grinning.

Booker introduced Atkins and Elizabeth Holleran to his old friend. The president and Steve Draper came over to join them.

Using the robot's control panel, Booker put Neutron through several maneuvers, which included manipulating the robot's powerful hydraulic "human extender" arms to lift the MK/B-61. The demonstration impressed Doc Murray. Neutron easily carried the four-foot-long, cylindrically shaped weapon.

"Not bad," Murray said. "I can see why you want that little guy to come along with us."

Booker then turned to a discussion of the arming-and-firing procedure he planned to follow with the MK/B-61.

It was Elizabeth's first good look at the weapon and its gleaming, stainless-steel housing. Like Atkins, she was struck by its small size. She'd expected something much larger for a one-megaton nuclear bomb. Atkins was right. He'd compared it to an elongated trash can.

Ross was among those who listened, hanging on Booker's every word. They were shielded from the flanking hillsides by a double row of military trucks. Several more squads of troops had moved into the woods that sloped up from the mine. There'd been a few shots earlier, but for the time being all firing had ceased.

Booker used sheets ripped from a yellow legal pad to sketch out the bomb's firing system.

Atkins took notes as he tried to keep warm. The sun had broken through the gloom, but it wasn't enough to take the chill out of the air. He tried to concentrate and stay awake. After the trip from Texas and now this, he needed sleep, craved it. Even half an hour would have been a blessing.

When this was over, he was going to lock himself up in a hotel room with Elizabeth and not come out for days.

Booker's plan was to use a time-delay fuse, which he'd set once they were in position in the mine. There was less risk of error or mechanical breakdown that way, he explained. The firing signal from the timer would release an electrical charge stored in the capacitors, which would set off the detonators. That blast, in turn, would ignite the high explosives that encased the nuclear pit.

The mechanics of the time-delay fuse were fairly simple: the electrical charge from the capacitors would open two normally closed contact circuits and close two other circuits that were normally open. The process would send an electrical pulse across a bridge wire, triggering the detonators.

"How much time are you giving yourself to get out?" Ross asked.

"Four hours," Booker said.

"Is that enough?"

Atkins wondered the same thing. Based on what Doc Murray had seen in the mine, the sooner they got out of there, the better. Four hours didn't give them much leeway in case something went wrong.

"It better be," Booker said. "Once the timer is set, you can't turn it off without going back. I don't think we'll want to do that. For that matter, I don't think we'll get the chance."

During their descent, Booker would set explosives at key points in the mine. They'd be timed to go off exactly one minute before the blast. The plastic charges were designed to seal off all four shafts to prevent any radioactive material from venting into the atmosphere.

"I'll use gelatin dynamite, a mixture of nitroglycerin and sodium nitrate," Booker said. "It's incredibly dense, highly stable, and water resistant. It makes a hell of an explosion."

"How do you plan to detonate it?" Atkins asked.

"With fuse tubing and a blaster," Booker said. "I wouldn't risk running wire for the weapon, but I don't see any other alternative for the explosive charges. They've got to be connected to a fusing network." He explained how he'd use a special nonelectrical or "non-l" fuse that consisted of plastic tubing filled with explosives. About the size of the clear tubing used in aquarium tanks, non-l didn't emit sparks that could ignite dangerous gases. It had long been a popular detonation device in mines.

"We'll use a PAL arming system for the bomb," the physicist went on. The letters, he explained, stood for Permissive Action Link, which consisted of a code that had to be set by punching in the right sequence of numbers before an electromagnetic lock would open, arming the weapon.

"We've come a long way with PALs," said Booker. "The coding can be transmitted automatically once a missile has been launched. On this shot, we're going to do it the old-fashioned way."

Booker programmed the weapon with an eight-digit number randomly selected from a coding device a presidential aide carried in the "black box," actually a battered, black leather briefcase. When they were ready to "arm enable" the weapon underground, Booker would punch in the same sequence of numbers.

For safety redundancy, they also used a fail-safe color coding system. Booker turned a red arming switch on the side of the bomb's hard case. Later, in the mine, he'd flip a corresponding green switch, which would arm the weapon.

An array of monitoring devices would be set up near ground zero. Electrical cables would be run from the equipment four miles to the red shack, an Army trailer, where Guy Thompson and other seismologists would track the explosion and its seismic effects. Thompson was already there, setting up.

Everyone would be withdrawn from the area two hours before the bomb was detonated. Two helicopters would be kept on standby with their engines running, ready to fly the party to safety as soon as they emerged from the mine.

"I'll be waiting for you when you get out of there," Ross promised.

"I beg to differ, Mister President," said his Secret Service chief, Belleau. "You can't be anywhere near here once they arm that weapon."

"I'm afraid I outrank you on this one, Phil," the president said in a soft, firm voice. He turned to the team that was going to make the descent. He shook hands with each of them, first Elizabeth, then Atkins, and the others.

"I'll be praying for you all," he said. He looked right at Belleau. "And when you come out of that mine, I'll be here."

DOC Murray laid the equipment out on the ground. Elizabeth, Atkins, and the others had gathered around him. There was time for only one safety session. So Atkins and the others listened to Murray as they'd never listened to anyone in their lives.

Murray picked up an apparatus that looked like a small oxygen tank. It was equipped with a mask.

"We call this a Drag-B," he said, demonstrating how the tank was strapped over the shoulders. The face piece slipped over the head like a scuba mask. "The full name is a Drager BG-174 Long Duration Closed Circuit Breathing Apparatus. It's the most important piece of equipment you're going to carry. The canister holds forty pounds of air, enough for four hours. It's got a scrubber that takes out the carbon monoxide. If I tell you to put the mask on, get it over your face as fast as you can. Your life will depend on it. You've got to know how to do this in the dark. We'll run a little practice drill once we get down into the mine."

Murray may have looked country, tall and rawboned with a mountain twang to his voice, but Atkins had found out from Draper that he had a Ph.D. in engineering from the University of Missouri at Rolla School of Mines.

Murray spent several minutes with each of them, demonstrating how to get the face mask on. Atkins had to try twice before he did it properly. Elizabeth got it right the first time.

"The main thing is to put it on as soon as I tell you," Murray said. "You don't want to wait for smoke. Carbon monoxide could already be present in the air. You won't see it or smell it."

Murray got them outfitted with hard hats and lamps. The five-pound battery for the lamp hung from a web belt. The lamp itself was attached to the helmet. Murray and Atkins would carry state-of-the-art dry foam sprayers in case they had to fight fires. The forty-pound canisters strapped to their backs. Each also would carry a hundred-foot coil of rope.

"Remember that the air shafts and skip shaft are you

primary escape routes," Murray said. "Once we go below ground, you'll see they're all marked with green reflectors."

"What's the worst thing that can happen down there?" Weston asked.

Murray didn't hesitate.

"Fire," he said. "I've been in three fires in coal mines. I don't want to go through another one. I'm all out of luck."

LAUREN MITCHELL WAS SHOCKED TO SEE HIM. AT first she wasn't sure it was the same man. He'd aged, but he looked and moved with the easy, fluid grace of someone much younger. The face was creased and heavily lined, but the real difference, the detail that focused her attention, were the eyes. She remembered how his blue, clear eyes had blazed out from his coal-blackened face when he came up out of the mine on that day so many years ago. His eyes were different. They'd lost some of their sparkle.

Lauren approached Murray as he lit an unfiltered Camel.

"You won't remember me, but I was here twenty-three years ago," she said. "You helped bring up my husband's body."

Murray, who'd been staring at the ground, quickly looked up. He hadn't mentioned the disaster to the scientists, figuring they probably already knew about it, and if they didn't, why give them another reason to lose their nerve.

"His name was Bob Mitchell," Lauren said.

"One of the best foremen in the business," Murray said, taking off his helmet. "I met Bob once or twice. He was a fine man."

He didn't know what else to say to the woman, who stood there smiling at him with her thick hair blowing in the wind. It had been the worst mine disaster he'd ever seen. More than forty men trapped a thousand feet below ground by methane explosion, sealed off in a tunnel and slowly suffocating as their air gave out. He'd led a rescue team, one of the lucky ones. Three men from another squad had been killed in a cave-in.

"I never thanked you for bringing him out," Lauren said. "It's a little late, but I want you to know I've never forgotten and never stopped praying for you."

Murray took her hand and held it. "I wouldn't mind a few more of those prayers."

Lauren said, "This is going to be bad, isn't it?"

Murray hesitated before he said, "These people have no idea what it's like down there."

When it was almost time, Lauren watched as Murray helped them slip into their fire-resistant bunker gear—thick leather overcoats, pants, steel-toed boots and gloves, hard hats. They strapped on their air tanks. Each of them also lugged a twenty-pound tank of dry foam for fighting fires. A coil of rope was attached to their web belts.

Booker carried the bomb's fusing components, capacitors, and timer in a canvas backpack. The remote control for Neutron—about the size of a laptop—was strapped around his neck. He punched a few buttons and worked the joysticks. The robot easily picked up the bomb, cradling it in its special alloy mechanical arms. It rolled onto the steel elevator cage that would take them down the man shaft to the eight-hundred-foot level. A large spool of non-l fuse was attached to its back.

"I'm gonna have to get me one of those," Murray said, smiling. "How much does that machine cost?"

"About $10 million," Booker said. "If you get us through this, I'll see if I can get you a deal."

THE elevator cage had just reached the four-hundred-foot level when the ground moved—a sharp horizontal tremor that made the cage sway on its steel cable. A sprinkling of dust fell on them. They all had their hard hat lanterns turned on.

"Better get used to it," Murray said, gripping the side of the cage for balance. "We're probably going to have some more of those."

Atkins knew he was right. Shortly before they'd made their descent, he'd spoken with Guy Thompson by radio. The most recent seismic data showed the fault was averaging ten or eleven mild shocks an hour and that they were building in intensity.

Murray carried a multigas detector. The size of a pocket calculator, the device was calibrated to detect such gases as methane, carbon monoxide, and oxygen. It emitted a beep and flashed a red light when it registered dangerous levels.

Murray checked the readings. "It's showing about 3.6 percent. That's up a little since the last time I went down. We're all right as long as it doesn't hit 5 percent."

Atkins was fairly sure the repeated tremors were responsible for the methane. The powerful shaking had probably opened up a pocket of the gas trapped in the ground. As soon as they'd started down the elevator shaft, he'd noticed another gas, hydrogen sulfide. He remembered the smell, the faint odor of rotten eggs, from the last time he'd gone into the Golden Orient.

He asked Murray if he'd ever encountered anything like that before.

"Not down in a mine," he said. "It sure as hell stinks, but I don't think it's gonna kill us."

Atkins figured the foul-smelling gas was escaping from deep underground pockets, much like the methane.

There were seven of them. Murray, Walt Jacobs, Elizabeth, Atkins, Weston, Wren, and Booker, who walked behind Neutron. The robot had glided along to the mine entrance, the wheels adjusting automatically to the changes in grade. It moved easily even weighed down with the bomb and the heavy roll of fuse.

The party carried two radios to stay in touch with the people on the surface.

"I feel like I'm going on one of my digs," Elizabeth said, shifting the weight of the two heavy canisters on her back. "I could use a couple grad students to help carry this stuff."

It was a feeble joke meant to cheer up Walt Jacobs. The man had looked feverish ever since they'd arrived at the mine. His face was pale. He glanced back and smiled at her and she sensed he was putting on a brave front. They'd just started, and she was already worried he wouldn't make it.

So was Atkins. Jacobs looked physically weak, unsteady on his feet. He'd also been concerned about Elizabeth, bu after watching how easily she carried her packs, he realized she was in better shape than any of them.

At the eight-hundred-foot level, they left the elevator cage. It was the place where the shaft had collapsed. It was totally blocked by fallen rock. They got their first look at the deep room-and-pillar cuts that tank-sized machines known as continuous miners had carved out of the rock face. They were on Level 8.

Atkins found the layout just as Doc Murray had described it. Each level was comprised of a gridwork of three or four parallel tunnels with crossovers that connected them at right angles. As many as twenty-five "rooms" opened onto each side of the thousand-foot-long tunnels. Only the central or main tunnel connected to the air shaft and skip shaft. The air shaft was at one end. The skip shaft, which had once carried the coal to the top, was at the other.

The tunnel's roof and walls were covered with a thick layer of white powder. Atkins had remembered that detail from his first visit.

"That's rock dust," Murray explained. "They mix it with water and spray it on the walls to keep down the coal dust. It reduces the risk of explosions. Dust can be volatile."

Booker placed his first explosive charges near the elevator cage, chipping out holes in the shaft for five sticks of plastic explosive. He attached the non-l fusing, crimping it onto the explosives with a special tool, and began to unreel the fuse from the spool attached to Neutron's back.

They advanced down a tunnel single file. Murray led the way, playing a spotlight on the walls and roof, checking for any sign of fresh cracks.

"Stay as close to the center of the tunnel as you can," he said. "The roof supports are better in the middle." The supports consisted of hundreds of steel bolts drilled up into the ceiling, each of them four feet long.

Looking behind a few minutes later to check on everyone's progress, Murray noticed that Weston and Wren had drifted over toward the side of the tunnel. In the disorienting, absolute darkness, it was easy to get out of line, even with a headlamp.

"Hold it," Murray told them. He'd noticed a thin crack in the ceiling. "Get back here behind me."

When the two men were safely out of the way, he jabbed at the crack with the sharp end of an eight-foot-long crowbar he carried. A sheet of rock about five feet wide and an inch thick crashed down, throwing up a cloud of white dust.

"Hope you got the idea," Murray said. "Stay . . . in . . . the . . . middle of the tunnel. The shoring along the ribs over on the side wall is pretty poor. I'm noticing a lot of cracks."

With the stop it took them fifteen minutes to advance about five hundred feet to the end of the tunnel. Murray led them into the air shaft. Thick, heavy sheets of plastic covered the opening to the shaft.

"That's a fire curtain," Murray said. "A fire breaks out, that'll give you a little protection. Maybe a couple minutes. They're mainly used to channel fresh air or to help seal off a tunnel from poisonous gas." He grinned. "Like I said, it'll buy you a couple minutes."

The air shaft sloped down at a steep incline. It was possible to walk on the grade, which had been designed to serve the double purpose of providing an intake for fresh air and an escape route in an emergency.

"We'll go down about seven hundred feet, then cut down a tunnel on Level 15 and take the skip shaft to the eighteen-hundred-foot level. That's the end of the line."

Ever since they'd entered the mine, they'd heard an intermittent rumble deep in the ground. It was the same unnerving sound Atkins remembered from before. It was far below them, the sound, Atkins thought, of mountains of rock sliding together in the earth's crust.

Before they started down the air shaft, Murray tied everyone to a lifeline. He looped the ends through metal rings in their web belts much like mountain climbers used carabiners to link up to a rope. It was a steep descent. They sometimes had to hold on to the walls to keep their footing. If someone stumbled, the line would keep them from knocking down the others. The air shaft was just over five feet high, so they had to walk hunched over. Neutro moved easily, its orange football helmet passing well below the roof of the tunnel.

There were frequent tremors, none severe. Their faces and hard hats were soon covered with the chalky white powder that fell from the roof like flakes of snow every time the ground shook.

Murray called a brief halt to take another gas reading. Jacobs rubbed his temples.

"What's wrong, Walt?" Atkins asked. "You okay, fella?" His friend looked like he'd been stricken with a crushing headache. His eyes were clamped shut. He put his hand against Atkins' shoulder to steady himself.

"I'm fine, just a little wobbly," he said, wiping sweat from his brow with his sleeve. "I forgot how hot it was down here. It's like a steam room."

It was warm, another of the details Atkins recalled from their descent nearly a week earlier.

"That heat's one of the things that's got me concerned," Murray said. "A mine's usually cool. Low sixties year-round. We've got readings in places nearly ninety degrees. This ground is really putting out the heat."

Atkins still found that puzzling. His best guess was that heavy seismic activity at great depth was causing it. Rock strain generated heat, and in this case, the strain was still building, still putting out energy.

They stopped several times so that Booker could place explosive charges in the shaft. He kept unwinding the yellow fuse line from Neutron.

Atkins marveled at the robot's ability to make the descent. The engineering was superb. The omnidirectional platform and unique tread system compensated instantly for sudden grade changes. The hydraulics automatically shifted the robot's center of gravity. It was designed to descend a steep grade.

When they reached Level 15, Murray moved them back into the mine tunnel.

"How far down are we?" Elizabeth asked Murray.

"About fifteen hundred feet," he said.

Except for a mild headache from the depth, she was holding up well, better than she'd expected. She quietly asked Atkins how he felt.

"Just like a walk in the country," he said, forcing himself to smile. It was tough, but he hadn't experienced any panic attacks, which was about as good as he could hope for. Having Elizabeth along helped him for a reason he hadn't considered: she gave him something else to focus on.

They started through another maze of dark tunnels carved out of the coal seam. The rooms were interspersed with thick columns left in place to support the ceilings. The damaging effects of the earthquake were more apparent at this level. Parts of the roof and walls had caved in, leaving only narrow passageways. With every mild shake of the ground, more dust and rock fell.

It was getting warmer.

Murray called another halt to check his gas meter. He'd been doing this often.

"I'm reading about 4.2 percent methane," he said. "That's a hell of a jump since the last time."

Looking up the dark tunnel, Atkins remembered what Murray had told them about sitting in the barrel of a shotgun.

GUY Thompson, resplendent in a broad-brimmed cowboy hat with an eagle feather in the brim, was monitoring an array of seismographs they'd set up around the periphery of the mine. The instruments were programmed to send signals to the red shack four miles away. The instruments would pick up the effects of the explosion, the intensity of the seismic waves it generated.

Thompson, who was at the red shack, had just gotten them on-line. The digital instruments indicated a pronounced increase in seismic activity.

"We're getting a mag 3 or better every ten or twenty minutes," Thompson told Steve Draper over the radio. "I'm thinking maybe we're building up to something."

President Ross and Draper felt most of the tremors, the alternating vertical movement and side-to-side swaying. So far, nothing serious.

Gunfire broke out again, more distant this time. Automatic weapons. Ross had been told that the 101st Airborne continued to run into pockets of resistance. The patrols were keeping the pressure on the rebellious National Guard troops and militia units still scattered in diminishing numbers throughout the surrounding hills. Remote, thickly forested, the country offered superb cover and the Kentucky soldiers were making the most of it.

The president's Secret Service chief, Phil Belleau, kept pushing him to withdraw to the red shack. The position—it was on a hilltop—was more secure and easier to defend.

Ross refused. Two UH-60 helicopters were parked near the entrance to the mine, ready to fly him out at a moment's notice. One was a backup in case the first was disabled. Both engines were kept idling, the crews on standby.

Ross was hardly aware of the shooting or the drone of helicopter gunships as they circled the hills, hunting for targets. He was engrossed, watching a strong-motion seismograph record the vibrations coming from the deep earth.

"See if you can get them on the radio," Ross said. "Let's find out how they're doing." He wanted to keep such calls to a minimum, afraid of distracting them.

Draper turned on the portable radio. There was a long burst of static before he got through to Atkins. "John, what's your situation down there?" he asked.

"We're starting to pick up some methane," Atkins said.

"How bad?" Draper asked.

"Over four percent."

That wasn't good news. If methane reached high enough concentration levels, there was always the danger of spontaneous combustion and an explosion.

Listening to this exchange, Lauren Mitchell remembered how the Golden Orient was notorious for the deadly gas. There'd been at least three methane explosions before the big one that had killed her husband.

Spontaneous combustion.

Those two words were a miner's curse.

The radio crackled again. "We're approaching the skip shaft," Atkins said. The long, steeply inclined tunnel had once housed the coal conveyor. "It shouldn't be too much longer before we're in position."

Lauren Mitchell knew it was time to leave. She'd done everything she could and wanted to get away from this place. She missed her grandson. Her house was in the evacuation zone, but she'd made up her mind not to leave or let anyone run her off. If the worst happened, she wanted to be on familiar ground.

She also knew what could happen in the mine and didn't want to be around to see it if it did.

She'd promised Murray she'd pray and had been praying steadily. But she knew what a 4-percent-and-climbing methane level meant. If it went too high, all the prayers in the world wouldn't stop the explosion.

THEY'D REACHED THE SKIP SHAFT. THE BELTED CON-
veyor that once brought a black stream of coal to the surface
had been dismantled, leaving a rough, steep tunnel that was
narrower with less headroom than the air shaft. They had to
walk in a stiff crouch, their hard hats often scraping against
the roof. Even Neutron's football helmet occasionally grazed
the top of the shaft.

Following Murray, they descended another three hundred
feet to Level 18. Slow going, it took nearly thirty minutes
to cover the distance. They were as far down in the mine as
they could go—eighteen hundred feet below the surface. Beyond that point, cave-ins had blocked both air shafts and the
skip shaft.

Atkins checked his watch. They'd been underground a little more than ninety minutes. He was surprised. The time
had seemed much shorter.

Murray took them another five hundred feet up the main
tunnel on Level 18 to the base of the collapsed man shaft.

"Here's what I was talking about," he said, playing his
spotlight on the gaping black hole where the elevator cage
had once descended another two levels to the bottom of the
mine. The earthquake had opened a crevasse that had swallowed the man shaft. A ragged hole about fifteen feet wide
descended to depths unknown. Murray shined his powerful
light on the jagged walls of the trench as Atkins and the
others cautiously approached the edge and peered over. They
couldn't see the bottom.

"God knows how far down that goes," Weston said.

Ever since they'd started their descent, Atkins had found Weston unusually subdued but had no complaints with his performance. He'd done whatever Murray asked without objection. So had Wren, who'd always been reasonably pleasant and cooperative.

"I tried this the last time," Murray said. He picked up a hefty piece of rock and dropped it into the crevasse. They didn't hear it hit bottom.

Operating Neutron's control panel, Booker had the robot gently place the bomb on the floor of the tunnel about five yards from the edge of the drop-off. "I suggest we lower it two hundred feet into that hole," he said. "That will put it at roughly the two-thousand-foot mark." That was the depth Thompson and the other seismologists had calculated was needed for the weapon's shock waves to achieve maximum effect on the fault.

"Will your climbing ropes support four hundred fifty pounds?" he asked.

"No problem," said Murray.

First Booker had to arm the device, punching in the coding sequence, the same eight digits he'd used earlier to activate the bomb's electronic circuitry. Then he flipped the red switch on the small control grid on the bomb's hard case, the fail-safe companion to the green switch he'd already thrown.

"The bomb is armed," Booker said quietly. He'd never done it manually before. Arming procedures at the NTS were carried out electronically, using cables that ran to the warhead, which usually sat at the bottom of an eight-hundred- to thousand-foot-deep borehole or in a tunnel carved into the side of a hill. This was definitely a first for him. He noticed that his hands were trembling.

He'd completed the first critical step. The second was to set the timer and firing mechanism.

Opening his backpack, Booker took out the capacitors and batteries. The four dry-cell batteries, taped together, would provide the electrical pulse needed to charge the capacitors, which, in turn, would activate the fuse and fire the warhead. The whole process would be triggered by a small, digitally programmed timer.

"Doctor Booker, that's as far as we're going with this."

Atkins had been watching Booker. Turning, he saw Walt Jacobs, who was holding something in his right hand. It was hard to make it out in the dark. Then Atkins recognized it. A small pistol.

"Walt, what are you doing?" he said, not believing what he was seeing. The man had finally snapped. Atkins was angry with himself for letting it happen. It was his own damn fault. He should have seen it coming, should have kept him out of the mine. Without thinking, he took a step toward his friend.

Jacobs held up a hand. "Stop, John. I don't want to shoot anyone. But I will if I have to. This bomb can't be detonated. It could start an earthquake the likes of which we've never seen. I can't allow that."

Atkins' head was swimming. He knew that he had to choose his words carefully, try to make a persuasive argument about why they had to risk it. But there wasn't time for more discussion, and he could see that Jacobs was in no mood for it anyway.

"Walt, you've studied the data, the seismic reports," Atkins said. "You know that strain energy is building up here. My God, you've felt the ground shaking. It's been moving ever since we entered this mine. We're going to have a big earthquake here. You know that as well as anybody."

"You . . . can't . . . do . . . this! Not a nuclear shot," Jacobs said in a burst of anger. He was about five feet from Booker. He pointed the pistol at the physicist's head.

"Put the capacitors and timer back into the backpack with your left hand," he said. "Do it slowly and carefully. Then set it down next to me." His voice was firm, deliberate. He moved a few steps closer to the edge of the fissure.

Atkins realized Jacobs was going to kick the bag over the side.

"I'm afraid I can't, Walt," Booker said. He sat down, both hands clutching the blue backpack to his chest. "I'm not trying to be brave or stupid. But you'll have to shoot me to get this. Do you really want to kill me?"

Elizabeth was standing next to Murray and Wren. She gestured to the on-off switch for their headlamps. It was on the battery pack attached to their belts. They understood. So did Atkins, who'd noticed what she'd done.

Jacobs fired a shot at Booker's feet. The explosion was deafening. The earsplitting echo blasted back through the tunnels.

"Put the pack down, doctor," Jacobs repeated, his face hard-set. "I'll shoot you if I have to." The pistol practically touched Booker's forehead.

Calmly staring at Jacobs, Booker continued to hold the backpack on his lap, gripping the sides.

"Fred, give it to him," Atkins pleaded. He realized that Jacobs' change of heart about a nuclear explosion had been a ruse. He'd gone to some trouble to pull this off. Shown a lot of nerve. He'd kill Booker. Atkins didn't doubt it for a moment.

Booker said, "Are you completely sure you're right about this, Walt?"

"For the last time. Give it to me," Jacobs repeated.

Booker set the backpack down on the ground.

"Turn out your lights!" Elizabeth shouted.

Within seconds, everyone switched off their headlamps. Jacobs pivoted, trying to keep all of them in sight, but the sweeping arc of his light wasn't wide enough for him to see everyone. He missed Atkins, who ducked down and crawled to his left, toward the collapsed man shaft.

"Stop right there!" Jacobs shouted. He'd heard movement in the darkness that pressed in around him. He turned just as Atkins lunged at him from the side, catching him hard around the waist and driving him to the ground.

The impact knocked Jacobs' helmet off. The lamp disconnected. Atkins groped for Jacobs' hands. He was trying to get the pistol. He couldn't remember where the edge of the crevasse was. He sensed they were very close to it.

There was another shot, a ringing explosion close to his ear. Atkins gripped Jacobs' gun hand. He felt the hot barrel of the pistol and was suddenly aware of light. Elizabeth and the others had switched on their headlamps. Atkins got a close look at Jacobs' twisted face. His eyes were bulging with rage. He looked like someone else.

Something crashed against the side of his hard hat. Jacobs had hit him with the pistol. Atkins let go.

Jacobs scrambled to his knees, clutching the backpack.

They'd rolled to within a few feet of the crevasse.

Murray stepped toward Jacobs, who whirled and fired, the gun roaring. The shot missed him. Murray, everyone, dropped to the floor of the tunnel. Jacobs fired at the bomb. Then another, the bullets making a slapping sound when they ricocheted off the metal casing.

Atkins grabbed Jacobs around the legs. Jacobs swung down hard with the pistol, slashing at him, clipping him on the shoulder blade. The pain burned, but he managed to hold on. Jacobs chopped at him again, and this time Atkins grabbed his gun hand and bent it back sharply at the wrist.

Crying out in pain and anger, Jacobs dropped the weapon. He pulled away, chest heaving, and stepped toward the drop-off. He still gripped the backpack.

"Walt!" Elizabeth screamed. "For God's sake, let's talk!"

Jacobs hesitated. He looked at her, his expression softening. He was only inches from the edge.

"Don't do it, please."

Atkins could see his friend's fear and anguish. The man had lost his wife and daughter, everything. He wasn't going to lose this last battle. Atkins wanted to help him. He slowly reached out his hand.

"Walt, take it."

He said it over and over, begging his friend to take his hand.

Jacobs took a slow, deep breath, clutched the backpack to his chest, and threw himself backward into the crevasse.

•

ELIZABETH DROPPED TO HER KNEES AND CRAWLED
to the edge. She looked down, her headlamp playing on the
walls. Jacobs had disappeared, swallowed up in the deep
black hole.

Atkins put his arm around her waist and gently pulled her
back. His shoulder throbbed where Jacobs had struck him
with the pistol.

Elizabeth shook her head. ''John, what happened to him?''
She could only imagine what losing his family had done to
him, how it must have affected his reason. Their deaths,
compounded by the overwhelming destruction he'd lived
with for days in Memphis. It was too much for him.

Atkins was in awe of what his friend had done. It left
him speechless.

Murray walked to the edge of the hole and stood there,
staring down into the blackness. His legs spread slightly for
balance, knees bent, he looked perfectly at ease. Weston and
Wren also inched forward to take a look. Both quickly
stepped back.

Weston said, ''That could be a thousand feet deep.''

Murray shook his head. ''More,'' he said. ''I've looked
down some deep holes in my day. I was listening hard.
didn't hear that man hit the bottom.''

''What exactly was in the backpack he took with him?''
Wren asked Booker. ''What's the damage?''

Booker didn't answer. Bent over the weapon, he was care
fully feeling the casing with his fingertips, searching for bu

let holes. One of the slugs had skipped off the metal hard case. The other had penetrated the housing an inch from the weapon's nuclear package. Booker couldn't believe it when he saw the hole.

"That wasn't supposed to happen," he said. "A bullet from a handgun shouldn't be able to penetrate a missile's hard case." He looked astonished. "If it had hit two inches more to the left, we'd all be dead."

"From an explosion?" Murray asked.

Booker said, "From plutonium radiation escaping from the primary. We would have received a lethal dose in about two seconds."

Repeating his earlier question, Wren wanted to know what was in the backpack that Jacobs had grabbed before he went over the edge.

So did Atkins.

"The batteries and timer," Booker said matter-of-factly. He continued to examine the surface of the bomb.

"Then how are we going to do this?" Wren said in a screaming burst of anger. It was the first time Atkins had seen him lose his composure. Normally easygoing, the young geologist looked like he'd finally reached the breaking point.

"What about the capacitors?" Elizabeth asked.

Booker stood up. "They're right here," he said, smiling as he patted the pocket of his heavy jumpsuit. He removed a small package of electrical components. "When all the lights were out, I managed to slip it out of the pack before Walt grabbed it. It's the only part that's crucial to the detonation. The only one I couldn't do without."

"We still need batteries and a timer," Atkins said.

"That's not a significant problem," Booker said. "We can use batteries from the flashlights. And I've got a backup timer. I'd planned for redundancy, at least I thought I had. I can't believe I forgot to bring a backup for the capacitors." He frowned. It was almost a fatal oversight. He should have known better, planned better. "I guess I'm older than I thought."

The ground trembled, an almost imperceptible shift at first, then much harder shaking. The sound of cracking, splintering rock boomed up from the depths of the crevasse. Another tremor hit, a strong sideways motion. Rock fragments fell on them. A cloud of dust formed in the tunnel. They heard a heavy rumble somewhere above them. It sounded like an avalanche.

"That's a cave-in," Murray said, coughing in the thick dust. "A big one."

"How long did it last?" Elizabeth asked. She held a hand-kerchief over her mouth in the dust. Murray and Booker had dropped to their knees to keep from being knocked down.

"Five seconds," Atkins said. He'd timed the shaking, the longest since they'd entered the mine.

"Folks, I suggest we switch to plan B and get moving," Murray said, clearing his throat as the dust settled.

Atkins agreed. The fault's seismicity was increasing. The pattern closely resembled the one that had preceded the 8.4 earthquake, a series of gradually intensifying preshocks, sometimes coming in flurries. Then the big one.

Booker took four double-A batteries from two flashlights and wrapped them together with tape, attaching them to the capacitors. The batteries would charge the capacitors, which would send an electric current across a bridge wire connected to the detonator.

The timer looked like a digital alarm clock. Booker had carried it in one of his pockets. He wired the timer to an enabling plug on the exterior of the bomb's hard case.

"It's time to raise the critical question," Booker asked. "Do we stick with the original plan and set it for four hours?"

"We might not have four hours," Elizabeth said. "This fault seems primed to explode." Like Atkins, she thought a major earthquake was imminent.

"I'd make it longer," Murray said. "We don't know what happened above us during that last shake, whether the passageways are still open. And we still need to lower the bomb into this hole. That's going to take more time."

"Then considering the differing opinions, I'd suggest we stick to the plan," Booker said. He pushed two buttons on the timer. One set the hour and minute. The other set the trigger.

Atkins watched the red digits begin to flash on the small device, which tracked the seconds and minutes.

Four hours.

Earlier, it had seemed like plenty of time. It didn't now.
He turned on the radio and got Steve Draper.

"We've started the countdown," he said.

The radio crackled.

"Then get the hell out of there!"

It was the president's voice.

Atkins explained they were going to lower the bomb into
the crevasse to reach the two-thousand-foot maximum-ef-
fect level.

He briefly described what had happened to Walt Jacobs.

There was no answer. Then the radio clicked again. It
was Draper.

"Did you feel that last shake?"

Atkins said, "I thought it was going to bury us."

"It was a mag 5.1, John. Get out of there as fast as you
can, pal."

BOOKER GENTLY SLID THE CAPACITORS AND BAT-teries into a canvas bag, which he looped over the front of the bomb. He lashed it down with cord and tape. Then he and Murray tied a three-hundred-foot length of rope to both ends of the MK/B-61. They wrapped the rope several times around a steel post that had once supported the frame of the collapsed elevator shaft. Murray tied a white handkerchief at the two-hundred-foot mark.

With Booker operating the joysticks, Neutron lifted the bomb, then placed it over the side of the crevasse while Murray, Atkins, and the others held on to the rope, keeping it taut as they slowly lowered the weapon into position.

Atkins stood behind Wren and was surprised at his strength. A thick pack of shoulder muscles moved under his coveralls as he gripped the rope. The geologist was much stronger and fitter than he looked.

"Let it down a little more," Booker said.

They lowered the bomb a few feet at a time until they reached the handkerchief. They looped the rope around the steel post and tied it down. The entire procedure had taken nearly half an hour.

Atkins went to the edge of the crevasse and took a final look at the bomb as it hung suspended against the rough wall of the trench. He could just make out the red glow of the timer, ticking off the seconds and minutes.

Would it go off on schedule?

Would it be a dud or a misfire?

Was it too powerful, or not powerful enough?

Booker put an arm around his shoulder. "Don't think about it," he said, guessing what was on Atkins' mind. "We've done everything we could."

"I hope so," Atkins said. He knew you never did everything you could. There was always that small or large detail you forgot, the potential for a screwup.

Murray quickly got everyone back in line for the ascent. The sooner they were moving, the better he'd like it.

They picked up their canisters of dry foam and extra coils of rope. Murray told them to recheck the straps on their oxygen tanks.

"Unless we find out different, nothing's changed," he said. "We're going back the same way we got down here, up the skip shaft to Level 15. Then up the main air shaft to the elevator cage on Level 8. Any questions?"

They started up the skip shaft. It was more difficult climbing up the steep incline than descending. What had taken nearly half an hour during the three-hundred-foot descent now ate up forty minutes of time. Tied together again, they had to lean into each step. Their leg muscles soon began to feel the strain and they had to stop once when Booker's calves cramped up. Only Neutron had an easier time of it, carrying the large spool of non-1 fusing as it rolled up the shaft once used for the coal conveyor belt. Freed from the weight of the bomb, the robot moved effortlessly up the slope.

When they reached Level 15 Murray checked the temperature gauge. They stopped beside the three-foot-high red-painted number on the wall—15.

"Man, I don't believe this," he said. "It's pushing ninety degrees. This ground's a furnace."

He didn't have to tell that to Elizabeth or Atkins. Both were soaked through their heavy clothing. They all were.

They started down one of the dark, forty-foot-wide tunnels that had been carved out of the coal seam. They squeezed through a narrow space where part of the ceiling had collapsed and were approaching a crosscut that linked two of the tunnels when the ground heaved. They'd gone about four hundred feet.

The force of the tremor hurled Atkins down. He fell hard

on his back, his air tank cracking against his spine. Elizabeth and Weston also fell. The ground kept moving, shaking back and forth like a vibrator. There was a deep rumble far below them, the sound of buried thunder.

"Get back! Move!" Murray was screaming at them as they scrambled to their feet.

Atkins heard the sharp crack and glanced up just as a section of the roof collapsed. A slab at least twenty feet long fell ten yards in front of them. Coal dust stung their eyes. They were coughing, spitting it up.

When the air started to clear, they made out the dimensions of the cave-in. They stood in the dusty haze, staring at a wall of broken rock that had sealed the tunnel from floor to ceiling. They'd almost been crushed.

"I noticed that weak spot coming in," Murray said, angrily shaking his head. He was mad at himself. He should have been more cautious. They were in a hurry, but that was no excuse for carelessness. He shined his light on the ceiling, looking for other dangerous fractures. They'd moved back just in time.

"How strong do you think that was?" Elizabeth asked.

"I'd say another 5," Atkins said.

"I don't like the way they're starting to bunch up," Weston said. "The ground's really moving."

Atkins couldn't have agreed more. He thought again about the huge fault that spread out twenty miles below them and how dangerously close it was to others that cut through the Mississippi Valley.

Murray laid out their only option.

"We're going to have to blast our way through that rock," he said. "I'll set the charge. Everybody get back as far as you can." They retreated down the tunnel almost to the skip shaft, nearly fifty yards.

Murray waited until everyone was out of the way. He checked his gas meter. Methane levels had climbed slightly, but still weren't at the danger threshold. He set two sticks of plastic explosives in a shallow crevice in the rock, positioning them at the base of the rib wall. Designed to blast escape holes through blocked passageways, the shaped charges of gelatin dynamite were called "rock busters."

The fuse cord was attached to a small blasting cap, which

resembled a shotgun shell. Made of aluminum, it was crimped onto the explosives. Murray ran the cord back up the tunnel nearly to the skip shaft and crouched behind a pillar.

"Get ready!" he said. He counted down from five, then shouted, "Fire in the hole!"

He pulled a metal trigger attached to the end of the fuse cord, which provided the spark that ignited it. Within seconds the black powder core of the fuse raced to the blasting cap. The explosion went off with a ripping blast that peppered the tunnel with rock fragments.

When the dust settled, Murray shined his spotlight at the cave-in. His heart sank. The hole the explosives had blown in the rock was too small. Barely two feet high, it didn't go all the way through.

"That's not going to do it," he said.

Elizabeth asked whether they could use the explosive charges that Booker had placed in the shafts on the way down.

Booker said, "They're much too strong. They're designed to collapse the tunnel. The whole thing would come down on us."

Murray didn't like the way it looked. Long cracks had opened in the ceiling. He was worried about another cave-in.

Booker had another idea. "Let's see if Neutron can widen that hole." Working the controls, he manipulated the robot's steel-composite "man extender" claws so they spun like a drill. Within twenty minutes, Neutron had widened the hole enough for them to scrape through.

Booker sent the robot in first, its orange football helmet still securely strapped in place. He switched on Neutron's powerful headlamp and television monitor and maneuvered it fifty yards down the tunnel. Beyond the cave-in, everything looked clear and open.

Pushing their air tanks and foam canisters in ahead of them, they crawled through the cramped opening.

Murray hurried them another six hundred feet to the air shaft at the end of the tunnel and immediately noticed something was wrong. He no longer felt fresh air moving in it. He shined his spotlight up the shaft. A row of green reflectors glinted in the light, extending at spaced intervals as far up as he could see.

"It looks clear," he said. That was good news, but Murray was worried about all that falling rock he'd heard earlier. Somewhere up there, they were going to run into trouble.

They started up the air shaft, the longest leg to the elevator cage on Level 8, nearly seven hundred feet.

"How much time do we have?" Murray asked.

Booker checked his watch. "Just under two hours," he said.

Atkins felt something turn in the pit of his stomach. They were eating up the minutes. He doubted four hours was enough time to get out of the mine.

As they crept single-file up the steep incline, Booker stopped to examine the explosive charges and fusing he'd inserted into the rock wall on the way down. Everything looked intact. As a backup, he placed more of the water gel explosives in the shaft, running a separate fuse line, which he would connect once they reached the surface. The charges were designed to explode with a delay interval of twenty-five milliseconds for maximum effect.

Murray called a halt when they reached Level 11. His gas meter had started beeping. A red light flashed. He cleared the meter and rechecked the reading.

"We've got a methane problem," he said. "I'm getting concentrations of 5.4 percent, and the damn thing is still climbing."

Atkins remembered what Murray had told them about methane danger levels. Five percent was the redline. Anything over that was bad news.

Murray announced more trouble. "The carbon monoxide levels have really popped," he said. "They're reading fifty parts per million."

"What does it mean?" Weston asked.

"It means there's a fire burning somewhere above us," Murray said. "It could be anywhere in the mine, in one of the tunnels, up a crosscut, in one of the galleries. Anywhere. We've got to worry about all that methane igniting."

Moments after he finished speaking, there was an explosion far above them. A single loud blast. The air shaft vibrated under their feet. Dust and rock rained down on them.

Atkins could tell it wasn't an earthquake. Something was

crashing down the air shaft, a wall of moving rock that was rolling in their direction.

"Everyone out of the shaft," Murray screamed. "Get up the tunnel!"

The noise grew louder as the rock swept down the air shaft, blasting it wider as the walls gave way.

They ran up the main tunnel on Level 11, moving awkwardly under the weight of their air tanks, rope, and foam canisters. They'd gone about a hundred feet when Murray shouted for them to huddle in one of the "rooms" that had been dug into the rockface. There wasn't time to go any farther. A cloud of coal dust and pulverized rock exploded down the length of the tunnel, pushed in by the collapse of the air shaft.

Coughing and spitting in the thick dust, Murray told them to put on their air masks until the tunnel cleared. When the dust finally settled a few minutes later, the entrance to the air shaft at the end of the tunnel had disappeared. It was completely sealed. There was no way to get through.

"That was a methane explosion," Murray said, taking off his mask. The air had cleared sufficiently to breathe without assistance. "My guess is the fire ignited a pocket of gas." He checked his meter. "Damn, we've still got a methane reading of 5.6."

Still in the danger zone, the methane level had even climbed slightly. The only good news was the carbon monoxide levels had dropped.

They had to find another way up to Level 8, assuming it was still there. With all that methane in the air, they weren't about to try to blast their way through the rock.

Murray said, "We've got three chances. The other air shaft, the elevator shaft, or the skip shaft. Let's hope one of them is open."

"What do we do if we run into a fire?" Wren asked.

"We try to get around it and keep moving," Murray said. "You don't want to have the fire get between you and an escape route." Murray made a brief reconnaissance. He returned a few minutes later and said, "The skip shaft looks open. I can't tell how far up it goes. At least one more level, maybe two."

They had no choice. The entrance to the skip shaft was

about eight hundred feet down the tunnel, which, to Atkins' relief, still looked fairly intact.

Before they moved out, Murray wanted to do a short practice drill with their air tanks. He wasn't happy with their first effort. Everyone had fumbled with the awkward mask and air canister.

Murray told them to put on their face masks, explaining they needed to familiarize themselves with the air supply system while there was still a little time. "When I give the word, turn off your headlamps," he said. "If we run into smoke or dangerous levels of CO or methane up there, it could hit fast. You've got to be able to get that mask on in the dark."

One by one, the helmet lamps went off as they squatted or knelt in the tunnel. Elizabeth was next to Atkins. The darkness was like nothing she'd ever experienced. Black, impenetrable. She couldn't see her hand when she pressed it against her nose.

As she fumbled with her mask and straps, Elizabeth noticed a faint green light. Barely visible in the inky dark, it was glowing and luminescent. As her eyes slowly focused, she could make out the greenish light more clearly.

It formed an oval design. She realized it was the luminous dial of a watch.

Seeing it more clearly, her hand shot to her mouth, and she bit down on it to keep from crying out. She stifled a scream. She remembered the last time she'd seen it, not understanding what it was.

The night someone had entered the equipment room when the lights were out. She'd glimpsed a faint green light, a momentary flash of color.

It was the watch of the man who'd stolen her computer.

"TURN YOUR LIGHTS BACK ON."

At Murray's order, Elizabeth and the others switched on their helmet lamps. Heart pounding, she looked to see who was sitting to her left. That's where she'd seen the luminous dial, or where she thought she'd seen it. Someone must have checked the time, momentarily revealing the glowing watch face.

In the darkness, it was hard to pinpoint exactly where an object was located.

Atkins and Weston were to her left. Murray, Wren, and Booker sat across from them. They were all bunched together.

Elizabeth focused on everyone's hands, looking for the wristwatch with the oval dial.

No luck. The long sleeves of their jumpsuits covered their wrists. With their headlamps on again, Elizabeth couldn't tell who was wearing the watch.

But he was here. Close to her.

She wanted to scream. It took every ounce of her frayed self-control to keep the look of anger and fear off her face. He was sitting within a few feet of her, a few inches.

"We better move out," Murray said. They were on Level 11. He explained that they were going to ascend the skip shaft about two hundred feet to Level 9. Moving back into the coal tunnel on that level, they'd try to see if the air shaft or man shaft was still open so they could climb up to Level 8, where the elevator cage waited for them.

They had to keep going at all costs.

Murray warned them it was likely they'd encounter smoke—possibly fire.

"Loop the air masks around your neck so you can get them on fast in an emergency," he advised. They headed down the tunnel to the skip shaft. Murray checked his gas meter. The carbon monoxide levels were rising. So was the methane, which had climbed to 6.3 percent.

"This keeps up, we're going to have another explosion," he said grimly. "It's just a matter of time."

They started up the skip shaft. Elizabeth hung back so she could whisper a few words to Atkins. "He's here," she said softly. "The man who stole my laptop."

The words startled him. They were totally unexpected. Atkins said, "Who is it?" He knew it couldn't be Booker or Murray. There were only two possibilities, Weston or Wren.

"I don't know," she said. "I saw his wristwatch when we turned off our lamps. I recognized the luminous dial from that night. It was the only thing I got a look at. I remember seeing a blur of something green. I didn't realize it was a watch until a few seconds ago in the dark."

"What did it look like?" Atkins asked, trying to keep his voice down.

Elizabeth described the watch.

"Get ready to take another look," he said. "I'm going to try something." He shouted to Murray up at the head of the line.

"Hey, Doc. Can we turn off the headlamps again? Just for a few seconds. I'd like to have one more try with the face mask. I don't have it down yet."

"Make it quick," Murray said.

Atkins noted where Weston and Wren were in the shaft. They all switched off the lamps on their hard hats. Instantly, the blackness swallowed them up, obliterated their presence.

Atkins waited, straining to see. Then he glimpsed the watch. It was just ahead of him, a green, oval-shaped dial. He wanted to reach for it, grab it, but held back.

The man with the watch had his arms extended, bracing himself on the narrow walls of the shaft.

"I've got it now, thanks," Atkins said, calling out to Murray.

Everyone turned their headlamps back on.

Ever since Elizabeth had told him what had happened, Atkins was sure it had to be either Weston or Marshall.

The man with the watch was the soft-spoken geologist, Mark Wren.

ATKINS and Elizabeth both got a clearer look at the wrist-watch as Wren kept his hands pressed against the sides of the skip shaft. Atkins was struck by the man's daunting coolness. During the descent into the mine, he'd spoken several times to Elizabeth, had helped her pick up her gear, offered his hand to her in some of the more difficult places. He'd given no indication anything was wrong, not the slightest hint.

It was a bravura performance, Atkins thought. But the question remained: Why was he taking such a risk? He already had the computer. What else did he want? Surely he had to figure there was a remote chance she might recognize him. It didn't make sense. Was he that sure of himself, that brazen? If so, he was more dangerous than either of them could have imagined.

They'd climbed about a hundred feet up the skip shaft and were nearly to Level 10 when another explosion ripped through the heart of the mine. The walls and floor shuddered. The deafening blast was much louder than before. Its concussive force knocked them down. Rock and powder fell on them. There was a cave-in somewhere far below them. They heard the shaft collapse.

"That's got to be another methane explosion," Murray said, getting back on his feet.

Fire curtains were drawn to each side of the opening to the mine tunnel on Level 10.

Murray, who was in the lead, saw it first, a ball of white fire rolling down the tunnel, spreading out through the other tunnels and crosscuts as it headed toward the skip shaft.

Murray pulled the fire curtains together. "Come on, fast!" he yelled. "We've got to get up the shaft before we're fried."

They tried to run, but their heavy air tanks and the other equipment weighed them down, and it was impossible to stand up in the low, steep tunnel. Hunched over, they were strung out. Murray was in front, followed by Neutron and

Booker. The robot was carrying Murray's forty-pound foam canister as well as the one that had belonged to Walt Jacobs.

Weston was the last to make it past the Level 10 opening. A tongue of flame obliterated the thick plastic fire curtains, roaring into the shaft right behind him.

Wren, the next in line, was forced to drop back. In his haste to get away from the heat, he threw himself against Elizabeth, driving her into Atkins. They rolled and slid down the shaft nearly all the way to Level 11.

Stopping his own tumbling fall, Wren got to his feet and faced the flames. He shouted up to Murray, but the roaring fire drowned out his words. Backing down the shaft, he joined Elizabeth and Atkins at the entrance to the tunnel on Level 11.

Atkins confronted him. "If we get out of this, I'm going to make sure you're charged with theft. You can tell the cops why you wanted Elizabeth's computer." He knew he should have held off, waited until they were out of danger, but he couldn't help himself. He was too angry.

Wren didn't look in the least surprised or shaken, but his entire demeanor changed. The soft-spoken geologist, ever deferential to Weston and his superiors, spoke with bullet hardness.

"I wondered if you'd ever figure out it was me," he said, shrugging. "It doesn't matter. We've got another problem to deal with here, don't we? We need to talk about the dam at Kentucky Lake and what you saw there. Those incredible cracks. I sure haven't forgotten them. I doubt you have either. Weston says you told him you'd seen them. That was very indiscreet, Doctor Atkins. And Doctor Holleran makes several references to them in notes she typed in her laptop. Did you know it was Weston's idea I steal your computer? I wish I'd thought of it myself. There's some very interesting information stored in zipped files on your hard drive."

He put his right hand in the pocket of his coveralls and took out a pistol.

Atkins recognized the automatic. It had belonged to Walt Jacobs. He'd lost sight of it after Jacobs had jumped to his death.

"I know," Wren said. "First Jacobs pulls a gun on Doctor Booker, and now it's my turn. Frankly, I wasn't planning on using a pistol. Didn't think I'd need one in a place like this where there are so many ways to get killed.'' Wren looked at his watch. "We've got one hour, forty minutes, and counting until blastoff. Turns out maybe it was a lucky break we got separated from the others. Gives us a chance to work all this out in private. In a minute, I'm going back up that shaft with your extra foam tanks and see if I can get by that blowtorch up there. You won't need yours anymore, and I wouldn't want them to go to waste.''

Atkins carried one of the two forty-pound foam sprayers they'd brought into the mine.

Wren raised the pistol. He was less than five feet from Atkins. The stubby barrel was pointed at his chest. Staring at the black hole in the muzzle, Atkins felt helpless, unable to move. He and Elizabeth unstrapped their tanks and set them down.

THE weather had slowly improved. The thick clouds and gray overcast had broken up. As the morning slipped into afternoon, the sun started to shine again.

Ross found himself checking his watch every few minutes. Fighting continued in isolated pockets, but, for the most part, the Army had brought it under control. Despite nightmarish logistical problems, the evacuations were proceeding. Troops were out in the country, escorting thousands of people out of the danger zone. Some of the convoys were a mile long.

Steve Draper quickly chilled even this meager dose of good news. He'd just gotten a radio message from the mine.

"They've got trouble down there, sir. There's been a fire. The flames have separated the group.''

"Where are they right now?'' Ross asked. Draper had drawn a rough map of the mine to follow their progress. He pointed out the probable locations.

"Some of them are huddled in the skip shaft right about here,'' he said, pointing to the map. "Just above Level 10. They've had a methane explosion down there. The fires are still burning. Three others are trapped on one of the lower levels.''

'Who is it?'' the president asked.

'Atkins, Elizabeth Holleran, and the geologist from the

Seismic Commission, Mark Wren.'' Draper's voice was
husky. He knew the odds.

"Is there anything we can do?"

"Nothing, sir,'' Draper said, shaking his head. "Doc Murray says they're going to lay down some foam and see if
they can get through the fire and reach them.''

"I don't know if they should risk that,'' Ross said slowly.
For all anyone knew, Atkins and the others were already
dead. It might be a fatal mistake to go looking for them.
The more prudent course, Ross thought, would be for the
survivors to keep looking for an escape route. The brutal
truth was they were running out of time. The bomb was
scheduled to detonate in about an hour and a half.

Ross stared hard at the ground, hands clasped behind his
back. "How do they propose getting through the fire to look
for Atkins?"

Draper smiled. He couldn't help it, even at such a moment
"They're sending down Neutron."

WREN took a step toward Elizabeth, who'd been holding
her hands behind her back. She threw a fistful of rock and
coal dust in his face.

Staggering backward, rubbing his eyes with a gloved hand
Wren started shooting. He fired blindly, the gunshots echoing
off the walls.

Atkins grabbed Elizabeth. They ran down the tunnel an
turned left into a crosscut. A large picnic table was there
along with a few wooden storage boxes and hand tools. A
kins had noticed similar places during the descent. Murra
had explained they were rest stations, where the miners a
lunch, took their breaks, drank coffee.

A long crowbar lay in the dust next to the table. Atki
picked it up. Nearly seven feet long with a pointed end,
was like the one Murray had carried. He couldn't believe h
luck. It wasn't much, but at least he had something in h
hands to fight with.

They turned a corner and entered another tunnel. It w
lined on both sides with room-and-pillar cuts, black hol
that looked like the eye sockets of a skull. They turned
their lamps and in the dark heard a noise, boots on grav
Wren was coming after them.

"I want you to stay here. Keep your light out," Atkins whispered.

"Forget it," Elizabeth answered. "I'm coming with you."

Groping their way down the tunnel in the dark, they came to another crosscut. Atkins knew they couldn't afford to play hide-and-seek for long. They might get lost, and besides, there wasn't time. Every second mattered.

"John, I'm happy as hell to leave you two in peace down here," Wren said, his voice booming out in the darkness. "I'm going to end this foolishness and head back to the skip shaft. Maybe I can get past that fire up on the next level and join the others. Wish me luck."

"We've got to follow him," Atkins told Elizabeth. "If we're going to get out of this, we'll need those extinguishers."

Using their headlamps, switching them on seconds at a time, they made their way back to the main tunnel. They saw Wren's light about fifty yards in front of them, swaying from side to side. He was running.

"Maybe we can get in front of him," Atkins said. They ran down another tunnel, slowing at every crosscut.

Atkins was sure Wren could hear them. Their footsteps were loud on the hard, tamped-down rock of the tunnel floor. Gunfire suddenly exploded in front of them. Three shots. Something stung Atkins' right forearm just below the elbow. He'd been hit. He couldn't tell if it was a bullet or a rock fragment. He felt a stab of pain when he moved his arm.

He pushed Elizabeth down behind one of the pillars that supported the roof.

They turned off their headlamps.

"You shouldn't have come back," Wren said. "Let's settle this quickly. Doctor Weston will breathe a lot easier if he knows you're dead. The fact is he's hoping I'll get killed, too, so he can blame those cracks at the dam on my negligence. He'll say I was taking payoffs, not doing the regular inspections. The very thing he's guilty of himself."

Atkins heard Wren's footsteps as he came closer to their hiding place. Before they'd turned off their headlamps, he'd noticed a pattern of large cracks extending across the roof of the tunnel. It wouldn't take much for the whole thing to cave in, another good tremor. He remembered how Murray had chipped away at the roof with a crowbar. A few light taps had caused an entire section to collapse.

Atkins gripped the crowbar in both hands and hefted it. His arm burned and was starting to stiffen up.

Do it near the rib, where the roof and wall meet, he told himself, recalling what Murray had said.

He peered around the pillar and saw the light from Wren's helmet coming toward him, moving in rhythm to his footsteps.

"Frankly, if I were you, I'd have waited for the bomb to go off," Wren said. "You won't feel a thing. You'll just turn into gas, probably some form of hydrocarbon. You should have stayed hidden. Now I've got to shoot you."

BOOKER made the last adjustments on Neutron's control panel. The robot was armed with Murray's forty-pound canister of fire-fighting foam and the twenty-pound canister that Jacobs had carried.

"You're sure that thing's fireproof?" Murray asked.

"He'll roll right through it," Booker said. "The trick will be getting him down the skip shaft. It's hard to gauge distances by remote control. I don't want him to pitch forward. Then we'd be in trouble."

Booker, Murray, and Weston were crouched in the skip shaft thirty yards up from the fire that was still pouring out of the main tunnel on Level 10. They'd managed to climb up as far as Level 9. The tunnel was partially smoke filled but there was no sign of an active fire. A few yards beyond that point, another cave-in had blocked the shaft.

Murray was sure another fire was burning somewhere else in the mine. The rock that blocked the skip shaft was warm to the touch.

They had their emergency air tanks turned on. Their masks were fitted with transistor-sized radio receivers and speakers that allowed them to talk to each other.

Weston wasn't saying much. He was preoccupied with worries. He knew what Wren had in mind for Atkins and Elizabeth. They'd discussed it in detail before they made their descent into the mine. If the two raised any questions about the cracks that had opened up in the dam at Kentucky Lake before the big quake, there might be serious trouble.

e thing might lead to another, all of it bad. He'd read
ough of Elizabeth's computer files to know she'd written
tensive notes on what she'd seen at the dam.

He also recalled Atkins' veiled threat about the cracks a
w days earlier. Weston thought Atkins was feeling him
t, trying to see how he'd react.

Fortunately, he'd kept no records of the money he'd re-
ved during the last six years from a contractor who'd done
utine maintenance on the dam. He'd allowed the contractor
pad his bills, not much, just a few percentage points here
d there, but over time it added up to nearly $2 million.
ere was no paper trail, and the work hadn't had any bear-
; on the disaster. No dam in the world could have with-
od an 8.4 quake. And yet if an inquiry began, it could
imately lead right to his door. He had to downplay the
iousness of those cracks when they first appeared.

In a sense, the disaster was a godsend. It had washed away
: evidence. All he needed to say about the cracks was the
th, at least part of it, that they'd tried to have them re-
red before the earthquake struck. An evacuation order
ght have started a panic. They'd done everything they
ild, but a horrendous act of nature had doomed their
orts.

The key was to make sure Atkins and Elizabeth Holleran
ver talked. And if everything went extremely well, maybe
en would also die down there. Wren and Stan Marshal
d both received kickbacks from the contractor. Marshal
d panicked and tried to kill Atkins and Elizabeth Holleran
blowing them up during those seismic reflection tests. It
s crude, stupid, and careless. Badly frightened, Marshal
uld keep his mouth shut, but Wren was another matter.
e man was quite capable of asking for more money. Wes-
, knew it was only a matter of time before he'd have to
al with him.

All things considered, this could work out splendidly. He
t needed to survive.

'How much time do we have?'' Weston asked.

'About an hour and a half,'' Murray said.

With Booker operating the controls, the robot slowly
rted to descend the steep incline of the skip shaft, clasping
heavy canisters of foam with its clawed ''man exten-

ders.'' It was briefly lost to view as it rolled through the
flames and smoke that continued to dart out of the tunnel on
Level 10. Booker glimpsed the robot's orange helmet through
the swirling smoke. Then, suddenly, it reemerged from the
inferno.

Outfitted with its television monitor, audio receiver, and
powerful spotlights, Neutron gave Booker a clear image of
its progress down the shaft.

"It's coming up on the entrance to Level 11," he said.
"There's some smoke down there, but it doesn't look too
bad." He carefully guided Neutron out of the shaft and into
the coal tunnel.

Watching the television monitor, he saw a miner's head
lamp burning far down the tunnel. It seemed to be moving.

Then he heard what sounded like small explosions. Three
of them. The sound was clear, unmistakable.

"Those are gunshots," he said.

HIS HEADLAMP TURNED OFF, ATKINS FELT A SHARP
pain in his right arm and shoulder as he reached around the
stone pillar with the long crowbar and chipped hard at the
tunnel's roof. He'd gauged the distance carefully before he'd
switched off his lamp and hoped he was hitting the right
place as he dug into the rock again and again, prying at it,
wincing at the effort. His arm felt like hot needles had been
shoved up under the skin.

Swiveling with his lamp on, Wren saw him and fired.
Gunshots hammering in his ears, Atkins ducked back behind
the pillar.

A section of the roof crashed to the floor. When the pow-
dery dust cleared, Atkins saw Wren standing there, his headlamp pointed at his feet. A six-foot-long block of stone had
just missed him.

Atkins realized that Wren had dropped his pistol and was
searching for it.

Before he knew what he was doing or had time to think
about it, he ran straight at Wren, driving a shoulder into his
chest, knocking him backward. They both fell down and
rolled. Every time Atkins' right arm scraped the ground,
sparklers of white light exploded in front of his eyes.

Pushing up on his knees, Wren threw a hard punch at
Atkins' head. The blow knocked him down. Stunned, he was
aware of footsteps. Wren was running off.

Atkins rolled over on his back and lay there, trying not to
pass out. He could smell the sweet, unmistakable odor of

blood. He touched his nose and felt cartilage move. It was broken.

He stood up gingerly, leaning against the wall as he fumbled with the switch to his headlamp. Elizabeth was at his side.

"We've got to go after him," Atkins said. "If he gets to the fire extinguishers and uses them we're stuck down here." He thought about trying to find the pistol that Wren had dropped. There wasn't time.

They started jogging, Atkins moving stiffly, and turned at the first crosscut. They came to another tunnel and turned right. Atkins hoped they were headed toward the skip shaft. He wasn't sure anymore. It was so damned easy to get disoriented in the dark. They had their lamps on and were making no effort to conceal themselves. Atkins checked his watch. They had about eighty minutes until the bomb detonated.

"It can't be much farther," Atkins said. His right arm throbbed where the bullet had grazed him just below the elbow. It hurt every time he moved it. The pain and tightness worried him. He wasn't sure he'd be able to stop Wren if it came to that. The guy was strong.

They felt a blast of heat, hot air moving down the skip shaft from the fires one level above them. They'd gone the right way.

Suddenly, a dark shape hurtled at them from a recess in the tunnel. Atkins heard the footsteps and turned just as Wren came at him, clutching something in his hands. He swung the object, and Atkins ducked and heard sharp metal chink into the wall. Coal fragments stung his face.

Wren had a pickax. He'd found it lying in one of th passageways, just as Atkins had found the crowbar. He wa enraged. He was desperate to kill them. He dug the pick ou of the coal and swung again, slashing sideways this time.

Atkins leaped back, pushing Elizabeth out of the way.

"Turn your light off!" he shouted.

Wren kept trying to catch Atkins in the light from h headlamp. He was wielding the pickax like a club, savage chopping at the walls and floor.

Atkins edged backward, one cautious step at a time, kee ing his right hand on the wall for balance. Wren was gettin close. Atkins knew he'd have to make a move soon. He w losing strength. He took another step backward and almost fell. There was nothing behind him, just open space. He knelt down and carefully felt in back of him with his hands. He'd nearly fallen into some kind of shaft or pit.

Groping on his knees in the darkness, he touched the edges of some kind of drop-off. It was a rectangular hole three or four feet wide. He remembered that Murray had pointed out narrow openings between the floors, runs for electric and water lines. Most were covered with steel plates. A few, like this one, had been left open.

A thought took shape.

Do it, he told himself. Don't wait.

Keeping his back to the hole, Atkins turned on his head-lamp and stood up. "Here I am, you bastard!"

Wren charged as soon as he saw him, gripping the pick with both hands like a baseball bat.

Atkins waited until Wren was almost upon him, then dropped to his knees and pushed up with his left forearm and shoulder as Wren stumbled over him. Falling through the opening, Wren managed to get his hands up and grab the edge of the hole. He hung there, his feet kicking at the sides of the narrow shaft, trying to get a toehold.

"Help me!" he screamed. "Please, for God's sakes."

Atkins hesitated, but knew he had no choice, not if he wanted to live with himself. He offered the struggling man his left hand.

Wren gripped it and started pulling himself up through the hole. He got his head over the edge, then part of a shoulder. Atkins reached down, trying to get the other arm when Wren, with a powerful thrust of his arms, suddenly pushed up and grabbed the shoulder strap of Atkins' air tank.

Halfway out of the hole and holding onto the edge, prop-ping himself there, Wren tried to yank Atkins down through the opening. His left arm pinned, Atkins could only swing with his injured right. He punched Wren in the face with no effect. Wren kept pulling him down in a steel grip.

Atkins felt himself starting to go when Wren suddenly let loose.

Atkins rolled over on his back and lay on the floor of the tunnel, trying to get his wind back, trying to suck air into his lungs. Elizabeth stood over him, clutching the pick. She'd hit Wren hard in the face with the wooden handle.

Blood pouring from his forehead, Wren managed to hold on to the edge of the hole. Screaming in rage, he started pulling himself up with both hands. Atkins tried to stand. His head was spinning. He got to his knees. Wren grabbed one of his legs.

Elizabeth swung again, catching Wren squarely in the head. The long handle of the pick made a dull crack when it hit his cheekbone.

Wren fell back through the hole. Atkins heard him slam against the floor of the tunnel below them. He looked over the edge. In the light from his headlamp, he saw that Wren had fallen about a hundred feet. His right leg was folded under him at a severe angle. He wasn't moving.

"Are you all right?" Elizabeth asked.

"Where did you learn to swing like that?" Atkins said, standing up slowly, gripping the wall for balance.

"Girls' softball," Elizabeth said, smiling.

The tunnel ahead of them was suddenly very bright. Someone was approaching with a powerful spotlight, playing it on the walls. It looked odd. The angle was all wrong. The light was low to the ground.

It was Neutron.

"FOLLOW the robot back to the skip shaft."

The voice was Booker's, amplified by a small speaker mounted on Neutron's video camera.

Atkins and Elizabeth hurried after the robot as it rolled quickly down the tunnel. It made a turn, then another and came out at the entrance to the skip shaft, which glowed a dull yellow from the fires burning one level above them.

"This isn't going to be easy," Booker said over the radio. "You'll have to get through the fire up on Level 10. Neutron's going to lay down foam spray. Stay as close to him as you can. We'll be fighting the flames from this end."

They heard Murray's voice. "Get your masks on. Button yourselves up real good. Don't leave any exposed skin. Get the collars up around your throat. Your bunker gear will protect you from the fire. Try not to stand in one place too long coming up that shaft. Keep moving and trust that foam

It'll knock the shit out of that fire. Good luck to you. Now let's go!''

Before they followed the robot into the skip shaft, Atkins took Elizabeth in his arms. They stood there a few moments, holding each other.

"Let's do this," Atkins said.

"You're on," Elizabeth said, her eyes as clear as he'd ever seen them. "We can do whatever a robot can, right?"

They put on their air masks and tightened them, then picked up their fire extinguishers. They made sure all their skin was covered. It hurt like hell when the edge of the mask grazed his broken nose. He winced again as he looped the straps of the foam canister over his shoulders.

Neutron moved into the shaft and started up the incline, gripping the nozzles of the two foam packs it carried on its back.

Crouched over in the tight space, Atkins and Elizabeth stayed close to the robot. Flames were still shooting into the shaft up on Level 10, long darting waves of orange and white fire.

"Steady now," said Booker, who was following their progress on his television monitor. "Get ready to turn on your extinguishers. Hold it—"

Shimmering waves of heat rolled toward them down the shaft.

"Do it!" Booker said.

Atkins and Elizabeth started spraying foam. So did Neutron, a wide, double jet that instantly knocked the flames back five feet.

They'd reached the tunnel entrance. Atkins saw nothing but a wall of fire. Every step forward seemed to take an eternity.

"When Neutron stops, move on around him," Booker said. "He'll buy you a few seconds of time. Get around fast."

The robot halted, pivoted so it squarely faced the fire, and laid down a thick blanket of white foam that continued to push back the flames. As Elizabeth and Atkins slipped behind it, Atkins noticed that his foam canister was losing pressure. So was Elizabeth's. Their face masks started to fog over and blister in the intense heat.

Atkins saw two dark figures looming a few yards ahead of them.

Murray and Booker.

They'd come down the shaft to meet them and were dousing the fire with more foam.

Murray motioned for them to hurry.

Atkins and Elizabeth kept climbing up the shaft. Elizabeth stumbled, and Atkins grabbed her around the waist and pulled her with him as he kept going up the steep slope, fighting for every inch. Murray and Booker followed them, moving backward a step at a time as they continued to throw spray on the fire.

When Atkins and Elizabeth reached the coal tunnel on Level 9, Weston was waiting for them.

"Where's Wren?" he asked.

Atkins shook his head. "He didn't make it." That was all he was going to say. They'd have to deal with Weston and what Wren had told them later.

Murray and Booker soon joined them. Neutron rolled into the tunnel right behind them. The paint had blistered on the front of the robot. The sides of the football helmet had melted. The top had flattened out and turned black at the edges. Orange goo had puddled on the metal surface like candle wax. But the alloy steel was undamaged. He was still operational.

On Murray's advice, they moved down the tunnel until they were a good two hundred feet from the entrance to the skip shaft. The smoke had diminished enough for them to take off their face masks. After checking the methane and CO levels with his gas meter, Murray left them there while he scouted ahead.

When he returned a few minutes later, he was smiling.

"I have a way out," he said. "But it's gonna be a bitch."

THEY HAD FIFTY MINUTES.

Murray's proposed escape route was the vertical air shaft, which ran up the center of the mine, paralleling the elevator shaft. Barely three feet wide, it was connected to a powerful fan at the surface. A kind of return air duct, it was designed to suck stale air from the mine.

Murray would go first, wedging his back and legs against opposite walls of the air shaft. Slowly, a few inches at a time, he would "walk" his way up the sides. The elevator cage was one level up, a distance of about a hundred feet.

When he got to the top, he'd lower a rope for the others and help pull them up. "I'm not trying to fool anybody. This is going to be tough," Murray said. "If you slip, you fall. It's that simple. And if you fall and break something, you're dead. The trick is to concentrate. Think ahead every time you move your arms and legs. Try to mentally visualize what you're going to do. Think it through before you do it. Don't rely on the rope. And don't rush it."

Murray checked his gas meter. The CO levels continued to hover at the danger mark, nearly fifty parts per million. The methane levels had fallen off some after the fire and explosions, but were starting to inch up again. They were back over the redline, reading nearly 7 percent.

"Keep track of the time," Murray said, hooking a coil of rope in his belt. "The clock's really running down on us. We got to bust it, folks."

A sharp tremor jolted them, another strong shake. Fragments of the tunnel's roof fell. Everyone instinctively dropped into a crouch position, covering their heads with their arms. The quake lasted only three or four seconds but was stronger than some of the others.

The sound came from far below them, a loud cracking noise that reverberated through the mine. Atkins was sure it was rock fracturing at great depth. The fault was continuing to slip, continuing to build toward a final rupture.

"They're coming more often," Elizabeth said. She didn't say the rest of it—that the tremors were also building in strength. She wondered how much more shaking the mine could stand before the tunnels collapsed on themselves.

Atkins and Booker helped boost Murray up into the shaft, which was cut into the roof of the tunnel. He got his back and legs in position in the cramped space and started up the rough rock walls, bracing himself hard with his feet and shoulders. He'd trained to do this very maneuver dozens of times. This was the first he'd ever tried it in a mine. He kept repeating to himself the advice he'd given the others: concentrate on every move, think it through from start to finish.

It took nearly fifteen minutes for him to climb to Level 8 He was pouring sweat when he pulled himself out of the shaft. Kneeling on the floor of the tunnel, his chest heaving from his exertions, he took a look at the elevator cage les than ten yards away. His heart sank.

"We've got a problem up here," he shouted down to th others. "The cage won't work. The cable's snapped."

NATHAN Ross was drinking a cup of hot coffee, trying t warm himself in the damp cold. The sun hadn't taken an of the chill from the air. He had the collar of his jack pulled up. His ears felt frozen.

Ross looked at his watch and frowned. They were cuttin this awfully close.

Draper ran up and told him about the broken cable. Book and the others were trapped far below ground.

"We're lowering ropes to them," he said.

"That bomb's scheduled to blow in forty minutes," sa

Phil Belleau. "Those people are down about eight hundred feet. We'll never get them all up."

"We'll damn well try," Ross said quietly as he walked to the elevator shack, where a squad of paratroopers had lowered two makeshift harnesses with basketseats down the man shaft. The ropes were attached to cables that ran to hoists on the two helicopters. The big UH-60s that had remained at the mine.

"Mister President, I've got to insist you leave here," said Belleau, not giving up. Ross was his sole responsibility. He was ready to force the issue if need be.

Ross ignored him. He was helping paratroopers carry more rope into the mine.

THERE was no changing Booker's mind. Atkins saw it in his eyes, the frozen, unblinking stare.

"I'm sorry, John. You know what needs to be done as well as I do. We can't risk any venting."

The last tremor had done more than snap the cable to the elevator cage. Booker had carried a small instrument that monitored the fuse circuit in the non-1 detonating cord he'd run through the mine. The device showed several breaks. He'd arranged the charges to fire in sequence, relying on a network of low-voltage electric blasting caps with multisecond delays to touch off the detonator cord and the explosives. The caps were equipped with special shunts to prevent any sparking that might have ignited methane gas.

The breaks in the circuit, Booker figured, were undoubtedly caused by the fires and cave-ins or the repeated tremors. It was impossible to know exactly where they'd occurred. Booker had set up two detonation lines: one during the descent, the other as they climbed back up. He'd positioned the explosives where they'd be most likely to collapse the shafts.

Atkins was shocked when the physicist calmly announced here was only one solution to the problem. Manual detonation.

Booker said he'd remain on Level 8 and explode the charges that would seal the main shafts and air vents. He made the decision sound as simple as going to the store to buy milk.

He caught Atkins completely off guard. Elizabeth and Weston had already made it up the air vent with Murray helping them. They'd gone up with ropes looped under their arms and around their waists. Twice Weston had almost fallen, only to be caught by Murray, who'd wrapped the rope for extra support around an electrical outlet box bolted to the floor of the tunnel.

The looped end of the rope now dangled in front of Atkins. Murray had shouted down for one of them to start climbing.

"Why in the hell don't you run the detonator cord up to ground level and set it off up there?" Atkins asked.

Booker shook his head. "If we get another good earthquake and that cord snaps . . ." He didn't finish the thought. "Any venting from a bomb this size, and the dust cloud could drift all the way to the East Coast."

"But you can't stay here!" Atkins shouted. He'd clamped his hands on Booker's shoulders as he tried to reason with him. He couldn't believe this was happening. Booker was resolute. There was no moving him.

"It's the right time and the right place," the physicist said patiently. "I've got plenty of explosives left. I can seal every vent at this level. I only wish I'd thought of this earlier. It would have made things so much easier. I wouldn't have had to lug all that extra plastic explosive and fuse down into this hole in the ground."

Atkins looked at him, shaking his head. It was hopeless. He was staying.

"John, you're running out of time," Booker said. "I'm not going to leave. It's a simple decision. I've made it of sound body and mind. I wish you'd go. Please go. If you stay, it's safe to say the end will come very quickly. You won't suffer. If by some miracle we survive the explosive charges, we can look forward to being vaporized. I must say I've always been curious about the chemical processes involved, all that radiation your bones absorb in a few nanoseconds. Of course, you won't feel it because you'll implode when all those gamma rays shoot through you. Photons, actually. Your body will light up, something like a flashbulb, I imagine."

"Dammit, your leukemia is in remission," Atkins pe

sisted angrily. "You don't have to do this, Fred. You can live another ten years. You don't have to commit suicide."

"Think logically," Booker said. "This is the only way we can make sure there's no screwup. If the ground vents from a one-megaton shot, you'll have a hot cloud rising to thirty thousand feet within four minutes."

"You two better get a fucking move on down there," Murray shouted. For the first time since they'd entered the mine, his voice showed fear.

Booker smiled at Atkins. "You get back to Doctor Holleran, John. Get back to her as fast as you can. There's going to be a lot of work to do after this. They're going to need both of you."

"We've got two harnesses up here," Murray yelled. "They're ready to pull us up the man shaft." Moments earlier, Elizabeth and Weston had started on their way to the surface, the rescue lines attached to the helicopter hoists. They were already nearing the halfway point.

Booker looked at Atkins and said, "It's your turn, doctor. Don't do anything foolish like trying to overpower me. This seal has to work."

Atkins wrapped the rope under his arms, gritting his teeth at the pain in his right forearm and shoulder. With a push from Booker, he started up the shaft, helped along by Murray and the rope. It was a hard go. He had to make a conscious effort every time he moved his arms and legs, which felt like lead weights hung from them. As he neared the top, he came close to passing out. He held himself in place, wedging against the walls of the shaft with his feet and shoulder blades.

"Come on, doc," Murray shouted. "You're too close to quit on me now."

Atkins looked up. He only had another five feet to go. He moved one leg, then another, inching his shoulders higher up the wall. Then Murray had him by the arms and he was out of the shaft.

When he looked down at Booker, the physicist waved.

"Remember to make sure everyone's long gone from this mine at D minus five minutes," Booker shouted. "That's when I'll fire the explosives. It's going to make a beautiful noise."

ATKINS WENT UP THE ELEVATOR SHAFT A FEW MIN-
utes after Murray. Strapped into one of the jury-rigged harnesses, he was halfway to the surface when a tremor hit. He
no longer doubted it anymore. These were preshocks—the
increasingly heavy seismic jolts that preceded a big earthquake. His seat bounced and swayed as rock fragments broke
off the walls. Grasping the ropes, he leaned forward as they
pelted his hard hat and shoulders. Several large pieces just
missed him and crashed onto the elevator cage four hundred
feet below.

The shaft was starting to crumble. The last two hundred
feet were agonizingly slow. Atkins kept waiting for the walls
to collapse on him.

When he was closer to the surface, he had to cover his
eyes in the glare of powerful spotlights. Squinting into the
painful brightness when he reached the top, he saw Elizabeth
waiting for him. She was standing next to the president and
Steven Draper. Both men were smiling. Draper grabbed Atkins' hand and pumped it hard.

"Now let's get the hell out of here," he said.

They had about twenty minutes until the bomb detonated.

Draper hurried them out of the metal building that housed
the entrance to the mine. They emerged into the soft, gauzy
light of a winter's afternoon. The sun was a dull, gray disk,
but Atkins and Elizabeth had to hold their hands over their
eyes to cut down on the glare.

As they trotted down a gravel path toward the mine's

parking lot, Draper explained there'd been a change of plans. They weren't going to use the helicopters. More fighting had broken out in the surrounding hills, mainly skirmishes between small groups of the Kentucky National Guard and Army patrols. It was considered too risky for the president to try to fly out. They feared another rocket attack.

They were going to drive out.

Draper wanted to reach the red shack, where they'd monitor the effects of the blast. It was about four miles south of the mine on a hilltop that had been heavily fortified against attack. The scientists had steadily added to the array of portable seismographs and other instrumentation around the blast zone to record the velocity and direction of the seismic waves, analyze the release of strain energy in the ground, and calculate the yield of the bomb. They were also ready to record and pinpoint whatever seismic activity the explosion generated on the Caruthersville Fault and those adjoining it.

As he jogged along next to Atkins, the president asked about Booker.

"He's still down there with the robot," Atkins said. "He's not coming up."

He explained.

There hadn't been many times in Ross' career, first as a lawyer in Evanston, Illinois, then as a politician, when words failed him. This was one of them. He didn't know what to say, how to respond. He wouldn't even try. He'd damn well do it later when he could hope to do justice to Booker's heroism. He'd make sure the man was remembered.

In a few brief sentences, Atkins also explained what had happened to Walt Jacobs—and to Wren.

Atkins had already noticed Weston staring at him nervously. This wasn't the time to deal with him. But he would make sure it all came out later. How Wren, Weston, and Marshal had deliberately withheld information about the extent of the damage to the dam at Kentucky Lake. How they'd covered up other problems there, falsified inspection reports, accepted kickbacks.

Atkins wanted Weston and Marshal turned over to the authorities as soon as they were away from the mine. But more immediate worries distracted him. He still wasn't sure the bomb would detonate.

He'd considered the risk of a misfire. There was no way of knowing if that flimsy-looking timer Booker had installed at the last moment would do the job, or if the flashlight batteries he'd tied together would have enough electrical juice to fire the capacitors.

He remembered Booker's confidence and thought again of the physicist, saw him standing in the darkness on Level 8, his face streaked with coal dust, gray eyes shining through the grime. He was smiling.

A fine, wonderful man.

"I should never have let him stay down there," he told Elizabeth.

"Stop it," she said, touching his hand. They'd reached the trucks that were lined up, engines revving. "There was nothing you could have done. He knew what he was doing. He wouldn't want you to start second-guessing yourself."

She remembered the first time she'd seen Booker. He'd just parachuted into Memphis. She'd thought his idea about defusing a big earthquake with a nuclear explosion was absurd and had a hard time believing he was serious. She'd changed her mind, mainly because she feared what would happen if they did nothing, but partly, too, because of Booker's persuasiveness. She liked the man and was grateful she'd had a chance to know him.

The ground suddenly rocked again. The motion was east-west, in the direction of the fault. These S waves were characterized by hard, side-to-side movement. A kind of shear wave, S waves moved through the upper crust more slowly than P waves, but their journey was a violent one. They vibrated like crazy and hit hard.

"That's very close," Elizabeth said.

Another, stronger shake followed the first by a matter of seconds.

"We may have a sequence starting," Atkins said.

If the clock on the bomb was still running, it was eleven minutes until detonation.

The next tremor almost knocked them down. An undulating lateral movement that rippled the surface of the ground

"Look at the hills!" a soldier shouted.

The surrounding hills, their sloping flanks thick with trees were moving, shaking as the earth rumbled. Atkins recog

nized the sound. He'd heard it before, something almost like
thunder, distant, more powerful. The trees were swaying as
if blown by powerful winds. Some of them cracked and fell,
the sound of splitting wood explosive and sharp. Jumpy from
the shooting, soldiers raised their rifles and looked for
targets.

Atkins recognized the look on their faces. They were
frightened. Most had fallen to their knees to wait out the
shaking.

The two UH-60 Black Hawk helicopters lifted off and
climbed rapidly, heading east. Everyone waited and watched,
holding their breath. There was no missile shot. The helicopters cleared the ridgeline and disappeared.

Soldiers started jumping into the trucks, Humvees and armored troop carriers. Orders were shouted, clipped words.

In the confusion, Belleau announced another change in
plans.

They wouldn't make it to the command center. There
wasn't time. "We'll be lucky to get beyond the next line of
hills," Belleau said. "That's three miles from here. We
ought to be just outside the blast zone."

"Then let's move it," Ross said.

Troop carriers armed with .50-caliber machine guns
flanked the convoy. They were going to leave the same way
they'd come in, following back roads and cutting across open
pastures. No one doubted that it was going to be a wild,
dangerous ride.

Atkins, Elizabeth, and Murray jumped into one of the
Humvees. "Tighten your belts to the max," said the driver.
He had a light blond mustache and a boyish face. "This
road's a bitch, and we're gonna be making tracks."

FRED Booker tucked up his legs and sat with his back
against the wall. The stone was warm. The amount of heat
being generated deep in the ground still amazed him. He
unzipped his jumpsuit. He was already soaked to the skin
with sweat, and it was getting more difficult to breathe. He
thought about putting on his face mask, then smiled to himself. The damn thing was hot and uncomfortable and in a
few minutes it wouldn't matter anyway.

He had his headlamp turned on, a tapering wedge of light

illuminating the darkness. The repeated tremors were knocking the hell out of the mine. He heard a tunnel collapse in the depths. Chunks of rock broke off the ceiling.

The temblors were coming with greater force.

He held three strands of non-l detonating cord. He'd already connected them to an old-fashioned twist-action blasting machine, which rested on his lap. When the moment came, he'd give the handle a hard, clockwise twist. The twist would supply just enough electrical current to trigger the blasting caps attached to the plastic explosives he'd placed in quantity on Level 8. He'd wired thirty sticks in the short time since Atkins had left.

That was more than enough to seal all of the shafts.

Neutron was positioned ten feet away in the middle of the tunnel. The robot's powerful mechanical arms were extended, holding up a section of the roof that had cracked wide open during the last strong shake. A block of stone the size of a garage door was sagging against the exposed steel roofing bolts. The bolts were starting to give way. The robot had pushed the slab back in place.

Booker took off his digital wristwatch and placed it on top of the blaster. Another ten minutes.

He'd detonate the plastic gel six seconds before the bomb exploded. He would have preferred to set it off two or three seconds before, but didn't trust the precision of the timer. Better to take a few more seconds and play it safe.

The risk of firing too soon was that the explosions might trigger landslides or a massive cave-in. If that happened the bomb could be damaged before it detonated. Booker doubted that was likely. The weapon's hard case was designed to withstand a severe impact long enough to hit a buried target. Years of field and laboratory tests had proven the strength of the design. And yet a bullet had easily punctured the case. That still worried him. So did the jury-rigged battery pack and timer he'd attached to the weapon.

He had less than eight minutes.

Booker took off his hard hat and placed it so the lamp shined directly on his watch face. It was a relief to take off. He took one last look at Neutron, who stood ten feet from him. The robot had performed superbly. He hoped Je

Burke would hear about that. He was sure John Atkins would tell him.

Booker remembered the old joke in the National Laboratory's Robotics Lab: it was time to switch careers when you started talking to the robots.

He smiled.

He wasn't going to talk to Neutron. He was going to sing—an old Appalachian song about working in coal mines. It had been years since he'd heard it, but he still remembered some of the lyrics.

He hummed the haunting bluegrass melody played by the Nitty Gritty Dirt Band, trying to remember the words. When he had them, he began to sing softly.

Where the dangers are many and the pleasures are few.
Where the rain never falls and the sun never shines.
It's dark as a dungeon . . . down in the mine.

He looked at his watch.
Five minutes.

THE DRIVER HIT A CURVE ON THE NARROW, BACK-country gravel road at fifty miles an hour. The rear end of the Humvee fishtailed through the turn, narrowly missing two big trees that formed a corner where the road veered sharply left. They were descending a hill single file, engines groaning in low gear as helicopters swept overhead, looking for snipers.

By Atkins' estimate, they had about seven minutes to get as far as possible beyond the hills that sheltered the Golden Orient.

Four miles!

They weren't going to make it. Not over this kind of muddy, rugged terrain, where the road was knotted with switchbacks. There was no way. They rounded another curve, then made a tight S-turn. The side of the road fell sharply forty feet into dense woods, then dropped some more, becoming a sheer cliff. Far below them, a band of silver twisted through the trees. A shallow stream or river.

"How many miles have we gone?" Elizabeth asked. She sat next to Atkins. Both were clutching the Humvee's roll bar, trying to hang on. They were pitched up and down, rocking like a carnival ride as the tires banged over ruts and washouts.

"Maybe two," Atkins said.

The driver, focused completely on keeping the vehicle from spinning out, didn't answer. The windshields were streaked with mud.

Strung out in a ragged line, the convoy hit the floor of a valley, smashed through a wire fence, and cut across a freshly plowed field, the tires throwing up rooster tails of reddish-brown dirt. If they could get beyond the next line of hills, they'd be out of danger.

Provided we've calculated correctly, Atkins reminded himself. He hoped that Guy Thompson's people hadn't screwed up when they ran their figures.

They'd concluded that a one-megaton bomb detonated at two thousand feet would have only minimal effect on the topography. The risk of significant ground subsidence extended up to a half-mile from ground zero. But they weren't absolutely certain of these conclusions. There were too many exceptions and variables. Some of the one-megaton underground blasts at the Nevada Test Site had cracked and settled the earth up to two and three miles from the bomb crater.

Atkins had a more serious worry: if they'd made a mistake about the venting hazard, huge amounts of radioactive debris, mainly dirt and crushed rock, would be hurled miles into the sky.

And at the top of his fear list: What if the explosion actually triggered a major earthquake instead of stopping it? What if it ignited other quakes along the many faults that ran like deep furrows through the unstable basement rock in the Mississippi Valley?

From the start, that had always been their biggest concern. Fear of that possibility was partly to blame for Walt Jacobs' death. It's what had pushed him—Atkins was sure of it—to try to sabotage their effort. They'd never know for sure, or how much the death of his family had affected his reason.

The Humvee banged up into the air. All four wheels momentarily leaving the ground. The earth had shaken again and the floor of the valley started moving in undulating waves two and three feet high. They'd hit one of them, then another.

A jet of muddy water, black sand, and lignite or "wood coal" blasted into the sky. A foaming geyser shot into the air fifty yards to their left.

A sand blow. First one, then another, and another. All of them shooting thick fountains of muck as high as trees.

The convoy changed directions to steer away from it. The

ground was churning, shaking. Yet another sand blow erupted, throwing up a stream of water, silt, and cottony-white sand. One bubbling hole after another opened up in the field. One of them was about a hundred feet wide.

"You better push it!" Atkins shouted to the driver. "We've got to get across before the whole field liquefies." If that happened, it would be like trying to cross a lake of quicksand. They'd never make it.

"John, over there!" Elizabeth said, pointing to steam billowing from a narrow fissure that had split the ground open. A couple feet wide, the tear ran up the side of the facing hill like a scar.

"Did the bomb explode?" Elizabeth asked.

"It's not time yet."

Elizabeth, like Atkins, knew these were all preshocks leading to a major earthquake. Strain energy was rapidly building toward a rupture. When this one hit, the tectonic explosion was going to be immense.

The convoy was climbing the hill, the studded, oversize tires churning up the soft ground. Elizabeth and Atkins were snapped back in their seats as the Humvee rolled over a fallen tree.

They were almost to the crest.

Another fifty yards, and they'd be out of the danger zone.

BOOKER gripped the blaster firmly in both hands. In the last strong shock, the roof had collapsed at the far end of the tunnel.

The detonator cord still ran free.

He sat against the wall, trying to steady himself and think clearly.

Neutron continued to hold up the weakened section of roof in the middle of the tunnel, but it was starting to sag and the cracks were spreading. It wouldn't be long before it caved in on them.

It was almost time, a matter of a few seconds.

Booker put his head back against the wall, closed his eyes, and took a breath. Images of his wife and daughters, of places they'd gone, tracked before him.

His two daughters.

He focused on them and remembered their faces as first

and second-graders and how cute they looked in their blue-and-white tartan school uniforms. He'd kept those faded pictures in his wallet for thirty years.

They were bright, good girls, far better than he'd deserved. He'd stayed close to them. One taught English literature at the University of Tennessee at Knoxville. The other was an architect in Kansas City. He hoped they'd understand the decision he'd made and why.

He glanced at his watch and started counting down from ten. . . .

Five . . .

Four . . .

Three . . .

Two . . .

One . . .

He gave the blaster a sharp clockwise turn with his right hand.

THE Humvee barreled over the top of the hill. Wheels spinning, it slid through a ragged clearing in the trees smashed open moments earlier by a heavy personnel carrier. Back in control, the driver started down the other side but immediately hit his brakes, skidding to a stop that spun them around in a sharp half-circle.

Atkins had heard the order to halt come over the Humvee's dashboard radio.

He knew what it meant: it was almost time for the explosion.

"Get out!" the driver shouted. Soldiers were jumping from the open backs of troop carriers. They were lugging rifles and packs and running hard down the side of the hill, some stumbling and rolling, then getting up and running again.

Atkins and Elizabeth got out of the Humvee and started after them. There was no cover, no shelter. They were going to take whatever happened out on open ground. It was as good as any other place, Atkins thought. At least they'd be able to see each other in case someone needed help.

A gorgeous valley spread open before them. The hills in this part of southwestern Kentucky were wooded. The fields lush with thick grass. Atkins couldn't help but think, as he

often had before, that it was fine horse country. Then he
realized something that he'd overlooked for days. He hadn't
seen a single horse or cow or sheep. The fields in this part
of the Bluegrass State had been abandoned by both man
and beast.

They saw the president at the bottom of the hill. He'd just
stepped out of a half-track. Soldiers had already formed a
protective shield around him. Others had moved up into the
hills and taken defensive positions. Helicopters buzzed the
ridgeline at dangerously low altitude.

"Here it comes," Elizabeth said. "Yes!"

She felt herself lifted up. It was like an ocean swell washing against her legs in a strong surf, causing her to sway on
her feet but not fall down. Two distinct ground waves rolled
past them, rippling the trees and tall grass.

They were ten yards from a stream that trickled along the
base of the limestone hills. Clear as glass only moments
earlier, the surface of the water suddenly shimmered.

"It fired!" Atkins shouted.

LAUREN MITCHELL HAD BEEN GIVEN A PERSONAL ES-
cort to drive her home—four Army paratroopers in two
Humvees. In the two hours since they'd left the Golden Orient, they'd covered less than twenty miles on unmarked
country roads. Following Lauren's directions, they'd frequently plowed across sodden fields and pastures to save
time.

Lauren had wanted to be back with her grandson when
the bomb exploded. She didn't make it.

Her driver, a nervous but alert corporal, pulled over on the
shoulder of a muddy road a few seconds before zero hour.

"Maybe we better get out of the vehicle," he said.

Unsure what to expect, they were well within the thirty-
to forty-mile radius for the bomb's maximum seismic effect.

"It should hit any second now," the soldier said, looking
at his watch.

They were on a steep hillcrest with a view of Kentucky
Lake in the distance, the gray-blue water visible through a
gap in the trees. Another five miles, and Lauren would have
been home. She wondered how Bobby was doing and longed
to be back with him.

"Listen!" one of the soldiers shouted.

The sound of muffled thunder rolled along the ridges. The
bomb had gone off.

"It's gonna wash right over us," the corporal said, looking
back toward a narrow valley they'd just driven through. The

hills were swaying. The ground was moving toward them in waves.

"Get away from the vehicles!" the corporal yelled. The Humvees had begun to rock up and down on their axles. They ran, half fell, down a grassy hill that sloped away from the road. The first wave staggered them, then the second wave knocked them off their feet. They fell hard.

"Jesus," the corporal said, trying to stand and falling on his back as the ground kept shaking.

Lauren sat up and dug her hands into the wet grass, trying to hold on to something, afraid she'd be thrown into the air. She stared out toward the lake. The water momentarily seemed to pull back from shore. She watched big waves whip up as the shaking intensified. Monster waves.

After a few minutes, the ground quieted again.

Lauren picked herself up, got her balance, and hiked back to the road.

The corporal followed her. "I think we can drive now, ma'am," he said. "Let's get you home."

Lauren shook her head and said, "Thanks, but I'll walk the rest of the way." She could be home in an hour if she put her mind to it. She didn't want to be caught in one of those Humvees if the road turned liquid or a trench opened up beneath them. Two of the paratroopers followed her on foot. The others drove.

The Mississippi Valley might keep shaking for days, Lauren thought. Sooner or later it would stop for good and when it did, they'd start rebuilding their marina. That was her unwavering plan. This was her country and her grandson's. They were going to survive this.

JUST AS BOOKER HAD PLANNED, THE PLASTIC EX-
plosives detonated deep in the Golden Orient, caving in all
four major shafts on Level 8. Roofs and tunnels collapsed
on themselves as the mine was sealed.

Seconds later and right on schedule, the MK/B-61
exploded.

The capacitors flashed their charge. The electrical circuit
closed, setting off the network of detonators. The blocks of
high explosives that Booker had painstakingly shaped at the
Pantex plant in Texas all fired, crushing the plutonium core
in the bomb's primary. At the moment of maximum compression, a small fireball of fission—boosted by the infusion
of tritium and deuterium gas—flooded the bomb's secondary
component, the part containing lithium deuteride uranium. In
the barrage of radiation from the fireball, the secondary imploded, setting off the thermonuclear explosion.

Deep in the mine, the bomb's supercharged energy was
released, blasting the temperature to about ten million degrees. The pressure spiked at a thousand times that of the
earth's atmosphere. The same kind of white-hot, incandes-
cent gas that forms the core of a star blasted outward, carving
a dome-shaped cavity the size of a ten-story building. During
the last few preshocks, the deep fissure at the bottom of the
mine had already begun to close. The explosion hastened the
process, sealing the fissure as great sheets of molten rock
collapsed into it.

Shock waves radiating from the core fractured the surrounding rock and liquefied it. The explosion created a nuclear earthquake that unleashed swarms of seismic waves rippling through the earth's crust. The P waves traveled through the rock as sound waves, a series of rapid compressions and dilations. These were followed by the much slower-moving S waves. There was an abundance of Love waves, converted S waves trapped within the earth's surface layers.

As the bomb exploded, the ground directly above the blast site billowed up like a sail suddenly filled with a strong gust of wind. Then the ground settled again, forming a concave-shaped subsidence crater on the surface one thousand feet in diameter. More settling would follow as the hot cavity continued to cool.

The mine's tall skip shaft and man shaft towers collapsed, shaken apart, their heavy timbers crashing through the metal building that housed the main entrance.

No cloud of radioactive dust escaped.

ATKINS was soon on the radio with Guy Thompson and the team of seismologists manning the red shack control center two miles farther to the west. They were monitoring the array of strong-motion seismographs and other instruments positioned near ground zero. The equipment had been geared up to make a quick determination of the bomb's yield by measuring the amplitudes of the P waves and the S waves.

Thompson had lost his scientific detachment, the ability to consider disturbing facts analytically without losing his composure.

He was terrified.

The ground had gone into spasm. The bomb, following predictions, had released strain energy comparable to an earthquake in the magnitude 6.5 range and exactly in the bull's-eye. The nuclear shock waves were directed right at the western end of the newly discovered Caruthersville Fault, its wide point of intersection with the fault from the 7 quake and the northernmost arm of the New Madrid Seismic Zone, the place where the greatest stress was likely to concentrated. The maximum band of seismic energy had radiated about forty miles, a little more than they'd anticipated.

"We're showing lots of Love waves," Thompson reported.

That was exactly what they'd wanted. Love waves were a good indicator that tectonic strain energy in the ground was being released as the deep rock fissured and cracked. The number of Love waves moving across the surface of the ground was considered a measure of the amount of energy released.

What they hadn't anticipated was the flurry of powerful aftershocks that inexplicably broke out along the entire length of the Caruthersville Fault. They were also firing with unprecedented rapidity along other segments of the NMSZ.

The first aftershock—nearly as large as the main event—followed within thirty seconds, a quake that measured a magnitude 6.

By then, the ground had been shaking intermittently for more than three minutes.

"This may be getting away from us," Thompson said, not hiding his fear. "The seismographs are swinging all over the place. I don't like the way these aftershocks keep hammering us."

"How many have we had?" Elizabeth asked.

"Five big ones within the last two minutes. Three over a mag 5. And maybe twenty smaller ones in the mag 4 or less range. They're popping everywhere. We just had a mag 5.4 seventy miles northwest of Memphis."

President Ross and Steve Draper stood behind Atkins and Elizabeth. The president listened to what Thompson was reporting, not saying a word, hands thrust in the pockets of his jacket. If he was frightened, he didn't show it. He was holding on to the edge of a portable table that had been set up to hold the radio equipment. It was difficult to stand during some of the stronger tremors. They were coming almost back-to-back.

The profound uncertainty of what they were doing had tormented them all along. Atkins couldn't help but wonder if their questions were being answered once and for all with each of these powerful seismic convulsions.

"Is there anything we can do?" Ross said.

"Nothing," Atkins said. The ground rocked upward again, the hard vibrations rippling up through his legs and spine.

The aftershocks weren't nearly as powerful as the 8.4 monster, but they were very strong. Atkins and the others, everyone in the field, continued to hear what one soldier called "ground thunder," the rumbling, otherworldly sound that seemed to rise from deep in the earth. Over the last few days Atkins had come to hate it.

What fools they'd been to think they could stop an earthquake, he thought. What arrogance to assume they could meddle with one of nature's most destructive forces.

He feared that's how they'd be judged. As arrogant, dangerous fools.

The Caruthersville Fault was going to touch off another killer earthquake. You had no options, he reminded himself bitterly, slapping his gloved hands together in the cold. You had to do something. You had to try to stop it.

He wasn't going to make any excuses. He wouldn't permit it. He'd never do that no matter what he had to face.

Later, he'd have difficulty trying to pin down how much time elapsed between this crushing feeling of depression and self-doubt and the moment Elizabeth gently touched him on the arm. He realized it could have been only twenty to thirty minutes at most. It seemed much longer, a black hole chiseled into his memory as he shivered with fear in that cold, bleak field.

Elizabeth said, "They might be slowing down."

The last few tremors were noticeably milder. And they were coming farther apart.

Atkins felt it, too.

The aftershocks appeared to be diminishing, winding down like a great engine coming to a halt.

For the next hour as the black sky seemed to press down upon their heads, so oppressively low they felt they coul touch it, Atkins and Elizabeth timed the aftershocks. Joine by the president, their eyes were glued to their watches.

Guy Thompson called back. He sounded excited. "It look like they've stopped," he shouted. "We haven't recorded significant tremor in ninety minutes."

His amplified words carried far in the cold, damp a Some of the soldiers who'd started a bonfire broke in loud cheers.

Elizabeth slipped her arm around Atkins' waist. Th

spoke to Thompson together. He told them the accelerations had fallen to almost zero.

IT was still too early to celebrate. They knew they'd be on edge for the next few days. They'd have to wait until they could get a definitive reading from the GPS system. The satellite data would tell them if the ground was deforming anywhere along the extensive seismic zone. A crucial test, it was the only way to assess how much elastic strain energy remained trapped in the ground.

Atkins doubted they'd released all of it. A one-megaton bomb simply wasn't powerful enough to do that, but they didn't have to. Their strategy all along was to discharge just enough tectonic stress or "critical asperity" to break the cycle of earthquakes without pushing the fault into a major upheaval.

The ultimate outcome still wasn't known, but for the time being, they couldn't deny there'd been a pronounced drop-off in seismic activity. Atkins wanted to believe it was happening, wanted to let down his guard, his scientific skepticism, and hope for the best.

"Excuse me, sir, but do you know you've been shot?" one of the soldiers said, a medic.

Atkins took his first good look at his right forearm. Wren's bullet had opened a shallow furrow that ran just across the wrist. The bullet had nicked the bone, but hadn't done any serious damage.

The medic quickly got a bandage on it and examined Atkins' nose.

"Good clean break," he said. "Looks like the second time, right?"

Atkins nodded. He winced when the soldier gently touched the bridge.

"I like it," Elizabeth said, smiling. "I think it helps."

She kept remembering how she felt when she'd climbed out of the mine. It had hurt to be out of his sight, not knowing what was happening to him as the shaking intensified. Leaving him below in the darkness was the most difficult thing she'd ever done.

When Atkins took her in his arms, something burst open inside him, an aching release unlike anything he'd ever expe-

rienced. Trapped in the depths of the mine, he hadn't allowed himself to think about this moment—hadn't dared. She'd taken off her hard hat. Her dark blond hair hung to the shoulders of her jumpsuit, which was caked with coal dust and white powder. He'd thought about her hair often during the last few hours, wondering whether he'd ever see it again. He wanted to run his fingers through it.

Just after 11:00 P.M., Army patrols reported the route was secure. They got back into their Humvees and other vehicles and drove two miles to the red shack, where they spent the rest of the night, drinking strong coffee as Thompson's team continued to monitor the encouraging seismic readings.

In the morning, as the sun began to rise in a clear blue-gray sky, Atkins and Elizabeth took a walk. They hiked along the ridge to an opening in the trees where they could look out over a wide valley.

Elizabeth noticed them first, the distant shapes almost obscured in the long shadows that had spread across the floor of the valley as the sun climbed higher over the hills.

Atkins had borrowed a pair of binoculars. He adjusted the eyepiece. The image snapped into sharp view—a line of brown-and-white cows that had come out of the woods single file and were grazing in the pasture. Farther off, he saw two horses with their heads down, a mare and a gray colt, feeding in the tall grass.

They were the first animals they'd seen in days.

Atkins finally let himself dare to believe it. Finally let himself go.

It was over.